when I
lost you

Also by Kelly Rimmer:

The Secret Daughter
Me Without You

kelly rimmer

when I lost you

bookouture

Published by Bookouture, an imprint of StoryFire Ltd.

23 Sussex Road, Ickenham, UB10 8PN,
United Kingdom
www.bookouture.com

ISBN 978-1-910751-90-9
eBook ISBN 978-1-910751-89-3

For Catie

PART ONE

CHAPTER 1
Molly – July 2015

I have realised that it is possible to love someone with your whole heart, but at the same time to hate them with an equal force of passion. These emotions can somehow balance each other out, leaving an exhausted sense of emptiness. In the ten days I've spent sitting by this hospital bed staring at my husband, I have wondered again and again how we got here. Not how *he* got here, into this ICU ward and in such a terrible state – that was almost inevitable. No, the surprising *here* to my current scenario is my ambiguity towards the man on the bed. Leo was – *is* – the love of my life. I will love him until I die. It still seems impossible that I can loathe him too, and yet here we are.

This comatose Leo is still handsome despite the uneven beard and the swathe of bandages he's been left with after the injury. He is pale and unconscious but he still looks dangerous... he *is* dangerous. Leo has always treated his body and his life as if they were nothing more than sacrificial offerings to be made to his work. Beneath the sheets and the hospital gown his body is covered in scars – those from this current disaster, and an endless series of faded marks from so many earlier incidents.

My husband has a way of dragging people along on a journey with him – even, apparently, when the journey is to nowhere at all. In the days since his accident I've become a member of the living dead myself – leaving his side only to sleep when my body forces me to do so, passing through the days in a strange kind of coma of my own. Unlike Leo, I have of course been conscious, but every non-essential function of life has been put on hold.

All that I have really done during these awful days has been to feel the full gamut of emotions arising from our situation. In the last few years of my life I have thought of myself as something of an expert in loneliness but for all those days apart from Leo, I realise now that I'd only ever experienced a shadow of it. For the last four years, through ups and downs and rough patches and good times, Leo has been my 'go-to' person. More than once lately I have picked up my phone to tell him about how scared I am and how lost I feel – but right now, I realise that *every one* of the layers of lost and alone in my life is his fault.

I was stunned when the doctors said it was time to reduce the sedation that had induced Leo's coma. In the first few hours I'd signed organ donation forms and discussed with his specialists at which point heroic measures would still be appropriate. I'd even made the awful call back to Leo's parents and his editor in Sydney to discuss a potential funeral. Even when he'd stabilised his doctors were determined to keep my expectations realistic, and so any time I displayed my habitual optimistic streak, I was quickly corrected with a dose of reality. The chances of a full recovery had been slim to start with and they grew less likely with each passing day. Even if Leo woke up, they said, there was almost no chance he'd still be the man he once was.

But then they started turning the respirator off for trial periods and I got to watch him breathe on his own again for brief stretches of time. I've so loathed the sound of that damned machine – the incessant *whoosh* as it filled his lungs with air, and the matching *hiss* as it sucked it back out again. Twenty-four hours a day the respirator has been a soundtrack to the waiting and the fear, grating on my nerves at times, leaving me feeling strangely ungrateful whenever I reflected on the safety net it had provided him. One night I went to the hotel for a shower and a bit of sleep and when I came back early the next morning, the tubes had been removed from his throat. Watching him breathe so steadily on his own has filled me with a hope that I desperately needed. Despite everything that has happened between us in the last twelve months, and the ocean of despair of these past weeks, I still can't bear to give up hope. I want people like Leo in the world, whether he's in *my* world or not.

❖ ❖ ❖

It's late in the morning of day eleven after my arrival in Rome when I am woken by the sound of Leo coughing and grunting. I have been asleep in the chair under the window, my head on one armrest, my legs dangling over the other.

'I'm here, Leo,' I call. I'm not sure if he can move his neck, so I lean over the bed as I reach it. I see frustration in his wrinkled brow, so I fumble for his glasses. It's a relief to finally slip them back onto his face. Now that the swelling and bruising are fading, he has looked so strange without his trademark tortoise-shell frames. I see his pupils shrink and expand as he adjusts to the lenses again and then his gaze fixes on mine. I offer a smile, but it's weak and wobbly because I am too scared even to breathe. At first, Leo doesn't react at all – and for a moment I feel the crushing swell of disappointment in my chest – what if this is as good as it gets? What if he is awake now, but will never speak or respond to my presence?

My hips and legs are stiff. I can't stand over him forever, so I sink slowly into the chair beside his bed. Suddenly, my emotions swing again – now I'm excited because he turns his head to follow me. He stares at me – concentrating intently, but then his eyes narrow suddenly and I'm sure I see something of an accusation in them. I am instantly defensive – is he questioning my right to be here? What did he expect me to do – stay in Sydney and leave him here alone? Once again, he has no idea what he has put me through. The hide of the man is incomprehensible.

But I can't snap at him – he's emerging from a coma, for God's sake. Just as this thought crosses my mind, Leo's eyes drift closed again.

The doctors warned me that this might take a while and that we have no choice but to be patient – but I have already been patient for far too long and I have well and truly exhausted my supply of that virtue. I realise belatedly that I am so hungry that the bitter taste of nausea lingers in my throat and I rise reluctantly to head for the cafeteria. As I leave Leo's room I ask myself what I really want out of the next few days. The answer is waiting at the forefront of my mind, but even as I acknowledge it, the guilt begins to rise.

I want Leo to wake up as quickly as possible and to somehow be completely okay. And then I want to go home and finally get on with my life.

CHAPTER 2

Leo – 2011

Hi Leo

I hope this email finds you well. I have been following your career – congratulations on the Pulitzer and the wonderful success you've achieved. My brother would have been so proud of you, he always told me you were going to do something great with your life.

As I'm sure you know, it was the tenth anniversary of Dec's death a few months ago. I was hoping you could spare me some time when you're next in Sydney to have a chat about his last days. I do understand that I'm asking a lot of you but if you are able to sit down and chat with me, I think understanding things a little better might bring me the closure I need. My contact details are below; please give me a call if you can.

Sincerely,

Molly

I was in a field hospital in Libya when I saw her note nestled in the first few entries in my inbox. It had been three weeks since I checked my mail. So many emails, so little care – hers was the only one out of the 200-odd waiting that I bothered to open. I was sitting on a stretcher, my left arm in a sling, a bullet lodged in my shoulder. I'd been lucky; there was minimal damage – supposedly. Still, it throbbed like hell and I was distracted when I first read Molly's email on the screen of my satellite phone, but that wasn't why I sent it straight to trash.

'So,' Brad Norse, my photo-journalist partner-in-crime, was seated on a chair beside me. 'Home we go?'

'Home?' I repeated, then I sighed. 'Brad…'

'When one of us gets shot, we get to go home for a while. It's one of the perks.'

'Please—' I turned off the satellite phone. 'This barely counts as "getting shot". The bullet missed all the important bits.'

'That's the morphine speaking.'

'They didn't have any morphine. I think they gave me paracetamol.' Or maybe it had been some kind of sugar pill because whatever it was I'd swallowed two hours earlier, it hadn't done a thing to ease the thumping pain in my shoulder. The truth was I almost wanted to go home too. The field medic had assessed me with the equipment he had available, but I wanted to be sure I wasn't going to wind up with permanent damage – and I really needed something stronger for the pain. But we had only been in Libya for a few weeks and I wasn't at all satisfied with the progress I'd made on my research. And now, if I went home to Sydney to recuperate, I'd have to face Molly Torrington and her uncomfortable questions about her brother's death.

'We're going home, Leo,' Brad said suddenly. I shook my head, and then winced as the movement inadvertently triggered a damaged muscle in my shoulder.

'There's more to do here,' I said, when I'd caught my breath again.

'There's *always* more to do. I'm going with or without you. Your psyche might be made of cast iron, but mine isn't – that bullet could have killed either one of us. I need a chance to regroup.'

In the end I didn't have any choice. I'd used the words 'flesh wound' when describing the incident to our editor, Kisani Hughes, but when Brad called her later that day, he gave a different assessment and she recalled us to Sydney. I grumbled, but by the time our plane touched down, I had a fever and signs of infection. Begrudgingly, I agreed that she'd made the right call.

I did not, however, agree with the medical leave the staff doctor then insisted I take. Several weeks of enforced time off was my idea of a nightmare. Within a few days I was bored out of my skull. I couldn't exercise or walk my dog, or ride my motorbike. I couldn't even run karate classes as I normally would when in Sydney between assignments. I did a lot of reading and an awful lot of thinking, but whether I was trying to focus on a novel, or awkwardly making breakfast with my one useful arm, my mind constantly circled back to Molly Torrington.

I'd always felt for her but I knew that any conversation about her brother's death was going to be painful for both of us. I could never give her the closure she was seeking anyway; there had never been any easy answers when it came to Declan Torrington.

I'd never really known her well. For years I'd floated on the periphery of their family life, but as an unwelcome guest at the best of times. The last time I'd seen her in person had been at her brother's funeral, when she stared down at the gravesite almost unblinkingly – a shocked expression on her face throughout the entire proceedings. Every other time I'd ever seen Molly, she'd been laughing or smiling – the kind of joyous and privileged child who approached every situation with a broad, generous beam. Declan used to joke that her riotous laugh always arrived at a room before she did – announcing her arrival like a town crier might have announced royalty.

His funeral was the first time I'd seen her look sad and the depth of misery in her eyes that day made me wonder if the sheer size and shape of this sudden grief would change her; maybe she would never wear that same brilliantly easy smile again? In this unexpected email all these years later the lingering grief in her words suggested that I'd been right.

I'd seen her in the press at times – Including the cover of a finance magazine only a year or two earlier when she was promoted to VP of something or other at *Torrington Media*. I remember spotting the magazine in a newsagent at Dubai airport and doing a double take – surely she was too young to be working for her father? I'd calculated the years and realised with some shock that she was in her late twenties. To me it seemed unfathomable that cheerful Molly Torrington would one day lead a global media empire, but in the article she was already touted as the logical successor to her father.

Molly was doing what Declan could not: forging a path from childhood to adulthood in the immense shadow of Laith Torrington's expectations and legacy. But judging by that studio-shot cover photo, the carefree kid I'd once known had altogether gone. She had cut off the caramel hair that she'd worn to her waist in her younger years and what was left was now a stark blonde. In the photo she was smiling, but the smile stopped dead at her lips. Her blue eyes were hard and her gaze was sharp as she met the camera, almost issuing a challenge – *you want to mess with me?* If I hadn't seen her new look evolve via the media, I'd never have recognised her – she had morphed from a fun-loving kid to a very grown-up corporate shark.

I wondered how much of that transformation was the result of the loss of her brother. Then I wondered what Declan would make of it all and what *he* would have me do. I'd never been a fan of leaving skeletons to rest – it went against my nature and even my training – but I'd also made a point of not applying that philosophy to personal matters. Deeply held moments should definitely be left to fade into history. Still, I accepted that I couldn't make that decision for Molly and I recovered her email from the trash folder. As I dialled her mobile phone, I ignored the sensation of dread in my gut. It wasn't going to be a comfortable call, but I was *fairly* sure I was doing the right thing.

'Molly Torrington.' Her greeting was abrupt.

'Hi – Molly – it's Leo.' When she didn't respond, I clarified carefully, 'Leo Stephens.'

'I know, sorry… I just… I didn't think you were going to call,' she said. I glanced at the email and realised it had been over month since she'd sent it.

'Sorry it's taken so long,' I said. 'I was on an assignment and then I was injured.'

'Are you okay?'

'Oh yeah, I'm fine. It's nothing.'

'Right, well…' she paused a little awkwardly. 'God, Leo, sorry to hear that, anyway.'

I tapped my toes against the carpet to expend the strange nervous energy I felt. The small talk felt unnatural and it was only prolonging the inevitable. 'You wanted to talk about Declan?' I said.

'Yes, I really did – do. Can we meet?'

'Meet?' This was unexpected, but as soon as she said the word, I realised it shouldn't have been.

'Uh, I'm…'

'Please,' she said quietly. The rhythmic tapping of my toes against the floor stopped. 'I won't take up much of your time, I promise.'

'Okay.'

'When suits?'

'I'm on sick leave. I can meet whenever you want to.'

'Now?'

'Now? But…'

'Later today then?'

'No, now is okay.' I sighed, then cautioned, 'I don't know what you think I can tell you, Molly.'

'But you found him, didn't you?'

At the memory I felt my chest contract. I could still see him in my mind's eye – Declan, lying limp on the filthy, threadbare carpet in a storage room in the basement of my cousin's building.

'Yeah.'

'Then…' she let the word hang.

I waited for her to finish the thought, but when it became clear that she wasn't going to, I said, 'Okay, where do you want to meet?'

✦ ✦ ✦

Declan and I met in the first few weeks of our course at Sydney Uni in the mid-1990s. We were paired together in a tutorial group to complete a joint assessment that in hindsight was most likely a cruel joke on the professor's part; the kid who still lived in a public housing unit with his unemployed mother partnered with the son of a billionaire who had been raised in a mansion on Sydney Harbour.

I was rough around the edges in those days, and I knew it. I remember sitting down next to Declan and feeling so intimidated I could barely bring myself to speak. Fortunately, I soon realised I wasn't the only person feeling out of my depth; Declan *looked* confident, with his uppity clothing and his carefully enunciated speech. The façade didn't last long – within one study session it was pretty apparent to me that he was going to need me to pass that assignment much more than I needed him.

Dec and I bonded deeply and quickly as only teenagers can, collectively stewing over a shared sense of injustice about our individual situations. As a young Aboriginal man in the sea of mostly white students in our class, I was an outsider and I was only there because of a special entry programme and my ability to write a convincing essay. But even as an exceedingly wealthy white kid, Declan did not belong in that group of students either – at high school he'd failed his final exams miserably. Were it not for his father's deep pockets, Declan would never have made it to university at all, let alone gained entry to a highly sought-after course at a prestigious institution like Sydney Uni.

With all his easy privileges it should have been easy for me to hate him and there were some days that I did. But Declan had one beautifully redeeming quality: he did not see money or lack thereof, or colour or race or any of the other trappings or categories that most people filter the world by. Right from the very beginning, I was nothing more or less than a friend; somehow, it never really occurred to him that there was any reason why I shouldn't be. When I finally, reluctantly, invited him to my home, he stepped into the tiny, dank apartment I shared with Mum and looked around.

'Shit, Leo!' he had said, genuinely confused and shocked. 'You're *poor?*'

'Yeah.'

'I didn't realise,' he said, and he shrugged and opened the fridge to look for a snack.

Declan was one of a kind – one of the good guys.

❖ ❖ ❖

Only an hour or so after our phone call I waited in a café at The Rocks for Molly to arrive. The dull thud of dread in my gut had not abated. There was no denying that the Torrington family had been embarrassed by Declan's death – the instant cover-up they manufactured for the media had more than proven that. I wondered whether anything I could tell Molly would comfort her.

'Sorry, I'm late…'

I hadn't noticed Molly approaching, but now she was standing right beside me and so I shot to my feet. We stared at each other for a moment, and then she opened her arms – offering me a hug. We'd never really touched before, not even at the funeral. Her father had made sure I was kept well away.

I accepted her embrace, turning my sling-clad arm away from her and gingerly reciprocating the hug with my good arm. Molly was much taller than I remembered – almost as tall as me – but as I had expected, she had the polished, careful air of a woman of significant wealth. She was wearing a lot of make-up – *too* much, to my eye – and a very heavy perfume. As we released one another and she took the seat opposite me, she fiddled awkwardly with the belt of her dress and then smoothed her hand down over the front part of her hair. Her white-blonde hair was so short – shorter even than mine. The only softness about her look was a slightly longer fringe that was brushed forward, curving down over her forehead towards her cheek.

'I can't thank you enough for this,' she said.

'Like I said – I just hope you're not expecting me to have any real answers. I can only tell you what I know.'

'Should we order coffee?' She was already flagging down a waiter, who nearly fell over himself rushing to greet her. I'd forgotten what it was like to be in public with a Torrington – Molly and Declan had never really been household names, but they were familiar to many people because of who their father was. Whenever Dec and I had spent time at bars in our uni days, we were always plied with free drinks – a bonus for me, who couldn't have afforded the drinks otherwise, but it amused Declan, who even in his late teens had access to a trust fund that was virtually limitless.

Once we'd each ordered a coffee, Molly and I got somehow stuck in a holding pattern, each waiting for the other to begin. After an uncomfortably long time, I found myself prompting her to start the conversation that I didn't even want to have.

'So, what *did* you want to know?'

'I know this is weird,' she admitted. 'I thought about getting in touch with you a lot, even right after it happened. But it was just such a mess and it had been such a shock. And I was embarrassed because of how Dad treated you at the funeral. I didn't know what to say to you or how to apologise.'

'It wasn't your place to apologise. It still isn't,' I told her.

She sighed heavily. 'Well, I *am* sorry. You deserved to be with us that day. No one knew Declan like you did.'

'Your brother was a particularly special kind of guy,' I said quietly. I still thought about Declan often, but I hadn't spoken about him in years. It felt odd – more than a little unnatural.

'Dad had a heart attack last year,' Molly said suddenly, and I frowned.

'I'm sorry to hear that.' I was also surprised that I hadn't heard that already, given that her father was one of the biggest names in the industry.

'Yeah. That's off the record, of course. Dad didn't want the shareholders to find out so...' Molly sighed wearily as she rubbed her forehead, then she looked directly at me. 'The thing is, Dad had a heart attack, and Declan *supposedly* died of an undiagnosed heart condition. So you'd think Dad would have his doctors look into Declan's illness to make sure it's not genetic, right?'

She looked at me, waiting for a response, so I opened my mouth to say something but no words came out at all. Molly seemed strangely satisfied by the shock I couldn't hide. She crossed her arms over her chest and peered at me as she continued quietly. 'Whenever I brought the subject up or even mentioned Declan's name, Dad yelled, Mum sobbed. Something *never* added up and I'm embarrassed to admit this, but until Dad's heart attack, it was just easier for me to pretend I hadn't noticed. Did Declan kill himself, Leo?'

She delivered that last brutal question without hesitation, but when I glanced at her I saw the way she braced herself as she waited for my answer.

'No – God *no*! He didn't.'

Molly's tight posture relaxed, but only a little.

'Well? It obviously wasn't some random heart problem. So what am I missing?'

'Just...' I exhaled heavily and stared at the table. 'Just give me a second, okay?' I thought for a moment I had been saved by the arrival of the coffees, but soon discovered that there was only so long I could stare into my latte while I tried to figure out what to say to her.

I knew that Laith and Danielle Torrington had lied to the world about Declan's death – and I almost understood why. I also knew that Molly had not known the truth about his illness when he was alive. He'd asked us all to keep it from her, and I could understand that too. He was terrified that she'd think less of him.

It had never occurred to me that the lies to protect her would have continued *after* his death. I despised Laith Torrington and everything he stood for, but not for one second had I expected that he would stoop as low as this.

'Leo?' Molly prompted me very gently. She was trying to tread lightly, assuming I was still hurting over the loss of my friend. But I wasn't – not really. Ten years had passed, and I'd seen plenty of other horrors in those years to harden me. My hesitation was only because I had just walked into a situation expecting to find sadness, only to discover it was an ethical minefield instead. I didn't take sugar but to busy myself, I reached for the sugar bowl and scooped a half-spoonful into my coffee then stirred slowly before I looked up at her.

'I have no idea what to say to you, Molly,' I admitted.

'But you know something I don't? Did you know he was sick?'

I stirred the coffee again, just so I had somewhere else to look – somewhere safely away from her pleading blue eyes. 'Yes,' I muttered. This time the simple word was layered with truth. Yes, I knew he was sick – he *was* sick, in the grip of a monstrous addiction that resisted any treatment any of us could throw at it. I had expected that she would ask me the details of his spiral downwards into addiction and that would have been difficult enough. This scenario was a whole new level of complicated. I cleared my throat.

'You need to ask Laith and Danielle these questions, Molly.'

'I can't – I've tried, honestly – I've pushed them as hard as I can. They won't – or they *can't* – talk about it. They won't even talk about him at all.'

The dread in my gut had turned to a churning. I pushed the coffee away towards the middle of the table before I slid my chair back and rose. 'Look, I'm really sorry I can't help you, but these are things you need to discuss with your parents, not with me.' I slid my wallet out of my pocket. After some awkward fumbling with the sling, I dropped a note onto the table that would cover both coffees; then I dared to glance at Molly's face one last time. Her eyes were narrow and her lips pursed – Molly Torrington was pissed off. It wasn't the first time I'd left a member of the Torrington family in that state, but I felt a pang of remorse.

Molly rose too, and she stared at me. 'Leo,' she stated calmly, but with some determination. 'I deserve to know, and no one else is going to tell me but you.'

I thought about the last argument I'd had with Laith at the hospital. I remembered Declan's body cooling on the bed behind him and Danielle, lying over her son, wailing. I remembered Laith's breath on my face and his spittle on my skin as he lost control of his emotions. I remembered the battle I'd fought with myself to resist an overwhelming urge to lash out at him – I *could* have taken him. With one punch or a well-placed kick, I could have silenced those cruel words that were barbs into my raw, grief-stripped emotions.

'*You filthy piece of scum! You did this to him. He would never have known where to buy this shit if it wasn't for your bastard abo family!*'

But it wasn't my problem. It wasn't my place to tell her. It wasn't going to help her even if she did know. I was tempted to just walk out and leave her standing there. Then I glanced at Molly and saw the desperation in her eyes. I sighed. 'This isn't a conversation for a café.'

Molly winced, but it was only a fleeting expression – she immediately flagged down a waiter.

'Can we get these coffees into takeaway cups?'

CHAPTER 3
Molly – July 2015

Leo wakes again just after lunch and this time from the moment his eyes open, it's obvious that he is much more alert. When I lift his glasses to his face, his hands meet mine and the contact feels strangely awkward. I realise that he wants to position his glasses without assistance and I smile to myself; this stubborn, independent man is the Leo I've known and loved.

'Hi, Leo,' I murmur softly.

'Hello,' he says, and I am startled by the hoarse and oddly formal word. Leo exhales deeply and for a moment his eyes close. His hands drop from his face to his throat, and when he opens his eyes again he croaks, 'Throat sore. Water?'

'I don't know,' I say, and frantically press the call button for the nurse. Immediately I hear footsteps and Alda appears. One of the youngest nurses, she speaks only a little English. Alda's dark eyebrows raise when she sees Leo and she beams at me and claps. 'He is awake!'

These weeks in Rome have only taught me basic Italian, but I've become a world-class expert at plucking English words from the tangle of a heavy accent. 'And he's *speaking*,' I say. Suddenly I realise just how amazing and wonderful this is and I feel a tear running down my cheek. I swipe at it with the back of my hand but I needn't have bothered. He's clueless when it comes to his own emotions, but Leo has never been left uncomfortable by tears. Having spent most of his adult life reporting from war zones, he is well accustomed to suffering.

'Can I have water?' Leo asks.

Alda nods enthusiastically. 'Oh, Mr Stephens – I check. This is very good!' she says, and then disappears from the doorway.

'Where am I?' Leo looks to me again.

'We're in Rome, Leo.'

'No,' he says immediately. 'Libya.'

'Libya? No, you were on an embed in Syria. You were medevaced here for treatment after a car accident. Don't you remember?'

'No, no...' Leo shakes his head, but the movement clearly causes him some pain – he winces and his hand lifts towards his skull. I glance at the clock and realise he's due for medication.

'It was a pretty serious injury – it's okay to be confused,' I murmur, but I've already reached for my phone and I quickly draft a group message to our friends and family back home.

Leo is awake and speaking. He is confused, but he's awake!! And speaking!!

As I hit the send button I feel triumphant. I knew he'd be okay – I just *knew* it. Leo Stephens has always been the kind of man who laughs in the face of other people's expectations of him.

'I'm not confused. I feel fine – except for the headache,' he says, and he's staring at me, his brow wrinkled. He shifts on the bed then wiggles his right shoulder around. He *was* shot there, but that was four years ago and I wonder why that injury would be troubling him now. 'I was in Libya. I know I was.'

'It doesn't matter for now anyway,' I say, as gently as I can. It's very late back in Sydney but already my phone is lighting up with text messages as people reply to the good news of his progress. Leo gives a sudden, exasperated sigh and my triumphant buzz fades a little at his arrogance.

It should not surprise me that Leo has woken from a coma with a serious head injury and still assumes that he knows better than me how he came to be injured. One of the things that attracted me to him in the first place was how well he knows his own mind. That same quality has driven me nearly insane over the course of our marriage.

'Why are you here, anyway?' he asks, and now I can't help myself – I glare at him.

'Seriously, Leo?'

He grimaces and shakes his head, then winces hard at the pain again. I try to suppress my frustration. It is actually a fair question but God, couldn't he have slipped in a 'thanks for coming' somewhere around it?

'I don't mean…' he clears his throat. 'I'm sorry.'

'It just didn't seem right for you to be here alone,' I say after a moment. 'I can go if you want me to.'

'Do you live here now?'

'What do you mean?' I drop my phone into my handbag and lean low towards him as I clarify, 'Do I live in *Rome*? No, of course I don't. I still live in Sydney.'

'Well,' Leo clears his throat and I recognise awkwardness in the way that he is avoiding my gaze. He looks to the roof for a while, then glances at me and says carefully, 'I mean, thanks – but…'

'Anne just couldn't come, Leo,' I say gently. His mother is petrified of flying, and even when it looked a lot like Leo wasn't going to make it, I couldn't convince her to get on a plane. I don't want to tell Leo that – it would surely hurt him, so I lie about the reason for her absence. 'She wanted to, but Teresa really needed her – she's is having a very difficult time with the boys and we weren't sure how long you'd be here for. And Andrew – well, he's so busy at the Centre and he's doing a lot with Tobias in my absence so we couldn't both be away indefinitely…'

I'm babbling, until I glance at Leo's face and see that his eyes are wide open and he's staring at me as if I've shocked him. I quickly scan over the words I've just said and am confused – although I'm sure he's disappointed that I'm the only person here, he shouldn't be all that surprised. His family is a wonderful group of people, but none of them are in a position to drop everything to be at his bedside.

'Leo? Are you okay?' I reach onto the bed to touch his forearm and immediately he recoils. I know this makes sense, but it still stings. I sit up stiffly and look away, hoping he can't see how much the rejection hurts me.

'Call the nurse for me?' he asks stiffly. I assume something is medically wrong and so I reach for the buzzer and hit it with urgency.

'What is it, Leo? Can you tell me what's wrong?'

Leo looks towards the door and is visibly relieved when another nurse appears. I am relieved too, because it's Edmondo, and his English is excellent. He is carrying Leo's pain medication and a large glass of water.

'Sorry for the delay, Mr Stephens – we had to check with the doctor if you could start oral fluids. Is everything okay?'

'Yes, thank you – and please…' Leo looks at me and clears his throat. 'Can I speak with him alone?'

I know this makes sense too and I remind myself that Leo has every right to his privacy. My internal lecture doesn't help – I'm still offended and now I'm annoyed. I've been sitting by his bedside for almost two weeks and the minute he wakes up, he asks me to leave? *Bastard!*

'Fine,' I say, and I rise, but before I take a single step I shoot him a sharp look just in case he's somehow missed my snarky tone. As I reach the door Edmondo looks at me curiously. I wonder what he's going to think of all of this – how odd it will seem to him.

I am embarrassed that our private issues are about to become public knowledge to the staff here. Leo would say it doesn't matter, and that the only reason I care at all is that I have a chronic need for approval. He'd probably be right about that – I feel shame at the looming judgement I'll receive from the hospital staff, even before they know the truth about us at all.

I leave the room, but I stay near to the door so that I can eavesdrop. Leo might think he wants privacy, but he has a serious head injury and whether he likes it or not, I'm still his wife and his only support in Rome. Until I'm sure that he's fine, I'm not going anywhere.

'How are you feeling, Mr Stephens?' I hear the sounds of movement, and then the whir of Leo's bed being adjusted.

'I'm okay.' There's silence for a moment, and I hear Leo slurping at his water. 'How long have I been here?'

'Almost two weeks,' Edmondo says, and there's the sound of intermittent typing as he updates Leo's notes on the computer.

'I have a head injury?'

'Your skull was fractured.'

'And why is my throat sore?'

'From the respirator, it will get better in time.'

'It's hard to speak.'

'It was a pretty significant injury, Mr Stephens. I'm impressed you can speak at all.'

'Molly – how long has she been here?'

I bite my lip at the ice in Leo's tone. How has it come to this? I have flown halfway around the world to be there with him. Surely that earns me some warmth?

'The whole time, sir. She arrived the day after you did.'

'And – do you know why?'

'Why *what*, Mr Stephens?'

'Why she is here?' Leo says. His words are clipped with impatience. I frown and lean closer to the door, wondering if I've misheard him. Surely he would at least understand why I came. Despite everything, I know he'd have done the same for me if our circumstances were reversed.

'You know who she is?' Edmondo asks.

'Of course I do, she's Molly Torrington,' Leo says. I note that he's already dropped the 'Stephens' off my surname and I flush. Poor Edmondo, I should have at least warned him. 'I know *who* she is, I just don't know why she is here.'

'What's your name, Mr Stephens?'

'I know my name.'

'Humour me, sir.'

'Leonardo David Stephens.'

'And your date of birth?'

'March tenth, 1975.'

'And do you know the date?'

'How long did you say I was in a coma?'

'A week and a half, sir.'

Leo doesn't hesitate. He answers the nurse with complete confidence. 'Then it must be February.'

I almost second-guess myself when I hear this response. I'm exhausted and I may have lost track of time a little – but I *know* that it's not February.

'And the year?'

There's a long pause, and the longer it stretches, the more anxious I feel. After a moment or two, Edmondo gives Leo a gentle prompt.

'Please, humour me, Mr Stephens. It is just procedure to check such things when someone wakes from a serious injury.'

'It's 2011,' Leo says the words with an impatient sigh. I wait for Edmondo to correct him, but there is only the sound of typing, then the screech of the keyboard tray being returned to its home beneath the computer.

'Why don't you rest now?' Edmondo says. 'The doctor will be in soon.'

'I'm just confused why she's even here,' Leo says. 'I hardly know her. She was talking about my family too. Something's not right.'

'I will ask her to wait outside until we figure out what is going on.'

My heart is racing as I hear Edmondo approaching the door and by the time he joins me in the corridor, I'm shaking all over.

'You were listening?' He chastises me quietly as he closes the door behind him.

'What was that? What was he talking about?'

'His injury is severe; he is confused. It is normal.'

'*Normal?*' I repeat the word incredulously.

'Well, maybe not *normal*.' Edmondo concedes. 'But it is nothing unexpected. The doctor will look him over.'

Edmondo's calmness is instantly irritating. I can barely stand still – I feel nervous tension all the way down to my toes.

'Will it happen now?'

'I think Craig Walker is here, Molly. I will ask him to do a cognitive review as soon as he can, okay? But because Leo is so confused, it's best that you wait out here until he does.'

Craig Walker is an ex-pat American ICU specialist and he has been a godsend since my arrival – checking on Leo often. He sometimes even stops by at the end of his shift to explain procedures to me. I pace the hall while I wait, and when he approaches I greet him as if he's a long-lost relative.

'Did Edmondo tell you?'

'Of course,' he says. He has a clipboard under his arm and he pulls it out to show me a questionnaire. 'I'm going to do a cognitive assessment on Leo now, and *you* are going to take yourself for a walk to get something to eat and some fresh air. I'll be a while.'

✦ ✦ ✦

It's over an hour before Craig leaves Leo's room. I don't go for fresh air or food – I sit on the bench in the corridor and I worry instead. When Craig closes the door quietly behind him, his expression is grim. He takes a seat beside me and asks gently, 'How are you holding up, Molly?'

'Good. I'm good, of course. He's okay? Is he going to be okay?'

'Well, as expected, I suppose. There are a few things not quite working as they should yet. Firstly, there's some motor issues with his lower body. He was a little freaked out by that, but I'm not too concerned – it's very early days.'

'He can't walk?'

'He's a long way from walking, I'm afraid,' Craig explains. 'I've just done some preliminary testing – it will take some time to figure out exactly what is going on there. He has sensation in his lower limbs but impairment in his control of the muscles – basically his movement is limited. I don't want to worry you too much until we know some more. There are plenty of good signs, and all of his other physical abilities are intact. With a bit of rehab, there's a good chance we can resolve this.'

'Does this mean he will be in a wheelchair?'

'For the time being, yes.'

I think this through, then shake my head as if it's a request I can decline on Leo's behalf. Like – *no thanks, Leo doesn't like scrambled eggs* or *no thanks, he won't read the tabloid paper, can we have the broadsheet?* Instead, it's just *no thanks, Leo won't cope with life in a wheelchair, could you just fix him instead?* Leo is a foreign affairs reporter who specialises in work in volatile war zones; he cannot do that work from a wheelchair. He is a fitness fanatic and a karate instructor in his spare time, and he lives in a three-storey terrace – his beloved office is on the top floor, his bedroom on the second. How can he even live in his home if he's in a wheelchair? Nothing works. There's no workaround that I could offer that would make this news anything other than devastating – not for Leo.

'He will adjust, Molly,' Craig says quietly. 'So will you. And like I said there's a very good chance that with the right therapy and some hard work, he can get past this. Please don't panic yet.'

'If it were *me*, I could live a very full life. But Leo won't cope with this.'

'You will both figure it out. And there'll be plenty of support along the way.'

I rub my eyes with my fists and sigh, but then I remember that this isn't even all of it. I grimace at the doctor.

'And the rest? Why does he think it's 2011?'

'It seems to be a case of what we call partial retrograde amnesia. Was Leo shot during the Libyan civil war?'

'Yes, in the shoulder.'

'That's actually the last thing he remembers. He feels like that happened earlier today and he's just woken up,' Craig says. 'Obviously you didn't know Leo in 2011?'

I'd known him as a kid, but I don't have the energy to explain any of that now, so I only nod.

'We met shortly after that, actually.' I try to figure out what Leo's last memory of me would be and realise that it would be of Declan's funeral. No wonder he was bewildered when he saw me. 'Did you tell him?'

'Yes.'

'What did he say?'

Craig smiles ruefully. 'He didn't believe me. I had to do a Google image search to show him some paparazzi photos of you two together. He said he needs to think about it. I am pretty sure he thinks we're playing a practical joke on him.'

'God!' I groan and rub my forehead. 'Doesn't this just complicate *everything*? So I'm a stranger to him?'

'Try not to panic,' Craig says quietly, and I suddenly wish I'd kept count of how many times he's said those words since I first met him. I suspect the tally would be into the hundreds by now. 'He's on the list for a full neurological assessment from the specialist in the next day or so anyway, but I'll try to speed things up. In any case, this kind of amnesia really is unlikely to be permanent. Hopefully, his memory will return quickly and in the meantime we'll just make sure he's calm and focused on getting better, okay?'

'How much should I *tell* him?'

'He's going to be very drowsy for a while yet, so I don't think you need to worry too much about bringing him up to speed. If he asks specific questions, answer them – but don't feel you have to repaint the memories for him. Just keep it vague enough to give him the chance to remember for himself.'

'Okay,' I sigh. So much for getting Leo home and getting on with my life. 'I thought things couldn't get any worse.'

'Ah, Molly,' Craig laughs and pats me on the back a little patronisingly. 'Things really could be a *lot* worse, trust me. This is the last series of hurdles, hopefully.'

✦ ✦ ✦

As instructed, I am trying not to panic but I'm failing miserably, and my own energy levels have reached an all-time low. I force myself to return to Leo's room and am relieved to find he is already asleep.

I have no idea what I'm going to say to him. What is there *to* say that will satiate the questions he will have, and at the same time help him to stay calm? Leo knows who I am, but not who *we* are. How exactly do you educate someone on the entire circle of a relationship – particularly one as complex as ours? So we met, fell very deeply in love, got married and then…

And then there's the worst part – the messy months in this current year of our life together. It is too much to contemplate and after all the tension and stress, this amnesia feels like one more blow to what has already been the worst period of my life.

Leo would snap at me if he knew just how sorry I am feeling for myself – *get some perspective, Molly! There are children starving to death in Syria, you can survive a few awkward weeks with me.* I try to console myself and to stay grounded. I need to calm myself too, and there are real positives here. Leo is alive, against all the odds. He can move – well, mostly – and he can speak. There could very easily have been infinitely worse outcomes from this accident.

I have somehow drifted into a light doze at Leo's bedside when I am woken by movement. Hesitantly I open my eyes and see Alda standing beside him, setting up a tray on the mobile table.

'I feel better every time I wake up,' I hear Leo murmur quietly.

'This good, Mr Stephens.'

'Please, call me Leo. It's Alda, isn't it?'

'*Si*, Leo,' Alda confirms.

I stay in my chair, watching from a distance, unsure of what I should do. Do I approach the bed, or does he want privacy? There has been no dignity in the care he's required in the last few weeks, but at least he didn't know about it – his consciousness presents a new layer of sensitivity that I will need to navigate carefully.

'I'm *unbelievably* thirsty and hungry,' he says now, and Alda laughs quietly.

'You no eat or drink for two weeks – I'm not surprised!' she chuckles. I hear her tearing open packaging. 'I feed you?'

'No. God, no!' he says, and he takes a spoon from her. 'Apparently I can't move my legs or remember what year it is, but I can definitely feed myself.'

He glances towards me and our eyes meet and lock. I have invested countless hours of my life staring into these beautiful brown eyes. I remember vividly the feeling of being close to lost in them when we first started going out – the sensation of sinking and drowning and feeling blissfully content to go to some other place with and through him. Leo's eyes have seen the world in a way that I could never have imagined before I met him and in all of the perfect moments of those intimate stares, he shared some of that with me.

This is not one of those moments. In fact, those moments have disappeared altogether from our lives this past year. I can't even remember the last time we really looked at each other – these days our eye contact has been reduced to passing glances and disdainful glares. Seeing the openness and curiosity in Leo's eyes, I am sorely tempted to pretend even to myself that everything is as it always was, even just for a moment. This thought is followed immediately by guilt, as if I'm using Leo while he's vulnerable – taking advantage of him even just in the way I'm looking at him. I drag my eyes to the floor before I greet him.

'Hi.'

'Hello, Molly,' he says quietly. We fall silent as Alda pushes the little bed-table over Leo's lap and then she flashes me a smile as she leaves the room. Then I am alone with my husband and there is no denying it – I am too nervous to even think straight and I have no idea what to do next. I stand but immediately regret it because I don't want to move towards the bed and make him feel even more uncomfortable. After a moment of leaning forward as if I might approach him, then hesitating and stepping back, I settle on standing stiffly with my hands clenched in fists by my thighs. I will wait for Leo to make the first move.

'I'm really sorry,' he says suddenly. 'About before. Was that earlier today, or was it yesterday?'

'It was a few hours ago. And please, you don't need to apologise, really.' I trip over my words in my haste to console him. 'You don't remember anything at all about us?' He shakes his head. 'That must have been bewildering for you.'

'It's still bewildering,' he says quietly. I can hear the uncertainty in his voice – he's still not convinced that we are telling him the truth. I walk to the small table beside his bed and withdraw my handbag, then reach inside for my passport which I flip open and then sit on the blanket beside his thigh.

'See? Molly Torrington-Stephens.' I show him the text beside the obligatory bad photo and then I raise the fingers of my left hand towards him to draw attention to my rings. 'And this, as I'm sure you remember, was your grandmother's engagement ring. You had a new stone set in it because the old one was cracked, but the design will be familiar.'

He silently stares at the rings on my left hand. We have never talked about it, because Leo does not cry and he does not talk about crying – but I am sure I saw tears in his eyes when he slid this band onto my finger at our wedding. We made each other happy, at least that day. It was the kind of happiness that grows bigger than a person or a couple and engulfs everyone there to witness it. It was the best day of my life.

In spite of everything that came after, the idea that the memories of who we were together might be for ever lost to him is unbearable. We were good to each other – good for each other – at least for a time. I lift my eyes to his face and find him staring at the passport again, his expression unreadable.

'If this is true,' he says suddenly. 'Why aren't I wearing a ring?'

'It's at home,' I say. His band is silver and, like mine, plain except for a single etched line around the middle. A line without an end, he'd pointed out to me as we stared at our hands in an exhausted bubble of bliss in the hours after the wedding. But quickly, that memory shatters and is replaced at the forefront of my mind by thoughts of the last time I saw Leo's ring. I had walked into the bathroom to check the cabinets for make-up I'd missed when I packed. The sight of the ring was a punch to the gut and I completely lost my breath. It was sitting in the little soap-rest in the moulded bathroom counter-top – partially submerged in a tiny but still-sudsy puddle. I spent hours that night trying to convince myself that Leo might have left it there by accident; it seemed impossible that he would have been willing to take it off so quickly.

'So, I took it off before I went to Libya,' Leo says. He stops and carefully corrects himself, 'to *Syria* – for safekeeping?'

I know I need to tell him the truth and this seems to be the right moment to do it – I'm just not sure how he's going to react. I hesitate, and while I'm wondering about this, Leo continues without waiting for my response.

'*No*,' he says, and he shakes his head violently. I see the echoes of pain that cross his face as he does so, then he raises his eyes and his glare issues me with a determined challenge. 'I don't buy it. It doesn't make any sense. What's really going on here?'

I clear my throat and sit gingerly on the bed beside my passport, close to him, but careful to avoid touching him. I try to slow my thoughts down so that I can plot out the best response. Here I am worrying about how to tell him our marriage is all but over, and he still doesn't believe it ever began.

'It's a long story,' I say. 'But I promise it *will* make sense once you remember the missing years. Why would I even lie about this? Why else would I be here? And I can *prove* the current date to you. I mean—' I pick up the passport again and show it to him. 'You think it's 2011, right? Well, this passport was issued in 2014.'

'It's not the *date* I can't believe,' he says, and he's impatient enough now to snap at me. He waves his hand between us. 'It's *this*. I *know* I wouldn't have married you.'

His dismissive tone stings, and although I'm determined not to get into an argument with him, there is no way I'm going to let him speak to me like that. 'And what's that supposed to mean?' I ask him pointedly. Leo winces just a little.

'Obviously we are just too different. If I was going to marry someone, and I wasn't – it wouldn't have been you.'

'If you can't remember past 2011, you don't even know me,' I raise an eyebrow at him. 'Besides which, it's too late to raise these objections now. Whether you remember it or not, we've been married for almost three years.'

'I don't need to know you to know that we aren't compatible. You're a *Torrington*. That's all I need to know. I wouldn't have gone there.'

'Leo, you're being an arse,' I say. The words are strained, not because I'm hurt by his stereotyping me, but because I'm infuriated by his arrogance and fighting hard to hold back my natural inclination to snap at him.

'I don't mean to offend you—' he starts to say, but his tone is so patronising that I finally snap. I slam the passport shut and throw it into my handbag by the bed.

'If you really don't want to offend me, stop *assuming* that you know who I am just because you know my maiden name. That's about all you remember about me, right? How dare you try to tell me that it would be impossible for someone like you to marry someone like me just because of who my family is. Imagine if our positions were reversed and I said that to you!'

Leo's mouth is still open. He slowly closes it, and looks back to his meal. I exhale and rub my forehead wearily, and I think the conversation is over until he mutters, 'I am *far* too old for you.'

'Leo!' I groan. '*God!* It's only ten years and it has never been an issue.'

'What would we even have in common? How did we even meet?' He pushes the empty apple puree cup away and frowns at me again. 'I don't even *want* to get married.'

I laugh a little at that, because I know his concerns were always about how a spouse might fit into the demanding schedule he keeps – and now, with the benefit of hindsight, I can see that he was absolutely right. He raises his eyebrows at me and I assure him, 'I know you didn't. But you obviously changed your mind because you proposed and then went ahead and married me.'

'But how? Why would I change my mind?' Leo's prompts are impatient and my laughter fades. I can see that he's tiring again already, and I make a mental note to check with Craig Walker just *how* much I should be shielding him from stress. If I'm supposed to be keeping him completely calm, I'm going to have my work cut out. I take a few deep breaths and slide off the bed, and then take the seat beside him. Leo just *has* to come to terms with this because I'm all he has here in Rome. There is no one else, and no one else is coming, and I still have no idea when we will be able to leave or even what awaits him back in Sydney.

The first thing I need to do is to make him realise that he can trust me – that he *used* to trust me – and there is probably only one way to do that. When I do speak again, I manage to do so very gently – conscious of the delicate subject I need to reference.

'I know that until you were thirteen or fourteen, you were sure that it was inevitable that you'd end up just like Mike.'

There are two words we don't ever use when we're talking about Leo's family. The first word is 'step' – although Teresa is technically his step-sister, and Andrew his step-father. To Leo they are simply family, and on the odd occasion when I've used the 'step' prefix by mistake, he has always corrected me instantly. The other word we don't use is 'Mike' – Leo's biological father's name. We have had exactly three conversations about Mike in four years, and I initiated every one of them. Leo does not dwell on the unhappy periods of his childhood and he prefers not to speak about them, but I have become convinced that those times have marked him in a way that is every bit as real as the tattoos that cover his arms and shoulders.

Now, when I say Mike's name, Leo's shock is palpable – as I knew it would be. With that one word I have proved to him that he has trusted me with the depths of his inner world. Nothing at all about his outer life these days would even acknowledge Mike's existence.

'You were actually completely wrong about who you are until you experienced a little bit more of the world and you learnt differently,' I say quietly. 'It was the same kind of revelation when we met.' I search for a way to articulate it. I hadn't understood the breadth and depth of real love before I met Leo. In the past I'd thought I'd loved boyfriends, but in hindsight I can see that those feelings were shallow and fragile. The love I had for Leo was something unique and special – something altogether different, although it's painful to acknowledge that now even to myself. I sigh and look at Leo again. His gaze is guarded, but he's watching me closely.

'It was as if I'd only ever felt in black and white before, and then falling in love with you was my first experience of colour. And I *know* it was like that for you too. We fell very hard, very fast, and every idea we had about the future had to be reconsidered because the world was suddenly a different place.' I wrinkle my nose as I fumble for the right words. 'It was just *that* good, you know?'

'It would have to have been,' Leo says. He's still frowning, but I can see that my explanation has gone at least some way towards convincing him. 'So, where *did* we meet, then?'

'I emailed you to ask you some questions about Dec. We met up to discuss that, and things evolved from there.' His face is set in a fierce frown. I recognise intense concentration and give him a minute or two. I wonder if he's remembering something and after a while curiosity gets the better of me. I touch his arm very gently. 'Leo?'

He sinks heavily back against his pillows. The frown gives way to weariness.

'I just can't remember. It still doesn't… none of this makes sense.'

'Give it some time?'

'Something is right there… I don't even know if it's a memory…' he mutters, pointing at his forehead. 'It's just like when a word is on the tip of your tongue, exactly that feeling. Maybe if I can figure out what it is…'

'Try to be patient, Leo. I don't think you can force this,' I say.

He sighs. 'I'm not good at being patient.'

'Oh, I know that!' I say wryly. He glances at me again.

'Did they tell you I can't move my legs properly?'

Tears loom as I nod, but I force them away with some determined staccato blinking. We sit in silence for a moment, then

Leo asks hesitantly, 'Since apparently I don't know my own life these days, tell me... does it work at all if I'm in a wheelchair? Because the way I remember it, it just wouldn't.'

I meet his gaze and I keep my expression neutral and it's possibly the most courageous thing I've ever done. As I raise my chin and stiffen my spine I force every weakness out of myself because I want him to see that I am facing this bravely and that he can too. I can blubber later, and I will. 'Firstly,' I say, 'no one is saying the wheelchair will be a long-term thing. I signed organ donation forms for you two weeks ago and now you're sitting up in bed, talking. You've already proven that you refuse to do what anyone expects of you and there's no doubt in my mind that you'll get those legs working again through sheer force of will. And until then, we'll adjust.'

But I'm not the strong one in our relationship. I'm the one who sulks at the drop of a hat and feels so deeply that I can't sort out a good decision from a bad one once my heart gets involved. If it's up to me to help Leo navigate this terrifying possibility, he's doomed – but he doesn't know that yet, and it's sure as hell not the time to show him. He seems surprised by the strength of my declaration, and after he ponders it for a moment, he offers me a weak smile. His eyelids look heavy and he's pale again but he's smiling and I feel an immense sense of satisfaction that I've brought him at least a little comfort.

'I feel like I'm having a really trippy dream,' he admits. He sinks further down into the pillows and I take a seat beside his bed and fish out my iPad from my bag. He glances at it. 'What are you doing?'

'I've got emails to deal with, and you have a date with some real dreams,' I tell him. 'We can talk some more later and I'll be here when you wake up.'

And I will be. Despite everything that's happened between us, I'll be here as long as he needs me.

CHAPTER 4
Leo – January 2011

Molly and I strolled in silence at first, sipping our coffees as we walked. I was still trying to figure out how to get out of telling her the truth about Declan, but at the same time I was also trying to plot a script as to how I would word it if I actually had to.

'How did you hurt your arm?' she asked me.

I glanced at her. 'It's my shoulder. I caught a stray bullet in Libya.'

'You got *shot?*'

'Occupational hazard.'

'Oh. Are you supposed to be resting?'

'I'm fine to walk.'

'I'm not, my legs are killing me,' she sighed, and then she laughed weakly. 'I did a Pilates class a few days ago. I have no idea what I was thinking. Can we sit somewhere?'

We made our way towards First Fleet Park, a patch of grass between The Rocks and Circular Quay, and automatically steered together towards the only empty park bench. It was sheltered by the branches of a peppercorn tree and as we neared it, a flock of seagulls swarmed around us. I shooed them away and we sat side by side.

'Go,' Molly said, as soon as we were seated. Suddenly every word that I'd planned on the walk from the café seemed painfully contrived.

'Dec was a great guy, Molly. And he doted on you.'

'I know that. I need you to tell me things about him that I *don't* know.'

'I want you to remember those things, though – the brilliant human being he was; the loving brother he was – *those* are the things that count. Not his struggles.'

'You can say that because you knew him properly. All I know of Declan is that he was popular and clever and charming. But if that was who he *really* was, we wouldn't be having this conversation, and my mother wouldn't shut down whenever someone says his name even ten years after he left us.'

'It sounds like you knew the guy he wanted to be, and there's probably a good reason for that. He never wanted you to know any of this.'

'Because I was his sister?'

'Because you were *you*. He adored you.'

'So you're saying Mum and Dad have lied to me for ten years because Declan "adored" me?'

'No, I can't excuse their part in this since his death. But when he was alive, it mattered to him that you looked up to him.'

'Who *was* he, Leo? Was he not at all like the man I thought I knew?'

I sighed and stared out to the harbour as I thought about that. 'He was some of those things you said. He could be charming, but he wasn't exactly gifted academically – he struggled terribly at uni and frankly, he was out of his depth on our course.'

'I always thought Dec was at the top of his class,' she said, but the words had a distant, airy tone to them, as if she was thinking aloud.

'Dec only got into university because your dad made it happen, Molly. And he only earned his degree because he retook subjects over the summer each year.'

'And these struggles you mentioned?'

'Yeah. Dec…' It was even harder to say than I'd anticipated. I cleared my throat. 'Like most kids at uni, we messed around a bit with drugs in our first year or two, nothing serious and everyone else we knew grew out of it and settled down. Declan just never learned when enough was enough, you know?'

'Declan was a *drug addict*?' Molly whispered.

How the hell was it falling to *me* to give her this information? 'I'm so sorry, Molly.'

'That's not true. It can't be! How could I not have seen this?'

'Weren't you living overseas somewhere?'

'Yes, but I'd only been abroad for a year. He was fine when I was in Sydney.'

'Actually, he wasn't,' I sighed, and she sighed too.

'I guess he wasn't.'

I waited for a moment, giving her space to digest what she'd just learned. I was sure she'd need to cry – and after a while, I glanced at her to see if she was. Her eyes were dry, but she was staring blankly at the harbour. I had a sudden and vivid sense of déjà vu – this was the same neutral expression she'd worn throughout his funeral. It spoke of a shock and loss too great to process on the fly.

'Are you okay?' I asked.

'I'm trying to convince myself you're a lunatic or that you're lying to me about this,' she muttered, then she shot me a side-ways glance. 'But it's not working because I know you're not.'

'I think his problems actually started in our second or third year of uni,' I said quietly. 'He was always surrounded by a veri-table swarm of eager potential girlfriends, but he never really knew how to speak to them and he was forever telling me that they were only interested in him for his money. He wanted to come out of his shell and he was a completely different guy when he was high – outgoing and confident – that's when he *was* the life and soul of the party.'

'Would *I* have seen him high?'

'I'm not sure. I remember he went to spend Christmas with you in that last year – he was completely out of control by then, so you probably did.'

'Why didn't I notice?'

'You weren't looking for it.'

'What drugs did he use?'

It would have been easier to list for her the drugs that he *didn't* use, but she didn't need to know that. 'It was heroin that he came unstuck on in the end.'

'Did you try to help him?'

'Of course I did. Your parents did too.'

'But nothing worked?'

'Some things did. Dec had a few periods of sobriety – including quite a long period just before his death – maybe a few months.' Ah, the false hope those months had offered me. Our friendship seemed back on an even keel and Dec had seemed almost at peace again.

'Did he go to rehab?'

'No,' I murmured. 'Your parents were worried about confidentiality – his privacy. So they always tried to organise his treatment at home.'

'You mean, they were worried about *their* reputation,' Molly surmised.

'That was probably a factor.'

'Do you think if he had gone to a proper rehab place, he would still be alive?'

'I wondered about that for a while, but I don't think it would have made a difference in the end.'

'So how did he die?'

I cleared my throat. 'He had a bad day – a bad meeting with the board, I think he said. He felt he'd embarrassed your father; he hadn't prepared something they were expecting. Dec rang me on his way home from the meeting. We had a long chat then made plans to go to the cricket the following night. That's how I know this really was an accident. When he hung up, he sounded fine.' I cleared my throat again and shifted awkwardly on the bench, then stole a quick glance at Molly. She was staring at her lap now but her eyes were still dry.

'Why didn't someone call me? Why didn't someone *tell* me?' she whispered. 'I wasn't a kid anymore. I was nineteen, I could have handled it.'

'He was ashamed of the place he'd ended up. It really mattered to him that you still looked up to him.'

'Tell me about the night he died,' she said, her voice barely a whisper now.

I drank the last of my coffee and rested the cup on the ground beside my feet. 'Dec had a network of dealers around Bondi near his apartment, but Laith had cut off a lot of those pathways – brute financial force, I think you'd call the strategy. So when he decided to use again, Declan went to my aunt's house, where my cousin was staying.'

'Your cousin?'

'Yeah. Dec gave him money to score for both of them.' I stopped, and exhaled forcefully. 'My aunt called me. She didn't know what they were up to or where they'd gone – she just knew Declan was my friend and she was worried that her son was bad news for him. But *I* knew as soon as she called that there was only one reason Dec would have gone to that neighbourhood.'

'And your cousin?'

'He was fine – well, fine in the sense that he didn't overdose. I did some research later, trying to understand it all… Most likely because Dec had been clean for a few months, he'd lost his tolerance. It took me a while to find them – they'd locked themselves in a storage room in the basement of the building – I had to break down the door to get in.'

I was lost for a moment – remembering my panic when I realised where they were and the splintering sound the door made as I kicked it in – and then the dread, because the minute I saw him, I knew it was just too late.

Molly stood suddenly, startling me. I looked up at her and marvelled at the fact that she was still not crying.

'That's enough for today,' she said flatly. She was furious, and I couldn't blame her.

'I'm so sorry, Molly.' Her expression softened, just a little.

'*You* have nothing to be sorry about. Can I call you again?'

'Of course you can.'

She rested her hand on my good shoulder and squeezed as she offered me a fragile smile. 'Thank you, Leo.'

I watched Molly as she left. I thought I saw a shudder ripple through her, but almost instantly she corrected herself, walking away from me with a perfectly straight posture and her head held high.

I waited a long time before I left the park that morning. I sat on the bench until my backside was numb and the pain medication had worn off and my shoulder was throbbing. I thought about Declan and the Torrington family and the life lessons I'd learned from his friendship – including the most important one of all. It doesn't matter where your life's journey begins; the path it takes is still entirely up to you.

CHAPTER 5
Molly – July 2015

I wake just before dawn. I've spent so many nights by Leo's bedside, I don't even know what day it is. From the moment I force my eyelids open, I'm conscious of an exhaustion that seems to have overtaken every muscle in my body. I can't remember ever having felt so drained.

I stumble down the hallway for a vending machine coffee and in my sleep-deprived state I don't even notice that Leo is awake and sitting up in bed again when I return to his room. I've made it all the way to my chair and am sipping the coffee before he startles me with a quiet, 'Good morning, Molly.'

I nearly drop the cup, and then I trip over myself trying to apologise for nothing much at all.

'Oh, hi – sorry, I didn't realise you were awake yet – I didn't get you a coffee, I can go back—'

'No, no, it's fine. Thanks.' He looks around the room and then frowns at me. 'Where have you been sleeping?'

'My hotel is just a block away,' I say. This is actually true, but I hope he doesn't notice that I didn't answer the question. Leo keeps staring at me and the pause quickly becomes awkward. 'I just didn't want to leave you alone last night – I mean, in case you woke up and didn't know where you were – but I will go back to the hotel tonight.'

'Do you at least have a stretcher bed or something to sleep on?' I take some comfort in this evidence that Leo's eye for detail is already returning.

'No, it's a trip hazard or something. But it's okay, I haven't felt much like sleeping anyway.'

This lie is so ridiculous that I'm embarrassed to even have attempted it. I look at Leo then quickly look away, because he's staring at me and I don't need to read his mind to see that he isn't buying it. He is silent for a while before he speaks.

'Thank you, Molly.'

'Have you remembered anything?'

'Not yet. But yesterday it felt like every time I spoke to someone there were more shocks in store and I was so exhausted, I could barely keep up. I feel more alert today, that's got to help.'

'So you're feeling okay about what I told you yesterday?'

'About us being married?' he surmises, and he laughs. 'Well, I do believe you're telling me the truth. Is that a start?'

'It'll do,' I say. It is actually huge relief. I'm not sure I would have had the energy to keep trying to persuade him today.

'The problem is that I don't feel like I have a portion of my memory missing. I feel as if I took a nap and woke up and people started insisting I'd been out for four years and my whole life is now completely different. I don't know how memories are supposed to come back when it doesn't actually feel like any are missing.'

'It sounds like a nightmare,' I murmur.

'The nightmare is my legs.' He looks down the length of the bed as he says this, then looks back at me. 'So you've been sleeping in a chair?'

'Only the last few nights since you started to wake up.'

'You must be dying to get home.'

'Lucien is going to be as fat as a house,' I sigh. When I moved in with Leo, I automatically adopted the standard apricot poodle he part-owned with his elderly neighbour. I'm not surprised when Leo brightens considerably at the mention of the dog. I was never really a dog person before, but Lucien is the kind of animal that it's hard not to fall in love with.

'So, I take it that means Mrs Wilkins is looking after him? She's still in her house?'

'Oh yes, and she's still well – we shared a cake with her for her ninety-second birthday a few months ago. She has a carer who comes in now and she doesn't really get upstairs much anymore, but she's still fighting fit, considering. And yes, she still overfeeds Lucien. I've got the dog walker coming morning and night but last time we were both away it took me six months to get him back to under twenty-five kilos.'

'Wait a second – are you saying we live in *my* town house?'

That question is far more complicated than either one of us is ready to deal with just yet.

'Of course we do.'

His eyes are wide with disbelief. 'There's no "of course" about it. You're still a Torrington, right? I figured we'd be living in some horrendous mansion in some uncomfortably affluent suburb.'

'*Not* a Torrington,' I remind him pointedly. 'I'm a "*Stephens*" now. But yes, we're still wealthy – you just didn't want to leave your precious town house when we got married, so we compromised on a few things and I moved in there.'

'What exactly did we compromise on?' he frowns, and I laugh at him softly.

'Don't panic, Leo. I know you love your house, and we didn't destroy it. We just updated the kitchen and the bathrooms. And we added a fresh coat of paint and replaced the carpet on the top floors.'

'So it sounds like we live in the same location but a completely different house.'

'It's the same building and the same layout, we just improved it.' I smile then shrug. 'And of course, we added a few little helpers for around the house.'

I know immediately that he's going to assume I mean staff, and although I feel a little bad to be playing with him, it's momentarily amusing to predict his reaction to these things. It took months of careful negotiating to plan our life together in that terrace and I know what each of the sticking points were for him.

'God – not – *staff*?' He is aghast, and I smile.

'We didn't build servants' quarters in the courtyard and hire a set of domestic workers. Our entire house is six rooms – what would they do all day? We just have a cleaner once a week and, most importantly, a dishwasher.'

His kitchen had been tiny before we renovated – more of a kitchenette, really. His gaze narrows when I mention the dishwasher and I know he's correctly assuming that to squeeze one in would have required some major renovations.

'How did you fit in a dishwasher?'

'You'll see for yourself soon enough,' I say. 'Don't worry, you survived the change once, I'm sure you'll get over it again.'

'And do you still work for…' He lets the question trail off, and I shake my head.

'No, I don't work with Dad anymore.'

'Is that because of me? Because of… us?'

I pause before I answer this question. I had no choice but to resign once Dad found out about Leo and me, but that wasn't actually *why* I did it. I left because I was working with him for all the wrong reasons, caught in a cycle of seeking my father's approval at the cost of my own happiness. But for our relationship forcing the issue, I'd probably still be working away at *Torrington Media*, trapped in a life that was never really mine. Leo was the catalyst, but the end result was my freedom.

At the time it seemed that there was something quite mystical about the way that falling in love with Leo had changed my world. But looking back on this now, I am torn between a sense of relief and gratitude to have stepped out of that life and a feeling of having been cheated out of the future I should have stepped into. Leo and I started a journey together, but he wandered off on his own after such a short time and left me to carry on in my new existence alone. I'm still glad to be where I am, and I'm still grateful to him, but at the same time even this train of thought leaves me feeling an aching sense of disappointment for what should have been. I thought I was leaving *Torrington Media* so that Leo and I could build a future together. It never occurred to me for even a second that we could fail to do so – I thought the love I had for him could overcome *anything*.

'I left because I wanted to,' I say eventually. 'I kind of fell into that career when Dec died, and by the time you and I met, I desperately wanted to leave but I just didn't know how. I run a charitable foundation now – it's a much better fit for me.'

There's a sound at the door as a woman pushes a cart of meal trays past. I hear the rumble of Leo's stomach at the thought of food, and he watches the door hopefully. When the attendant doesn't return, he sighs.

'If they tell me I can only eat apple puree today, I might cry.'

'You *don't* cry.'

'If you know me as well as you seem to think you do, that statement should tell you how much I need some real food,' he says, and one corner of his mouth turns upwards and I see the smile echo in his eyes. That's Leo's charming smile – and while I haven't actually been the target of it for a very long time, I find that I'm still not immune to its powers.

'Give me a minute and I'll go see if I can talk them into letting you try something more substantial, okay? If you're allowed to eat, I can sneak something else in for you later. The hospital food looks awful.'

I return a minute or two later, a triumphant smile on my face and the tray in hand. 'They said I have to watch you like a hawk but you can try solid food if you're really that determined to,' I tell him wryly.

'Thanks,' he says. I feel his eyes on my face as I organise the tray for him and I'm suddenly very self-consciousness. As I peel the lid back on the packaging of some jam-like substance, a thick strand of hair falls over my face and I press it away with my shoulder awkwardly. The wayward lock of hair immediately falls forward again and Leo reaches forward hesitantly, then very slowly tucks it behind my ear.

I feel a million things at once. There's a tenderness in the gesture that has been lost to us for so long that I've actually forgotten to miss it. I'm almost floored by how wonderful it feels to have him touch me like that again. There's a dangerous pummelling of emotions right at my gut – our attraction has always been intense, even when everything else went to hell – *that* side of our marriage still worked. But there's a grief in it all too for me – because I know that once Leo gets his memory back, this automatic affection will disappear again and it needs to, because our marriage is over. At this thought, I want to step away and protect myself from the hurt that's inevitably going to return, but I don't want to confuse him further. Instead, I smile almost shyly at Leo, and then I push the tray towards him.

'Did I make you uncomfortable?' he asks. 'It just seemed like a natural thing to do.'

'No, no,' I shake my head hastily. 'I just know this is all new to you. It must feel like you met me yesterday.'

Leo shrugs and peers at me thoughtfully. 'I felt as if I'd done it a million times before, even if I don't remember. Strange, isn't it?'

When we met, I had a pixie-cut – Leo eventually told me he hated it. It was such a severe look – not one that suited me at all – but toughening my image up had seemed necessary when I was trying to forge my way in that world. I remember the raised eyebrows from the board at the first meeting I attended in my floral dress and with my hair loose and swinging to my waist. I'd quickly learned to at least present an air of authority and ruthlessness and had changed my look completely to match, but it had never *felt* right to me.

When I finally resigned, I donated my working wardrobe to charity and I grew my hair out over our first year together. Leo used to tuck it behind my ears all the time; sometimes he'd stand right in front of me and tuck both sides at once and then he'd kiss me playfully until I was all dishevelled again. I flush at the memory and step away from the bed. Leo's attention, thankfully, is on the tray of food.

'What a magnificent feast,' he observes wryly. It's dry white toast, jam, strong black coffee and some unidentifiable stewed fruit with yoghurt.

'Remember, little bites, chew carefully, swallow slowly.' He raises his eyebrows at me and I lift my hands as if in surrender. 'I *know* that you know how to eat, I'm just repeating what the nurse told me.'

Leo takes a bite of the toast. He chews slowly and thoughtfully, then swallows and there's visible relief on his face as the food makes its way to his stomach. By the time he turns his attention back to me, I've resumed my place in the chair beside his bed and am sipping at the awful hospital coffee again.

'So, how long have we been married?'

I glance at him. Is this the time to tell him? His attention is back on the tray again and I don't want to distract him. I should check with Craig Walker too – how much upset can Leo take? Better to wait. I keep my answer simple. 'Three years in December.'

'What date?'

'Trust me, that's one thing you've never remembered.' I'm trying to make a joke, but it's not at all funny to me and it shows in my tone.

Leo winces. 'Can you tell me anyway? Maybe I'll try harder this year.'

'December third.' He's trying to be funny but I don't want to smile at him because this is Leo and it's his fault this is a sore spot for me. I think back to our first two anniversaries – both of which I spent at home alone. The first year, I was almost proud of the noble sacrifice I'd made in allowing him to work. The second year, I felt nothing but seething rage because he didn't even call.

'Right,' says Leo with some determination. 'December third. There's some kind of rule about anniversary gifts, isn't there? What's three years, paper or glass or something?'

'I have no idea. But the first year, you were in Iraq and the second year you were in Syria, so if you really are going to make an effort to buy me something, buy me *three* of whatever you pick and that might just make up for the other two years.'

I watch the flickering slide show of emotions pass over Leo's face. First there's a frown, but it's quickly replaced by curiosity and then concentration. I lose his focus in an instant – but I know exactly what he's thinking. He's wondering what happened in Iraq and Syria to inspire a visit from him, and he's wondering what the resultant stories were. He's wondering how quickly he can get up to speed with everything he's forgotten, and how soon he will get back to work.

I don't want to be angry with him, but I am instantly furious. Head injury or not, I want to thump him and yell at him and storm out of the room. I try to calm myself, but I unthinkingly crush the paper coffee cup in my fist and it makes a lot more noise than I would have expected. Leo's gaze shoots towards me and he interrogates me with his eyes. I feel the tension of my fury all the way from my head to my toes.

'I know what you're thinking,' I say. There's a tremor in my voice. Leo watches me silently. 'I'm telling you about the anniversaries that you missed because you were on assignment, and you're already wondering what stories you were working on. You've just woken from a coma and you can't move your legs or remember a thing about your life three weeks ago, but you're already thinking about getting back to work. Right?'

There's silence for a moment, then Leo murmurs, 'And yet, you're still here.' An expression of bewildered wonder suddenly crosses his face as he stares at me. 'I must be the luckiest bastard on the face of the planet.'

I stare at him blankly. We have had arguments about his work so many times I couldn't even guess the number of them and I am bone-weary of the fight. I have been *crushed* by this – all of my hopes for our future together ground to dust by this very problem and the fury of us each trying to figure it out. But now, without the memories of those previous fights, Leo has gone off-script and I don't know what to say. He's supposed to argue about how important his work is, and I'm supposed to argue back that I'm important too – and then we each get riled up, and the yelling turns to screaming and the bitterness rises in each of us and drowns everything else out.

This very argument ruined the best thing in my life and I'm still grieving for what might have been. And now, far too late, Leo has inadvertently suggested that it doesn't need to end the way it always did. A tiny glimmer of gratitude like that could have changed everything.

I'm annoyed to look up and find that he is still staring at me, his gaze searching. My irritation is not his fault because he can't even remember marrying me, let alone anything that came after, but then again, it is his fault, all of it, and I'm still angry and I'm still hurting. I can't stand the eye contact for more than a second, so I wrap my arms around my chest and frown at the floor.

'The skull fracture must have done more damage than they realised,' I mutter. 'This is not how our arguments go.'

'How *do* they go?'

'They quickly escalate to yelling.'

'My head still hurts too much for yelling. How about I promise that this year, not only will I be in the right country for our anniversary, but I'll organise something appropriately romantic and sufficiently meaningful to undo the damage I did the first few years?'

This is more familiar. When I'm upset, Leo has always had a tendency to make promises he won't keep.

'I'll believe it when I see it,' I sigh, and then in a clumsy shift of topic that Leo is apparently happy to allow, ask him, 'How's the breakfast?'

'Amazing, although I'm still going to let you bring me some proper food later in the day if you really insist on doing so.'

I laugh weakly. 'Okay. I'll go out later if you like.'

'Actually, why don't you go back to your hotel and have a shower and a decent nap, and come back when you're ready?'

Automatically I shake my head. I don't want to leave him. I feel I need to stay in case he needs me – there's no one else here who knows him. I move to argue, but instead a yawn creeps up on me and I try to stifle it.

Leo looks at me pointedly and says, 'I'll be okay for a while.'

'Are you telling me I look terrible?' I reach for my messy fringe and pat it self-consciously.

'You look beautiful. I still can't believe for even a second you'd marry someone like me.' The compliment and his self-derisive comment are so unexpected that they undo me altogether and the tears rise. This time they won't be stopped. I blink compulsively and then stand and turn away from him, hoping he won't notice. He gently touches my back. 'I was trying to make a joke, Molly. I'm sorry.'

'You've always been terrible at jokes.' I give up on my quest to hide the tears. One escapes and runs down to my chin and I wipe at it with the back of my hand. 'I'm just tired, and well…' I shrug and turn back to the bed and cover his left hand with mine. I squeeze his fingers gently. 'It's just so good to have you back, Leo.'

Leo turns his hand over and links his fingers through mine, and his hand contracts. It's another automatic gesture, I'm sure, but I can see the very slight hesitance in his face after he's made it – an internal battle between who he knows me to be – a stranger – and who he is being told I am – his wife. He's probably thinking that he will feel more comfortable about me once his memory returns, and now I feel entirely guilty that he's about to discover the opposite. A second tear runs down my face.

'Get out of here,' he says. 'Go rest. I'm okay, I promise.'

'Okay,' I whisper, and then release his hand and move away from him. He watches silently as I pick up my handbag and walk to the door, where I hesitate again. He's only been awake for a day. What if he takes a turn for the worse and I'm asleep?

'*Go*!' he says the word with feigned exasperation, and I nod and leave the room.

I do desperately need sleep – I'm going to need my wits about me to get through this.

CHAPTER 6
Leo – January 2011

I have always hated text messaging. I hate the lack of context and tone, and the abbreviations and spelling mistakes that seem rife with the medium. But I had spent the entire day after that discussion in the park feeling a confused mix of guilt and concern for Molly Torrington and I didn't want to crowd her. As darkness fell, I looked up her number and sent her a message. *I hope you're okay after this morning, Molly. Leo.*

Her response came before the phone was even out of my hands. *I'm really sorry I've made you drag all of this up. I appreciate your honesty with me. There's not really anyone I can talk to about this and I think it's going to take some time to process.* I read her message a few times and then it struck me that for all the times I'd asked myself, *what would Declan have me do?* in the last twenty-four hours, this time at least, the answer was obvious: *You can talk to me about it whenever you need to.*

The truth was, I wanted to talk more about it, and that was quite a shocking realisation. The night Declan died, when I finally left the hospital and arrived back at my apartment, the silence had been suffocating. I tried to sleep but couldn't, and eventually went to my parents' house. Dad and Mum both got up and I told them the news, and they tried to offer me condolences but I just couldn't explain my grief to them, or give voice to the terrible guilt I felt. After that, I'd never really spoken about it again. It had been too shocking and too raw at first, then life moved on and I put it behind me.

Molly didn't reply straight away to my offer of a further chat, and I put the phone down and went into my kitchen to scout around for some food. When I heard the text tone sound, I wandered back to scan the screen. *Do you have plans tonight?*

❖ ❖ ❖

We met back at the café, but this time I actually paid attention to it as I approached. It was the kind of hipster inner-city place I'd normally avoid. Nestled in a cobblestone laneway up a steep hill, and decorated with odd placements of vintage items, it was populated with exceedingly trendy young people.

Molly was sitting at a table by the front window. When I approached, she was reading something on her phone and for the first time I had a chance to look at her properly. This adult Molly, for all of her career success, seemed somehow fragile – or perhaps it was just the circumstances we were meeting under.

'I shouldn't have asked you to come. I've taken up way too much of your time already today,' Molly grimaced at me as I sat opposite her. I pointed to my sling.

'I'm not allowed to work, I can't type, I can't work out – I am literally sitting at home counting down the hours until I'm well again, so if you had to take up a bunch of my time, this *was* the time to do it.'

'I can't believe you got shot. And that it doesn't seem to be a big deal to you at all.'

'If you go into a war zone people are going to shoot at you or at least *near* you at some point, so…' I shrugged. 'It would be ridiculous to moan about it.'

'Is this the first time you've been shot?'

'The first time?' I repeated, and then laughed softly. 'No, this would be the third time. How are you doing after this morning?' I changed the subject.

'Honestly?' she sighed and massaged her forehead with both hands. 'I'm torn. I'm devastated that he had to go through all of that. And I'm both enraged by and sympathetic to Mum and Dad's decision to keep it all a secret. Dec had a problem, it beat him. It's not fair, but it happens and it's nothing to be ashamed of.'

'I'm pretty sure your dad was always thinking Declan would turn a corner at some point and he didn't want the board to find out and hold Dec's problems against him. It didn't seem to matter how messy your brother's life got, Laith was always expecting better of him.' I could barely believe I was defending Laith Torrington, but I had at least partly sympathised with the man.

'But that's the problem, isn't it? He does the same bloody thing with me.' Molly's face contorted and she ran a hand through her hair, exasperated. 'He can delegate the most complicated, difficult project to me and I take it and make it a success. And when he looks over what I've done, all he sees are the flaws – he's always expecting me to do a better job. There is no such thing as "good enough" for my father—' Molly broke off suddenly and picked the menu up. She stared at it for a long time, but when she spoke again the anger and frustration were entirely gone from her voice. She'd pushed them down into some internal compartment and sealed the lid. 'I'm starved. Do you want to eat?'

We ordered our meals, and while we waited for them, Molly prodded me for more details about my adventures in the field. As I spoke, she listened closely. I'd seen this same reaction from women I'd dated – a keen interest and fascination was usually the first response to the 'danger' aspect of my work.

The second response was hesitation, and the third was fear. I'd had a lot of special women in my life over the years, but that pattern of how those relationships progressed was inevitably consistent. It was one of the reasons why I'd long since decided that I'd never marry.

After a while I turned the conversation back to her job.

'I read an article about you once,' I told her quietly. 'It sounds like you're actually very good at what you do at TM.'

'I am,' she said easily. 'I work hard and I learn quickly.'

'Were you always going to work for the family business?'

'No.'

'Well, what were you going to do?' I asked.

'I didn't have a plan. I thought maybe I might start my own business one day. But then…' she sighed and shrugged. 'Then Declan died and everything changed.'

'You're only working for TM because Dec died?' I couldn't hide my surprise. She grimaced again.

'I had been studying in Manhattan, but I transferred back to uni here in Sydney. Mum and Dad seemed to really need me close and that made sense. Then once I was back, Dad assumed I'd go to work with him when I graduated. At first, I thought I'd bide my time and eventually tell him I'd decided to do something else. But then I *did* graduate and I didn't have the heart to hurt him. Plus, what difference does it make, really? I'm either working at TM, or I'm working somewhere else. It's the same at the end of the day.'

'Is it?'

Molly paused, then she sighed.

'No, it's not.'

'So, what would you be doing if Dec was still here?'

'That's part of the problem. I think if I'd had a firm plan – you know, something I *really* wanted to do – it would have been easier to let Dad down. But I didn't. And Dad so wanted to pass the mantle to one of his kids… There was only one set of shoulders left to take it on.'

'One set of *Torrington* shoulders,' I corrected her. 'There are probably tens of millions of people in the world who could successfully lead your company. You're not *that* special.'

She laughed softly and shrugged.

'Maybe. But Dad doesn't see it that way.'

'You can't live your whole life pleasing your father.'

'It seems to be working okay so far.'

'Is it?' I asked again, but this time I saw the way her brow wrinkled and her eyes narrowed. I'd clearly stepped way over a line with that comment, so I held up my palms towards her in surrender. 'Sorry, I know it's none of my business.'

'I made it your business by talking about it,' she muttered. The waiter brought our meals and I looked down at the pork fillet I'd ordered and realised I was going to have to take my sling off to cut it. As I started shifting my arm around to wiggle out of the sling, Molly leant forward.

'I can cut that if you like.'

'*No!* But, thanks.' I winced. 'I can cut my own food, it's fine.' I struggled out of the sling and cut the entire meal methodically, then glanced at her as I slipped my arm back into the sling. She was watching me, a half-smile on her face.

'That's funny?' I said, raising my eyebrows at her.

'That stubborn independent streak is funny. It's such a *man* thing to do. You obviously caused yourself pain while you cut the food just to avoid accepting help that would have been easy for me to give you.'

'It's about dignity.'

'It's about stupid male pride and ego,' Molly muttered in response, and I set down my fork to stare at her. 'Did I upset you when I asked you about working for your dad?'

Molly surprised me. She paused and frowned, but then she laughed suddenly and nodded. 'I suppose you did; given I've automatically flipped over into insult mode. I'm really sorry, that was completely uncalled for, especially after how kind you've been to me today. What can I say – I can be a defensive bitch sometimes. You didn't deserve that.'

Something about the flooding smile she offered disarmed the bristle that she'd caused and the tension dissipated in an instant because I couldn't help but smile back.

'As long as you don't literally shoot me I think I can handle it,' I said, and we laughed quietly together before Molly went back to her food.

'There's one thing I don't understand,' she said quietly.

'Only one thing?'

'Okay, there are dozens of things, but one thing in particular that you might be able to explain,' she said wryly. 'Why did you stay friends with Declan? My father was a complete arse to you, wasn't he?'

'Yeah.' That was something of an understatement. Laith had made me feel decidedly unwelcome from the first visit I made to the Torrington mansion, right up until the times I'd seen him at industry functions in more recent years. Even a decade after we last spoke, he still made a habit of boring holes in me with his death-stare whenever we were in the same room.

'And Dec?' Molly added. 'From what you've told me today, he was hard work as a friend.' She smiled at me but there was so much sadness in her eyes. I set down my fork and leant in a little as I said quietly, 'You know, Molly, that question is exactly why I told you this morning to focus on the good things you know about him. The human side to your brother was remarkable. He was one of the most generous, genuine people I've ever had the pleasure of knowing.'

'Tell me about that side to him then,' she prompted. 'I mean – he was a great brother, but I'm not sure I'd ever have thought of him as generous – and genuine? How does that work given what you told me today? It sounds like he was living a lie for most of his adult life.'

I hadn't intended to tell her any other secrets about Declan, but there was a cynicism in her voice when she spoke about him and it stung me to realise that I'd put it there. Plus, I really wanted to show her that my 'stupid male pride and ego' could actually accept help when I needed it. And so I set down my fork and I looked at her as I told her a story about her brother that I'd never shared before.

'We met in our first semester at uni and at the time my living situation wasn't ideal. I was living with my mother and she was at a real low point. Anyway, eventually Dec came to visit me at home. I'm sure he'd never seen anything like where we were living – a public housing unit in one of those huge towers in Redfern. Back then those places were dangerous and uncomfortable. I'd seen *your* house so there was no way I wanted him to see where I lived but he kept asking and eventually I had him around…' It was an uncomfortable memory. Mum had hit a real slump when my biological father finally left, and it had taken her a few years to find herself again. Meanwhile, I was trying to find my place at uni and working two part-time jobs to get some money behind me, and not at all sure if I was up to the task of juggling it all.

'Did Dec give you money?'

'Not directly,' I said, and then I laughed. 'I would have been mortified if he'd offered and that probably would have been the end of our friendship. But the Dean called me into her office late in that first semester, and she told me that I'd been "selected" for a scholarship. Within a few weeks I had enough income coming in that I could live independently while I finished my degree. It was an embarrassingly long time later that I realised my "scholarship" was personally funded by your brother. Although he always denied it – the Dean admitted it when I finally graduated.' I picked up my fork again and pushed the food around the plate for a moment, then admitted, 'I just don't know if I could have finished uni without that money. And if I hadn't… Well, there was this whole other world around me then that would have sucked me back in. I'd been in a lot of trouble in my early teens and the vultures were already circling. If I'd slipped back into that lifestyle, it would have changed everything. My life would look completely different now.'

'I don't believe that,' Molly said as she frowned at me. 'Twenty minutes ago you were telling me nonchalantly about getting shot in the pursuit of your career. Would you really have let money stop you?'

My immediate reaction was to rip that statement to pieces. I gave myself a firm mental lecture – trying to remember that Molly had grown up with a kind of privilege that was as blinding as poverty itself could be. And she'd had a very tough day. Her ignorance was not malicious, but it was still infuriating.

'Money stops people from my background from doing all kinds of things, Molly. When I started uni, I was the first person from my family to do so. If I'd dropped out, the best case scenario for me would have been to find some shitty, menial job and stagnate there for fifty years. The worst-case scenario…' I shrugged. 'Well, my other friends weren't exactly model citizens and our pastimes weren't always legal. Even if I'd been arrested just once, I'd never have had the freedom to travel the way I do now. It was the dream of this job that kept me out of trouble – but the path from there to here wasn't exactly well-worn. No one else I knew back then had a professional career – God, half the people I knew had never worked at all.'

'But if you're determined enough that you would literally put your life on the line to do this job, time and time again – and talented enough to build the career you've achieved – I just don't understand why you think you would have let anything stop you,' Molly said quietly.

'The thing most people don't understand about poverty is that it feels like an impossible wall holding you back from a different life. When you're on the ground looking up at it, it seems insurmountable. When you learn how to build a ladder, you realise it's just a wall. That's what education was for me – it was the way out.'

'Isn't there something like income support payments? From the government?' Molly's gaze wavered, and she pressed those words out towards me hesitantly. I had embarrassed her. I hadn't intended to, but now that I had, I wasn't entirely sorry it had happened.

'There are, but they are very small and studying is a very expensive past-time,' I said carefully. 'I couldn't have sustained it without the scholarship.'

'I guess there are good things I never knew about Declan, as well as bad things.'

'Your brother taught me to look for the good in people. Yes, our friendship was difficult and weird at times but it was worth it. Declan was a good guy. If what I told you today makes you think otherwise, then I shouldn't have told you.'

'No, you did the right thing. I'm just adjusting to the reality that he had a whole other side that I didn't even see,' Molly said. She glanced at me. 'Dad was mortified when he started bringing you to our place, you know. He and Dec used to fight about you all of the time.'

'He was trying to protect his son,' I said quietly. Defending Laith *twice* in the one day? God, I'd lost my mind. 'Maybe he was right to do so.'

'Why on earth would you say that? You can't seriously blame yourself for the decisions Declan made about his own life.'

'It's not about blaming myself, I'm just a realist.' I was suddenly finding it difficult to look at Molly again, so I turned my attention to the centrepiece in the middle of the table. 'There's surely a good chance he'd still be alive had our paths never crossed. I never intended it of course, but he *was* exposed to that world through me.'

'That is complete bullshit,' Molly said. I raised my gaze to her and shrugged.

'Perhaps.'

'Look at my father, Leo – he's sixty-four years old and he hasn't taken a day off work since he left school. When Dad had that heart attack last year, the doctor told him that if he didn't slow down, he was going to die. So he fired that doctor and found a new one who prescribed medication instead of rest. Dad's every bit as addicted as Declan apparently was – his drug of choice is just work. If it wasn't heroin via your cousin, it would have been something else through one of his wealthy friends instead. It sounds like what you actually did was to provide my brother with a soft, private place to land whenever he crashed, and I can't even imagine how much that took out of you.'

She reached across and placed her hand on my wrist and squeezed gently, and I was startled by the contact. I didn't expect her to touch me – and I certainly didn't expect to find myself immediately distracted by the softness of her hand against my forearm.

I couldn't have missed Molly's beauty if I'd tried, but up until that moment I'd observed it with a sense of detachment. Her skin against mine changed everything because suddenly, she wasn't just a beautiful woman, she was a beautiful woman who was touching me and staring intensely into my eyes. Something shifted in the conversation with that contact. The vague curiosity and sympathy I felt towards her faded until I was simply *aware* of her. It was as if my pulse had grown loud within my body, and with each thump of my heart against my chest, that awareness grew. I noticed her scent in the air and the gloss on her lips. These things were all innocent, but suddenly my thoughts towards Molly were not. There was an undercurrent between us – hiding deep beneath the nostalgic conversation and the drama of what she'd discovered about her brother. Did she feel it too? Her hand lingered on my wrist.

'You have a lot of tattoos,' she murmured suddenly. Her gaze lingered on the place on my forearm where her hand rested. 'Do they mean something?'

I realised that her fingers now rested right beside the tattoo that I'd had made immediately after her brother's death. I'd never explained my body art to anyone before, but I felt a sudden compulsion to. The meaning behind my tattoos was intensely personal, but the only reason I had never shared it aloud before was that I'd never actually wanted to – it was my truth, and only mine. What did it mean that I wanted to share this with her? I barely knew her but I knew one thing: she had lost Declan too, and she would understand my grief for his loss.

With the fingers of my sling-bound hand, I awkwardly pointed to the symbols on my forearm beside her hand – two heavy arches around a series of circles – and I said quietly, 'This tattoo was actually for Declan. It's a dot painting – it represents two men sitting together – it signifies friendship. Do you know what "sorry business" is?'

She shook her head.

I said softly, 'There were hundreds of Aboriginal nations here in the past and each had their own sort of culture, but death was always a time of ritual. That's what "sorry business" means. It is different ways of remembering and commemorating a person lost. All of my recent ancestors were city people and most of those traditions are lost within my family, so what I learned about traditional customs mostly came from books. But Declan's death was the first time I'd been scarred by grief, and I didn't really have a framework to understand how to deal with it so I made my own ritual.'

Molly lifted her hand off my arm slowly, but her forefinger immediately landed on the next tattoo along. She traced the shape almost absentmindedly, and I watched as her finger moved along my skin. Her touch was much more familiar than our fleeting acquaintance dictated and it felt to me to be almost intimate; bewildering given we were fully-clothed, near strangers and sitting in a public café. I could feel the heat rising in my blood.

'Do these tattoos go all the way along your arm? And the other arm?' Molly murmured. I was so distracted by the gentle friction of her fingernail against my arm that I almost missed the question, but once it sunk in, I suddenly regretted the turn the conversation had taken. Silently I nodded and tried to think of a way to redirect the chat. But I was too slow in doing so – she asked me next, 'So, what do the others represent?'

'The same idea,' I admitted reluctantly. 'Each one is for a time I've seen someone lost in the field. Each represents its own story. They're a reminder of a life or lives that touched me somehow… and then ended.'

'Goodness,' Molly whispered. I flicked my gaze to her face and found her staring back at me. 'That's a lot of grief for one lifetime, Leo.'

'It's a closure thing. A way to honour those people.' I suddenly felt exposed and awkward about it. Withdrawing my arm gently, I sat up straighter in my chair. 'I don't really talk about this much.'

'I was thinking about you today,' Molly said suddenly. She too had withdrawn the hand that had been against mine, but now she leant her elbow onto the table and rested her chin on it. 'You could have taken the truth about my brother's death to any newspaper in the world and swapped it for any position you wanted. And you didn't.'

'Of course I didn't.'

'There's no "of course" about it. I know plenty of other journalists – I think most of them would have written that story.'

'Any decent human being would have kept it to themselves if it was about someone they cared for like a brother. God, who would embarrass a grieving family like that?'

'Maybe someone who was embarrassed by that family at the funeral of their best friend?' Molly suggested quietly.

I shook my head briskly. 'I would never have considered it.'

'That's my point – I wasn't having a go at you, I was just...' She sighed and smiled at me. 'Thanks, the way you handled this whole situation says a lot about who you are.'

'Well, you weren't as upset as I expected you to be this morning.'

'I did cry a bit when I left you,' she admitted easily. 'But I already knew something didn't add up. And you know, I've already grieved Declan. This is so tragic but it was always tragic. I guess contacting you was more about finding out the truth for myself, rather than trying to deal with losing him – which I've kind of done by now. Also,' she grimaced. 'I'm not really the weepy type. I've spent most of my life "in public". I'm pretty good at keeping myself together when I need to.'

She picked up her fork, and resumed her meal. I did so too after a while and we ate in silence for a few moments. I just couldn't assess that silence. It wasn't the kind of familiar, comfortable silence two old friends share – but it wasn't exactly the awkward silence of strangers, either. I felt unsettled; I'd exposed parts of history that I'd never intended to, and I was now acutely conscious of the woman opposite me and I wasn't quite sure what to do with that.

When our conversation resumed, it was small talk again, as if we had silently agreed to lighten the mood a little. We chatted about her job, and she asked me more questions about mine. After a while, when we'd finished eating dinner, the conversation faded to a natural close and we split the bill and walked side by side towards the train station.

When I turned to enter, I extended my hand to shake hers. 'Good luck with everything, Molly. If you ever want to talk, you have my number.'

She looked at my hand, then gave a little laugh and threw her arms around me – wrapping them right around my waist. I hugged her back with my free arm, and we paused just like that. The embrace was an innocent gesture on her part I was sure, but that didn't change the effect it had on me. She fitted so beautifully against my body – the perfect blend of softness and strength as well as a gentle warmth that I could feel through my clothes. Even as she stepped away I was sure that the scent she wore had bound itself to me, as if she'd somehow imprinted herself upon me. We'd walked through tough memories over that day, and shared grief has a way of forging a bond.

'You don't mind if I call you again?' she asked.

'Of course I don't.'

'Thanks, Leo. For everything.'

I nodded, offered her a smile and walked away. Within a few footsteps I was already trying to figure out a way that I could see her again without our focus being on her brother.

CHAPTER 7
Molly – July 2015

I set the alarm on my phone for lunchtime and crawl into the extraordinary comfort of my hotel bed. I take only a moment to luxuriate in the sensation of being stretched out on an appropriately comfortable surface before sleep overtakes me.

When I wake, I immediately realise that it is late afternoon and I've slept through the alarm. I shower and wash my hair, then dress in the first outfit I lay my hands on. I run the block back to the hospital, stopping only to pick up a large box of hot *supplì* from a restaurant on the way. As I race down the hallway towards the ICU, I catch a glimpse of myself in a mirrored window and groan. Somehow, a decent stretch of sleep and a shower have left me looking even worse – my hair has semi-dried into a frizz ball and I'm wearing a geometrically patterned skirt in shades of orange and pink with a blue and yellow striped top. It occurs to me that I look exactly like a clown and I laugh a little hysterically at the thought.

Craig Walker and a doctor I do not know are in Leo's room. I can see from the expression on his face that Leo is not hearing good news. I pause at the door, my fingers at the handle, and Alda approaches me.

'You go in,' she says softly. 'This is neurologist. Leo has tests today; they talk about results now.'

I steady myself as I push the door open. The three men look at me and I focus on Leo. 'Sorry to interrupt. Do you – do you want me in here? I'm so sorry, I slept through my alarm.'

'Come in,' he says. 'You should hear this too, I guess.'

'This is Dr Fida,' Craig tells me. 'He's Leo's neurologist. I've been helping to translate.'

'Hello, Mrs Stephens,' Dr Fida says, and he extends his hand towards me. I shake it and return his greeting.

'I had some scans and a proper neurology assessment this morning,' Leo informs me.

'Dr Fida was just explaining our theories about the issues with movement in Leo's lower body,' Craig says quietly.

I listen for the next few minutes, trying to make sense of the doctor-speak as Dr Fida and Craig explain the findings. Leo's ability to coordinate the muscles of his legs or balance himself when he stands is impaired. These symptoms are likely a result of the location of the fracture and underlying bruising to his brain. It's too soon to tell if this will be lasting. The doctors recommend an intensive rehabilitative programme to support him as his brain continues to heal.

'Are you optimistic?' Leo asks.

The tone of this discussion is making me nervous for Leo, and I want to take his hand, but I don't want to make him uncomfortable.

'It's really too soon to tell much about your long-term prognosis, Leo,' Craig says. 'We can see on your scans that there's been some damage to your brain – but it's a remarkable organ. It will heal with time, and with therapy it can adapt, even when there is permanent damage.'

'I just need to know that I'm going to walk again,' Leo says, very carefully. 'It's really – well – beyond imperative that I can walk. I mean, if I can't walk…' He breaks off. Now I do take his hand and squeeze it. I will let go if he pulls away, but unless he does, I will hold it so tightly that he will never forget for a second that I'm here to support him through this.

Dr Fida and Craig converse quietly in Italian for a few minutes. I watch Leo's face. He is terrified and trying very hard not to show it. After a while, he finally meets my gaze and I offer him an anxious smile. He doesn't smile back, but he doesn't look away either.

'Your best chance at restoring your mobility is to commence rehabilitation as soon as you can. We can't give you any guarantees, Leo.'

'I know that millions of people in the world live wonderful lives in wheelchairs,' Leo says stiffly. 'But I can't. I can't do my job in a wheelchair. Nothing in my life would work if I can't walk.'

'There are ways of adjusting and coping,' Craig tells him gently. 'But you're getting way ahead of yourself. Step one to your recovery will be to rest a little more, and then the next step is going to be to get you into a rehabilitation programme. There are some world-class brain injury programmes in Sydney.'

'And – Leo's amnesia?' I prompt hesitantly.

'We are confident it will resolve in its own time.' Craig turns back to Leo. 'In cases like yours, where the patient is able to form new memories and has only lost a portion of the previous memories the prognosis is actually very good. It's likely most of your missing memories will return as the swelling recedes.'

'I've already had a few memories return,' Leo tells us, and I glance at him in surprise. I can tell by the way he looks immediately to me that he's remembered something about us, and judging by the warmth in his gaze, the memories are early ones.

'That's very encouraging,' Craig tells him.

'Is there anything I can do to speed it up?' Leo asks, and I nod enthusiastically at this idea.

'Yes,' I say. 'Is there medication? Or some kind of therapy we could enrol Leo in?'

'No, I'm afraid not in this case. The "cure" is time and patience.' Leo and I both sigh. 'Now for the good news,' Craig continues. 'You can travel whenever you're ready – but only by air ambulance. You're not in any shape to attempt a commercial flight.'

'I'll organise a medical crew for our jet,' I say, and Craig nods, but Leo laughs weakly and says dryly, 'Of course. "Our jet" – how could I forget?'

I *hate* the sarcasm and it's an immediate reminder of how things used to be between us, unsettling me more than it should. 'Do you want to go home, or not?' I snap, and I immediately feel the doctors' eyes on me. I flush, and then work hard to follow up my sharp tone with a gentle explanation: 'It belongs to my parents, but I can still use it. We can get home whenever we want to – if you want to, Leo.'

As the doctors prepare to leave, I tell Leo that I need to visit the bathroom and on my way out, I hand him the box of *suppli*. As soon as Craig steps out, I waylay him in the corridor.

'How are you holding up, Molly?'

'I'm okay,' I say. 'I just wanted to ask your advice.'

'Happy to help if I can.'

'We were…' I freeze up when I try to say the words to explain our situation. I don't want to admit the terrible mess we've made of things, not even to this doctor whom I will soon bid farewell to and never see again. 'You said to keep him calm. How calm did you mean? There's so much that he has forgotten, I don't even know where to start. I just don't know *what* to tell him.'

'I'm inclined to suggest that you trust your instincts. I think you'll know when he's ready to hear the things you need to tell him.'

I stare at the floor, trying to figure out what that will look like in practice. Craig adds gently, 'I think you need to ask yourself what he *needs* to know, Molly. Your role between now and when he's well again will be one of tour guide – let him experience the world again for himself, but give him the information he needs to understand it.'

I take a moment to collect myself, and when I return to his room I find Leo busily eating the *supplì*. He's sitting up in bed more easily now, not leaning into the pillows anymore. There's a newspaper on the table beside him. Leo is definitely on his way back.

'These are amazing,' he says.

'There's a wonderful pizzeria between the hospital and my hotel. I've had more carbs in the last two weeks than I've had in the last year. It will be so good to get home.'

'But where will I go? Surely rehabilitation centres have waiting lists.'

This has occurred to me too, but I have a back-up plan. If we can't find Leo a suitable place, we'll have to get therapists to come to us. He would have to move into my apartment, though – his house has too many stairs.

'Money talks, Leo. It'll be fine.'

We both fall silent for a moment, then Leo pushes the box of *supplì* towards me. I take one. 'You said you'd remembered something,' I prompt.

'I remembered meeting you a few times, when we were talking about Declan. When you mentioned it earlier, I had a…' He struggles for words, then says, 'It was just like… maybe like déjà vu? It was familiar, as if it had been there all along but I'd forgotten how to access it.' He hesitates again, and then mutters, 'Very hard to explain. But I do remember thinking…' Leo pauses, and seems to select his next words very carefully. 'I remember thinking that, if I'd met someone like you under any other circumstances, I might have asked you out.'

'How far do these new memories extend?'

'There was certainly nothing romantic going on in what I've remembered so far.'

'Do you remember the night we met up for a drink at Darling Harbour?' He frowns, pauses to concentrate, then sighs in frustration and shakes his head.

'Do you think you could take me there?' he asks suddenly. 'To Darling Harbour – and maybe some other places we went together – you know – if I'm allowed out once we get back to Sydney, and if the memories still aren't back.'

I glance at him quizzically. I don't know how I feel about the idea. It makes sense to take Leo to some of our old haunts, but this is hard enough already without literally taking myself back to remember the things we've lost. I remind myself that the most important thing is for him to be well, and even if it's a little uncomfortable for me to revisit those days, he has been such an important part of my life. I need to do what I can to help him.

'Sure, if you think it'll help.'

'Thanks, Molly. Anything I can do to speed things up, I'm willing to try. It's frustrating to have more questions than I can figure out how to ask. You said before that Laith isn't in our lives? But we use his jet?'

'We don't usually. And he's not in *our* lives, but *I* still see him occasionally and I speak to Mum often. When I called to tell them you'd been injured, they told me to use the jet. It's not such a big deal – Dad has a second one for the company anyway.'

'I still can't believe I got involved with you,' Leo says, and when I laugh softly he hastily adds, 'I just meant...'

'I know what you meant.' I glance at my watch and calculate the time difference in my mind. 'It's very early morning at home, but I did tell Anne you'd call her tonight. How are you feeling after all the tests today? Are you tired?'

'I'm fine, Molly. I had a rest before the doctors came by. Why don't you tell me something about yourself? I really need to get to know you a little.'

'What do you want to know?'

'What's your favourite colour?'

'*That's* where you want to start?'

'Seems as good a place as any. And I can't really tell from the clothes you're wearing.'

I look down at my quasi-clown outfit and grimace. 'Yeah, I was in such a rush to get back, I didn't really look at these before I put them on.'

'I wondered if fashion had changed in the last four years.'

Leo's wardrobe consists of dozens of pairs of identical chinos and identical casual shirts. He has no sense at all of style.

'As if *you'd* know what's in fashion,' and we laugh together. It feels good to laugh with Leo again. Once upon a time our life together was punctuated by easy laughter and shared smiles. 'My favourite colour is yellow.'

'Do you know mine?'

'That's a trick question. You don't have a favourite colour.'

'What's your favourite food?'

'I like anything I don't have to cook. And you like simple food. You'll eat pretty much anything, especially when you travel, but when you're at home you crave simplicity. When we first moved in together, you came back from your first long trip and I was so excited to have you home I made you an elaborate four-course dinner. I don't cook so that was quite a big gesture from me. You didn't have the heart to tell me you had a little routine that I was getting in the way of so after I'd gone to bed, you snuck downstairs and I caught you at the table with a cup of tea and your precious vegemite toast.'

Leo laughs and nods, as if he knows immediately what I'm referring to. 'It started off as a practical thing. I always kept some bread in the freezer and vegemite lasts forever, so it didn't matter if it was stupid o'clock and I'd just come from the airport. Nothing feels more like coming home to Australia than good old-fashioned vegemite on toast. I never meant for it to become a ritual.'

'Anyway, I learned not to bother you when you came home. I would just wave at you from the couch and wait until after you had finished.'

Leo frowned at me. 'Surely I didn't just ignore you until I was done eating my snack.'

'That *is* pretty much what you did, actually.'

'Didn't that annoy you?'

'I think it was about decompressing, actually. Yes, it annoyed me sometimes, but for the most part I understood that it was your way of compartmentalising your work. It was your pause before you came back properly into our home life.'

The truth is, the only way I could actually tolerate his stupid ritual at all was because right up until things between us really broke down, he always made it up to me. There was a second ritual that came immediately after the toast in the kitchen and that was long embraces with me on the couch, moments layered with affection and emotion. Even when he was exhausted, he always made such an effort to really come home to me. Leo never said sorry, but I interpreted every affectionate move in those blissful moments of reunion as an apology anyway.

'What's our favourite thing we do together?' he asks me now.

I think about this for a minute, then say casually, 'We love watching reality TV.'

'Okay, now I know you're lying. I do *not* watch reality TV!' He's aghast, as I knew he would be. I grin at him, and for a moment I'm lost in my own memories of nights on the couch with Leo's warmth against my body through our clothes, our limbs entangled, his scent around me and the soft glow of the TV before us. That's who we *really* were together when things were good – just me and Leo and the natural entwining of our hobbies and habits.

'We usually sat together after dinner and I watched reality TV shows while you read next to me,' I explain. 'Every now and again you pulled your head out of your book to make disparaging comments about whatever show I was engrossed in. I usually pretended to be offended. It's a bit of a game we played.' Even the banter was perfect in the early days, tinged with tenderness and affection and a warmth that went all the way through the very layers of who we were as individuals.

God, I miss us.

'Ah, snarky, judgemental comments about reality TV while reading a good book does sound more like me,' Leo laughs, but then another thought strikes him, 'And my family? Is everyone okay? Has anything happened that I need to know about before I call Mum?'

I'm glad of the change of topic. I don't want to spend too much time reminiscing about our happier days together – I really can't bear to think of it at all, the loss is still too raw. I spend the next few minutes bringing Leo up to speed on the Stephens family news. I tell him about his nephews – Baxter and River – two unbelievably energetic children who run his step-sister Teresa ragged. I show him photos on my phone and Leo tells me that he thinks they look a bit like him. I laugh at him, because he has no biological link to those children but this is exactly what he said when he saw each of them as newborns.

I tell him that his mum is fit and well as usual, and that his step-father Andrew still works far too hard but is also well. I don't tell him about the work Andrew and I do together yet – there's just too much to explain, and it will be easier in Sydney when I can let him see for himself.

Later, a nurse brings a tray of food, which Leo devours and then I set up a video call to his parents. Anne sobs most of the way through the call and keeps forgetting it's a video call and keeps lifting the phone to her ear, but both Andrew and Leo are typically busy trying to maintain their tough macho façade. Each man spends an awful lot of time clearing his throat and turning away from the camera, but I know them both too well to fall for it for even a second. When the call is finished, I see Leo is starting to tire.

'You'll sleep at the hotel tonight, right?' he asks me.

'Unless you don't want me to? I can stay but I've got a heap of calls to make later,' I tell him.

'I'm fine now. Just get a decent night's sleep, okay?'

This interchange feels strange but it's familiar, because in the beginning that was exactly how Leo was: attentive, sensitive, thoughtful. But it's also unfamiliar, because this year he's been so distant. I had almost forgotten how cared for I felt in the beginning.

Back at the hotel, I spend half the night on the phone trying to find a suitable specialist rehabilitation centre with a vacancy. I manage to line up accommodation for Leo, but it's on the other side of Sydney and even as I accept the place, I wonder how we're going to make it work. Next I catch up with my assistant Tobias and he offers to organise the jet and necessary staff for the following afternoon.

When I finally hang up, the still silence of the hotel room around me belies the frantic pace of my thoughts. I can barely believe that we're actually going home... *both* of us.

I climb into bed, but unable to sleep, I lie staring up at the ceiling, trying to figure out what to tell Leo and when. It will be an equation I have little hope of solving alone, but I can't exactly ask for help either, because I don't think anyone other than Leo and I could ever understand what went wrong between us.

CHAPTER 8

Leo – January 2011

I have never considered myself an impulsive man, but I am instinct driven. When my gut tells me to do something, I almost always do it – without always thinking things through. It is both a strength and a weakness when it comes to my work. When instinct tells me to pursue an angle, I do so with a single-minded focus on pushing for the *rare* stories – the stories that happen outside the safe zone and past the front line, probing deeper than the surface level happenings that most of my colleagues would capture in the field.

When it came to Molly, my instincts sounded loudly after that dinner at the café. I needed to see her again. I didn't just want to – I *needed* to. It was the only way I was going to figure out if the connection I'd felt with her was falsely induced by the depth of the discussions we'd had around her brother's death. I did hesitate a little – I knew that I couldn't exactly call her and ask her out on a date without some kind of segue from the tone of our first chats. Declan was both my excuse to see her again, and the reason I had to tread carefully.

By Thursday, I had decided that I would organise a catch up and check in with her about Dec, then see what happened if I led our conversation away from him. When I had a clear plan in my mind, I called her.

'Hello, Leo,' she greeted me warmly.

'Hi, Molly. Did I catch you at a good time?'

'There's *never* a good time,' she sighed, but there was a smile in her voice. 'How are you? How's the shoulder?'

'I'm delighted to say that I have graduated from the sling.'

'That *is* good news. Back at work, then?'

'Not yet, but soon – I'm still not allowed to do much. But at least I can cut up my own food now.'

She laughed softly. 'I'm glad you called, actually.'

'Oh?' This was very pleasing. I sat carefully on my couch and propped my feet up on the coffee table.

'Yeah. Do you have time to catch up for a drink?' she asked. 'I realised some things after we talked the other night. If you can spare me some more time, I'd really like to chat again.'

'Of course I can spare the time,' I said quietly. My mild tone belied my elation as I accepted her offer.

We arranged to meet at a bar on Darling Harbour that evening.

❖ ❖ ❖

Once again, it was an odd kind of place for me to find myself – given the uncomfortably pretentious décor and the trendy and affluent crowd. Molly was fifteen minutes late arriving, and I started to wonder if I'd misunderstood her instructions.

'Hi,' she breathed a greeting as she took the seat opposite me. I could see a little flush on her cheeks beneath her make-up, and she was buzzing with a flustered energy as she sat down and drew in a deep breath. 'God, I'm so sorry I'm late – my phone has been ringing off the hook. We posted record dividends this week and there's been a bit of a flurry of media stuff to do. And you know what journalists are like.' She flashed me a wry smile.

I smiled back. 'No problem. So you're okay?'

'Yes, but I'm exhausted and frazzled. Actually – you know what? I need wine.'

I laughed. 'That sounds good.'

Once we'd secured our drinks, we took a table out on the waterfront, sitting beside one another on a long, cushioned bench seat. I angled myself slightly towards Molly so that she was within my natural line of sight. She was framed by the glitter of the restaurants and bars and the harbour behind her. I was struck by how much she stood out in this crowd – an exceptionally beautiful, well-coiffed young woman in a sea of well-dressed but bland inner-city types.

'So, record dividends, huh?' I prompted.

'All *my* doing, naturally,' she said with a grin.

'Of course.'

'Actually, it was just a good year. But our shareholders expect good years now so it's always nice when we deliver.'

'And… the stuff we talked about?'

'Yeah, I'm good,' she said, and she smiled at me. 'I haven't talked to my parents yet – I don't know if I will. I can't even say they are clinging to this false idea of who he was and how he died – they are just completely shut down to acknowledging his life at all.' She glanced at me, and said hesitantly, 'You know, if you ever spot my father in a dark alleyway, you should probably run in the other direction. He *really* seems to have an issue with you.'

'I think I can handle Laith but if he has bodyguards with him, I'll definitely take your advice,' I said, and she laughed. 'I'm really sorry that your parents are still closed to discussing him.'

'It's fine,' she said. 'At least I know the truth now. Quite often when I was at work I'd wonder if I was living up to the role he once filled. But these last few days I have felt I can be myself for the first time, and that's marvellous – and it's all thanks to you.'

'Oh, no!' I cringed at the praise, uncomfortable with her gratitude. If only she knew how non-altruistic my motivation for *this* catch-up was. 'Don't say that. I didn't do anything at all, but – congratulations. Here's to being yourself,' I said, and I raised my glass to her. She shuffled closer to me and we clinked glasses.

'And to healing,' she added, gesturing towards my shoulder.

'And to healing.' We each took a sip, and I realised how close she was sitting to me – close enough that if I just moved my knee to the left, it would brush hers. How would she react? It was far too soon to find out, but just the idea was captivating. I leant back a little so that I could glance down beneath the table. She was sitting with her legs crossed, her knees angled towards me. I dragged my gaze back up to hers.

'Sometimes, I think about leaving TM,' she murmured as she stared out to the harbour. 'Not yet, but maybe someday.'

'That would be a brave move.'

'Please. Brave? A trust-fund kid thinking about leaving her cushy job at the family firm to loaf around and binge-watch the back catalogue of *The Bachelor* is not brave.'

'Taking a step into the unknown is.'

'It's only brave when you don't have a safety net. And I have *three* safety nets – I have my shares in TM, I have Declan's shares in TM, and I have a trust fund. I don't need to be there at all, really.'

'Actually,' I said wryly. 'When you put it like that, you're right. That's not brave at all and I can't believe you waited this long to do it.' Molly laughed and elbowed me gently on my forearm. 'Have you really *no* clue what you would do next?'

'I'd like to do something for Declan,' she said. 'I don't know what, yet. But that's my first goal. I'll do something to honour his memory and to…' She turned to glance at my tattoos as she continued, 'to memorialise him for the person he really was. I'm trying to think of a gesture I can make for him. Maybe then I'll be ready to start my own life.'

She flashed yet another smile at me and took a long, slow sip of her wine as she turned back towards the water. I watched her lips connect with the glass and noted the way that she licked them after she'd swallowed the wine. As she lowered the glass back to the table, I realised what I was doing and felt a flush creep up my neck. My close observation of her movements was instinctive and I was struck by that odd way an attraction can make every innocent physical gesture seem somehow sensual. Even so, I was surprised by how quickly my thoughts had shifted from the very serious matter of her grief. I stopped myself, drew in a deep breath and tried to keep my whole focus on the conversation.

'So, once you're back at work, will you go back to Libya?' she asked suddenly.

'Yes,' I said. My voice was unexpectedly rough, and I cleared my throat before I continued, 'We need to go back to finish what we started.'

'We?'

'I work closely with a photo-journalist; his name is Brad Norse. We've done most of our work together over the last few years – we co-won that Pulitzer together, actually.'

'Which article won the prize? I remember seeing you on television but don't remember the details.'

'It was a series of articles about the impact of war on the life of four Iraqi families.'

'I'll have to look it up. It sounds amazing,' she murmured.

'Apparently we did an okay job of it.' I tried to make a joke, but I was startled when Molly burst out laughing as if I'd actually succeeded in being funny. I saw several people around us turn to look at her. The laugh was back – the riotous, inappropriately loud laugh that had defined her as a child. She twisted a little in the seat, turning to face me more as she asked, 'So what inspired this series?'

'The whole thing started with some photos Brad took of children playing in rubble in Fallujah while the war raged around them. But what inspired *Brad* was his son waiting back home. Sometimes it's like that – you have to run two lives almost, there's the adrenaline-fuelled life in the field and the ordinary "pick up the groceries and do the laundry" life back home. And every now and again, like with Brad and those Iraqi kids, you see this fragile link develop where you see the common ground, and then you see the difference. They're the best stories because they really connect with readers.'

'I just realised what I want to do with my life,' Molly said suddenly.

'If you say "war journalism", I'm pretty sure Laith *will* hunt me down and kill me.'

'No,' she laughed again. 'I prefer my overseas trips to end at a luxurious five-star hotel in a peaceful country, thank you. It's not the *thing* you do, Leo. It's the way you talk about it. Like you genuinely love it. You talk about your job the same way people talk about their partner or their kids – there's pride and passion and real drive.'

'I couldn't stop doing it even if I wanted to,' I agreed quietly. 'It's not a job to me, it's a calling.'

'*Yes!*' she said, and with so much enthusiasm that once again, heads turned to look at us. I wondered what they were thinking when they saw me sitting beside her. We were sitting close together, talking intently at a table on the water at a fancy bar, sharing a drink and staring at one another. Would people assume we were on a date? I liked that idea very much indeed. A young guy in a suit at the table behind Molly had turned when she made her exclamation and his gaze lingered. I stared at him long enough to catch his eye, then let my stare sharpen until he looked away.

I had no claim to Molly – no right to any feeling of possessiveness – but even so, if he was going to gawk at her, he wasn't going to do it while I was sitting right beside her.

'That's what I need,' Molly continued chatting, completely oblivious to the eye-contact power struggle that had just happened right behind her back. 'I need a *calling*. What made you realise that you wanted to be a journalist?' She tilted her head as she stared at me, and I stared right back, altogether distracted by the deep ocean-blue of her eyes and the intense focus she was directing at me. After a moment or two, she raised her eyebrows and the hint of a smile hovered over her lips. 'I'm in no rush. Do you need to be somewhere?'

There wasn't a place in the world where I'd rather have been in that moment – quite literally, I realised with some surprise.

'I saw an interview on the news one night during the first Iraq war – a teenager about my age had seen his mother shot right in front of him. Mum was pretty important to me, and it kind of rocked me that things like that could go on in the world. It put a lot of things into perspective, actually. I thought the guy who was standing there interviewing that kid was a superhero. He was *in* a war zone and giving that kid a voice. So...' I shrugged, 'that was that.'

'But print, not television?'

'That was an easy choice. I wanted to *do* the groundbreaking interviews, I didn't want anyone to watch while I did it. I do get asked to do some television stuff occasionally – giving commentary on conflict events mostly – but I don't love it. I much prefer having the space to tinker with words until they express my thoughts properly.'

'Right,' she said, and she drew in a deep breath. 'So I need to get myself a defining moment like that one.'

I chuckled and said, 'I don't think you can just buy them at a shop.'

'Leo,' she smiled at me patronisingly. 'I'm Molly *Torrington*. I am the kind of person who can make things happen.'

'I'm not suggesting for even a second that you are anything *other* than extraordinary,' I assured her. 'I like your attitude.' I loved the confidence behind it too. 'I really hope it works out for you.'

'It will,' she said with some determination, and she finished the last of her wine and sat the glass down heavily against the table. 'God, I need another drink.'

'Allow me,' I said, and I shuffled along the bench so that I could stand. 'I could do with another too. Should we split a bottle?'

'That wasn't a hint,' she said, and she fumbled for her purse. 'I can get it.'

'Oh no, I insist,' I said, and I tried for a joke. 'I know your company posted record profits yesterday, but you can't just go buying drinks willy-nilly for every person you meet up with. You still need to watch the pennies.'

I just wanted to get her a drink. It was a macho thing – a stupid male ego thing, Molly might have said. But whether she was a bazillionaire or not, she was just a beautiful woman, I was enjoying her company and I wanted to be the one to buy the wine – although I was well aware that she was probably earning more money from investments while we sat there chatting than I would make all year.

She wrinkled her nose at me and was laughing as she nodded. 'Thanks for the financial advice, Leo. I'll make a note of that. Wine would be lovely.'

✦ ✦ ✦

Over the next few hours we nibbled on finger food from a tapas platter and shared a bottle of wine as we chatted. The sun set over the buildings on the west side of the harbour and I got to watch Molly's expressions change as the light shifted and faded. Eventually darkness settled and soon we were chatting by the softer light of the restaurant's table lamps. The people at the tables around us gradually moved on and were replaced by new patrons, but Molly and I stayed. The passage of time became irrelevant. My entire focus was on her.

With the tension and the secrets out of the way, we shared common memories of her brother that were wistful rather than fraught. She reminded me of all of the times when she'd follow him around the house like a shadow and marvelled that Declan always used to play with her whenever she asked, even if he was studying.

'He was such a great brother,' she sighed.

'He actually told me that he'd learned the quickest way to get rid of you was to play with you for a few minutes and wait for you to get bored and move onto something else,' I told her, a little reluctantly.

'Well, that probably explains it,' Molly laughed. 'Even so, he *was* so tolerant of me.' She glanced at me. 'You were his first rebellion, you know. I don't remember him ever disagreeing with Dad until you started turning up at our house.'

'You never really spoke to me,' I said suddenly. 'I had a feeling I scared you.'

'No, you didn't scare me, I just knew Dad didn't like you. And I *always* do what Dad wants.' There was a bitterness in her tone. She sighed suddenly and shook her head. 'It's pathetic.'

'He likes me even less now,' I pointed out. 'And yet, here you are.'

'Yeah, but you watch me panic if he happens to walk around the corner.' She rubbed her forehead as she sought my gaze. 'Sorry, I wish I wasn't like this. He's just always moving the bar, you know? His approval is *my* addiction. Whenever he asks me to do something, I try so hard but it's never quite good enough so I get sucked into this cycle of always trying to make him happy and it means my whole life ends up as an endless quest for his favour.'

'You don't *have* to live like that, Molly,' I said. I wanted to cup her face in my hands and smooth away the worry lines that surfaced on her forehead and around her eyes whenever the subject of Laith arose. I leant towards her and added, 'With the resources you have, you could do literally anything you can dream of. What a waste to spend a life with such potential stuck doing something you don't have a passion for.'

'I wish I were braver,' she murmured, and her gaze sought mine, as if she could find the impetus to solve the problem somewhere in my eyes. 'I wish I was someone with real courage, like *you*. If you were in my shoes, you'd probably resign and use your trust fund to solve world hunger or something. You must think I'm a spineless fool.'

'It's only natural that you don't want to disappoint your parents. But life is pretty short, and you only get one shot at it.'

'I realise that living my life trying to please Dad is completely ridiculous,' she murmured, fiddling with her wine stem. 'I know we were joking about finding a defining moment but I do have a bit of a plan. I'm going to make myself open to the possibilities and see if I can find something that really brings me to life. *Then* I might have the guts to leave.'

I shifted on the bench seat so that I could rest my arm against the backrest and face her fully. As I did so, I accidentally brushed my knee against her thigh. We both tensed, and my gaze flew to her face to watch for her reaction. She bit her lip for just a second, and then she lifted her gaze from the wine glass to my face. I was close enough that I could see the way her pupils dilated, and when she released a withheld breath, I felt the air warm against the skin of my neck. Molly's gaze was curious; she was assessing my reaction, just as I was assessing hers. She didn't seem at all hesitant – but she wasn't really giving much away either.

'So…' I murmured. 'How will you make yourself "open to the possibilities"?'

'I don't know yet,' she admitted. Her voice was low and she spoke slowly. 'Do you have some ideas?'

Oh, I had plenty of ideas – and more were coming to me by the second.

'Why don't you go after some new experiences and see where they lead you?' I suggested quietly.

'Oh, I've had a *lot* of experience already,' Molly said, and she leant her elbow on the table. She rubbed at the back of her neck with her hand, staring at me from beneath her lashes, waiting for my response.

'You have, have you?'

'Not *too* much, although I'm not actually convinced there *is* such a thing,' she said suddenly. 'Actually, I'd say I've had just the right amount.'

She spoke so casually that I started to wonder if I was completely misreading the situation. I continued to stare at her for a moment, then realised my addled brain wasn't going to make sense of it – that there was only one way to find out.

'What kind of experiences are *you* talking about?' I asked her.

'That depends what *you* were talking about,' she said pointedly.

'I was going to suggest travel,' I said, and then we both started laughing.

'You were bloody not!'

'I was!' I protested, and Molly straightened her posture. Her gaze dropped to my mouth, and I thought for one shocking second that she was going to kiss me, right then and there. My chest felt frozen – too tight to draw in enough air to speak normally. She leant closer still, her eyes fixed on my lips, but then when her face was right before mine, she lifted her gaze to mine. Our eyes locked, and from the corner of my eye I saw Molly's lips part. I was literally holding my breath by that stage, unable to move, other than to lean towards her ever so slightly.

'Li-ar,' she whispered very slowly, and then she grinned at me as she pulled away and straightened in her seat to face the harbour. I laughed – but it was a weak and uneven laugh. In equal parts I was shaken by her game and delighted by her playfulness but one thing was certain – I was completely under her spell. I reached for her elbow and very gently turned her back to face me. Our eyes locked again, and this time the playfulness was gone altogether.

'Have dinner with me tomorrow,' I said.

'We had dinner here tonight,' Molly pointed out. She wasn't going to make this easy, but that was just fine with me – I loved the challenge of this more pointed interplay between us.

'Not like this,' I said. 'A proper dinner.'

'You mean a dinner where we don't spend half the night talking about the tragic death of my beloved big brother?' she said, one eyebrow high.

'Would that be okay?'

'Can I pick the venue?'

'Why?'

'There's a place I'd like to go with you.'

'Okay,' I said. She could have asked for the moon that night and I'd have found a way to get it for her. Letting her choose yet another swanky, rich-lady dinner place was fine. It saved me trying to figure out where the hell to take her anyway.

'Seven o'clock?' she prompted.

'Where will I meet you?'

'I'll text you tomorrow.'

'Okay,' I said, and then, just to make doubly sure we were both on the same page, I added quietly, 'It's a date.'

'It's a date,' she echoed, and then, flashing me a quick smile, she scooped her phone up from the table and glanced at the screen. She pressed a few buttons and then murmured apologetically, 'I really need to go.'

'Okay,' I said, and we slid out of the bench seat and automatically started walking back towards the road behind the bar.

'Can I get you a taxi?' I asked her.

'No, the town car is on its way. Do you need a lift somewhere?'

'Thanks for the offer but I think your driver would have a panic attack if I told him my address. I'll get a cab.'

'Where *do* you live?'

'I live in a terrace near one of the public housing towers in Redfern.'

Molly frowned at me and shook her head. I responded with a quizzical frown of my own.

'How can you live in Sydney and *not* know the Redfern towers?'

'I don't really know anything about Redfern, I just know it's a rough place,' she admitted.

'You'll probably be pleased to know gentrification is well and truly underway, it's not nearly as rough as it once was. Plus, it's actually a great place to live,' I said. Molly nodded and smiled, but I could see that she wasn't convinced. I was about to launch into a spiel about the suburb I loved, but she distracted me by pointing into the distance behind me. I glanced over my shoulder and saw a taxi approaching, but I shook my head. 'I'll wait with you until your car comes.'

'I don't need a babysitter.'

'I don't mind. Frankly, I could do with some back-up in case your father is waiting in hiding in my cab.'

She grinned at me. 'I have a feeling you can handle yourself, Leo. Take it, I'll be insulted if you don't.'

I hesitated, but Molly stepped in front of me and waved vigorously, calling the cab to a stop beside us. 'Text me when you get home safely?' I asked. It seemed wrong to leave her standing alone by the side of the road at night, even though we were in a busy and perfectly safe part of the city.

'God, listen to you,' she rolled her eyes. 'I agree to have dinner with you and suddenly you're my bodyguard.'

As I opened the cab door, I swept my gaze over her. Molly slowly reached up to smooth her fringe down over her forehead, trailing a finger behind her ear and down her neck, then she rested her hand against her shoulder as she stared back at me intently. Whatever the chemistry was, it was alive and humming between us, and there was no doubt in my mind now that she was as conscious of it as I was.

'See you tomorrow,' I said.

'Oh, you will,' she assured me quietly, and then she closed the taxi door.

CHAPTER 9
Molly – July 2015

It's a twenty-hour flight from Rome to Sydney, including the brief stop at Singapore where the plane is refuelled. Leo is in a hospital bed that has been fitted into the jet, and he sleeps on and off, around meals and brief chats and long stints reading the newspapers that someone thought to load onto the plane for us. When we're finally coming into Sydney and I look out my window to see the Harbour Bridge below us, I find myself unexpectedly teary as I breathe the sigh of relief that I've been holding onto since I flew out.

Several more hours pass before Leo is admitted and settled in the hotel-like room that will be his home for the foreseeable future. The rehab centre is plush, and he's treated like a celebrity from the moment we enter the front doors. I know he'll be comfortable there – and most importantly, at least for a while, he'll be safe. This is not something I have *ever* been able to take for granted with Leo.

My phone has been ringing off the hook since we landed – his friends and family are dying to come and see him, but with the exception of his parents, I've asked them to wait until he's had a chance to settle in. And then, once a nurse has finished Leo's induction, we're left alone for the first time in a day. Leo flicks through the paperwork they've given him while I sit at the end of his bed and stare out of the large window at the beautifully landscaped gardens that surround the rehabilitation centre.

'What do you think?' he asks. I drag my eyes back to him from the window and smile.

'It's great, as long as you're happy with it.'

'I can't believe you organised this so quickly.'

'I told you,' I smile weakly. 'Money talks. There have to be some benefits to marrying a trust-fund kid.'

He smiles wryly. 'I'm sure this isn't the only one. What are your plans? Home for a very long sleep in your own—' he catches himself, 'in *our* bed?'

I *am* going home to our bed – not to mine. I have organised for the terrace to be aired out, and I'm going to sleep there, at least tonight. I have absolutely no idea why.

'Unless you need anything else?'

'New legs?'

'Your legs are fine,' I remind him. 'It's your brain that's wonky, and soon that'll be fine too.'

'I hope you're right.'

'If your memory was intact, you'd know that I'm not often wrong.' Leo laughs at me, and I slide off the end of his bed and stretch. 'Can I bring you anything tomorrow?'

'I was hoping you might bring me a few things. I'm guessing I would have had a sat phone with me in Syria and that's probably lost?'

'I'd say so. Brad was travelling with you, but I doubt he went back for your gear.'

'He was with me?' Leo visibly brightens at this news, and not for the first time I am irrationally jealous of the great love he has for his work. 'Do you think he'll visit me soon?'

'He's already texted me this afternoon to ask when he can visit, and so has half of the *News Monthly* team and the guys at the gym. Your parents will come sometime this evening, but I've told the rest of them they have to come over the next few days. I hope that's okay?'

'Thanks, Molly. That's great. So – do I have another phone? A mobile?'

I hesitate before I nod, because God only knows what's on his phone. There will definitely be a history of text messages between us – snarky ones at least, brutally nasty ones at worst.

'You do. I'm not sure where you left It,' I lie.

'Unless my routine has changed it'll be in the safe in my office. Do you know the code?'

'I do. I'll see if I can find it. And something to read? Your main Kindle is probably lost in Syria, but I'll bring the spare.'

'Kindle?' he raises an eyebrow at me. 'An E-reader? I don't like to read electronically.'

'That's what you said when I bought you one for your birthday the first year we were together. Now you own two. It took you a while to come round to the idea of reading on a device but once you caught on, you *really* caught on.'

'Really?' He is a little sceptical, but I know he'll change his mind about a chapter into his first book. 'Right. Well, in that case, yes – the spare Kindle too, please. And some of my own clothes if it's not too much trouble.' He holds out his hand to me, and I automatically slide mine into it as if to shake hands. I'm surprised when he pulls me close, and then envelops me in a hug.

'Thank you, Molly – for everything,' he whispers into my hair. There's such sincerity in his voice that I'm almost taken aback. It's not that Leo is an ungrateful man… it's just that he isn't the kind of man to wear his emotions on his sleeve. There's a degree of vulnerability in the warmth in his tone, and a shaky edge to it, almost as if he's overwhelmed – but surely not. Leo doesn't do overwhelmed, particularly not when it comes to gratitude.

I return his hug, and it's amazing to have his arms around me again. Greedily I absorb the moment – I want to stay here, just like this, to revel in the peacefulness between us. For a moment or two, I let myself wonder what it would be like if Leo never recovered any more of his lost years than he has, just so that I could keep him like this: warm, caring – *friendly*.

But I don't let myself cling to that thought for more than a second. I gently pull out of the embrace, but brush a soft kiss against the scruffy beard on his cheek before I leave.

❖ ❖ ❖

I call Brad Norse on my way home. I've been putting this call off, but there's no more delaying it. I put the privacy screen up between the driver and my backseat, and dial with shaking fingers.

'Molly! How's Leo?'

Brad is the closest thing to a best friend that Leo has. They often travel together – Brad taking the photos, Leo writing the words. In the last few years we've all become fairly close – Brad's wife Penny is one of the few people I know who understands what it's like to have a husband work in such a dangerous job.

I haven't spoken to Brad since the accident. I didn't want to speak to him, because I figured he probably knew the truth about Leo and me, and I couldn't bring myself to face his con-demnation. I love Brad but he's the kind of friend who would take sides, and I know which side he would take.

'He's doing really well, Brad – really well. He's almost back to normal already – except he can't move his legs and he's alto-gether forgotten me,' I laugh uneasily.

'Yeah, Anne told me about all of that. How's he coping?'

'He's doing great considering but the memory loss has com-plicated things.'

'I'll bet it has.'

'I don't know what he told you… before the accident, I mean. I know you're close,' I say awkwardly. Suddenly I realise I should have had this conversation with Brad in person so that I could watch his reaction.

Brad, unsurprisingly, is protective of Leo and is not going to make this easy on me. 'About?' he asks, a little tersely. I pick at imaginary fluff on my skirt while I try to figure out what to say. The silence stretches, and then Brad apparently softens. 'It was pretty obvious that you two were going through a rough patch. Is that what you mean?'

'Yeah,' I whisper. Rough patch? Leo obviously has not told him.

'You know Leo even better than I do, Molly. He's not the sort of guy to sit around and talk about feelings. But yes, I knew things weren't great because… well, there was that god-awful dinner party we had with you guys just before Quinn was born… plus he was as cranky as a bear with a sore head and crazy-distracted.'

'Distracted?' Great. Now the accident is my fault too.

'Honestly, Molly, we should have pulled out of that embed the day after we got there – God, we should never have been given permission to go. Am I right in guessing you'd fought about him going? He seemed pretty determined to make it worthwhile even though we both knew it was just too dangerous. I thought he was maybe making a point of it.'

'Of course I didn't want him to go,' I mutter. 'And you shouldn't have gone, either, Brad.'

'That was always going to be my last crazy war-zone trip with him. Even more so once he got injured, I'm just…' Brad sighed. 'I am just done with trying to be a hero, you know? Anyway, sounds like Leo's heroic days are over too.'

'No,' I say automatically. 'They won't be. Leo lives for that stuff. Anyway, he just has no idea we were in a rough patch. I don't know if I've done the right thing but he has so much to catch up on, and I didn't want to overwhelm him.'

'Do they think his memory will return?'

'He's already remembered a few things. They're pretty confident it will all come back in time.'

'He'll understand, Molly. He'll probably appreciate you shielding him from it so he can concentrate on getting well. Is that why you called? You don't want me to tell him?'

'*Please* don't. Not yet.'

'Got it.'

'You'll go see Leo tomorrow?'

'Yeah. Should I take him anything?'

'Do you have any of his stuff?'

'There wasn't time to recover anything from the car but I did go back to the camp before I left, so I've got everything else.'

'Great. And do you have any photos to show him?'

'Do I have photos…?' Brad feigns outrage. 'Of course I have photos. I even have photos of your husband with his head cracked open if he wants to see them.'

'Probably leave those at home for now.'

I wrap up the call as we arrive at the terrace. Tobias has been during the day to restock the fridge and air the place out, and he's left the doggy door at the back of the house open – I can tell this last part before I even open the front door, because Lucien is already waiting on the other side. I can hear the rhythmic swish of his tail as it wags against the floorboards. When I open the door, there's a ball of apricot fluff waiting for me. I drop to my knees and he leaps into my arms.

'I missed you too!' Leo always mocks me for talking to Lucien, but I've caught him doing it himself when he didn't realise

I was in earshot. Lucien tries to lick my face and I lean away. He is far too large to be a lap dog, but that's never stopped him from trying, and if the warmth and weight of him is physically uncomfortable, emotionally it's an overwhelming comfort. He has seen me shed more tears than any human has, and he always seems to know how to console me. He settles with his paws against my shoulder and rests his ear against my head. I wrap my arms around him and I sob.

I am overwhelmed with relief at the simple reality of being back in the terrace – in my home, which is no longer my home. And yet from the moment I knew we were leaving Rome, this was where I wanted to be. I try to tell myself it's Lucien I wanted to be close to, and as he nuzzles himself into my neck, I can almost convince myself that's true – almost.

I climb the stairs and fall into the bed fully clothed – Lucien at my side. I curl up around Leo's pillows and I breathe in deeply, and think about my husband. I am trapped in this situation with him, at least for now, and I feel a bewildering sense of panic as I consider the possibilities for the next few weeks or, God forbid, even months.

I have so much going on in my own life; so much healing to do – so much planning to do. I don't have the time nor the brain space to deal with scaffolding and guiding as Leo recovers… nor could I ever abandon him – not now, when he needs me. But can I handle the continuing walk down memory lane? I feel dread at the very thought of it – it's too soon; things are too raw. I am still too angry with him and I am too vulnerable. And what if he never recovers?

That thought is like cold water dumped onto my self-pity. I take a few deep breaths. My situation is crappy, but his is infinitely worse. It's uncomfortable and scary, but being here for Leo during this time is the least I can do.

CHAPTER 10
Leo – February 2011

Friday was a day devoted entirely to anticipation. By the time I headed to Circular Quay to meet Molly, I felt as though I'd been waiting a very long time to see her again, although it was actually less than twenty-four hours.

I took a seat at the bar where I could keep an eye on the door and ordered some water as I surveyed the place. It was, as I'd expected, an exorbitantly priced restaurant. But there were cosy booths and tea light candles on the tables and folksy music playing in the background; this was a place constructed for intimate dinners. I could forgive the pretentious nature of the establishment given the unmistakable message Molly had sent with her choice of venue.

I looked at the door just as she entered, and saw her scanning the room, looking for me. She was wearing a soft pink dress with delicate folds across the front. The skirt fell to her knees, the neckline was high, and the sleeves were elbow-length. There was nothing at all seductive about her attire, but there didn't need to be – I would have been equally captivated had she stepped through the door wearing a hessian sack and gumboots.

'Ms Torrington, lovely to see you,' the waitress approached her as I did, and after a quick glance at me, returned her attention to Molly. 'Your booth is ready.'

'Hello, Molly,' I said quietly.

'Hi, Leo,' she smiled back at me almost shyly, and we followed the waitress to the table. Molly slid into the booth and I followed her but sat opposite her – I wanted to keep my thoughts clear.

It had occurred to me as we flirted the previous night that Molly had met every challenge I'd issued head-on. I was confident that I knew how to speak to women – I'd had plenty of chances to hone my dating game to a fine art over the years – but I might just have met my match in Molly Torrington. The challenge she presented was enthralling,

'I've been thinking about you a lot this week,' I said, as soon as we were seated. 'And you have been thinking a lot about me.'

She stared back at me, unfazed. 'Oh, I *have*, have I?' she laughed softly.

'You have. If you hadn't, you wouldn't have worn that dress.'

'Why? What's wrong with my dress?' she glanced down at herself and frowned at me.

'It's beautiful. And so are you.'

'Well, what did you mean, then?'

'I bet when you pulled on that dress tonight, you were thinking about the look I'd have on my face when I saw you walk in here.'

'You are awfully cocky, Leo Stephens,' she raised an eyebrow at me. 'And actually, that wasn't what I was thinking,' she added pointedly. I looked at her questioningly, and she leant forward and said softly, 'When I pulled this dress on earlier, I was thinking a lot more about the look I'll see on your face if I decide to let you take it off later.'

The image she'd painted was so vivid that my mind completely shut down. For a moment or two I stared at her blankly, then cleared my throat and shifted in the seat as I said unevenly, 'Now who's being cocky?'

Molly shrugged and picked up the wine list as if we'd just been discussing the weather.

'I'd like to remind you that *you* started this conversation. White or red?'

I was still trying to re-engage my brain. 'Lady's choice. How's your day been?'

'It's been good. Productive. And yours?'

'Peaceful,' I said. 'I convinced my physiotherapist to let me get back to work on Monday, although I'm not cleared to head back to Libya yet, but at least I'll be able to start writing up the story I was working on.'

'Congratulations,' she said, and put the menu down. 'I'll order bubbles then, since we're celebrating again.'

We ordered drinks and our meals, and I told her about the Libyan article I was planning and she told me about the acquisition she'd just completed.

That night I was so captivated by Molly that even her business talk about takeovers was fascinating. I tried to understand what it must be like to work in a demanding, high-pressure job like hers and to pursue success that she didn't actually want or need.

For me my work was everything: it was my reason for breathing. Molly had to work just as hard as I did – maybe even harder – but at the end of the day, every minute she spent in that role she was effectively giving over to Laith. I was surprised by how much that bothered me. I knew it was none of my business, and I was generally well-accustomed to turning from any urge to solve other people's problems – that was a necessary skill in my work. But this was Molly, and although I barely knew her, I felt sure she deserved better.

'Where is our meal?' Molly asked suddenly. 'I always lose track of time when I'm talking to you,' she murmured, and then looked around. A waitress hurried over to us. 'We ordered almost an hour ago…'

'I'm so sorry, Ms Torrington,' she said, 'There's been a staffing issue in the kitchen. Your meals are on their way, but it might be another ten or fifteen minutes. I'll organise another bottle of wine on the house as a small token of our apology.'

When the waitress left, Molly glanced at me and said, 'I do come here fairly often, so I'm sure the free wine isn't because she recognised me and feared the Torrington dynasty falling on her head if she delayed my food.'

'Doesn't a place like this lose its appeal if you come often?' I raised my hand and waved generally towards the view. 'Surely overexposure just makes it too familiar?'

'It's like a family member you really like, or a favourite piece of furniture. You still like them even if you see them every day, right?'

I stared at her blankly. If I could have forgotten for even one second just how vastly different our worlds were, there it was.

'Did you really just refer to a Michelin-rated restaurant as a "favourite piece of furniture"?'

'My apartment is a sixty-second walk from here. The food is fantastic. Why *wouldn't* I come regularly?'

'Because you've taken something exceptional and made it everyday.'

'Or, am I just lucky enough to be in a position that the exceptional *is* my everyday?'

I paused, and then frowned as I considered her words. 'Your apartment is a sixty-second walk from here? You don't. . . tell me you don't live in "the toaster".'

'It's actually named "The Bennelong Apartments", Leo,' She laughed at the popular nickname I'd used for one of the wealthiest addresses in Sydney. The building did look like a giant toaster, plunked unceremoniously among the city's most famous landmarks. 'I take it by that haughty tone that you're not a fan of it.'

'It's an eyesore,' I winced. 'I remember back when you could see all the way from Circular Quay down to the Botanic Gardens. That building completely changed the tone of the gateway to the city.'

'When you say things like that, you make yourself sound quite old,' Molly remarked, and she grinned at me. 'A lot of people disliked that building in the nineties when it was built, but you're the first person I've heard express such hatred for it recently. Now that it's been around for a while no one really cares anymore. And yes, I live in the Bennelong Apartments – it's a great place to live.'

'Is there even a sense of community in a place like that? That's what I love most about Redfern,' I said suddenly. Molly's face twisted a little – my comment had offended her. Right then, the waitress returned with the second bottle of wine, which she presented with grand aplomb. When she left, I raised an eyebrow at Molly. 'I believe you were about to make some snobbish comment about Redfern?'

'I just – it's…' I rather enjoyed watching her flounder for words, but after a moment, she looked at me and said with an easy shrug, 'I am not a snob, but that area doesn't have a very good reputation, does it?'

I leant back as I surveyed her. 'I grew up in Redfern. I went to a public primary school then high school there, and that was long before all of the trendy parts popped up.'

'You said that last night, but I'm still not sure there are trendy parts,' she said. At this I sighed, and she muttered hastily, 'Sorry.'

'Next time we meet,' I said suddenly. 'We meet on my turf.'

'Don't you feel unsafe there?'

'*Unsafe?*' I repeated incredulously.

'I mean, there are so many…'

'Filthy poor people? Or do you mean filthy black people?' Now my hackles were up and my comment was snarkier than it was playful.

'Well, *no*, of course not – just...'

'Molly,' I interrupted her, because I couldn't bear another second of her uncomfortable back-pedalling, 'you do realise that more than half my career has been reporting from war zones? Are you really asking me if I feel unsafe in an inner-city suburb of *Sydney*? Redfern is a wonderful community. There's a rich heritage there, cultural and physical. My neighbour is an eighty-something woman who still lives in the house where she was born. At my gym the community comes together every week-night to donate meals to kids to make sure they have good nutrition after they work out. Yes, there have been some problems and yes, there are a lot of underprivileged families, but the underprivileged families are not the problem – they never are.'

Molly's intense focus on my rant was flattering, but when I finally stopped talking, she tilted her head to the side and said quietly, 'You should go into politics.'

'I wouldn't last ten seconds on the campaign trail.'

'True. Your controversial and antiquated views on "the toaster" building would offend too many wealthy people,' she laughed.

I glanced around. The waitress was looking towards us, but she was empty-handed and visibly nervous. She kept glancing at Molly, as if she was likely to throw a tantrum any second. I wondered if Molly was generally a difficult patron or if it was just her family's reputation that made the waitress so anxious.

I looked back at Molly and found she was staring at me. Our eyes locked and the moment stretched and intensified; neither of us seemed capable of looking away. The world seemed to have paused all around us, and only picked up again when another diner brushed past us on his way to a table.

We hadn't even had our first course yet, but I already wanted to touch her – take her hand, or touch her face, her hair. She smoothed her fringe across her forehead. I was already familiar with the gesture but I hadn't figured out yet how to interpret it.

'So, you grew up in Redfern,' she said suddenly. 'Is your mum still there?'

'She lives in Alexandria now, with my step-father – although I don't actually call him a "step" father,' I said. 'He is just my dad – he's earned the title.'

'That's nice.'

'He's an incredible human being.'

'Do you have siblings?'

'Just the one – my sister Teresa; she and her husband Paul live at Cronulla. She keeps telling me she's the favourite child at the moment because she's going to give them a grandchild at last. She's probably right.'

'Are you the eldest?'

'Yes, Teresa is quite a bit younger than me; she's only twenty-nine. She's a beautician; her husband is a graphic designer.'

'Quite a bit younger,' Molly repeated, and she laughed. 'She's the same age as me. How old are you?'

'I'm thirty-eight,' I admitted.

'Jesus, you're *ancient!*' she feigned horror. I laughed reluctantly. 'Seriously, thirty-eight and not even retired yet. That's remarkable. Is it some kind of world record?' she said cheerfully. I sank back into my seat and stared at my wine, processing this. It wasn't an outrageous age gap, but it was still the widest I'd dealt with in any woman I'd gone out with. 'Well, who cares if you're a senior citizen?'

'I'm so sorry for the wait,' the waitress was back, but this time she was carrying our main courses. Her eyes were swimming with tears and her hands shook as she set Molly's plate down first. Molly opened her mouth – I knew immediately that she was going reproach the waitress because we hadn't yet had our entrées. I leant towards her and tapped her wrist gently with my hand. She shot me a confused glance, but only murmured a quiet thanks to the waitress as she left.

'She's having a pretty bad night,' I whispered, as soon as she left us. 'Give the kid a break; she's already close to tears.'

Molly looked back at the waitress, who had immediately moved to a booth further along the wall, where some other frustrated diners were now loudly expressing their disappointment at their delayed meals.

'I should have noticed that,' she said, a deep frown crossing her face. 'I don't mean to be hard on people. What is it they say about familiarity breeding contempt?'

'You live a pretty unique existence,' I said, and I smiled at her. 'Not many people think of Circular as a suitable venue for a quick after-work dinner but I have to say, in spite of the delay, this meal is amazing.'

And it was – the food was exquisite – both of our dishes were a culinary work of art. As we each finished eating, I reached for the carafe of water at the same moment Molly did, and our hands collided awkwardly. I withdrew mine automatically and felt almost guilty, as if the accidental contact might have happened through sheer force of will on my behalf. It struck me that Molly had also pulled her hand back. I gazed at her face, expecting to see awkwardness or embarrassment, but I only saw the same quickening that I felt running riot within myself. Even in the dim light of the restaurant I could see that her eyes had darkened somewhat. She was staring at me with an open, unashamed hunger.

Her hand was on the table, away from the carafe but resting near her cutlery. I now moved my own very slowly across the table. She watched its passage, and I sensed her holding her breath. Millimetre by millimetre I brought my hand closer, and then carefully brushed the back of my forefinger all the way along the top of hers, from her fingernail down to the back of her hand. When I reached her wrist, I curled my fingers away from hers, leaving our hands just touching.

I was giving her the chance to pull her hand away, but I knew she wouldn't take it – what I was really doing was prolonging the delicious tension and anticipation that had been humming between us all night. Although it had been a simple movement, in no way could it be misconstrued. Our gazes locked again and there was only us, and only that moment – a *first* moment of brutal, unspoken honesty between us.

The desire was palpable. It was intense, it was strange, and it was a beautifully mutual thing. She raised the fingers of her hand upwards and towards mine, pressing her palm into the table. I repeated the motion, then linked my fingers through hers and twisted our hands so that mine rested over hers. And then I swallowed, hard, because even this palm-to-palm contact was good. Very good.

She stared down at our hands, my dark fingers linked through her pale ones, and then she looked back at my face. 'Have you ever been inside the Bennelong Apartments?' she asked me softly.

'No, I have not,' I said. I looked at her sharply as a sudden, shocking thought struck me. 'Is *that* why you picked this restaurant – because it's close to your home?'

Her fingers contracted around mine just a little, and the corners of her mouth turned upwards. If I'd caught her out, she didn't mind at all.

'I like to be prepared for all possibilities,' was all that she said, but the intensity in her eyes left me in no doubt at all that I was right. I glanced at her plate, which was clean.

'Would you like some dessert?' I asked her.

'Oh yes,' she murmured. 'Let's go.'

CHAPTER 11
Molly – July 2015

It's early afternoon before I make it to the rehab clinic the next day. The quick visit to the office I'd intended stretches to several hours, and then there is the long drive across the city to reach Leo's temporary home. I'm feeling harried and guilty by the time I reach his room.

I find him sitting up in a wheelchair talking to Teresa, who is curled up on the couch near his bed. I'm relieved that she hasn't brought the kids with her – the hospital room is not at all child-friendly; the boys would have wreaked havoc.

Teresa's eyes are red, and she's clutching a tissue in one hand and her mobile phone in the other. Her relationship with Leo is generally defined by their non-stop insults, but I know that beneath the bravado, they almost revere one another. I give her a hug then I sit next to her.

'Sorry I'm so late,' I grimace. 'Busy morning. Everything okay here?'

'I've been busy too,' Leo assures me. 'It's been like a production line of visitors and bossy therapists since you left last night.'

'Good,' I smile. 'You're feeling okay?'

'Better every hour.'

'Do you just love his new haircut? Have I not been saying for years that he should cut it shorter?' Teresa says pointedly, and I realise belatedly that Leo's bandages have been removed.

The hasty buzz cut he'd been given before his surgery is now exposed, and so is the huge scar running vertically along his skull. I can see the marks of the thick staples that were holding him together. It is daunting – but Leo's hair grows so fast, the scar will disappear beneath his thick dark waves in no time.

'He looks terrific,' I say. It is difficult to believe this is the same Leo who was still in a coma a week ago – harder still to believe it's the same man who was so furious with me that, just a few weeks before his accident, he left his wedding ring sitting on our basin for me to find.

'Teresa has spent the last hour or so catching me up on the entire history of her children's lives,' Leo tells me, motioning towards the phone in her hand. 'I think we were up to the photo of Baxter's fourth or fifth nappy change and his second bottle of milk. Continue?'

'You'll feel bad for that when your memory returns and you realise how much you love them,' I tell him.

'I can take them for rides on my wheelchair,' Leo says. He tries to keep his tone light, but there's no way Teresa or I are going to miss the negative undertone.

'You'll be chasing them and tickling them again in no time,' she assures him. 'You're far too stubborn to be permanently injured.'

'I'm not sure "stubbornness" is the criteria they use to assess whether a traumatic brain injury will be permanent or not, but thanks for the vote of confidence,' Leo says, and he pushes himself forward and ruffles her hair as if she's a child. Teresa swats at him with obvious irritation and I laugh, because it feels so wonderful to see the two of them in sparring mode again.

'Now that your lovely wife is here to keep you company, I'm going to head home and save Paul from our sons. We'll come together soon, when Mum can babysit for us. Unless you want us to bring the kids so you can "meet" them?'

'Actually,' Leo says quietly, 'They've told me I'm free to come and go as I please – I'm really hoping to get out and about soon. Maybe I can come to you?'

'Tobias has organised a wheelchair-enabled van,' I tell him, 'so that should be easily arranged.'

'That's great news,' Leo says. 'Please give Tobias my sincerest thanks. Whoever "Tobias" is.'

His sarcasm triggers instant irritation in me. My gaze sharpens – it would be so easy to throw out a retort or snap at him. If Teresa wasn't sitting next to me, I probably would. She is notoriously blunt and protective of Leo – if I reveal so much as a hint of impatience with him, I know she'll be onto me and the last thing any of us needs right now is a family squabble.

'Poor Leo,' she winces. 'This must be so confusing. Tobias is your superhero wife's loyal side-kick at the Foundation. He's her assistant.'

'Ah, "the Foundation".' Leo glances at me. 'Your charity?'

I nod silently, and Teresa stands. 'Will you let me know when you're coming? I'll even pick the Lego up so you can get the wheelchair past the front door.' She kisses Leo on the cheek as she leaves. 'Thanks for bringing him home to us, Molly.'

'You haven't told me anything about your charity,' Leo says, as soon as Teresa is gone.

'I know. It's easier to show you, that's partly why I asked Tobias to organise the van.'

'When can we go?'

'I guess that's up to you.'

'This may be difficult to believe, but my dance card is fairly empty.'

'Don't they have you doing therapy and classes like twenty-four hours a day here?'

Leo leans across and picks up a laminated piece of paper from the coffee table.

'Let's check the schedule… so there's physical therapy every morning and I'm pretty sure I want that. Then occupational therapy some days, which I'm not entirely sure I understand, but I think it might be useful, and on the alternate days there's hydro-therapy.'

'You do like to swim,' I remark.

'I do, so maybe I'll stick around for those sessions too. But then there's lunch and right after *that*, there's something called "group talk therapy".'

Leo looks traumatised reading those words aloud. I burst out laughing. 'Oh dear!'

'That's between 3 p.m. and 4.30 p.m. – every day.' Leo glances at me. I don't think he's entirely pretending to be horrified. I am still laughing, and he raises his eyebrows at me. 'Maybe you don't understand, Molly, it's *every single day*.'

'Perhaps it would do you good to talk about your feelings more?' I suggest, and he rests the schedule on his lap and narrows his eyes at me.

'If I *have* to talk about feelings, at least let me talk about pleasant ones. Do you think you could come with me to visit a few places? See if we can jog some more memories? And I'd like to see your charity, of course.'

'Okay.'

'How does 3 to 4.30 p.m. every day this week sound?'

It sounds completely impossible given that I've missed two weeks of work already and it will take me at least two hours of travel to get here and back. But Leo smiles at me and it's the charming smile; the one he flashes at cranky airport staff when he can't get the flight he wants or the embassy staff when he needs yet another rushed visa. It's reflex to smile back, and even my posture softens; I find myself slumping just a bit, as if my spine is melting.

'Has Brad been in yet?' I ask.

'Nope.'

'Well, he's coming at some point, so we'd better let you stick around here today and start our alternative talk therapy tomorrow.'

'Fantastic, it's a date.' He pauses after he says the words and then the realisation dawns on his face. 'I think I said that to you, didn't I? We were at that bar… the one on Darling Harbour. We were going to have dinner together and I wanted to be sure that we were on the same page.'

I'm back at that moment in an instant. I remember tall, strong Leo sitting beside me at the bar and the closed-in feeling of the darkness that had fallen… and how intense his stare had been. I'd barely been able to sleep that night so instead of sleeping, I had schemed. My spoilt, selfish little mind schemed until the wee hours – I planned the venue and the atmosphere of the dinner we'd agreed to share, and I even decided on the dress and the perfume I'd wear.

I was a shark tracking her prey.

'Do you remember that whole night?'

'I remember that *moment*, but so far, it's just a fragment – those words jumped into my head but the rest hasn't come back yet. It's kind of like seeing a scene cut from the middle of a movie,' he says wryly. 'So, where did we go?'

'Circular Quay. We did a lot around there, actually. Maybe that's where we should go tomorrow.'

'That sounds good. Thanks, Molly. Did you bring some clothes I can wear?'

I point to the bag I've left sitting on his bed. 'Yes – clothing and Kindle, as requested. I picked you up a wallet and I've put your spare credit card in it in case you need to buy anything. I just can't find your phone – I'm really sorry, so I organised you another. It has the same number, and you'll find the code for the credit card saved in the phone too.'

'I was really hoping for my old phone. It's not in the safe?'

I shake my head. I'm lying – I haven't even checked, but I suspect he's right – that's where it will be. I tell myself that I'm withholding his old phone from him to protect him – if I handed it over, ready or not he would immediately have to deal with the reality of our situation. Just from his text message history there would be no doubt at all that we are no longer happily married.

But if I'm really honest with myself, that's probably only half of the reason why I am lying. I'm feeling oddly curious about Leo, which seems ridiculous because I know him better than I know myself. But I'd forgotten what it was like to be with him, before all of the layers of bitterness settled over our relationship. Yes, I am sensitive towards him and a little too easily irritated by him – but I also thought he was going to die, and then he didn't, and now he's here and he's charming to me again and… I guess, I'm just not ready for things to go back to the way they were.

'Next to my bed?' he prompts. I shake my head, and he sighs. 'That's so strange.'

'I'll keep looking if you like but I guess you must have taken it with you.'

'It seems really odd – you said I had the sat phone too, right?' I nod, and he frowns. 'Why would I take two phones into the field?'

I'm kicking myself now because he is right – he *never* takes two phones with him.

'I'm not sure,' I say. I'm really hoping he doesn't notice the flush on my cheeks.

'How were we communicating?'

We weren't, I think and I'm panicking a little now. The last communication we'd had before he flew out was his awful email suggesting I find a lawyer, and a curt text telling me to clear the last of my things from his house. Just thinking about those messages causes me pain, even now, weeks later. They were the first few lines in the new chapter of my life that was supposed to be titled *After Leo* – but they were also a confrontation, and what those messages lacked said as much about them as the actual words they contained. Those messages were business-like and curt – there was no undertone of familiarity or warmth. We were strangers at the point – even more so than we are right now when Leo cannot remember much at all of our life together.

But I don't want to think about this. I don't want to lie to him, and I especially don't want to be caught out lying to him. I need to move the conversation on as quickly as I can, but before I can think of a story that will be convincing enough for him, he speaks again.

'Did I lose everything I took to Syria?'

'Brad has your bag, but he said everything you had with you in the car was lost, so if you did take it to Syria, it's likely it's gone.'

Leo sighs, but as I hoped, he is finally satisfied by this. 'I just figured it would have been a good way to get a feel for what I've been doing recently. I don't really use text messaging but I thought my phone history would give me some clues what I was busy with when I was last using it.'

'About the text messages...' I say, and he looks at me questioningly. I laugh softly. 'You text a lot now.'

'Oh?'

'I mean... I always do. I don't think you liked to, but you still used to do it.'

'Are you sure? I *really* hate them.'

'I know. I guess you compromised.'

This thought is actually startling. I think of Leo sometimes as a man who does *not* compromise, and yet, I have just accidentally reminded myself of one of the small ways that he did meet me halfway. It's such a minor thing but it's also not, because we really have relied on text messaging a lot over the years to stay in touch.

'Now I'm even more disappointed about the lost phone,' he sighs. 'That would have been a great insight into who we are together.'

Oh, you have no idea. I wonder what he would think if I did let him see those last few messages. Would he be embarrassed at his coldness? I have a feeling he would be, just as I'm embarrassed by some of the things I have done in recent months. The problem with losing a passion like ours is that it can drive a person a little crazy, and when the heat of the moment passes and you're left to face the aftermath, it can be hard to justify what seemed like a perfectly sensible decision when the anger was running hot.

'Sorry, Leo,' I say.

'Hey, it's not your fault,' he smiles at me.

'Are you settling in okay here?'

'I'd rather be home, but I know I need to be here.'

'It's not for ever,' I say softly. He nods.

'I know. How are you going? Are you okay by yourself?'

I laugh, but it's a sharp sound. My bitterness turns instantly to guilt as Leo winces.

'I guess you're used to that.'

'I'm well and truly capable of looking after myself,' I assure him tightly. 'It's never been the same at home when you're not there, but I can handle it.'

'Do I travel less now?'

I really wish I could tell him that he does. That *was* his plan when we got married – no more than three weeks away at a time, no more than six trips a year. It's not at all how things have panned out. 'No, your work is very important to you… and the world has been pretty messy the last few years so you've had an endless array of great assignments to choose from. You've told a lot of stories no one would ever have heard without you, and you want to focus on building your career for a bit longer.'

I take a moment to ponder the strange pang I feel inside – and it suddenly occurs to me that the reason I'm feeling so conflicted is that I'm justifying to Leo the decisions that he has made which have essentially ruined our marriage. I don't *want* to justify these things. When we've argued over this, Leo has always been closed – so determined – he would say all of the things I've just said, but he would make them seem so irrefutable. Then I would counter with my own demands – basically for *some* of his attention – which I was also utterly determined about. The end result was always a form of relationship violence – not that either one of us ever raised a hand towards the other – but there are ways to use words to do damage too.

In all of the dozens of times we have argued over this we have been two opposing forces of equal strength, and regardless of how often we collided, we somehow failed to wear each other down even a little.

For a split second I ponder all of this – because right now Leo is vulnerable and open and I could take advantage of that. Instead of parroting back at him all of the excuses he's given me time and time again, I could calmly point out to him now how unfair it all is to me, and how cruel the situation was – me waiting at home, loving him with such desperation, but always coming second to the rest of the world's problems.

I know immediately that I can't do it. Leo is too vulnerable, even more so than in our most intimate moments. For that reason alone, I can't take advantage of him – as much as I'd like to.

'Do you hate it?' Leo interrupts my mental debate, and he asks the question with urgency. I frown at him.

'Do I hate what?'

'My job.'

Stunned, I stare at him, unsure how to answer. We really don't talk about this – we argue about it, we bicker about it – but we don't *talk* about it. In the beginning, I didn't bother to discuss it with him. I figured it was obvious, for a start, but I also assumed we'd both change and our future would be forged from some natural compromise. I'd adjust to his job, and Leo's drive to work so hard would ease off too.

'It's hard,' I say carefully. I can't expand on this any further because if I do, I'm not going to be able to hide my fury. Already it is starting to bubble away inside me and all it will take to unleash it is one wrong step or even another question on the subject. Leo is certainly not up to any kind of screaming match. He wheels himself to my side and places his hand over mine – and suddenly it's just too much because this softness is *exactly* what I've needed from him and it's coming far too late to make any difference.

I withdraw my hand sharply and rise. He frowns but moves back to give me space to pass him.

'Don't leave,' he says, and he sounds bewildered. 'I just wanted to talk to you.'

'No, I really have to go,' I say, and I slip my bag onto my shoulder and add with artificial brightness, 'My driver is waiting in the car. But I'll see you tomorrow afternoon?'

'Molly,' he says quietly, 'did I upset you?'

I smile and shake my head, 'No, it's just time for me to go. I'll see you tomorrow.'

'We can talk tomorrow, then?' he says, and he's frowning at me.

'Sure,' I say. My tone is short, and I leave immediately – and I feel as if I'm running away. As I sit in the back of the car travelling across the city towards home, guilt settles over me because I know I will have confused Leo and he has enough confusion to deal with already.

I console myself with a reminder that his memory will soon return, and that means it's only a matter of time before he no longer cares.

◆ ◆ ◆

I arrive at the rehab clinic just before 3 p.m. the next day. I'm in a strange, prickly kind of mood. I am still a little jet-lagged and finding it hard to sleep, I'm increasingly conscious of the backlog of work waiting for me at the office, I'm even a little regretful at the awkward end to my conversation with Leo yesterday – but even with all of those things on my mind, I can't quite put a finger on why I feel so out of sorts.

I stop at the door to Leo's room and try to push away the lingering sense of irritation so that I can focus on the afternoon with him. Suddenly I realise why I feel so off – the word I have been looking for materialises in an instant: I feel trapped.

I am stuck in this situation for God only knows how long, and it's forcing me to put my own life on hold. This isn't what I'm supposed to be doing right now; I'm not supposed to be helping Leo recover, I'm supposed to be recovering *from* Leo. These are meant to be my post-Leo days – setting up my new life, preparing myself for my future without him.

Instead, I am here, and even in being here I am forced to re-live the good times – cruelly being reminded of the things I have lost, instead of grieving and moving on. Now I have identified it, I'm mortified at the self-absorbed source of my bad mood and I give myself a stern mental berating before I try to get Leo's attention. He is waiting in his wheelchair, but completely engrossed in his Kindle. This is typical Leo behaviour – when he's reading, the house could burn down around him and he'd probably not notice.

I pause and remind myself of what I'm here to do today; I have a plan for these outings and I need to keep it in focus. Today, I'm going to take him to the *News Monthly* offices to see if we can jog some of his memories – and his work is so vital to him that I know they will be important ones – but they won't be memories of us.

There's so much more that is important to Leo than me, and I have decided that any approach that keeps his focus elsewhere will be much safer for both of us.

'Hi,' I say, and he sits up hastily as if I've startled him. 'Ready to go?'

'You were right,' he says, and he waves the Kindle towards me. 'This is brilliant! Do you know I've read over six hundred books since I got this thing?'

'It's never far from your hand so I'm not surprised,' I nod. 'Does this mean you get to read them all again? I guess that's an upside to the amnesia.'

'Actually, no. It's completely bizarre – I remember what's in the books, but I can't remember reading them. I asked the neurologist this morning at my check-up and apparently it's all to do with the way memories are stored. So I've lost my episodic memory, but my semantic memory is intact. It's fascinating, although it's also a little annoying that I can recall great detail from the nine hundred-page Margaret Thatcher biography I read in 2014, but I can't remember our wedding day.'

'Spoiler alert,' I say lightly, 'I looked *amazing*!'

Leo smiles and rests the Kindle on the coffee table. 'So, are we still heading to Circular Quay today?' he asks.

'Actually, if you're up to it, I thought I'd show you some other places. There've been a lot of changes to the *News Monthly* office that you probably don't remember, so I thought we'd start there. I mean, you've probably been to Circular Quay a million times, right? And *it* hasn't really changed.'

Leo shakes his head slowly. 'I want to go to the office eventually, but my priority right now is remembering *our* early days together.'

I stare at him. He seems sincere, but the words he has said make no sense at all.

'It *is*?'

'Yeah. I mean, I still have the same job. And getting our memories back is the most important thing, right?'

For a moment I can't even figure out how to respond. Do I tell him that he has made no secret of the fact that he values his work far more than our relationship? How do I word that without seeming cold, or bitchy, or resentful, which is what I am?

It is actually completely heartbreaking to hear Leo assume that if he married me, he must think that I'm more important than his career.

I do then contemplate telling him the truth, just so that I can assess his reaction.

Actually, no, our memories are not the most important thing. In fact, I'd fall somewhere towards the bottom of your priorities list – after adventure, adrenaline, your hero complex and even your employer.

'Our relationship must have been a revelation to me,' he says slowly. 'I can't wait to remember that, Molly. Please, take me to the places where we first fell in love so that I can learn "us" again.'

I am numb, even my lips feel numb. I nod, because no words will come out of my mouth.

'Good,' he smiles. 'Let's get going.'

I step further into his room and move to take the handles on his wheelchair. Leo shifts sharply away from me and shakes his head as he snaps, 'God, no – Molly, don't do that! I'm not a baby in a pram, my hands are absolutely fine.'

'Oh – sorry.' It's awkward, and now I'm really not sure what to do – do I walk alongside him? Behind him but not touch the chair? In front of him? I glance at Leo and he still looks irritated, which instantly irritates me too. 'You have to tell me what I'm not supposed to do – I don't know the rules for how this works.'

'Neither do I,' he points out with a frown. 'But don't assume you need to baby me. I'm still the same person I was before this, you know.'

This stubborn, independent attitude is one I know far too well. I groan at him in frustration.

'I'm just trying to help you, Leo. I thought you might still be feeling weak.'

'I am *not* weak!'

'How do I know that? A week ago, you were *unconscious*.'

'If it wasn't for the headaches, I could almost forget my legs are stuffed until I try to get up out of this thing,' he sighs, and he takes a deep breath then points to the door. 'Why don't you walk in front, until we're in the corridor? Then walk next to me, okay? Like we're just walking side by side, except I'm using the wheelchair instead of my feet.'

'Okay.'

I step into the corridor, and once he's joined me, Leo says quietly, 'I think the key is going to be to communicate. There's going to be lots of things like this that we don't automatically know how to navigate. We need to talk about everything that's going on – even these little things, so they don't become big things.'

God! Now he wants to talk? Where was *this* a few months ago, when I so desperately needed it? If we had talked about the little things in the beginning, where would we have ended up? I have no idea, but the possibilities the question raises make me feel unsettled and fragile, and the defensiveness he has triggered since I arrived kicks up a notch.

'This from the man who's convinced his wife to help him play hooky to get out of "talk therapy"?' I snap at him.

'I don't need to sit in a room with the other residents and whine about how bad my headache is. I've got it easy compared to most of them anyway.'

Is that humility in his tone? That's such a startling idea that I pause, and my anger towards him recedes just a little. 'I wouldn't say you have it easy, Leo.'

'I still know myself, and I can speak, see, hear and read,' he says. 'I'm not loving the wheelchair and the memory loss, but it could have been so much worse. Some of the other patients here have lost everything.' He suddenly sits up higher in the chair. 'There's something else I wanted to say to you too – about yesterday.'

We are at the front doors, and the van is waiting right in front of us.

'That's our car,' I say, hoping to distract him. Leo stops the wheelchair and takes my hand, forcing me to stop with him.

'Yesterday, there were things you needed to say to me that you held back because I've been injured. I wanted to talk to you about how you felt about my job, and you shut down.'

I'm gazing at the car as if it's there on a time limit, and trying to think of a new way to avoid looking into his eyes. Leo waits patiently, and after a while I sigh and give in, meeting his gaze. Ordinarily, Leo is just a little taller than me when he stands at his full height but today I am standing and he is sitting so I'm forced to look down at him. I instantly hate it and I wonder if he hates it too.

'I "shut down" because it wasn't the time, and it's definitely not the place,' I say, very calmly. 'You asked me if I hate your job, and the truth is, if I let myself start talking about how *much* I hate it, I might never stop. So for now, it's better that we just focus on getting you back on your feet and we can figure all of that out later.'

'Is there a part of you that hopes I never go back into the field again?' he asks quietly.

I shake my head instantly. 'No.'

'Not even a *little* bit?' He is incredulous, but I am actually telling the truth.

'No.'

'Why not?' he seems bewildered, and I laugh at him.

'Because your job is a part of who you are, Leo. I hate watching you spar at karate tournaments too, but I can't wait to see you back on the mat, getting the shit kicked out of you.'

Leo offers me a half-smile. 'I feel like that was a back-handed reassurance, if there is such a thing.'

'It was, and there is,' I laugh, and then tug at his hand. 'Can we please go?'

He sighs and maintains a firm grip on my hand. Apparently Leo wasn't kidding when he said he wasn't feeling weak anymore.

'I want things to be honest and open between us. I don't *know* you, Molly, and I don't know if you're trying to protect me or you just don't like to tell me what's on your mind. But – I really want you to be honest with me. Is that okay?'

'Yes, that's fine,' I say, although obviously I'm lying, because I'm still not about to dump the entirety of our mess on his lap.

I need to make a plan to tell him the truth about our separation – and given how off-guard he's made me feel today, maybe that's going to need to happen sooner or later.

But I'm not ready yet, and neither is Leo.

CHAPTER

Leo – February 2011

Molly released my hand when she left the booth, and after we'd split the bill and were standing close to one another at the counter, she glanced towards me and said very quietly, 'I want to hold your hand again, and I *would*... but every now and again paparazzi...'

'I get it,' I interrupted her very quietly. 'You don't need to explain.'

She nodded and smiled, and I put my hand gently on the small of her back and turned her towards the doors. We walked towards her apartment in silence and when we had covered the short distance, a concierge held the doors to the lobby open. Molly greeted him only with a smile and a nod.

I had been walking in step with her, conscious only of the moment – of the blood thundering through my body, and the spiralling intensity of anticipation for what might happen next between us. But when we stepped into her brightly-lit lobby, I had a somewhat startling return to reality – as if I'd sobered instantly after a night of intoxication. I surveyed gleaming tiles, plush furnishings and staff. Maybe I'd fallen down the rabbit hole during the week and only realised it when we entered her building.

I wouldn't allow myself to feel intimidated, instead I held myself straighter and taller as I walked. When I caught a glimpse of Molly beside me in a mirror, I acknowledged for just a moment that although I might not feel at home in that place, the beautiful woman beside me in the alluring pink dress literally *was* at home, and she wanted me there with her. As I reflected on this, the man who looked back at me was strong and proud.

An attendant greeted Molly warmly at the elevator and hit a code into a security panel, and we stepped inside. The doors closed almost instantly, and as soon as we were alone, I reached for Molly as if I'd been waiting for her for decades. I cupped her face in my hands and she tilted it towards me. Our breaths mingled – ragged now, as if we'd sprinted from the restaurant. I wanted to savour her glistening lips and the dark blue storm of her eyes as she stared at me – but Molly hooked her arm around my neck and pulled me against her. She kissed me – hard and impatient – and I met the demands of her mouth against mine with demands of my own.

✦ ✦ ✦

Later, I lay on my back in Molly's bed, staring at the blurry shadows on the ceiling. She was lying with her head resting on my chest, one leg curled over my thigh, our hands entwined against my hip.

I didn't even try to untangle the mess of feelings in my chest. Even if I could put names to them, I wouldn't know what to do with them. Instead, I tried to focus on Molly.

'What are you thinking?' I asked her. I brushed my hand along her bare back in gently sweeping strokes, and she breathed in and out slowly.

'I was just wondering what you would do if I asked you to tell me something about yourself. Something no one else knows.'

'You already know things about me that no one else knows.'

'I do?'

'About the scholarship. I've never told anyone else that,' I admitted. 'And…' I lifted my arm and twisted it to expose the tattoos towards her. She shifted the hand from my hip to touch the inked skin, running her finger over each of the dot artworks, making her way along my arm. 'I mean, obviously people can see I have tattoos, but no one else knows what they mean.'

'These go over your back and shoulders too,' Molly whispered. 'And every one represents a death?' She twisted to stare up at me. I met her gaze, unflinching.

'Or deaths,' I said. I sounded hardened, even to my own ears.

'What about this one?' she traced the line of a symbol with her fingernail, and I felt trapped and exposed. I wanted to retreat. I wanted to gently extricate myself from her embrace and her bed and go back to my apartment to sleep by myself. But Molly waited, and there was a gradual unfurling within my gut. I stopped wanting to leave, but I still didn't want to talk to her about this. Then I stopped wanting to avoid the discussion altogether, and I started wanting to talk to her just a little – just enough to sate her curiosity, which was, I told myself, natural after all. But then I started talking, and the gentle flow of words became a torrent.

'I was in Darfur in 2005. I wasn't meant to take the assignment – I had been working in Iraq for months and I was due for a break, but Brad had been shooting there and he called me and asked me to come over. He said it was bad and that it needed more media attention, and that we should do a series together. We saw a lot of bad shit that trip – a lot of really, *really* bad shit.'

My memory bank was full of images that I wished I could erase and those from that particular trip began to stream through my mind. Brad and I had quite deliberately exposed the worst human rights abuses we could find in that crisis, in as much detail as we could – cataloguing the horror, trying to ensure that ignorance would not be an excuse for the world's failure to act.

But I did not want to tell Molly about those things – about the mass graves and the sickening stories of abuse and the immensity of the refugee camps – the sheer scale of it bewildering and overwhelming; it was if I was living a horrifying dystopian novel. She was confident and intelligent and – I'd quickly learned – bold, but she was also optimistic and quite sheltered. I felt that to expose her to the detail of those moments would be to sully her somehow. So I summarised, and I sanitised – techniques my editor forced me to use when I had written a piece and the content was just too brutal for my audience.

'That tattoo represents a refugee camp I visited.'

'What about that long one across your shoulders? Is it a snake?'

'Ah, that one is particularly special,' I admitted. Her fringe had fallen over her eye and I brushed it back gently. 'That's the only other tattoo I have that isn't about a piece I've written. It's about the loss of my culture.'

'As in…' she hesitated a little, then asked carefully, 'Aboriginal culture?'

'Yeah. Forty thousand years of culture passed down in oral stories and songs and rituals and paintings – and within two hundred years almost all of it was lost. I wish I could understand how I *miss* that knowledge. It should have been my birthright. My mum's family is so disconnected from our cultural heritage, so that means I have always been too, and it's so easy to feel like I should have had a grounding and a framework to understand the world and I just never got that. I had to build my own.'

It was too much – I'd said too much. Molly was still looking at me, doe-eyed and engaged, but I felt raw and naked in a way that had nothing to do with the fact that I *was* naked. I cleared my throat. 'So that's the two things you know about me that no one else does.'

'Thank you.'

'What for?'

'For showing me yourself.'

I paused. Now that I had finished forcing myself to be vulnerable, I was really glad I had. I liked how pleased she was that I'd made the effort to do so. I liked the way that her acceptance made me feel. I wanted more – not more sharing on my part, not yet. I wanted to know her at a deeper level too.

'Now it's your turn. You owe me two secrets.'

'I don't really have many secrets.'

'Everyone has secrets.' I paused, then asked her, 'Do you do this often?'

'*This?*' she repeated, and she looked up at me. 'You mean, bring men I barely know back to my apartment for several rounds of intense but thoroughly satisfying sex?'

'Several rounds?' I repeated, and she grinned at me.

'Well, the night *is* young. Was that presumptuous of me?'

'I wasn't complaining,' I assured her.

'Did it bother you that I was forward?' she asked and her eyes narrowed a little.

I laughed and shook my head. 'Did it bother me that a beautiful, intelligent, amazing woman came at me as hard as I was planning to go after her? Let me think about that… No!'

'When I know I want something, I don't like to play games – I just like to go after it. I know that sounds spoilt, maybe it is. Maybe some people would think it's unbecoming for a woman to say such a thing. You know – some people – like people from *your* generation.' The lilt in her tone left no doubt that she was kidding, and so I made a joke about my age too.

'Yeah, back in my day, your father would have had to offer me some cows or something to convince me to sleep with you.'

She laughed, and I touched my hand gently to her cheek. Her laughter faded to a soft, contented smile. 'I *am* a modern woman, Leo. I find no shame in enjoying sex and I'm not the kind of girl who is looking for a fairy-tale romance and a happily ever after – I wanted you tonight, and I could see that you wanted me, and I had a feeling that you could handle it if I skipped the nonsense games. I was right.'

'You were.'

'I just don't think an encounter has to end with a lifelong commitment to have been worthwhile, you know? Wherever a relationship ends, I'm always glad for the time I shared with that person.'

'I completely agree.' I was actually excited to hear that her thoughts on the matter aligned almost perfectly to mine. Closely aligned expectations meant that whatever happened between us, there was less chance of someone getting hurt.

'Good.'

'But, now that I think about it,' I said slowly. 'I actually asked you for two *secrets*, and I don't think that your philosophy on romance really counts.'

Molly shifted away from me, so that she was on her side looking towards me. After a while, in a very small voice, she murmured, 'I *desperately* want to leave TM, Leo.'

'I already know that. You don't really hide it that well.'

She sighed. 'I can't let Dad down. I don't even know what else I'd do with my life anyway. Imagine if I left TM and just sat around doing nothing – it's just not right.'

I wanted her closer again, so I rolled onto my side to mirror her posture and I cupped her cheek with my hand. 'So you hate your job. That's one secret. What's another?'

'I only have one more.'

'Well?'

'I think this was a really, really good idea.'

I laughed softly and shook my head. 'You're not getting out of it that easily.'

Molly's lips curved in a coy, secretive smile – then she brought her face closer to me and tried to distract me with a kiss. I let her try for a minute or two, then I pulled away and whispered, '*That's* not going to distract me either, although you're very welcome to keep trying.'

Molly giggled and dropped back onto her pillow. 'All right,' she sighed. 'But I really don't have any other secrets. Give me some ideas; what do you want to know?'

'What's the best thing about being Molly Torrington?'

She rolled back towards me and rested her chin on my chest to stare up at me. 'The best thing about Molly Torrington is that I don't even know how lucky I am.'

'Is that a *good* thing?'

'Up until that conversation with you on Tuesday, it had never occurred to me that people who want to get an education would be prevented from accessing one because of money – not here in Australia, anyway. In the world I live in if you want something, you just get it. You said poverty feels like an insurmountable wall – well, so is wealth. I don't even have a clue what's on the other side of that wall, that's how sheltered I've been, and I'd never even thought about it until I felt like an ignorant, privileged idiot talking to you the other night.'

'I asked you what the best thing was, not the worst,' I laughed softly, and she grimaced at me.

'It's both. But this definitely does meet the criteria of "things I've never told anyone before", so I think we're even.' Molly reached up to brush her lips gently against mine, and she asked in a whisper, 'Will you stay over tonight?'

I opened my mouth to tell her that I needed to leave but it suddenly occurred to me that the alternative was to fall asleep in her bed. I *wanted* that – I wanted to encircle her in my arms and to sleep with her body pressed against mine. And then I could wake and yes, there might be an awkward morning after to face – but the flip side of that meant that there would *be* a morning after. I would see her again – just as soon as my eyes opened. Suddenly, I couldn't wait to go to sleep, just so I could experience what it felt like to wake up beside her.

'I'd love to,' I told her.

CHAPTER 13
Molly – July 2015

It's always busy on Circular Quay. When we arrive, there are hordes of tourists and inner-city types swarming around the ferry wharf and along the foreshore enjoying the afternoon sunshine.

'Where to first?' I ask Leo, and he glances back at me with a wry smile.

'You're telling this story, Molly. Where does it start?'

I look around the Quay. There's First Fleet Park, where he told me the truth about my brother. then there's the café up in The Rocks where we shared coffee and then dinner and I caught my first glimpse of the exhilaration that came from hearing him talk about his work with such passion. Just around the corner there are the Botanic Gardens, where we shared countless walks when we were dating, and God – right in front of us is my apartment building, and we had countless significant firsts there.

'We spent a lot of time together around here in the early days. There's just so much here…' I say, and I tail off, suddenly uncertain. 'I don't even know what you *do* know, Leo.'

'Forget what I do and don't know. I remember some things about our early days together, but it's so patchy and I have no way of knowing what memories are missing. Why don't you just tell me about your favourite memory of us here?'

That narrows it down. Those early memories are all good – but the thought of only one night can still make my heart race.

'Let's go to Circular,' I say, and I point eastward towards the restaurant beneath the Opera House. We make the short journey around the ferry wharf and along the pier beneath my apartment building. We opt to sit at a table by the big glass windows, looking out over the harbour. After we order coffees and I convince Leo to share some cake, we're alone again. I look out at the bridge for a moment, and when I turn back to him, I find he is staring at me.

'We had dinner here, right?' he asks.

'We did.'

'I think I remember some of that night,' Leo frowns as he focuses. 'You wore that dress... was it pink?'

'Yep, rose pink chiffon,' I say, and I'm surprised. 'I can't believe you remember that.'

'I can't believe I ever forgot it – you looked incredible.'

I'm strangely touched by the thought that Leo had tucked that little detail away in his memory at all. I smile to myself, and I ask hesitantly, 'So, do I still feel like a stranger to you?'

'No. When I first woke up, all of this seemed completely impossible. I couldn't imagine how *we* could have happened... It felt like everyone was playing a particularly complicated trick on me. The details of my memories are slowly coming back, but it's very different with the feelings – they're kind of simmering below the surface, and every time we talk I'm reminded that you're actually familiar to me. It's like....' he raises his hand and points to his head. 'I've forgotten you up here...' his hand lowers, and he points to his chest, then grimaces again, as if this is a painful admission to make, 'but I always knew you here.'

My breath catches in my throat. I am devastated to realise that already Leo has rekindled emotions for me – that seems like a brutally unfair thing of me to allow, given that we are actually separated, and what he's remembering is long gone. When he told me he wanted to separate, we had a conversation that was drenched in sadness, but neither of us even had enough passion left to fight for the marriage – it felt almost inevitable. So I know that Leo really doesn't feel this way anymore – if he did, he would never have walked away.

At the same time I feel I am being drawn back towards him, even as our eyes lock. Leo is a charmer – he is someone who knows how to work with people and how to make them feel comfortable enough to open up to him. But he's not great at talking about feelings, particularly *his* feelings, and he's not a romantic by nature – he's the kind of guy much more likely to flirt than woo. This quiet declaration seems like an unusual level of vulnerability from him, although I suppose he feels safe to make it because he knows that we are married.

I love the way he's looking at me, as if he could drink me up with his eyes or find contentment just by keeping me in his gaze. And I connect very suddenly with a realisation that just as the feelings might be 'simmering below the surface' for Leo, they are doing so for me too. That thought is so startling that I panic and try to lighten the mood with a joke.

'You do realise that is the *corniest* thing you have ever said, right?'

Leo smiles at me, gently and kindly. 'Why do you think I'm wearing this face?' he says, and then he pulls an exaggerated expression of disgust and points to his cheek. I burst out laughing, and then we laugh together, and the two sounds mingle and I feel that just for a second, we're truly connecting – somehow, through that laughter, we're one again, just as we used to be – and I love that every bit as much as I miss it. I stop fighting my resurging feelings for just a second and I let them be. The ugliness will return, I know it will – but I make the most of this brief moment of togetherness. Leo quite casually reaches across and entwines our fingers, then rests them on the table between us.

'Do you remember when we held hands the first time?' I ask him. Leo stares at our hands, and I watch the laughter lines around his eyes relax and the way his expression shifts and morphs into something very intense. After a moment he raises his eyes back to me and searches my gaze.

'I remember being completely lost in you.'

'That's exactly how I felt,' I whisper, and staring deeply into Leo's eyes, I'm suddenly feeling that way all over again. 'I felt like your hands were made to hold mine, and I never wanted you to let me go.'

'Now who's being corny?' he says, but he whispers the words and the intensity in his eyes doesn't diminish.

I laugh softly, and look past Leo. The waiter is approaching with our coffees and the beautiful moment is passing already. I hold onto his hand much tighter than I did that first time because now I know what it feels like when he lets go.

'Why me, Molly?' Leo asks suddenly.

I smile at him quizzically. 'What on earth does that mean?'

'You could have been with any man you set your heart on.'

'Well, you really hate it when I go all "poor little rich girl" on you,' I say softly, and when he grimaces, I laugh freely for a second because I know that he doesn't need his memory to know that statement is true. I quickly sober though, and I plot my answer to his question. 'The truth is you showed me how to see the world through new eyes. I fell in love with you because of who you are, but I *married* you because of who I became when I was with you.'

He smiles at me, and he brings my hand to his lips and kisses it very gently, then rests it on the table again. I look away from him, towards the harbour, and think about my own words.

All that I have said is true but it strikes me now that soon, I will *not* be married to Leo, and I have no idea what a post-Leo Molly Torrington-Stephens even looks like. She is more hardened than the innocent woman who married that man almost three years ago, but she is also kinder – more socially aware, more generous.

Will she be happy? This thought is terrifying. I glance back to Leo, and find him still staring at me. He's not seeing *me*, he's seeing the pre-Leo me, who was different again.

She was spoilt, and selfish, and manipulative – and yet he loved her anyway.

CHAPTER 14
Leo – February 2011

I woke as soon as the sun hit Molly's windows the next morning. She was sprawled diagonally across her bed, her face squished against my chest, one arm draped loosely over me. Despite the slightness of her build, she had helped herself to most of the mattress, trapping me on a thin section towards the edge. She was snoring with surprising volume and I grinned as I thought about how mortified she'd be if I told her.

I shifted positions very carefully so that I could look down at her face and took a moment to soak in the sight of her. Her hair was standing up at wild angles after our energetic night and her make-up had smudged around her eyes. I pondered the almost irrational affection I had for her in that moment; she was beautiful to me, even in her sleep-rumpled state. What was it about Molly that drew me towards her? I thought about the amazing night we'd shared, but I immediately understood that the chemistry between us was only a part of the puzzle. Maybe another part of that puzzle was her confidence, and the challenge of her boldness, and perhaps even her surprisingly positive energy.

She was complex, and so was my attraction to her – too complex to really understand at that stage. I couldn't wait to see what the day would bring, and whether I'd get a chance to explore it – and explore all of the facets of her some more. As I thought about this, I grew impatient. I tried to wake her up subtly by shifting positions a few times but when that failed, I resorted to more drastic measures.

'Wake up,' I whispered. Molly peered at me from beneath one fluttering eyelid.

'Please don't tell me you're a morning person.'

'I'm not normally, but then again I don't usually wake up with a beautiful woman in my arms.'

'I have a feeling you'd wake up with a beautiful woman in your arms just about as often as you *want* to,' she murmured. 'What time is it?'

'I have no idea. Will you spend the day with me?'

'I usually work Saturdays,' she said, but then her eyes opened and she blinked a few times.

'Do you need to?'

'Not technically.'

'Do you want to?'

Molly rolled away from me and stretched and yawned. After a minute, she rolled back until she was leaning on my chest. She stared up at me and smiled. 'Not even a little bit.'

'Then play hooky with me.'

'What will we do?'

'Make ourselves open to the possibilities,' I said, echoing her comments at dinner two nights earlier. She reached up and kissed me.

'Sounds perfect,' she murmured, against my lips. 'Where did you want to start?' I scooped her into my arms and flipped her onto her back, and she squealed and then grinned at me. 'Yes, we definitely didn't finish exploring *those* possibilities last night.'

'It seems highly irresponsible to leave a task like that unfinished,' I murmured, as I bent to kiss her neck. 'So let's get it out of the way and get some breakfast.'

❖ ❖ ❖

When we finally climbed out of bed, Molly ordered coffee and breakfast, and we spent the next few hours on the balcony together. I sat with my legs propped up on her coffee table, she rested lengthways along the rattan loveseat, using my thigh as a pillow and dangling her legs over the armrest.

It was a casual morning – a relaxed morning filled with the strange tenderness I felt towards her and punctuated by the sound of her laughter. She'd amuse me with an anecdote or observation, and I'd caress her gently as she talked, or bend to kiss her without agenda. Although she wouldn't have known it, I knew that this wasn't my style. In the past I'd had more than my share of flings, but I couldn't actually remember the last time I wanted to just spend time learning someone.

I wanted to know Molly; I wanted to unpack all of the parts of her that made her who she was and to be as familiar with her as I was with myself. I wasn't thinking about the future, or even the past – I was in the moment with her, focused completely on her, and I felt content.

As the morning stretched on and we began to think about lunch, I realised I'd have to get some casual clothes – I was still wearing the dress trousers I'd donned for dinner at Circular.

'I really need to change out of these clothes.'

'I don't want you to leave.'

I looked down at her, and found her staring up at me. I felt the smile spread across my face.

'Come with me. Let's go get some lunch, then we can go back to my place.'

'Should I call a town car?'

I laughed. 'Nope. We're going to *my* place, so let's do this *my* way.'

✦ ✦ ✦

We walked away from Molly's apartment, back towards the city. She was wearing a cap and sunglasses, and it occurred to me that she'd donned a type of casual disguise.

'So, should we talk about the ground rules for being seen together in public?' I asked her quietly.

'Yeah. It doesn't happen often, but I've been papped a few times. Usually when I'm doing something embarrassing or un-glamorous – like wiping my nose or wearing tracksuit pants.'

'And if that happens today?'

'I wouldn't mind at all, except for Dad... but there *is* that, you know... so I really hope it doesn't happen. And it probably won't, it's not like photographers go looking for me – more they'll take a snap or two if they happen to be stalking some unfortunate celebrity and I wander past. So, I guess the takeaway message is – no getting handsy while we're out.'

'No getting handsy,' I repeated, and we both laughed.

'I'm not worried that other people might think we're together, you know. It's not that.'

'It's fine, Molly. It works for me too – God, imagine if people thought I was sleeping with you! How embarrassing!'

She giggled. there was something about the carefree way that sound escaped her lips – it relaxed me, and made me smile too. My life was full of purpose but it was not a life of laughter. Perhaps that was what had drawn me to her in the first place.

'We're not walking a long way, are we?' she asked me.

'Not far. Why, do your shoes hurt?' I glanced down at the casual shoes she'd pulled on.

'No, but I'm unfit and lazy,' she laughed. 'I love the idea of being fit, but I hate the reality of making it happen.'

'I think you'll like my dog,' I told her. 'He always tries to join me when I go for a run and sometimes he'll run like a machine and still be jumping around like a crazy thing when we get home. But other times, we'll get half a block down the road and he'll decide he's had enough. And when Lucien decides he's had enough running for one day, that's usually the end of the story.'

'What kind of dog is this Lucien?'

'He's a ruthless, ferocious, extremely macho…' I paused for dramatic effect, but then sighed. 'Actually, he's a poodle.'

'Sure he is!' her laughter echoed around us.

'Truly,' I put my hand over my heart. 'He is a pure-bred standard poodle and his hair is a very fetching shade of apricot.'

'You do *not* strike me as a poodle owner.'

'Well, I'm not really his master, he kind of owns me.'

'How do you even care for a dog with all the travel you do?'

'My neighbour technically owns him, but she's getting older now and couldn't manage his activity levels.'

'If you're trying to impress me with what a big softie you are, it's not very convincing.'

I laughed. But before I could say any more, we reached the train station. The look of sheer horror on her face stopped me in my tracks. 'You have caught a train before, right?'

'Of course I have,' she said, but she looked away from me as she said it, and then, 'Maybe I haven't caught a train before,' she murmured and she clutched her handbag to her chest.

'How did you think we would get back to my place?'

'I assumed you were walking to the cab rank,' she muttered.

I laughed. 'Wait here, Molly. I'll get you a ticket.'

'You'd better keep me safe,' she said, as she followed me through the turnstiles.

'If it makes you feel any better,' I remarked, 'I have a black belt in karate.'

'That actually *does* make me feel a bit better. No wonder you think Redfern is safe, you're probably the most dangerous resident in the suburb!'

'You might just be right about that.' Her father would certainly have agreed with that statement.

She still had a death-grip on her handbag when we reached the platform and I burst out laughing. 'Molly, you can see your place from here.' I gently spun her round to the window behind her, from where she could see the Bennelong Apartments just a hundred metres away. She huffed and turned around to face me.

'I've had a driver since I learned to walk. It feels *weird* to be here.' But she released her grip on her bag. I could almost have had second thoughts about taking her to my part of Redfern if she felt that uncomfortable already, but I was far too busy giving myself a mental pat on the back for coming up with the idea. If she really wanted a 'defining moment', she was probably not going to find one if her entire existence revolved around Sydney's city centre. I walked to a bench and sat down. Molly followed me, and sat gingerly on the edge of the seat. She was probably onto something there – the bench was filthy.

'I'm going to take *you* somewhere completely out of your comfort zone and see how you like it,' she muttered.

'Do you think I felt at home in Circular?'

She pondered this a moment, then said, 'Fair enough. So what's at the other end of this adventure?'

'Totally Thai,' I told her. 'It's a restaurant near my place.'

'Okay,' she said, and then grinned. 'Don't think I didn't notice that ticket you bought me is one way. Should I have packed an overnight bag?'

'I doubt you'll want to spend the night at my place – but I assumed you'd call your car rather than make the trek back on the train.' I laughed.

'Why wouldn't I spend the night at your place?'

'It's a terrace. Please don't misunderstand me – I love my house but it's hardly the Bennelong Apartments,' I said, a little stiffly.

Molly shrugged. 'I just can't wait to see where you live and meet this spoilt dog of yours.'

I wasn't convinced. 'Shall we play it by ear?'

'Who says I want to sleep with you again anyway?' she said pointedly. 'Maybe I prefer bed partners who *don't* wake me up at seven on a Saturday morning.'

I grinned at her 'You weren't complaining for very long.' Her cheeky smile faded to one of reminiscence as her eyes darkened.

The train was approaching and Molly took my hand to pull herself up, then immediately released it. I wanted to link my fingers back through hers and hold on tight. I understood the need for discretion, and I would respect it, but it was immediately frustrating.

As the train pushed forward into the tunnels that would take us to Redfern, I watched Molly's reflection in the glass of the window on the other side of the carriage. She was looking around the train, her wide eyes lingering on informational posters decorated with random pieces of chewing gum and graffiti.

'Now isn't this better than Circular?' I quipped. She met my eyes in the reflection of the train window.

'You have got to be kidding me.'

❖ ❖ ❖

If I thought her eyes were wide on the train, they were positively saucer-like as we walked through Redfern towards the restaurant. She walked closer to me than she had as we walked together in the city, but stepped immediately out of the way whenever anyone walked past us from the opposite direction. It was a strangely submissive gesture, and I knew it gave away the discomfort she felt at her surroundings.

It wasn't as if I'd taken her into a war zone. In reality, Redfern was a rapidly gentrifying suburb with a chequered and changing demographic. There were exceedingly trendy cafés filled with affluent locals in designer clothes – the kind of places Molly herself would have frequented had they been a few kilometres further north. However, as we neared the area closer to my terrace, we passed empty shops with heavily graffitied shutters and a burnt-out car, half-parked on a footpath and marked with police tape. There was a shopping trolley full of rotting rubbish right near the restaurant, with a discarded syringe resting on the ground beneath it. Molly stared at all of these things, but she walked in silence.

'What are you thinking?' I eventually asked her.

'I'm feeling very uncomfortable,' she said, and when I opened my mouth to reply, she cut me off with a pointed, 'And *not* because I'm a snob. It's because as I *warned* you, I am lazy and yet here you are, making me walk all over the world in search of this probably mythical restaurant.'

I laughed and rested my hand low on her back to turn her towards a doorway.

'We're here.'

Molly looked back at me. 'Now I *know* you're kidding.'

The restaurant was tucked in behind a pharmacy, but without its own street front was only accessed via a long, cement corridor that was frequently vandalised. The light bulb at the entrance to the corridor was on the blink, and it flickered on and off.

It looked a lot seedier than it actually was.

'Trust me,' I laughed, and I stepped inside, gently dragging her with me. She sighed and stepped closer to me again, and we walked along the corridor, arm in arm.

'It's like you deliberately picked the only place in the city down a dark, creepy corridor just to make a point,' she muttered accusingly.

'I come here *all* the time. This place is amazing.'

As we stepped inside, we were greeted with great enthusiasm by the owner, who had us wait in the tiny lobby while she found us a table.

Molly had fallen silent again. She was surveying the restaurant floor and I watched emotions flicker across her face. She was fascinated, she was uncomfortable, and she was nervous. She adjusted her posture and reached up to smooth her side-swept fringe into place. I suddenly realised that the gesture meant she was anxious.

'The food really is amazing,' I assured her.

Totally Thai made authentic and delicious food, but the décor was terrible – mismatched furniture, including plastic garden chairs at some tables – not even the tablecloths or cutlery matched. I thought about the contrast to Circular and it was a stark reminder of how different Molly and I were.

I suppose I was so used to the setting that I hadn't really thought about how tawdry it was compared to the culinary opulence that Molly was used to. I'd wanted more to blow her away with the fresh, delicious food and the personalised service. As I stood there watching her, I felt momentarily unsure of my choice of venue – but even as I acknowledged this, a stubborn determination rose in me.

This was who I was. This was a place I liked to go, and a place where I felt comfortable. I couldn't change the way she reacted to Totally Thai, or even my house when we visited after lunch. She would either deal with this glimpse into my life, or she wouldn't. I wanted her to enjoy our day together. I wanted her to enjoy the window into my world. But even if she didn't, I wasn't going to shy away from showing it to her. I was proud of who I was, and I was actually proud to be exposing a different side of Sydney to Molly. She had been sheltered long enough, and even she knew it.

'Never judge a book by its cover, right?' She flashed me a smile, but it was unconvincing.

'Not everything worth having in life comes wrapped in a fancy package,' I shrugged nonchalantly. The owner waved to indicate we should join her at a table, and although I knew she wanted me to be discreet in public, I slipped my arm around Molly's waist.

CHAPTER 15
Molly – July 2015

Leo thinks that this little trip down memory lane is going well. By the time we've finished our coffees and gone for a relaxed wander through the Botanic Gardens nearby, he's remembered all the way up to the end of that night. I know when he remembers going back to my apartment after dinner because he suddenly stops pushing the wheelchair and says, 'Oh!'

The expression on his face is one that I know all too well. I giggle a little as he exhales and shakes his head in disbelief.

'You were amazing that night.'

'You did okay yourself,' I say.

'Is it just me or is it hot out here?' He does look a little flushed and I laugh.

'God, Leo, if this is how you react when you remember that night, wait till you remember the honeymoon!'

'I can't wait for *that* one.'

On our way back to the rehab clinic, Leo takes my hand and holds it tightly against his thigh. He stares out the window, but his thumb brushes against the back of my hand. I watch the movement for a while, soothed somehow by that familiar, tender gesture, then I glance at his face. He's lost in thought, and I'm torn right down the middle. Reliving these moments with him is so painful for me, and with his memories returning so easily I know that this brief period of renewed closeness will end soon. But suddenly I'm grateful for this time with Leo. Every second I can have with him like this, I will greedily take for myself and I will hold these new memories close to my heart long after I've lost him all over again.

'What are you thinking?' he turns to me suddenly, and I feel myself flush. Even that question is so familiar and so lost that it causes a physical pain in my chest.

'You used to ask me that all the time,' I whisper.

'Why did I stop?'

You don't want to hear the answer anymore. 'I guess you don't need to ask these days,' I say. Leo smiles at me and squeezes my hand. 'Thanks for today. What's on the agenda for tomorrow? Do you think we can visit the terrace?'

'The terrace? But you'll only be able to see the ground floor.'

'I'm worried about how you fit a dishwasher in my kitchen,' he mutters, and I laugh.

'Okay, Leo. We can visit the terrace. Lucien will be glad to see you anyway.'

✦ ✦ ✦

After the renewed closeness during the afternoon I find that when the night draws in, I don't want to say goodbye to Leo. On some level, I do understand that this is *not* my real husband – this is a temporary version of him: one not shaped by the years that have passed because he has momentarily forgotten about them. But this version of Leo still loves me, and it's a version of him that I still love. He will go soon enough as the memories return, and my anger and my disappointment will definitely resurge as the real Leo emerges. But for now, I find excuses to stay at the rehabilitation centre with him until late in the evening. He convinces a nurse to find a spare meal for me and we have a 'romantic date' in his room.

'This is awesome,' I say, when I sit down with my hospital-food tray on my lap.

'It's not exactly Circular.'

'It'll do for now,' I say. 'It's much better than whatever I would have ordered in at home.'

'When I get home, I'm going to cook you a soufflé.'

'A *soufflé?*'

'There's a class here next week as part of the occupational therapy programme. I think it's actually meant for people who have trouble with cognition and sequencing or something, but I'm going anyway – I'm going to learn, and then when I'm released, I'm going to cook you the best damned soufflé you've ever eaten to say thanks for everything you've done for me lately.'

'Just getting you home will be thanks enough.'

'I wonder if I'll be home by December?'

December feels a long way away. I frown at him. 'I really hope so. But why December?'

Leo shakes his head at me in feigned disappointment. '*Now* who's forgotten our anniversary?'

CHAPTER 16
Leo – February 2011

After lunch, we walked the remaining blocks to my terrace. The traffic faded as we moved deeper into residential territory until we were on the jacaranda-lined streets around my home.

'What did you think of the restaurant?' I asked Molly.

'I think you enjoyed watching me squirm,' she said. I glanced at her and grinned. She thumped me hard in the chest. 'But the food *was* good – great, even. So we're going to your place now?'

'Right. It's just around the corner.'

As we turned into my street, Molly's eyes immediately flew to the public housing tower that loomed above it. The tower was a startling landmark among the terraces in the area – twenty storeys of depressing grey cement that housed hundreds of low-income families.

'That's not where Dec…' Molly said suddenly.

'No. It was in a similar building, but a few blocks south.' I stopped at my steps. 'But this is me.'

I walked up past the small veranda and unlocked the front door. Molly trailed her hand over my chest as she went in, and then curved it around my waist. She raised her face towards me, as if she was going to kiss me, but then Lucien came skidding into the living room just before us. At this she released me altogether to crouch down towards him.

'You are just beautiful,' she murmured.

Lucien approached her, sniffing carefully, and Molly leant forward to pat him.

'He takes a while to warm to new people,' I warned her. But Lucien's caution suddenly disappeared, and his tail started wagging at top speed. He brushed himself past her, wound his way around my legs, and then returned to lick Molly's hands. She stood up and looked around. 'This is nice. Do I get the guided tour?'

I walked towards her and entwined our hands. 'First stop is the kitchen. I know you have one in your house too, but this one actually gets used.'

'What an odd concept,' she laughed.

'It's small,' I said. 'But it works. The laundry and a bathroom are through that door.'

She released my hand to lean on the kitchen bench and peer out through the window, and when she turned back to me, she was grinning.

'You have a motorbike?'

'Yep.'

'I've never been on a bike.'

'I have a spare helmet,' I said. I could imagine the feel of her breasts against my back and her arms tight around my waist. 'Maybe we could go for a ride sometime. My shoulder just needs a few more weeks.'

Molly followed me up the first narrow flight of stairs into my bedroom and the full-sized bathroom. 'Speaks for itself,' I said.

She walked lazily towards the windows and pushed back the lace curtains I'd inherited with the house to look out onto the tiny veranda. 'It must be amazing to sit out there when the jacarandas are in bloom.'

'Yeah, for a while each summer the view from that veranda looks like a postcard.'

'And the top floor?'

'That's my office,' I led the way up the last flight of stairs to my favourite room in the house – my favourite place in the whole world, actually. It was a small room, half the size of the floors which housed the bedroom and living areas, and the east-facing wall featured a large peaked window that gave a view of the top of the jacaranda tree outside.

'This room is *beautiful*.'

'I like it.'

'I'm starting to think you might like reading.'

'What gives you that idea?' I said wryly, and she released me to walk further into the room. I'd lined three of the four walls with bookshelves, and every space on every shelf was taken. My desk was in the centre of the room, facing towards the window, and beside it sat a comfortable but rather unattractive recliner I'd picked up at a charity shop when I was at uni. Molly wandered along the bookshelves, surveying my eclectic collection of travel books and novels and autobiographies.

'Sometimes I think it would have been better if the bedroom and the office were reversed. I've probably overloaded this floor, maybe it'll crash down on me while I sleep one night.'

'Imagine that. You spend your entire life dodging bullets in the field but it's your bookworm side that will get you killed.' She laughed, and then turned to face me. 'I really don't know what you were so worried about, Leo. Your place is nice. It's quaint.' I raised an eyebrow at her. 'It *is*,' she insisted. 'It's a really cool little house.'

'Want to head back downstairs and get better acquainted with my mutt? He's due a walk.'

'Not *more* walking,' she groaned and shook her head. 'No way, Leo! Let's go downstairs and you can make me a coffee and I'll sit and pat him.'

✦ ✦ ✦

It felt strange having Molly Torrington sitting in my living area while I cooked dinner that night; stranger still that she and Lucien appeared to be bonding so quickly. I'd convinced her to walk him to the park with me, but as soon as we returned home she'd kicked off her shoes and curled up on the couch with the remote in her hand.

'What do you want to watch?'

'I don't really…'

'I was talking to Lucien,' she interrupted me with a laugh. 'I could tell you wouldn't have an opinion purely from the amount of dust on this remote control. What do you do to relax?'

'I don't watch rubbish on TV, that's for sure.'

'You don't know what you're missing out on. *The Bachelor* is on tonight – will you watch it with me?'

'What's *The Bachelor*?' I said. I was joking but I needn't have bothered, given that Molly missed my pitiful attempt at humour anyway.

'*Leo*! For such a well-travelled man you're remarkably naive about the things that really matter.'

We watched the evening news – and then when the theme music to the reality TV show started Molly squealed in excitement. 'I love this show!'

'I wish you'd told me that *before* I slept with you,' I sighed, and she laughed. She settled into my arms and then Lucien jumped onto the couch and made a place for himself, his head on her lap.

'I'm only letting you sit there to impress Molly,' I told him.

'I'm already impressed,' she said and turned back to brush a kiss over my lips.

I realised that I was in over my head with Molly when she convinced me to sit through an entire hour of reality TV. It was mind-numbing; the only entertaining aspect to the experience at all was her heart-felt explanations as to the background of what I was seeing in the show.

'You're an educated, cosmopolitan woman. A career woman,' I said, during an ad break.

'Yes.'

'And the idea of a group of women all competing for the attention of a man just to win television ratings isn't offensive to you? Even *I* want to storm that mansion and stage an intervention.'

'It's all good fun.'

'But it's demeaning.'

'It's all good fun, Leo,' she repeated. 'Those girls are getting exactly what they want – fifteen minutes of fame. No one is getting hurt. Lighten up, will you?'

'But don't you think that as a society…'

'Leo, the ad break is over and now you need to be quiet again so I can explain to you what the rose ceremony is,' she told me. I laughed, and heard the echo of her laughter too. 'You just need to watch it some more and you'll get it, I'm sure of it.' When the credits rolled, Molly sat up and grinned at me expectantly.

'Well, what did you think?' she asked, when it was over.

I burst out laughing. 'Well, I enjoyed having you here more than I hated the show so let's call it a success but next time I might read while you watch it.'

'Next time,' she repeated softly, and playfully leant in to kiss me, which soon took on an urgent, passionate edge that wasn't to be deterred. She pulled impatiently at the bottom of my shirt, feeling for the bare skin of my chest.

'Do you really want to stay here tonight?'

'Just try and get rid of me at this point,' she muttered. She threw my shirt over my shoulder then surveyed my chest and arms as her eyes grew darker. I caught her face in my hands and kissed her. Lucien slid off the couch and walked towards the back door, shooting a look our way as he passed.

'Come upstairs,' Molly commanded softly. She tugged on my hand, and I rose to follow her. As we climbed the stairs, I thought how much I liked having her in my house. I knew she was out of place there in my very ordinary surroundings, just as I was in her startlingly luxurious home. Somehow, it didn't seem to matter.

On Monday morning when it was time for Molly to leave, I kissed her at the door. When she took a step away towards the town car at the kerb, I caught her hand and drew her back for one last lingering kiss.

'Text me?' she whispered.

'Can I call you instead?'

'Okay, Grandpa,' she teased. 'Why don't you just send me a telegram? Or a note via carrier pigeon?'

'I'll text you,' I promised. I kissed her one last time, then watched as she left. The second her car was out of my sight, I missed her. I wouldn't interrupt her work day, and I knew she wouldn't interrupt mine, but the minute I left my office that afternoon I was going to find out when I could see her again.

Four amazing weeks passed before I was cleared to return to the field. But for the distraction of Molly, it would have been a frustrating, maddening time. But while I was grounded, those weeks belonged only to Molly and me. We didn't talk about our relationship – we didn't need to. We just enjoyed each other's company. That was okay, and it was more than enough.

During that time no one in the world knew about us. We were ensconced in a bubble of necessary secrecy, and the isolation of that was the catalyst for an intense intimacy. When Molly had finished her long working day, and I'd finished mine and spent some time at the gym, we'd find our way to each other and the day would finally come alive.

As our affection grew, we were increasingly cautious about being seen too much in public together. On some occasions when I wanted to wow her with a romantic date, my options for planning generally extended only as far as to where to get takeaway food and how to find a suitably private venue where we could share it. And there were time constraints too – Molly worked insanely long hours, starting early and finishing late every single week day.

She communicated with me a lot with damned text messages, her words drenched with emoticons and punctuated with string of x's and o's that grew or shrank depending on how her day had been. So I had to compromise a little, and then I compromised a lot until eventually we were in one continuous text conversation throughout the working day. I'd scroll back up the history every now and again and stare at it incredulously, unable to believe I had finally succumbed to a hated technology that I'd resisted for so long. Each time I did, I'd feel grateful – the text string was a visual reminder of her presence in my life – the silly icons a reminder of her affection.

It's a remarkable thing to be a part of a connection that is so satisfying that you feel lucky whenever you consider it. This made me want to try harder and to be better – I wanted to bring my A-game to every hour with Molly.

Sometimes, I struggled to find a balance between offering her support and challenging her about her relationship with her father. There was no doubt that she was unhappy with the direction her career was taking, but I could see that she actually revered Laith as much as she resented him; I could also see that she was too afraid of losing his approval to admit that last part even to herself.

The day that I was finally cleared to return to the field, I saw the doctor at lunchtime and Brad and I had flights booked to return to Libya by the time I'd left the office. I texted Molly to tell her and she suggested we meet for dinner at Totally Thai to celebrate. Afterwards, we shared a bottle of wine on the balcony off my bedroom.

We had only had a handful of nights apart in the month we'd had together, but as my trip drew near, I almost regretted allowing so many nights with her in a row. I wasn't used to missing someone, and I was almost nervous at the thought. Molly didn't seem at all concerned about the impending change to the way things were. Was she ready for a break from the somewhat full-on relationship we'd tumbled into, or did she not understand what my trip would mean for us?

I wasn't sure which alternative was worse, so I put off a discussion until late on Sunday afternoon and then I tried to make it a casual, natural conversation as I packed my suitcase.

'I have a satellite phone,' I said quietly. 'But…'

'I know you won't call me,' Molly said. I glanced at her and she shrugged. 'I get it.'

'I *might* call. I just can't promise it.'

'It's fine. And it's only for a few weeks anyway, right?'

'Most likely. I'll let you know if that changes.'

'So no texting, huh?'

I smiled at her as I dropped a flak jacket into my case. 'You'll have to find someone else to text forty times a day for the next little while.'

'Forty times a day!' she repeated, flattening her palm against her chest in mock outrage. 'You exaggerate. It's rarely more than thirty-five.'

'You can email me. I'll make sure I check it every few days. I'll write back when I can.'

'And when you get back?'

'When I get back…'

'What will it look like? Do you think this is the start of frequent trips?'

'Yes.'

'How regular?'

'It depends. If it disintegrates into a full-blown civil war, I'll probably spend a lot of time there until it resolves.'

'So what are we talking? Five trips a year? Ten?'

I thought about this as I retrieved my ballistic vests and rested them over my clothes in the suitcase. I glanced at Molly hesitantly before I answered. 'Last year, I was in the field for nine months.'

I saw the shock on her face and I turned back to the wardrobe, feeling a flush creeping up my neck. The conversation was necessary, but I didn't want to have it; I wanted to pretend that this was a one-off, and that in a few weeks' time I'd return to Sydney and we could resume an easy togetherness. I withdrew my helmet and gas mask from the drawers and when I turned back to the bed, Molly was staring at them in horror.

'What the hell?'

'It's a gas mask.'

'I know what it is. Why do you need it?'

'It's just a precaution.' I opted not to explain to her why I now carried it with me religiously after a close encounter during my first military embed in Iraq, when the patrol I was travelling with had stumbled upon a cache of shells laced with sarin.

Molly shifted forward on the bed and gingerly flicked through the items in my case.

'Leo, there are four outfits in here and the rest is protective gear.'

'In the field I don't really change clothes much… It's a war zone – no one is going to notice or care.'

Molly looked from the suitcase to the first-aid kit I was now nursing in my elbow and burst into tears. I had never seen her cry before, not even when we talked about Declan. I sank onto the bed beside her and rubbed her back.

'I don't understand,' I said slowly. 'How can any of this be a surprise to you? You run a media business.'

'I don't know,' she whispered. 'I just didn't let myself think about it.'

'Look, you knew my job was dangerous.'

'Of course I did,' she said, raising her chin. 'That doesn't mean I have to like it.'

We slept at her house that night, and we didn't say goodbye. Instead, we made love and fell asleep in each other's arms, and then I rose in the middle of the night to go to the airport.

As the plane left the runway at 6 a.m. that morning, I looked out of the window at the city below, and for the first time in my life I wished I didn't have to go.

CHAPTER 17
Molly – August 2015

I'm on my way to pick up Leo for our outing later that week when my phone rings. I look down at the caller ID and consider ignoring it, but at the very last second I pick up the call.

'Molly, this is Melissa from Dr Walton's rooms. I realise your husband has been ill, but you've missed two appointments now. Are you still requiring Dr Walton's care?'

'Yes – yes, I am – I just… It's been so busy. We've been overseas and I'm still trying to get back on top of things here. Maybe the week after next?'

I hear shuffling papers at the other end of the line.

'Are you sure you should leave it that long? You haven't had any of the tests Dr Walton ordered, and it's been five weeks since your last check-up.'

It has been necessary for me to compartmentalise my life lately, just to stay on top of things. The challenges in *this* particular compartment are just going to have to wait a few more weeks.

'No, I really can't spare the time until then. It has to wait.'

When I hang up, I don't put the appointment in my calendar, which I know means I'll probably forget it.

We have to enter the terrace from the alleyway behind to avoid the cement steps leading to the front door. As I unlock the back gate, I hear the sound of paws on the paving stones in the courtyard next door. I grin to myself as I swing the gate open, and Lucien leaps through the opening in the fence from Mrs Wilkins' yard and makes a beeline for Leo. He's running so fast that his paws skid, and I don't think I've ever seen his tail wag so hard.

Leo doesn't say anything at all, even as Lucien leaps onto his lap and licks his face, which would normally earn a stern word or two. Lucien is so excited that he cannot sit still. After a minute or two, he settles enough to accept a pat and Leo rubs the dog's back and his ears. He leans low so that their heads are close and I hear the surprisingly strained voice of my husband as he murmurs, 'It's good to see you too, buddy.'

And then Lucien loses his mind again, leaping off Leo's lap to jump up against my thighs and then run around in circles in the tiny courtyard space, chasing his tail. Leo laughs quietly for a moment, and then glancing at me, says incredulously, 'After everything you've been through in the last few weeks, it's the sight of me holding the dog that makes you cry?'

'I've cried plenty,' I mutter, and wipe the tears away with the back of my hands. There's another sound from the courtyard next door and then we hear Mrs Wilkins calling.

'Leo? Leo, is that you?'

Mrs Wilkins' cane appears through the gap in the fence, quickly followed by the rest of her. She clutches her spare hand to her chest in delight at the sight of Leo in our courtyard and makes a sprightly shuffle towards us.

'Hi there, Mrs Wilkins.'

'Welcome home, Leo! Oh, I'm so glad you're all right. You gave us such a scare.'

'I think I gave myself a scare this time too,' Leo says, and Mrs Wilkins bends to kiss his cheek.

'I didn't know you were coming home today. I would have cooked for you.'

'It's just a visit,' I tell her quietly. 'I'll let you know when his real homecoming is so you can bake him a feast.'

Mrs Wilkins smiles at me. 'Come, Lucien! Let's give these two some privacy.'

Lucien is still chasing his tail and panting now as if he's going to collapse, but as soon as Mrs Wilkins indicates that he should follow her, he shoots one last look towards Leo and disappears with her through the fence. I walk to the back door and unlock it, and I wait for Leo to comment on the extensions.

'Molly,' Leo says suddenly, and cautiously. 'Where is my motorbike?'

'You sold it.'

'Why would I sell it?'

'Because your beautiful new wife wanted to extend the kitchen. And that meant there was nowhere to store it.'

'Oh.' I hear the disappointment in his voice.

'It was *your* idea, you know,' I said, frowning at him.

'I hope you realise how much I loved that bike.'

'Apparently you loved me more.'

'I find that hard to believe,' he mutters, and when I gasp at him, he laughs at me and raises his palms in mock surrender. 'I'm kidding. I obviously do.'

'Well, you *did* sell it voluntarily… but I could see you missed it, and then you loved me even more when I bought you a new bike for our first wedding anniversary. We keep it at a storage facility over in Surry Hills.'

'What kind of bike is it?'

I pause and concentrate, trying to remember. 'I think it's a Ducati – maybe a pan – panimari? Something like that.'

'A *panigale*?'

'Probably.'

'You're right. I do love you even more now.'

'That's all it takes?'

'Yep,' Leo laughs, but quickly sobers and I wonder if he's thinking about whether he'll ever be able to ride it again. I force myself not to think about that. He and I rarely rode together, but every time we did, it was amazingly freeing. I loved trusting him like that, holding on and closing my eyes and letting the world fly past us.

I felt invincible on the back of Leo's bike, because he seemed invincible. On some level, I still can't quite believe that he is actually stuck in that wheelchair at all.

'Come inside,' I say as I swing the door open. I've already been through the ground floor with a tape measure, so I know his wheelchair is going to fit. Leo moves inside and I carefully step around him and flick the coffee machine on. When I turn back, his gaze is sweeping over the entirely new kitchen.

It was a difficult project – it took months to design and then even longer to complete. I was proud of the end result and the modern country look we'd achieved, with marbled bench tops and beautiful French doors on the cupboards. I was fairly sure Leo agreed at the time, but staring at him now, I'm starting to wonder if that was the case at all. I can see the tension in his upper body – the muscles of his shoulders are locked tense and there's a vein pulsing in his neck.

'You know, when we did this renovation, you told me you were cool with it,' I frown at him. He tears his gaze from the kitchen to me.

'I don't care about the kitchen. I'm trying to understand what you just told me about the motorbike.'

'I told you, we needed the space—'

'You misunderstand me. You bought me a motorbike – the bike I'd been dreaming of for years, apparently – for our first anniversary. And I wasn't even *here* for it?'

'No,' I said, and I turned away from him to the coffee machine again.

'Were you furious about that, Molly?'

'I wasn't the first year.' I really hadn't been – I had been sad, of course, but I wasn't angry – I knew there was a good reason as to why he wasn't there. It was only when he missed our second anniversary that it finally occurred to me that what had seemed like a one-off was actually going to be the standard.

'And the second year? What was that like?'

I don't answer him.

'Molly, for God's sake!' He's frustrated enough to raise his voice and I turn back to him and frown. 'Don't you understand how frustrating it is when you drip feed me information like that? What happened on the *second* year?'

'You didn't come home. You didn't call. You didn't even email me,' I snap at him, and Leo stares at me in disbelief.

'What? No, I wouldn't have done that.'

'That's exactly what you did. So forgive me if I don't really want to reminisce about that day with you.'

'Did you… Did you remind me?' he asks. He sounds uncertain, and it strikes me how infrequently I have heard Leo use such a tone. I shake my head at him. 'Maybe I just forgot?'

'You did. You were busy in Syria – it just slipped your mind.'

We'd had a number of icy phone calls in the days that followed, with Leo apparently bewildered as to why I was so furious with him. I know it was stupid and passive aggressive and immature, but I didn't ever remind him. Something must have jogged his memory a few days later because he sent flowers. I was so livid I threw them straight into the bin.

I open the fridge to take out the milk and automatically begin to make us each a coffee. Leo is still behind me, and after a minute or two, I glance back at him.

'What else have I missed, Molly?' he asks.

Everything. Every other damned time I needed you. I gave up my family for you, and you're never here for me. 'A lot.' I slam the fridge door closed and the sound echoes throughout the apartment. 'It's not fair to talk about it with you when you don't even remember it, plus we're just going to argue about it and I can't do that right now. So can you please just drop it. When your memory is back, if you want to talk about how I feel about your travel, I'll talk to you all day and night until you're satisfied but for now – *please* – can we just make this topic off limits? I can't see how any of this is going to help you get your memory back.'

Leo falls silent, and I make the coffees and then carry them through the dining room and into the lounge. I set the cups on the low coffee table and then push the sofa out of the way so Leo will be able to reach his cup. He comes through behind me, and I watch as he pauses at the wall of photos I've hung beside the new dining room table. Silently he surveys the twelve large images, his eyes scanning the neat rows of identical black frames. There's a candid shot that I took at the beach of Teresa and Paul and the boys, and there's also a photo of Brad and Penny and their kids. Then there's a photo of Anne and Andrew on our wedding day, and finally one I took of Lucien with Santa Claus at a charity day at his vet clinic one Christmas. But the rest are all of Leo and me together. I watch Leo's face as he scans them, but his expression remains neutral. I think about the portrait of a marriage I have painted through those photos. We are smiling in every single one; we are embracing in most of them.

They are all from when we were dating, or our first year of marriage. I think about the rest of the room, and the endless arguments we have had here, and the countless times when I have been alone in this space and acutely aware of Leo's absence. I have spent more time alone here now than I have had moments with Leo anywhere: the wall of photos is a lie.

He touches the new dining room table and he smiles a little to himself when he sees the silk irises in a vase, then moves on to the living space where I am waiting. There are new couches here – a plain beige upholstered set that I've brightened up with some bold pillows.

I had desperately wanted to stay in my beautiful apartment on the harbour, but Leo was determined not to move from this terrace. Gradually I came to understand that it was important enough to him that I should be the one to compromise and I was happy to do so, if it meant he would be more comfortable.

And so instead of shifting Leo into my world, I moved here, into his world – and then we set about turning *his* space into *our* space. By painting and replacing the furniture, we have gradually turned Leo's somewhat dark bachelor pad into a beautiful, fresh space where I can feel at home too. But Leo does not remember all of the careful negotiation that went into making this new look happen, and I am suddenly nervous. He is looking around, taking it all in, but he's guarding his reaction so closely that I know he's not pleased.

'I promise, Leo. You really were on-board with all of this,' I tell him. 'There's no change here that you didn't approve.'

'*Approve*?' he repeats, then he laughs. 'From what I remember of you, I'm finding it hard to imagine that you're a well-behaved, submissive wife.'

I laugh too. 'But I mean – we worked on all of this together. You even helped me pick the shade of white on the walls.'

'There are shades of white?'

'There are actually hundreds of whites to choose from when it comes to painting. It was kind of fun – you picked your favourite five and I picked mine, and then the next weekend we painted patches of them onto the walls and finally we agreed on this one. I think this was called something like "True White".'

'So you're telling me we spent several weeks trying to decide on a white, and in the end we went with white?'

'When you put it like that...'

'Did I *tell* you I was having fun? Because, I hate to break it to you, I was probably lying if I did. That sounds like my worst nightmare.'

Leo speaks absent-mindedly and I know he's only making one of those wry jokes that he throws out all of the time and he doesn't mean anything by what he has said – but even the idea that he might not have enjoyed those weekends has shocked me.

I am stunned to realise that the *only* part of the entire renovation that he'd actively participated in was the paint selection, and if my memory serves me correctly, we were actually part way painting those samples onto the wall when we had a minor squabble about the spacing between them. Leo painted a streak of paint onto my cheek, and when I squealed in protest, he rubbed his face all over mine – inadvertently getting paint all through his beard. I remember that playful encounter ended with us making love on the drop sheet. But now that I really think about it, I can't remember if Leo actually helped make the final decision at all.

'Don't you like the house like this, Leo?' I ask him suddenly.

'I don't *not* like it,' he says, unhelpfully. 'I mean – it's beautiful. I'm sure I told you how hard I had to save for this place, and when I moved in here, I felt like I'd *made it*. Although, looking at what you've done with it now, I realise it was a pretty dingy sort of shoebox back then. Anyway, I'm sure I'll get used to it again, it just doesn't feel like my home anymore. Not yet, anyway.'

God! What if he'd always felt like that? I thought I was the hero of our relationship when we negotiated our living arrangements. I thought *I* had done all of the compromising – all of the peacekeeping. For the first time ever, I wonder if what I actually did was agree to the geography, then force my home onto him anyway.

What if he never felt at home here after I changed it? Had that been part of the reason why he never seemed to want to come back here to me?

'What would you do differently?' I ask him. He had been staring at the new television, but his eyes sweep back to me.

'I don't hate it, Molly,' he says. 'I told you, it's beautiful. I'll adjust.'

'Do you remember anything here yet?' I desperately want him to reassure me with some very positive memories of *loving* the changes we made. I'm disappointed when he shakes his head.

'I thought today would be like yesterday at the Quay when the memories just reappeared easily. But today – maybe I'm trying too hard. I can't remember ever being here with you, let alone renovating it.'

Something about this statement reminds me that I was going to try to keep his focus on the rest of his life, other than me, and I sigh a little as I realise how badly I am failing at that task.

'Can you remember anything else of the last few years here? I mean – do you remember working on any of your articles here? Your office is virtually the same as it was when I moved in – you weren't so keen for me to change that space.'

'I wish I could get up there, maybe that would help.'

'I've already ordered chairlifts,' I tell him. 'Once you can move yourself in and out of the wheelchair, you'll be able to get up and down the floors. They'll be installed next week.'

'Thank you – that's wonderful – but how will I get from the first flight of stairs to the second? Will I need a wheelchair on each floor?'

'Oh no, they're going to install the rail so that it goes all the way from the bottom to the top and if you want to go to the bedroom, you'll just stop it there. And you'll fold the wheelchair up and hook it to the side so it goes with you.'

Leo tilts his head to the side and I see the faintest smile hover on his lips. 'You really do love me, don't you, Molly Torrington?'

'Molly Stephens,' I correct him automatically, but then I think about what he has said.

Do I really love him? Still? *What if I did?*

If I still loved him, then it is for nothing anyway, because he doesn't love me anymore and even if he did, he would always love his job more. If I still loved him, then at some point very soon his memory is going to return and I'd have to lose him all over again. If I still loved him, then my plans to move on and start afresh without him would be doomed to failure.

So I have to *not* love him – I have to make sure that I don't love him.

My eyes fill with tears and I know immediately that I'm not going to be able to stop them. I lower the coffee cup back towards the table, but move so fast that it spills all over my thighs and then I panic. I'm flapping my hands and the tears are turning to sobs and Leo is watching all of this with a bewildered kind of shock on his face. He catches my shaking hands in his, and then he says very gently, 'Did you burn yourself?' I shake my head, and I look at him, stricken and embarrassed. 'What's wrong? Did I say something wrong?'

'I just need a minute,' I say, and I pull out of his grasp and run to the bathroom at the back of the terrace near the laundry. I close the door behind myself and I lean on the basin and stare at myself in the mirror, then I splash my face with cold water again and again, but it's not working. There's a gentle knock against the bathroom door, and Leo calls hesitantly, 'Molly? Can I open the door?'

'No,' I choke.

'Come on, Molly. Come out.'

'I can't.'

'Why not?'

'I can't stop crying.' Admitting this aloud makes me cry even harder and I'm mortified. Leo doesn't remember me well enough to know this is a one-off. He's going to think I'm one of those weepy women who cries at the drop of a hat. He's going to hate me. He already hates me – he's just forgotten. *Oh God! This is all so miserable.*

Leo pushes the door open. The sight of him there and the concern in his eyes only makes things worse. He catches my hand and gently tugs me towards him and when I'm close, he pulls me all the way down onto his lap. I try to pull away. 'I'll hurt you, I'm too heavy,' I protest.

'Don't be silly, you're a lightweight,' and he pulls me against him and wraps his arms around me, and after a minute, I relax to lean against him. 'Cry,' he says.

'You must think I'm some kind of hysterical idiot.'

'You're telling me what to *think* now,' he says wryly. 'What a nag!'

I manage a laugh at his pitiful joke, and then realise I'm just going to have to ride this out and deal with the aftermath later. So I press my face into his neck and I breathe in his scent and I feel his arms around me and I let it all out. I'm relieved and

I'm grieving and I'm ashamed all at once. I cry and I cry, and he waits patiently, rubbing my back and occasionally murmuring comforting words into my hair.

When I finally feel the storm has passed, I extract myself from his embrace and stand. I straighten my dress, and I step back into the bathroom. I wash my face, and dry it on the hand towel, and then I finally make eye contact with Leo.

'I'm sorry,' I say stiffly.

'I've put you through hell,' Leo says quietly. '*You* have nothing to be sorry for.'

I look down at the floor. He has no idea just how right he is about that first statement – he *has* put me through hell. But he also has no idea yet how wrong he is about the second. I really do have my share of the blame for the way I'm feeling right now.

CHAPTER 18
Leo – March 2011

I was gone for six weeks in the end. We emailed a bit, and I called Molly a few times to satisfy myself when the missing became too distracting. I kept those calls to a minimum, though, because each time I spoke to her, I felt the sound of her voice pulling at me. I'd ring expecting to feel relieved to talk to her, and hang up desperate to go home.

Our return flight landed back into Sydney airport mid-morning. I watched the hours tick past on my phone, waiting for 5 p.m. so that I could call her. When I did, she answered on the first ring. 'Are you back?'

'Hi. Yes, I got back this morning.'

'Oh,' she said, and I could hear disappointment in her tone. 'What's wrong?'

'Why are you only calling me now?'

'I thought you'd be at work.'

'I don't give a *shit* about work if you're back. Can I see you?'

'Please. Yes, I'd like that.'

She was on my doorstep within twenty minutes and as I opened the door to her, she barged inside and pushed me hard up against the wall. Her kiss was hot and hungry and it took me some time to realise there were tears on her cheeks. I pulled away from her and stared at her flushed cheeks and the puffiness of her eyes.

'I missed you so much,' she blurted.

'I missed you too,' I admitted.

'I was so worried about you.'

'I told you I knew what I was doing.'

'I know you do. It's not *you* I don't trust, it's rogue governments and rebel militia.'

'I'll have to go back. There's something bad spiralling there.'

'Don't tell me that now,' Molly shuddered, 'let me pretend it's over. At least for a few days.'

She had been hurt by my absence. I studied this realisation for a moment and then was struck by another: *I* was hurt by it too. The strange angst I'd felt being separated from her had gone deeper than just 'missing'. It was a pain and a *wrongness* – something which had only been made right in that very moment when she was back in my arms.

'What *is* this, Leo?' Molly whispered suddenly.

'This?' I whispered back.

'Us.'

It was the first time we'd addressed our relationship directly – the first time we'd needed to. I drew in a deep breath, and shook my head. 'I don't know. I thought we were just having a fling,' I was speaking to myself as much as I was speaking to her. Perhaps it indicated my lack of self-awareness when it came to Molly, but it was only now that we were back in the same room that I realised how deeply relieved I was that she was beside me again. I met her gaze. 'This isn't a fling.' We stared at each other. 'Do we have to know what to call it?' I asked and after a while, she shook her head.

'Of course we don't.'

'Let's just call it "*us*", then. And when the time feels right, we'll give it a proper name.'

'Okay,' she agreed softly, and then I kissed her again.

From that moment on we were inseparable. I didn't spend much time thinking about what the future might hold for us but I was absolutely sure that our present was pretty bloody amazing. My life looked lighter and brighter than it ever had before.

Just a few weeks after my return from that first trip, we realised we'd be at the same industry function together the following Saturday night. We didn't discuss the logistics, but we both understood that we would be at the same event – separately. I wasn't thrilled about this situation, but just like her request that we avoid public affection, I understood where it came from.

The ceremony was held each year at a plush function centre on Darling Harbour and it was a glittering event – black tie, formal dress. That Saturday morning, we stayed in bed until noon and then Molly spent the afternoon at a day spa, having her hair and make-up done.

I walked into the city centre from Molly's apartment and had a haircut and a long overdue clean shave. Afterwards, I took a shower then pulled on the tux I'd hired. I stared at myself in the mirror of Molly's stupidly oversized bathroom. I looked good, I supposed – but I felt uncomfortable. The tux was much more constricting and felt much less natural to me than my body armour.

'Dear God! Someone has broken into my apartment and swapped Leo for a handsome, clean-cut stranger!' Molly's lightly teasing voice came from the door and I turned back to her. She was wearing the skin-tight red sheath dress she'd laid out on the bed earlier that day, with some heavy jewellery that I figured was probably worth more than my bike. I ran my eyes over her body and settled them on her face, and had to force myself to breathe.

'You look amazing.'

'Don't I always?' she did a playful pirouette, and then came close to brush her lips very lightly over mine. When I tried to kiss her properly, she laughed and swivelled her head away from mine.

'Hell no! I can't fix this make-up if you mess it up but if you behave tonight, I'll let you mess it up properly later.' She leant on the bathroom counter and stared at my reflection in the mirror, then said a little reluctantly, 'Leo… you know Dad is going to be there tonight, right? He always comes to this dinner. I'll have to sit at his table.'

'I did assume you'd be seated with the important people.'

'You're important.'

'I'm not exactly "*Torrington*" important. It's fine, I can admire you from afar.'

'You can come home with me, if that's any consolation.'

'I like it better when *you* come home with *me*.'

Molly stood behind me, and wrapped her arms around my waist. She rested her head against my back and murmured, 'Okay, your place tonight.'

There were hundreds of people in the function room by the time I arrived. I automatically scanned it, looking for Molly, and saw her standing next to her father at the front of the room by the stage. We'd probably been to this function at the same time in previous years, but I'd never even said hello to her in the past, so I knew it wasn't all that likely I'd find myself at her end of the room. Instead, I found my place-setting at the *News Monthly* table and started chatting with some colleagues. Brad's wife Penny was beside me. I took a glass of wine from a passing waiter and glanced at her.

'Must be good to have Brad home,' I said to her.

'It is, although you know as well as I do that it won't be for long,' she said. I didn't need to ask her what she thought about this – her opinion was clearly written on her face. She was staring at me as if his working habits were somehow my fault.

'He's in a rush to get back?' I surmised, but I wasn't surprised. That was the curse of the war correspondent – we were never *really* anywhere – when we were at home, our eyes were on the world stage, looking for the next adrenaline rush. And when we were in the field, we were constantly thinking of home and how amazingly blessed our peaceful real lives were. After enough years, 'field' and 'home' both felt a little wrong, because nothing really felt like home anymore.

'Aren't *you* in a rush to get back?' Her eyes accused me. 'He told me you two will probably be focusing on Syria for at least the next year.'

'Yeah, I'd say so.'

Penny sighed and reached for her wine. She brought it to her lips for a sip, then tipped it back and downed half the glass in one smooth motion.

'You're smart, you know,' she turned her gaze on me again.

'I am?'

'To stay single. It's just too hard otherwise.'

She'd said that to me many times before. Ordinarily I took it as a compliment – that night, it was an uncomfortable reminder of the realities of the life I'd chosen. I shrugged again and scanned the room.

'Where is Brad?'

'Somewhere here. Look – over there with Kisani.'

Kisani Hughes was our editor at *News Monthly*, and she was standing in a group of other senior staff. Brad was at her side, staring at the floor, clearly bored out of his mind. As if he felt our eyes on him, he suddenly turned and started walking towards us.

Penny sighed and tapped her wedding ring against the stem of her wine glass.

'He just needs to stick around here long enough for Imogen's birthday in a few weeks. Do you reckon you can help make that a reality, Leo?'

'I have a few things here I need to take care of before I can even think about getting back on a plane.'

'Good.'

'Christ!' Brad sat down heavily beside Penny and rubbed his eyes. 'Why is it that when people get promoted to a job with a title that contains the word "executive" they are instantly batshit boring?'

'It's the way of the world,' I said smoothly.

'Hey, Leo,' I heard Molly say quietly, and she took the seat beside me – the seat marked with Kisani's place-card.

'Hi,' I said softly, but I quickly scanned the shocked expressions of my companions.

'Just thought I'd pop by and say hello.'

'Molly, this is Brad and Penny Norse,' I said, leaning back in my chair and motioning towards Penny at my left. Molly leant across me to shake her hand, and then Brad's.

'Lovely to meet you both,' she said. 'I've heard a lot about you.'

'You've – *what*? You have?' Penny said blankly.

'Molly and I know each other from way back,' I said smoothly. 'I mentioned some of our exploits in the field, Brad.'

'*Exploits?*' he repeated, and shot me an incredulous, questioning look that I avoided with some determination.

'Are you having a nice night?' Molly asked me quietly.

'Fine so far,' I told her. 'Are you?'

'I was seated between my parents tonight, I had to swap the place-cards. It's as if I couldn't be trusted to be here without strict supervision, even by the organisers,' she laughed. 'In any case, I'll be on my best behaviour.'

She looked up towards her own table and I saw her smile disappear in an instant. I followed the path of her gaze and realised Laith Torrington was staring at her, the skin on his face beetroot red. Danielle was pulling on his arm, as if trying to get his attention.

'I'd better go,' Molly muttered, and I saw that she too was flushed. She shot me a look of frustrated impatience as she rose. It took quite a bit of energy to stay in my chair, and even more to stop myself from catching her arm and suggesting she stay right by my side, where I could protect her from the disgusted look in her father's eyes.

'Talk to you later,' I said softly. We all watched her walk away, and then Brad and Penny spoke at exactly the same time.

'What the hell…'

'You didn't tell me that you knew…'

'Guys,' I cut them both off with a determined smile. 'I'm *sure* I would have mentioned at some point that I went to uni with Declan Torrington.'

'You did,' Brad said. 'You forgot to mention that you wanted to bone his sister, though.'

'Leo,' Penny said, wide-eyed, 'surely you noticed that she was all but drooling over you?'

'Don't be silly,' I muttered, but I was delighted to hear Penny say it. Brad barked a laugh.

'Oh God! Can you imagine it? You could swap war stories. She could tell you about the horrific time they ran out of gold-plated toilet paper in their mansion, and you could tell her about the time your hotel was bombed in Egypt. You'd have so much in common.'

'She's actually quite down to earth.'

'That is complete bullshit and you know it,' Penny laughed. 'Down to earth? *Please*! She probably has someone on staff to tie her shoelaces.'

'You're both hilarious, do you know that?'

'Just promise me one thing, Leo,' Penny said suddenly, her tone very serious, and I turned to her expectantly. She took a deep breath, and looked me right in the eye. 'Just make sure that if you marry her, you get a pre-nup. I just don't want her going after your money.'

This time, the whole table laughed and I rolled my eyes at Penny and looked back across the room. Molly was standing with her parents. Her back was to me, but a small crowd of Torrington executives were staring at her, and I assumed she was telling a story that had caught their attention. She seemed okay, and the simmering in my blood started to cool.

✦ ✦ ✦

Much later, I heard the first whispers of trouble at the Torrington table. Kisani had been to the bathroom and when she returned to her seat, she stared at me quizzically.

'Everyone in the "ladies" is talking about you.'

'Aren't they always?' Brad quipped. Kisani shook her head and laughed.

'No, Brad. No, they aren't always.' Her gaze returned to me. 'What did you do to Laith Torrington?'

I felt the muscles through my torso tense in readiness for... something. I frowned at her.

'Nothing. What do you mean?'

'Apparently, Laith tore strips off Molly earlier and had her in tears. Their whole executive team saw it.'

'What's that got to do with Leo?' Penny asked.

'One of the TM wives said that the whole thing was *about* him, that's what.' Kisani laughed a little. 'So, tell me. Did you upset Laith, or was it Molly? I know you think you're invincible, but you really should be careful going around making enemies at *that* end of town.'

'He made her cry?' I repeated slowly. Suddenly I could hear my pulse in my ears and there was a throbbing anger rising in my chest. The muscles in my arms had locked as if I was about to step into a ring to spar.

'Apparently. What happened?' Kisani prompted.

'She was only here for a minute,' Penny interjected defensively. 'Leo barely said hello to her.' When several seconds passed and no one spoke, she tried to lighten the mood with a joke, 'I mean, he all but undressed her with his eyes, but Laith was on the other side of the room – he wouldn't have seen that.'

'Exactly *what* did Laith say to her?' I asked Kisani. My tone was so dark that Kisani's eyes narrowed.

'I don't know – wasn't actually there, remember.'

'And you're sure Molly was crying?'

'Leo, where do you think you're going?' Brad spoke very slowly and he had risen, and I realised belatedly that I had done so too. I was stuck on autopilot, acting without thinking. Molly was upset and I had to go to her – there was no alternative course of action. My entire table was staring at me now.

'I'm going to see if she's okay.'

'Whoa! That is a really bad idea,' Kisani said, and she stood and lifted her arms as if she could block my path. 'What's gotten into you?'

'Leo,' Brad said quietly. 'Take a deep breath and think about this. There's been a misunderstanding – it's just going to be awkward if you go over there. Why would Laith even care if she came and said hello to you?'

I brushed Brad's hand off my elbow and walked across the room. I was all the way across the floor when I noticed that the presenter was walking towards the middle of the stage to give a speech, and the rest of the guests were returning to their seats. I walked faster, and made it to the *Torrington Media* executive table just as the announcer reached the podium.

Molly turned and I knew in an instant that Kisani was right; her eyes were puffy and still red. It was the pain in her gaze that burnt me – she was hurt and embarrassed and be-wildered.

I felt an internal snap as surely as if I'd broken a bone.

I forgot that I was one of the only people standing in a room of four hundred of my peers. I forgot that I was standing beside a table that was right next to the stage, and I no longer saw the announcer staring down at me in bewilderment.

'Hi,' I said, and I was impressed with my own ability to sound polite when pure fury was pulsing through my veins. 'Laith, Danielle – it's so wonderful to see you both again. Entrées were fabulous this year, weren't they?'

But Laith was not going to pretend to be polite. He nar-rowed his eyes at me and I watched the tide of furious red creep along the skin of his cheeks. In the ten years since I'd known him he had aged – his hair and body seemed the same, but the skin on his face had sagged, pulling his mouth down and creas-ing his forehead into a permanent frown.

'What do you want, Stephens?'

No one moved – the entire auditorium seemed to have fallen silent. I took a moment to ponder – was I really so out of line, approaching them? The timing was bad, yes. But I'd done noth-ing wrong – so far.

I was making a total idiot of myself and maybe I'd regret it later, but I knew I would have regretted it more if I hadn't checked in on her. The only thing that mattered to me that moment was that Laith had made her cry.

I wanted to kill him. I wanted to speak to him with my fists and make him say sorry to her. I wanted to teach him to respect her for the person that she was, not the person he was trying to force her to be. I wanted to make him pay for all of the ways that he'd hurt Molly – and Declan – and the way that he'd always treated me.

Laith and I locked gazes. I could see the utter loathing in his eyes, and I hoped that he could see it mirrored mine. I slammed my hands into my pockets to hide my clenched fists and turned my gaze to Molly.

'I just wanted to come and see how your night was going, Molly. And to make sure you're okay.'

'No,' she said, calmly. 'I am *not* okay. I would like you to take me home now, please, Leo.'

She rose slowly and slightly unsteadily – and held her hand out towards me.

I stared at her outstretched fingers and then I took her hand. We entwined our fingers in a way that left absolutely no doubt as to the relationship between us, and I smiled at her tenderly. 'It would be an honour, Molly.'

She slipped out from her chair and lifted her purse from the table. Danielle was gaping at us and I looked pointedly to Laith, just in case he had somehow missed the body language between his daughter and me. 'Have a good night,' I said, nodding at him calmly, and then with a smile at the rest of the table, I turned away from them to find that the entire auditorium was indeed staring at me – at *us*. I raised my chin and quickly lead Molly towards the exit.

❖ ❖ ❖

We didn't say a word at first. My phone, nestled in my pocket, was vibrating continuously – I checked it briefly, and saw several missed calls from Brad, Penny and even Kisani – but they could all wait. As soon as we were outside, Molly started to cry.

'What the hell happened?' I whispered, and I turned to cup her face in my hands. I stared down at her in the semi-darkness and the sight of the tears rolling down her cheeks was enough to make me want to storm back into the auditorium. 'All you did was say hello to me.'

'He told me I wasn't allowed to talk to you, can you believe that? Not allowed,' she whispered. There was a stubborn set to her jaw but misery in her eyes. 'I told him he had no right to tell me who I could or couldn't talk to. He said some things about you…' She broke off, and her gaze fell.

I tilted her face towards mine. 'What did he say about me?'

'I don't even want to repeat it, Leo. He used words that would hurt you,' Molly whispered, and her gaze dropped. 'And I lost my shit at him.'

'That's not what I heard,' I said gently.

Molly laughed weakly, then her face fell and the tears started to flow all over again. 'And then *he* lost his shit at *me*, and he's much better at it than I am.'

'God, Molly! I'm so sorry.'

'I'm not. It was overdue.'

'Did I do the right thing coming to your table? I kind of lost my mind.' My phone vibrated again, and I sighed and released her to slip it from my pocket. A text from Brad – *What the hell is going on?*

I suddenly realised the very obvious option I'd overlooked.

'*Fuck*,' I groaned. 'Molly, I should have just sent you a text.'

'Yeah,' she laughed, and then I started to laugh too. 'That would have been slightly less dramatic.'

'I heard he made you cry and my brain kind of melted.'

'Who told you that? I did *not* cry!'

'You obviously did,' I said wryly, and I ran my thumb over her cheek.

'Well… still… I *am* a professional, you know – except for the whole arguing with Dad in front of the staff thing. Any crying I may or may not have done, I did in the bathroom. God, this industry is full of bloody gossips!'

'Isn't that kind of the point?'

'I'll bet it was someone from TM,' she muttered, and suddenly wrapped her arms around my neck, moving with such force that I stumbled backwards a little. 'I don't care what he thinks, or what anyone thinks. I think I'm falling in love with you, Leo Stephens, and I don't care who knows it. Do *you*?'

I replayed the words over and over again before I spoke.

Love. That's what this was. How had I not realised it yet? I'd been too busy enjoying it to step apart from it and identify it, but now that she'd said it, it made perfect sense.

'I think I'm falling in love with you too,' I whispered, and Molly gasped.

'You did *not* just say that!'

'You said it first,' I protested, confused by her shock.

'God, Leo! I've been known to say it to the clerk at the bakery for giving me a cupcake! I mean it, of course, but I just didn't expect you to say it back. I figured I'd be hanging on for years and years, hoping you were thinking it, never really being sure…'

I laughed and shook my head at her. 'Well, this whole night hasn't been a bust, then.'

We kissed again, slowly, savouring the moment. *Love.* I kept saying the word over and over again in my head, marvelling at it. *This is love. I love her. I am in love with her.* I wasn't sure where it would lead us but she mattered to me, and I mattered to her. It was beautifully simple, and simply profound.

After a while, I broke the kiss to gaze into her eyes.

'Are you going to have a job to go back to on Monday, Molly?'

'I don't know,' she said, and then she shuddered. 'God, Leo! I don't even know if Dad will forgive me. We embarrassed him and Dad is *all* about saving face.'

'It will be okay,' I promised her. 'We'll figure it out together, whatever happens.'

CHAPTER 19
Molly – August 2015

I am fragile after my breakdown at the terrace. I am clingy with Leo too, and although he doesn't seem to mind, I'm embarrassed about how reluctant I am to let him out of my sight. We stay at the terrace together for hours, and even when I see him tiring, I ignore his hints about heading back to the facility. Instead, I order a meal to be delivered from Totally Thai and we sit at the new dining table to eat. Leo asks me questions about our life together. They're innocent things – carefully selected discussion items, I suspect, because he stays entirely away from the issue of his travel or the periods of our marriage we have spent apart.

We talk about the easy moments and I try to frame my answers about things that should feel familiar. I remind him about how he *always* insists on taking the left side of the bed, and how he was adamant when we met that it was just as easy for me to put the toilet seat down before I used it as it was for him to put it down after he'd finished with it. He laughs when I tell him how I'd go to the bathroom in the middle of the night, forget that he'd been there and fall into the bowl. I thump him for laughing.

He asks me about our best moments together, and I tell him about the quiet ones. Those small moments really are my favourite memories of us. It was Leo doing the dishes in the early days so I wouldn't complain about the dishwasher, and me being so overwhelmed with love for him that I'd come up behind him and wrap my arms around his waist just to hold him.

It was Leo recording *The Bachelor* for me when I was stuck at the office one night, even though he hated the show and teased me mercilessly for watching it.

It was the mornings when we woke beside one another and the first communication that we had of the day was just a contented smile.

It was Leo kissing me in public, which he always liked to do – he was just so proud to be with me, and that made me feel proud too.

It was the way he'd stand in front of me and smile, and run his hands down over the back of my hair and then cup my shoulders to gently hold me in place, as if he wanted to show his affection for me from head to toe.

That was who we were before we broke. And just like the previous day at Circular Quay, reliving those moments with him is both unbearably painful and a precious gift. I want to keep talking about these light-hearted things all night, and Leo is treating me so tenderly after my tears earlier in the day that I have a feeling he'd let me. I battle an irrational urge to beg him to stay with me. I don't ask, but I want to.

Eventually I broach the subject of his return to the clinic and he calls for the van.

'Please let me go with you,' I say for the fourth or fifth time when the van arrives at the gate, and Leo smiles sadly at me and shakes his head.

'Molly, you are absolutely exhausted. You are going to take yourself up to bed and get a proper night's sleep. Promise me.' I am still holding his hand tightly within mine and he brings my wrist to his lips and kisses it gently. 'Good night, Molly.'

He releases my fingers but I hold onto his. I can't bring myself to let go. I bend, and although I know it's completely wrong, I gently kiss him. Leo responds with surprising enthusiasm for the kiss, and before I know it, I end up sitting on his lap and we are making out in a laneway like teenagers while the driver waits patiently in the car beside us.

Eventually, I pull away from him. As soon as I do, Leo wraps his arms around me and pulls me close again. 'God,' he whispers, and his breath is hot on my neck. 'You're amazing, Molly *Stephens*!'

He doesn't just say those words – they burst from his lips, as if he couldn't *not* say them. When was the last time he said that? When was the last time he even complimented me? I can't remember, and I doubt he's thought warm things about me at all over our last miserable months. It's the reminder I need that the night must end, so I turn and kiss him again – briefly but passionately, and then I say goodbye.

CHAPTER 20
Leo – March 2011

For all of her bravado at the function on Saturday night, Molly woke on Sunday morning in a miserable funk. I'd never seen her like that before. She was quiet and pale, and lethargic as if she was physically sick. I had to work hard to convince her to get out of bed, and when she dressed, she wore track pants and a hoody but no make-up. I made an endless series of pathetic jokes to try to cheer her up, but was rewarded with little more than a weak smile each time.

We walked to a café near my house – hand in hand in public for the very first time. I would have been celebrating any other day, but with Molly's dampened mood I didn't even draw attention to it. At the café she ordered only a coffee, which she sipped without enthusiasm. We shared the paper, and I silently scanned for any coverage of the scene I'd inadvertently caused. I wasn't surprised that I wasn't actually named, but Molly and Laith's public bust-up was referenced in all of the coverage of the awards night.

The annual Journalism Australia awards ceremony was held last night in a glittering function on Darling Harbour. Rumours are growing of a family rift between Torrington CEO Laith Torrington and his VP daughter, Molly – with a very public family argument played out during the dinner.

TM publicity staff declined to comment when contacted today.

'Leo,' Molly said suddenly, and I looked up from the paper. She was white-faced. 'I have to leave TM.'

'Not if you're not ready,' I said cautiously. 'This will blow over.'

She shook her head, knocking the tears onto her cheeks. I quickly glanced around to check for photographers. It was unlikely, but the last thing she needed was an image of her sitting sobbing in a café to make the news.

'No, I do. Dad is never going to tolerate…' she waved a hand between us.

'Don't do anything rash, okay?' I suggested. 'Don't jump yet. Wait and see what happens.'

I did want her to leave – but for her own sake. But I didn't want her to blame me for further damaging her relationship with her father: Molly had to be sure.

That day, it was like Molly's personality had been forced into mute mode. Her smiles were half-strength at best. I thought it'd pass quickly, but the following day, as we sat down to breakfast, she said, 'I'm going to resign today.'

'Are you sure?'

'I'm sure,' she whispered, and then she gave me a wobbly smile. 'This is what I want, what I've always wanted – it's not even about you, I just needed the push. Please don't try to talk me out of it, I'm not being impulsive.'

I helped her draft the email.

Dad, for the sake of the company but also for my own sake, I won't be returning to TM. I know this will be disappointing to you but it is something I have been thinking about for a very long time. I will try to touch base with you in a few weeks' time when the dust settles. I love you, Molly

Laith didn't respond that day, but the next morning, she woke me with her phone in her hand.

You have deeply disappointed and embarrassed your mother and me. You are welcome to call me when you have come to your senses and are ready to apologise.

I could feel her pain, but I didn't actually get it. I wanted to, but I just didn't understand how deeply his disapproval could hurt her. It was as if she'd lost her reason for living, and that seemed ridiculous to me. She still had so much – she still had *everything* – except for a job that she'd never really enjoyed anyway.

If she'd been sad before that email, she was positively miserable after it. I had another trip looming and I wasn't exactly sure what I was supposed to do if she was still this depressed when the time came to fly out. I started to worry – I dragged her out of the apartment for walks and sunshine, brought her meals and tried to persuade her to eat them – and generally did my best to be both patient and supportive. When I tried to talk to her, Molly only assured me she was glad to have had an impetus to force her to make a change. The relief of those words did not at all match the misery of her behaviour.

I wanted to be supportive and encouraging, and I think I was – at first. But by day I was working on a plan to dig deeper into the growing civil unrest in Syria and the increasingly difficult conditions people there were facing, and by night my extremely wealthy girlfriend seemed to be in deep mourning over the loss of a job she *hated*! It was maddening.

When I could no longer postpone my trip overseas, I decided it was time to take drastic action. I rang her as I left the *News Monthly* office one afternoon. 'How about you get dressed?' I suggested quietly. 'I'm taking you out.'

'What for?' she asked, in that almost monotonous tone that did awful things to my soul.

'I think it's time to show you my gym,' I murmured.

'I'm really not in the mood for a workout, Leo.'

'I'm not taking you there for a workout,' I said, and I sighed. 'I'm taking you there for perspective.'

'Oh God,' she groaned, 'I don't like the sound of that either! Can't I just wallow in my self-pity for a bit longer?'

'Wear running shoes and jeans, I'll pick you up in half an hour.'

CHAPTER 21
Molly – August 2015

'I'm taking you somewhere positive today,' I tell Leo when I arrive at his room the next afternoon.

'There were *lots* of things that were positive about yesterday,' he replies, and he winks at me as he switches his Kindle off. I know he's talking about the kiss that I should never have initiated, and I flush.

'I'm sure there were, but perhaps not the part where the wife you barely remember virtually drowned you in tears for no apparent reason,' I mutter.

'Actually, yesterday I felt like a man supporting his wife instead of a useless invalid.' I try to think of a profound way to respond to that, but Leo saves me. 'It's not *all* about you, you know,' he teases. I smile in spite of myself.

'Where are we going today then?' he asks.

'I think it's time I show you the Foundation.'

'Ah, the famous Foundation that I know almost nothing about, other than the fact that Tobias works there. Who I *also* know nothing about.'

Sarcasm, again. I draw in a breath, hold it while I count to five, then release it. 'I am trying to help you with that, Leo.'

'There's no need to be defensive, I was just making a joke.' The casual dismissiveness of his statement is fuel to the fire of my irritation.

'Well, it's not something you should—' I start sharply, but he reaches out and takes my hand, and the gesture surprises me into silence. I try to tug my hand away, but he holds it with determination.

'Molly,' he says, gently. 'I am only trying to poke fun at my situation. I am well aware that it's not actually funny – I hate every second of this. I am just trying to keep things light. Please, don't think that means I'm not appreciative of everything you are doing for me.'

I sigh and tug at my hand one last time. Leo releases it, but he watches me closely. 'Should we go?'

'Not yet.' He lifts his hand and points towards his lips. His eyes are on mine. 'Well, you just got stroppy with me, so I think we need to kiss and make up before we go anywhere.'

I bend to kiss him stiffly. 'There,' I say, but before I can rise, he lifts his hands to very gently cup my face, sliding his fingers into the hair behind my ears. He used to kiss me like that *all* the time, holding me close, as if our lips connecting weren't enough contact for him.

'I know you still like to kiss me – you showed me that last night. Let's do it properly,' he whispers, and then he leans forward and kisses me very tenderly. It's awkward because I'm bending down to reach him, but the gentle movement of his lips against mine softens the last of my irritation. He does not release my face as he kisses me; instead, he maintains a gentle hold on the back of my head. When he breaks away after a moment, he brushes his thumb over my cheek. 'Truce?'

'Okay,' I whisper back weakly. I feel as if my heart is going to beat its way out of my chest. He's right – I do still like kissing him. I have always loved the feel of his mouth against mine. When I am close to him, his scent instantly makes me feel safe

– it's the very reason I used to put off washing the sheets on our bed when he travelled.

'We should go,' I say. I don't want to be as affected by the kiss as I am and so I overcompensate with a too-tight tone, but I can feel the flush on my cheeks and as I straighten, I feel a little giddy from the intensity of the moment.

I hear the sigh in his voice, but Leo nods towards the door. 'Lead the way, sweetheart.'

◆ ◆ ◆

I'm surprisingly nervous about showing Leo the work I've been doing for the past three years. I don't do this for him – I do it because I want to make a difference in the world. But it feels so much as if *old* Leo has travelled forward in time to see where I wound up, and regardless of anything else that's happened between us in the years since, that version of Leo changed my life: I want him to be proud of me.

When we round the corner to the street to the *Redfern Sport and Recreation Centre*, I watch for Leo's reaction. I see the deep-set frown that crosses his face, and then I see his eyes widen as he realises what he's seeing. The run-down, ramshackle auditorium that once housed Leo's gym is gone, as are several buildings that surrounded it. In their place is a new multi-building community centre and behind it, the ultra-modern office block that houses my foundation staff.

When the van pulls to a stop in the disabled parking space at the front of our campus, we're right next to a series of signs guiding visitors through the maze of modern buildings.

Redfern Sport and Recreation Centre – Sponsored by the Declan Torrington Foundation

'Holy shit,' Leo whispers, and he turns to face me. His eyes are wide. 'You did this?'

'Not me,' I say automatically, then I flush. 'I mean, I run the Foundation but I have a whole team – *they* did it.'

'Molly,' Leo drags his gaze back to the buildings beside us, then back to me. He is as shocked as I have ever seen him. 'But – how? *Why?*'

'Do you remember that first night when you brought me here?' I ask him. Leo frowns as he concentrates, and shakes his head. The driver has stepped out of the van and I see him walking around to open the door. 'Let's go inside and look around. Maybe that will prompt some memories.'

As we enter the sports centre I keep a close eye on Leo. He surveys the lobby, and then moves immediately to the room directory near the door. As he reads it, his expression is guarded. I follow him, standing beside him to cast my eye over the facility list.

'So you said I brought you here?' he says eventually.

'Yes. I'd just left TM, and I was pretty upset about the state of things with my parents. I'd been quite depressed for a few weeks... You told me I needed some perspective.'

Leo is still staring at the room directory.

'You were upset about your job.'

'My *job*? No, I was upset because I'd spent years trying to keep my father happy, and in a single night I lost both him and Mum from my life completely. I felt like the rug had been pulled out from under me. Is this ringing any bells?'

'Well, I'm starting to remember you being upset, but I don't think I understood why,' Leo says. His voice is low, and he's still staring at the facilities list as he concentrates.

'Maybe that's my fault. I didn't want to tell you what I was thinking – I was worried you'd feel guilty,' I sigh and shrug. 'Anyway, however it came about, I needed to leave. And faced with a choice between *that* life and a life with you...' I stop, because I've been so focused on watching for Leo's reaction that I have been speaking without thinking. As I think about the words I have just spoken, a lump forms in my throat. It's true – there wasn't a thing in my life I wouldn't have sacrificed for Leo. Why didn't he feel that way about me?

'So... you were upset,' he says. 'And I brought you here to give you some "perspective"? I remember saying that,' he says, then he glances up at me and winces. 'God, Molly, I'm sorry! What a jerk.'

'Actually, it all worked out very well, as you're about to see.' I turn back to step further into the lobby, and Leo sighs as he follows me. As we approach the basketball courts, automatic doors slide open to let us through. Leo follows me inside and looks around the immense and empty room. 'You brought me here that night, and I met some of the kids and suddenly my own problems did seem embarrassingly small.'

'Tell me about that first visit here,' Leo murmurs. He's looking around the hall, his face still set in a frown. I see his gaze linger on the electronic scoreboard and the huge air-conditioning vents in the ceiling.

'Well, *that* night doesn't actually matter all that much, Leo. There's a lot to see...'

'Molly, the last time I remember standing on a basketball court in this centre, the building was a draughty warehouse and we couldn't afford to replace the backboards on the basketball hoops. Now I'm looking at a state-of-the-art sports centre and it obviously started with you and that night.' There's unmistakable frustration in his voice and he holds himself stiffly, as if he's angry. 'The last thing I remember is you sulking and me feeling frustrated because I didn't know how to help you. Fill in the gaps for me. *Please.*'

'*Sulking?*' I zero in on the word and it's like a red flag to a bull. In the same breath, he's telling me he needs me to help him remember and throwing out an insult like that. I have half a mind to leave him to figure it all out for himself. 'What was that you were saying ten seconds ago about being an insensitive jerk?'

'I just said "jerk",' he reminds me, and he offers me a slightly pleading smile. 'You *were* sulking. Maybe you had a good reason to, but that's still the right word, isn't it?'

'I was *grieving*,' I say. I cross my arms over my chest and stare at him.

'Okay, *grieving*. Sorry. Come on, sit down?'

He pushes his chair towards the bleachers without waiting for my response and I sigh and follow him. My shoes squeak on the court surface as I walk. I take a seat at the end of the bottom row of chairs and Leo parks his wheelchair in front of me.

'So?' he prompts.

'You picked me up on the motorbike. It was the first time we rode together.'

That gets a reaction. He leans back in his chair and smiles at me. 'Did you like it?'

'Not at first,' I say. 'Actually, at first I was annoyed with you because you told me to wear jeans with my running shoes.'

'Ah,' he brightens further at this. 'Yes, *that's* familiar. Yes, I did, and you told me it was a "crime of fashion".'

'It *was* a crime of fashion,' I laugh softly.

Leo almost squints – he's concentrating so hard. 'But you didn't listen anyway,' he says slowly, then he closes his eyes for a minute and when he opens them, his eyes are wide with surprise. 'You were wearing heels and a skirt when I arrived to pick you up.'

'Well, I didn't realise you were taking me on the bike. I did get changed eventually.'

'You sulked about that too,' Leo says, then grimaces at my automatic glare. 'Well, you can't say you were *grieving* over being forced to wear practical clothes.'

I roll my eyes at him. 'You took me for a ride around the city and eventually you brought me here. Do you remember now?'

'Keep talking, I'm starting to,' he murmurs, then chuckles suddenly, 'Actually, I remember you *squealing* when we came up Cleveland Street.'

'You were going too fast,' I protest. 'I thought I'd fall off.'

'I liked how tight you held on to me when I sped up,' he murmurs. Then, 'Do we still ride together? On the new bike?'

I shake my head and say vaguely, 'No, I can't even remember the last time you took it out of storage.'

I am only half-listening to Leo for a moment – totally distracted by memories myself. Although I never lost them, they have been long buried by the creeping chaos of our life together. I suddenly remember sliding myself off his bike at the front of the gym, my legs shaky and my muscles aching, and Leo pulling off my helmet. He smoothed my helmet hair and kissed me, and told me how good it felt to hear me laugh again. I don't think I'd ever felt quite so cared for before – the way that our feelings had entwined seemed almost mystical. When I was sad, Leo looked pensive and worried. When I smiled, he was happy – and I wanted for him to be happy even more than I wanted to feel better myself.

But then he had turned me towards the Sport and Rec Centre and from the outside the building had seemed so run-down, I wasn't even sure I wanted to go inside. There had been a group of teenagers mingling around the front doors smoking, a smashed window high on the wall, and layer after layer of graffiti on every conceivable surface. Even in the circle of Leo's arms I was more out of place in that moment than I had ever been in my entire life.

'What are you thinking about?' Leo asks. I glance at him.

'I haven't thought about that night in years.'

'Tell *me* about it,' he reminds me gently.

'At first, we just sat and watched a basketball game – your dad was refereeing.'

'You were uncomfortable here, weren't you?'

'I was,' I admit. 'I was intimidated.'

Leo frowns again. 'I remember being frustrated… Angry…'

'I said some stupid things,' I sigh. I can barely believe how naive I was in those days. 'I had no idea. Just being here made me feel guilty at how easy my life had been. As soon as I walked through the door, I was trying to tell you and Drew how things should be done.'

'Is that what *this* is?' Leo asks, and he sweeps a broad arc with his hands to indicate the building we are sitting in.

I look at him blankly. 'What's that supposed to mean?'

'The new buildings. Is this what happens when Molly Torrington tries to fix a broken black community?'

I gasp. That stings, and I stare at him, bewildered by the attack. 'That is not fair, Leo.'

'It is a fair *question* though, isn't it? Are you going to tell me you didn't throw a heap of your own money into this place just to make yourself feel better?'

I sit back against the backrest and stare at him. I think of the thousands of hours I've invested in this community in the period Leo has forgotten. This has become my life's work, and that work has benefited hundreds of people, including the community Leo loves. And all of it – every minute of every hour and every tear I've shed when I've failed and every drop of sweat I've expended – all of it was inspired by Leo, and that brutal wake-up call I'd had that first night he brought me here. I am so incensed at his attitude that I can't bring myself to speak.

'Well?' he prompts.

'If you're going to be a bastard, Leo, you can show yourself around the place,' I snap at him, and rise. 'I have plenty of work to do. The buildings are all wheelchair accessible, give me a call when you're done.'

'Why are you getting so defensive? Can't I even talk to you about this? I'm not saying you haven't done good work here – I'm just trying to understand *why*.'

'What would you have me do, Leo? You *brought* me here for perspective. Do you remember what this place was like? Every damned day Andrew and his team worked here there was some vital need they couldn't afford to meet.'

'So *explain* it to me.' I soften a little at the pleading edge to his voice. I don't sit back down, but I do slide my hands into the pockets of my jeans and meet his gaze again. 'What happened?'

'You insisted I help set up.' This new facility has a permanent martial arts studio with proper flooring, but back in those days space was at a premium so safety mats had to be packed down after every class to expose the basketball court. The mats were surprisingly heavy and unyielding, and I'd been covered in sweat by the time we finished.

That night was the pivotal point in my life. Drew had set up an anti-truancy programme with the local high schools – by attending school consistently, kids could earn a pass to fitness classes and a meal afterwards. Leo explained the purpose of the programme as I watched the karate class, then while he helped instruct the kids I moved into the cafeteria and got chatting to some of the basketball students while they ate spaghetti.

If I live to be a hundred years old, I'll still remember the way I felt talking to those kids that night. I didn't go looking for their darkest secrets, but even in the course of small talk with them,

I caught my first glimpse into lives marked by struggle and dis-advantage. I am wiser now – I understand that these are basic aspects of human existence – but at that stage in my life I had no concept of how other people lived or the challenges they faced.

There was no way I could walk away and go back to my old life after that night. I'd always figured that was why Leo brought me there in the first place.

'You helped set up for the karate class?' Leo prompts now, dragging me back to the present.

I nod. 'I asked Drew why he didn't just hire another room for the martial arts classes, some place he could leave set up all the time. He quite patiently explained that other than a tiny gov-ernment grant, the whole place was funded by the local commu-nity and the budget only just covered the rent and staff salaries. To me it didn't make sense that Andrew wasted so much of his time trying to raise money from a community that had so little. That's what started it all.'

'So you gave him money?' Leo surmises, and I frown at the distaste in his tone.

'Don't say it like that, you make it sound *sordid*. Anyway, would it have been a problem if I did?'

'I just know how this works. People like you—'

'People like *me*? We're back to that?' I gasp, and I throw my hands in the air. 'You still have no idea what kind of person I am.'

'I'm just trying to understand if what I'm seeing here is the wealthy white person coming into our community and telling us how to fix it,' Leo says tightly.

I'm done with this – the pinch of disappointment in my chest has twisted so tight that I feel like I'm going to snap. I thought I'd show Leo around the new centre and watch him explore it with joy and excitement, and I'd get the added bonus of pride in his eyes when he looked at me. It didn't occur to me for a second that he'd be somehow *offended* by it.

He has never given me any indication that he wasn't on board with the work for the Foundation, but I pause and reflect on his attitude over these last few years. He certainly had moments of enthusiasm, especially when the new gym was taking shape. Recently, he's been more distant, but I'd only thought about that in the context of *his* work, not mine. Could he have been resentful all along?

I only take a few steps back towards the exit before my indignation grows too great. I spin on my heel so that I can glare at him again.

'I didn't *give* Andrew any of my money, Leo – although it would have been none of your damned business if I had. I set up the Foundation with Declan's shares, and the Foundation bought this building and funded the renovations. The charity is just a conduit – people like your father register programmes and corporations get tax deductibility by sponsoring them. I don't have a bloody clue how to enact positive social change, all I do is enable the people like Drew to do *their* work. If you'd stop making assumptions about me for five minutes so I could explain, you'd see that the model here works *because* wealthy white people don't get a chance to tell communities what they need.'

Leo stares at me unflinchingly. 'You didn't explain yourself properly,' he says stiffly.

I realise that *this* is the version of Leo that has been missing since his accident – the arrogant side, the somewhat superior side – the ugly side to him that I saw only later in our marriage. *This* is the side of Leo Stephens that I hate – if only because I have no idea how to deal with it.

'At what point in this conversation did you give me enough space to explain *any* of that?'

'I'm sorry, Molly,' he says, and he exhales heavily. 'This is confronting. This place meant so much to me, and it's nothing at all like I remember it.'

'Isn't it *better*?' I ask, bewildered.

'It's… overwhelming.'

The fight drains out of me. 'Maybe this was a bad idea.'

'No,' he says, and he moves towards me. 'I'm sorry. This is amazing, and you are amazing, and I am an idiot. Can you please show me the rest? Where's the martial arts studio?'

'Are you sure? We can leave it here today. We can try again tomorrow.'

He shakes his head. 'No, let's do this today.'

It takes hours to show Leo around the facilities we have built. He is a little quiet, but he seems engaged, and he's particularly excited when he sees the weights room and the martial arts studio.

'I can't wait to get back on my feet and use some of this gear,' he says. 'And air conditioning? Heating? This is brilliant!'

This reaction is the one I was looking for, but I'm feeling so tender and bewildered by that argument on the basketball court that I can't enjoy his enthusiasm as much as I want to.

As the afternoon progresses the kids start to filter in after school and gradually Leo is mobbed by adoring fans; he's always been something of a hero to the kids at the Centre. His theory has always been that his karate classes have earned him that respect but I know it's much more than that: Leo is proof that a poor start to life does not have to limit them. More than a role model, he is living, breathing hope.

Andrew joins us eventually, and we stand at the back of the studio talking while the kids for the first class of the afternoon assemble at the front.

'I'm thinking I might stay and watch this junior brown belt class, if you don't mind,' Leo tells me. 'I don't remember most of the kids in the class and I can't help, obviously, but...'

'Of course,' I say, and I motion towards the chairs in the viewing area behind us. 'I'll wait too – I haven't watched a class in a while.'

'Sensei Leo, please, will you run the class tonight?' the young instructor calls suddenly from the front of the room. All of the kids in the class turn to stare, and Leo winces.

'Not really in a position to do that just yet, Joe.'

'But you *could* just coach us. It's a brown belt class so we know our stuff – we're mostly working on fitness and technique – just assign the exercises. If you need anything demonstrated, I can do it.'

'Do I teach this class often?' Leo asks Andrew quietly.

'You haven't really been here to teach, especially this last year or so. But all the more reason to do so now if you're up for it.'

Leo hesitates a moment or two, but then I see his posture straighten and he moves the wheelchair to the front of the studio as he barks at the class, 'Three minutes skipping for warm up, let's go!'

'He's looking good,' Andrew remarks.

'Definitely better every day.'

'His memory?'

'Returning quite quickly, I think.'

'And walking? Standing? *Anything?*'

I shake my head, and Andrew sighs.

'I've been doing some research. There are modified styles of karate for students in wheelchairs – I reckon we could advertise... Find enough kids to run a class or two if he was keen, maybe it will help him to accept what's happened. I'm just not sure if I should suggest he look into it yet.'

'He doesn't need to accept this, he needs to focus on his recovery.'

'Okay, love. You know best,' Andrew says quietly 'He's lucky to have you.'

'He'd be fine either way. You of all people know what that man is like when faced with a challenge.'

'And how are *you* doing? You've had to deal with so much of this on your own.'

'I'm tough.'

'You are bloody not!' Andrew laughs gently. 'You're the biggest softie I know.'

'I'm tough when it comes to Leo,' I say. 'I've *had* to be.'

'This might mark a new chapter for you two.'

'If he's stuck in a wheelchair, you mean?' I speak sharply to my father-in-law, but Andrew's expression doesn't change. He's well accustomed to moody teenagers, so my defensiveness is nothing new to him. 'I refuse to think of Leo having a permanent disability as a *positive*. If he can't work, he won't cope. We have to get him back on his feet.'

'Sometimes opportunities come to us wrapped up as problems, Molly.'

'What's that supposed to mean? I can't celebrate this. He would be miserable.'

'I think you and I both know that if he recovers and goes back into the field, one of these days he'll be coming home to us in a coffin. He has had no rationality whatsoever about the risks he has taken in the last few years. He *can't* regulate himself. Maybe fate is going to regulate him instead.'

I'm not sure how Leo would react if he knew his dad thought he was better off in the wheelchair, but I'm sure it wouldn't be good for him. Andrew sighs and hugs me.

'I never wanted to pry, love, but I've seen how unhappy you've been. This really could be a fresh start, couldn't it?'

I think about Andrew's comments as Leo and I travel back towards the rehabilitation clinic in the van. Do I even want a fresh start with Leo? And would I take one if it came at the cost of him being anchored to me – not by choice, but because of an injury?

I am softening towards Leo, just as I can see his affections growing towards me. But there's not just water under the bridge behind us, there's a veritable flow of toxic waste in our history and Leo's arrogant display in the basketball gym is a brutal reminder of the things about him that I only discovered after we were married. There is a side to him that I despise, just as there are aspects to him that I will always love, but at the end of the day we *are* done and the sooner I can figure out how to tell Leo that, the sooner I can extricate myself from this pretence that everything is okay.

Leo *has* to get well; he *has* to go back to work and his life. What would he be left with otherwise? Almost nothing now and I couldn't wish that on him – I just couldn't. I take a deep breath and I turn to face him. He notices my movement and he speaks before I get a chance to.

'About earlier—'

But I know where he's going with this and I wince. 'Let's just forget about it.'

'No,' he says. 'We need to talk about this. I was a jerk back there, and I'm really sorry. This life I have now is just so different to the one that I remember, and all of these changes here are good, but it doesn't feel like my life anymore. I don't want to push you away, Molly – I know that I need you. Will you forgive me?'

'You didn't need to say that,' I say, and my words are stiff with guilt, as if he has read my private thoughts.

'No, I really did,' Leo sighs. 'I am trying to take all of this in my stride, if you'll pardon the pun, but this is the hardest thing I've ever faced and I just don't know how I could have survived it without you. I can't afford to treat you like shit when you're the best thing in my life and I'm going to try harder, I promise you.'

If the last few years have built calluses around my heart, these simple sentences wipe them away effortlessly, and I feel the pull of our connection all over again. Two minutes ago I was ready to dust my hands and walk away – again – and all that it has taken to suck me right back in is another hint of humility from Leo. That's not because the words are magic: it's because the love I have for him is alive and well beneath the surface pain. I see that with sudden, startling clarity. I have been and I *am* angry. I have been and I *am* bruised. I have been and I *am* jaded. None of that is fixed. But the reason I went to Rome – the reason I *stayed* in Rome – the reason I am running myself into the ground to help Leo find his memory again isn't because I feel obligated to: it's because I want to. For all the hurt that lies between us, I want the very best for Leo. And if there *was* some miraculous chance to start our life together over again, I would give everything in my life to be able to take it with both hands.

'I can see that I've hurt you, Molly. Not just today, I mean. And I *hate* that.' Now I really don't know what to say to him. I can't deny it – I won't deny it. I let him slip his fingers through mine.

'I'm going to do better. I don't know if I've said that before, and if you already know that I won't, but I can promise you that I'm going to give it everything I've got this time. Okay?'

I nod mutely. When he brings my hand to his lips, I feel weak inside, like my resolve is dissolving and I'm being drawn back to him with every breath we take together. Leo looks at the window, but I stare at our hands in his lap, and wonder how much he means that.

And then for the first time I wonder if Andrew is right. Could this be a fresh start for us? A chance to do it over – and to do it with the benefit of hindsight?

✦ ✦ ✦

We take Lucien for a walk to a park the next day to make the most of a warm afternoon. I hold the lead and Lucien walks close to me at the left, with Leo pushing himself along on my right.

At the park, I unclip Lucien's lead and he trots off into the centre, but is immediately distracted by a butterfly. Leo and I watch as he does a series of insane acrobatics trying to catch it in his mouth.

'How was physiotherapy this morning?'

'The same,' Leo says. His words are curt. He hasn't said so, but I can tell that he's starting to worry about the lack of progress he is making with his physical therapy. 'But I had this random thought this morning. I thought it might have been a memory surfacing.'

'What was it?'

'It's actually really silly. I knocked some toast to the ground and wondered if it had landed on the buttered side. As I thought about that, you came to mind quite strongly.'

'Did you think anything in *particular* about me?' I can't help myself – I giggle and I feel a warm flush creeping up my cheeks. I take a few steps away from Leo and sit on a park bench.

'Maybe. Why?'

He comes closer, pushing the wheelchair easily off the path, but moving the wheels with more effort as he nears the chair. To my surprise, as soon as he's lined it up beside me, he leaps out of it to sit on the bench seat. He moves himself along until he's right next to me and then slides his arm around my shoulders. I relax into him instantly, and it's pure bliss to feel the strength of his body against mine again. He is still so strong and solid. I was always particularly taken by Leo's heavily muscular frame.

'I'd actually forgotten about that myself until you said it,' I murmur. 'But when we were first dating, we used to play this really silly game…' I stop laughing, and clear my throat a little awkwardly. 'It was a silly ritual we got into the habit of. Say we'd order a coffee in a café and you'd say something like, "I bet you it's going to have latte art on the froth." And I'd say, "Nope, I reckon it won't this time."'

'And?'

'And the loser of the bet had to…' I gesture towards his groin with my elbow. I'm blushing, which is ridiculous – because this is Leo, my husband, the person I played this game with – but our relationship was immensely different back then. 'Let's just say, we were usually both winners in the end.'

Leo chuckles and the sound reverberates in his chest. I lean into him even more and he rubs his hand up and down my upper arm.

'Well, that's actually a relief to hear,' he murmurs into my ear. 'I have to admit, I got a bit worried when a piece of toast falling off the table was enough to give me a raging erection.'

I laugh, and then pause. 'Actually, I think we *did* have a bet over a piece of toast on the floor at some point.' It comes back to me slowly. It was a lazy weekend and we were having breakfast in my dining room. Maybe I knocked the toast or maybe it was Leo – but before I could reach down to get it, he caught my chin in his hand and held my gaze. The need in his eyes was intense before the game had even begun. *I reckon that landed on the buttered side down. Usual stakes?* I looked under the table and saw that the buttered side was up, but I glanced up at Leo and smiled as I slid off my chair onto my knees.

'I'm remembering more and more of those months,' Leo says, startling me out of my daydream. I clear my throat again and resist the urge to fan my cheeks with my hand.

'That's good. What's the last thing you remember?'

'It's not really like that… I get fragments of memories and I don't always understand the meaning or the timeframe at first. Like the toast. I knew there was something there, but I didn't actually understand it until you explained it.'

'And now?'

'I'm pretty sure that later… I saw that the toast was *actually* butter-side up,' he says. The unseasonably warm day suddenly feels quite scorching. I pull away from him and turn to face him. Our eyes lock – the current between us is intense. He leans forward and kisses me. 'I think I miss you, Molly.'

I miss you more.

'How long has it been?' he asks me, his voice a whisper.

'Since we…'

'Yeah.'

I swallow. 'A few months.' The last time had been in Istanbul, where I went to surprise him on one of his trips. It was a disaster and I shut the memories down immediately. It's not even the sex that I miss – it's the closeness.

'Months?' Leo repeats, and he sighs. 'I was away too much, wasn't I?'

'Yes.'

'I wish I could stand up out of this chair and walk home and be your husband again.'

It amazes me how the conversation flips from our recently non-existent sex life to Leo's wheelchair. I frown at him and say carefully, 'You *don't* need to walk to be my husband, Leo.'

He flicks his gaze away from me, towards Lucien in the park. 'If I am in this wheelchair,' he says quietly, 'I can't be the man I need to be.'

'That's not true. You're still the same man you always were. And you won't be in the wheelchair for long. I know it's frustrating, but you *will* get there, I know you will.'

He looks back to me. My heart aches at the sadness in his gaze. 'And if I don't?'

'I haven't given it a moment's thought,' I lie.

'You should at least think about it.'

'I won't. And you shouldn't either. Keep your focus on getting better.'

'I just don't know how I'm going to get back to work if I can't walk,' he murmurs absent-mindedly. As I disentangle myself from him and slide off the bench, he tries to catch my arm to stop me leaving. I pull away from him easily. 'Don't go, Molly.'

'Lucien has gone too far,' I point into the distance, where Lucien is on the other edge of the park, still chasing the butterfly by the looks of his sporadic leaps into the air. I start to walk after him, and then I break into a jog and then the closest thing to a sprint I have any desire at all to ever achieve. I am running to the dog – but much more than that, I am running away from Leo.

As I run, I give myself one luxurious minute to be completely selfish, and I send up a prayer into the universe that Leo will be stuck in that wheelchair for the rest of his life, just so that I can keep him in mine. I feel immediately guilty and I'm furious with myself, and I try to chase the thought right out of my mind.

By the time I reach Lucien, he is flat on his belly in the grass and I know immediately what that means. I groan as I clip the lead onto his collar and then again when, as feared, I take a step back towards the bench and the dog refuses to budge.

'Come on, Lucien,' I mutter. I drop the lead and run ahead of him, which sometimes gets him moving again, but he just stares at me. My frustration quickly mounts and I pick up the lead and tug gently. 'Don't do this today!'

'Lucien, come,' Leo is approaching at speed on the pathway and he calls to the dog. Lucien leaps to his feet and runs for Leo, pulling the lead from my hand. I puff the air from my lungs and run my hands through my hair. Lucien heels at Leo's side – I know he's just a dog, but I swear he is trying to look innocent.

'I hate it when he does that!' I exclaim. 'I spend so much of my life trying to be good to him and it's like he's trying to *punish* me for it!' Leo leans over to scoop up Lucien's lead and I snatch it out of his hands. This time, Lucien follows me and I walk past Leo in a huff. He quickly catches up with me again. 'Doesn't he understand that the more he does that, the less likely I am to walk him? What's the point of having a pet if all he does is cause me frustration?'

'He's a dog, Molly. I don't think he's analysing his decisions in any depth,' Leo says carefully. 'He's just lazy, and he used up all his energy chasing the butterfly. It's not personal.'

'Well, it's not *good* enough. And I'm not going to put up with it anymore. He can't have it both ways,' I say sharply, and when Lucien gets distracted by a piece of rubbish on the ground, I pull him back into line. I'm not rough with him, but I'm not as gentle as I would normally be. Immediately I feel guilty again and that unwelcome sensation adds to the turmoil of bad feelings simmering in my gut.

'Molly,' Leo says quietly. 'You're angry with me. Don't take it out on Lucien.'

'Don't tell *me* what to do!' I snap, and I know I'm being childish and churlish, but we were having a moment back there and really connecting. Why did Leo have to bring up his work right in the middle of it? It was like a slap in the face – a disappointing, painful reminder of why all of this closeness and tenderness between us is utterly pointless. 'I think we should just go back to the rehab centre.'

'No.'

'What do you mean, "no"?'

'No, I'm going to stay until you cool down and then we are going to talk about what just happened back there.'

At this I stop dead in my tracks and I hook the lead over the back of the handle on Leo's chair, then I all but stomp back in front of him.

'I *am* going back. You and Lucien can continue your walk, I've had enough for today.'

But Leo and Lucien are right behind me the whole way – despite the wheelchair I still can't outrun him and even that is frustrating. When I reach the gate to our courtyard, I grudgingly hold it open for Leo and then wait at the back door, where he unclips Lucien's lead and gives him a gentle pat. Lucien makes a beeline for Mrs Wilkins's place and Leo looks at me.

'Let's talk,' he says quietly. He goes to the couch and lifts himself onto it, and I look at him from the kitchen. He is getting stronger by the day – more accustomed to working around his injury – and sitting there on our couch, it could almost be an average day in our ordinary lives and as much as I don't want to, I love even the thought of that. 'Love,' he says gently. 'Come on.' I approach him slowly. I sit on the couch, but not close to him. 'What did I say, Molly?' he prompts, and I glance at him. *How can such an intelligent man be so completely stupid?* 'Is it the wheelchair? Is it too much?'

'Leo, I don't give a shit if you're in a wheelchair! I mean, I *do* – but only because I know how hard it is for you. It's not the wheelchair I'm worried about, I promise.'

'So, what is it?'

'You're going to walk again, Leo. I know you are,' I say, and I can see his bewildered frown at my tone, so I add in a whisper, 'And then you're going to go back into the field.'

'Yes?' he prompts.

'It's that simple, and it's that impossible: you love your job, and I hate it. There is no middle ground.'

'So, what do we do about that?' Leo asks me, frowning. 'You're not suggesting I don't go back to work…'

'No.'

'So…' He's looking at me as if I have the answer, but if either one of us did, we wouldn't be in this situation at all. I shake my head.

'I don't know, Leo.'

Realisation dawns on his face. '*This* is what the tension be-tween us is about, isn't it?'

'Most of it,' I whisper.

'This is *also* why I was never going to marry,' he murmurs and then he sighs. 'I just fell so hard for you, I think my brain glitched out.' I offer him a weak smile, and he leans across and takes my hand. 'Do we need to figure this out today, Molly?'

I shake my head, and he tugs me towards him. I let him pull me all the way until I'm pressed up against him.

'Do you want to watch TV for a while?' he asks softly against my hair.

'Now I know you have lost your mind.'

I know that there is only so long we can put this discussion off, and I'm conscious of the fact that this was my chance to tell him that we are separated and about everything else that has happened this year – and I have squandered it. But I'm only sorry for a minute because if I had come clean with him, I wouldn't have been spending the afternoon on the couch in the strong circle of his arms. Sooner or later, this will catch up with me but it looks like I'll keep on choosing later until it's no longer possible.

CHAPTER 22

Leo – May 2011

Molly tossed and turned in my bed after we left the gym that night. I kept drifting off to sleep but waking again when she moved.

I'd insisted that she help set up for a class when we'd arrived at the gym, but even the simple task of laying out the mats had been maddening to perform alongside her – she moved slowly and put as much energy into complaining as she did working. But later, she drifted off to talk to some of the kids, and every time I saw her, there was no doubt that she was connecting with them. I'd been able to keep track of where she was by listening for the bursts of laughter she gave off. She seemed happy again – brought back to life somehow by the spirit of the kids of my community, and that's all that I'd been hoping for. When we got back to my place, she'd quietened a little, but she seemed thoughtful rather than sad… But then at two in the morning, I realised that she was still wide awake.

She was lying on her stomach, staring at me in the darkness. I rolled over to mirror her position and reached to rub her back.

'Are you okay?'

'Leo,' she said. 'Tell me about your childhood.'

'*What?*' I was immediately aghast. 'Where's this coming from?'

'You grew up like those kids I met tonight, didn't you?'

'You can't generalise,' I said, withdrawing my hand from her back. 'I grew up black? Yes. I grew up poor? Yes. That doesn't make them the same as me any more than it makes *you* the same as the Queen of England because you're white and you grew up in a big house.'

'I was *not* generalising, Leo. I meant only that you had to struggle just as some of those kids do. You *saw* my childhood. You have an unfair advantage in this relationship because you know why I'm a spoilt brat.'

I laughed, but Molly stared at me.

'Please.'

'There's not much more to tell,' I said. I reached for her back again, and watched the gentle massaging motions of my fingers so that I could avoid her gaze. 'Mum fell pregnant with me when she was sixteen. His name was Mike. He wasn't around much when I was young, and Mum had no real skills and couldn't get a job. We lived in one of the worst public housing towers. And Mike was a bastard. That's about it.'

'Please, Leo. If it's too hard to talk about, you don't have to tell me but I'd really like to know more – if you can.'

I frowned as I looked back to her face. She'd rolled up onto her elbow and she was staring at me. I recognised reverence in her eyes, and it terrified me. Who was the man Molly thought she saw when she looked at me? Did I really deserve such respect? It felt like these moments with her were my reward – the culmination of decades of hard work building a new life for myself. At the same time it was almost too much – like when Brad and I heard that we'd won the Pulitzer and we'd almost convinced each other it was a clerical mistake.

I felt my breathing coming faster, and anxiety rising in my chest. She knew all of my other secrets and she was still here. I wanted to tell her, I didn't want to talk about it – but I also wanted her to know me. It was the same battle I always faced whenever it was time for new intimacy with her. And just like all of the other times, I waited a while and as the minutes passed, I started to want her to know me more than I needed to hide.

'He used to beat Mum. I hated him – I *still* hate him. He'd go away without telling us if he was coming back, and he'd leave us with nothing – no money at all. There were months on end when she'd be begging from welfare agencies for food packages, or we'd be relying on her family to keep us going. Then he'd waltz in as if nothing had happened. Looking back on it, I think he probably had another family somewhere.'

Molly shuffled closer to me and rested her face against my chest. She draped one arm over my torso, and then tightened it. Automatically I held her closer as the memories buffeted me. I would *always* remember the shame of not being able to protect Mum. I didn't dwell on it because I would not be a victim of those days, but they shaped me. Some of the shaping was good – because it made me strong. The rest of it I could only hope I'd pushed down deep enough that it couldn't burst to the surface too often.

'Did he hurt you too, Leo?' she whispered.

I didn't say a word; I didn't need to. She was close enough to feel the way that I had tensed. I could still hear the sounds sometimes; the creak of the door and the stumbling of his feet and the realisation that he'd drank all our money again. He would be angry to have been cut off at the pub, and he'd be looking for someone to punish. I'd hear Mum trying to defend me, and the tenor of her voice would rise and rise as she grew more desperate, but regardless, Mike would still come closer to my room. I was a magnet to his rage – and while I never really understood why, I was a teenager before it had even occurred to me that I didn't actually deserve it.

Sometimes Mum would sob at the sickening sound of a fist striking flesh. Other times, I'd hear that same ghastly sound – the crunch, and then the wailing – but then my door would fly open and it would be my turn to cower. He always seemed so immense and his anger and the violence of his rages seemed unstoppable.

Other kids I knew watched superheroes on television, but I felt that even they would be powerless against the vastness of Mike's power: I was helpless, and I was hopeless.

'I was always in trouble in those days,' I said stiffly. 'I hung around the kids from the building – we'd break into a few houses, steal a few cars – and the older I got, the more I convinced myself that I was just like him. I thought that was who I was.'

'What changed?'

'I had a growth spurt after I started high school. Mike did his disappearing act one time and when he came back, I suddenly realised I was big enough to stand up to him. This was years before Andrew's anti-truancy programme – in those days he just ran martial arts classes at the gym, and I'd heard a bit about him from kids at school. I couldn't afford the fees of course, and Andrew wouldn't let me come for free unless I stopped skipping school and came for tutoring twice a week, so I did that too, and I quickly learned that I wasn't the dumb shit I'd always assumed.

'The harder I studied, the more classes he let me join and then I realised that I actually *did* know how to work hard. I trained like a maniac and I studied like a scholar and everything just turned around. The next time Mike tried to hit Mum, I got in the middle of it. I broke his jaw and we haven't seen him since.'

'Leo…' she whispered. I heard the pain in her voice and I tensed further.

'Don't,' I said. The word was clipped and much harsher than I intended, but I was struggling hard to remain open to the conversation. Every instinct within me was telling me to shut it down. I hadn't intended to go this deep – I was going to keep it lighter, and to summarise the high level points. *My father was an arsehole. I survived. Life goes on.* 'Don't feel sorry for me, Molly. I don't need your pity. The night I hit that bastard was the night I was *born*. When he scurried out the door I knew that I was a better man than him. I woke up the next morning and I felt like I ruled the world – and it was that night I saw the news article about the Iraq war. I redefined my own destiny. I could be someone important – someone good.' I felt moisture strike my chest from her cheek and I realised Molly was crying. Tears I could handle – tears for *me* were a whole other story. 'Don't cry about it,' I whispered, and I was suddenly struggling not to cry too and it was humiliating and infuriating.

Could she tell? God, I hoped not. I clenched my jaw and stared hard at the ceiling.

'I can't help it,' she whispered into my chest.

'Don't. *Please*.'

'I love you,' Molly said suddenly. 'I love the way that you see the world. I love the way that you show it to me. I love the way that you care for me. I love the man you *are*, Leo. But I *hate* that you had to go through that to become this man.'

I love you… I gently lifted her shoulders and she raised her face towards me. Her cheeks glistened in the semi-darkness.

'I love you too,' I said. I was looking right into her eyes and the words left my mouth as easily as any other words would on any ordinary day.

But that was no ordinary day… That was the day that I knew I wanted to spend my life with her.

CHAPTER 23
Molly – August 2015

It's Sunday and it's raining outside – a steady drizzle that makes me very glad that I don't need to leave the warmth of the house until later in the afternoon – Leo and I are going to have dinner together at the rehab clinic.

Before I go downstairs I dig out our wedding album from the top of the wardrobe in our bedroom, and I cradle it against my chest as I walk.

I take a seat at the couch and rest the album on my lap. The couple who stare back at me from the cover feel like old friends that I have long since lost touch with. *I wonder where they ended up*, I could ask, and Leo would smile at me and respond with a reassuring, *They were so in love, I'm sure wherever they are, they're happy.*

Before I have time to look further, I hear a sound at the back door. I push the album on the shelf under the coffee table and leap to my feet, smoothing a hand over my fringe as I run towards it. I assume it's Mrs Wilkins, but she always calls out so as not to startle me.

'Hello?' I call uncertainly as I approach.

'It's me,' Leo replies. I unlock the back door and he smiles at me. The driver is standing beside him, holding an umbrella over his head. 'Hello, love.'

'What are you doing here?' I ask him, scanning his face for signs of anger or pain – has his memory returned?

He smiles quizzically, and he gestures towards the door. 'Can I come in?' I hastily move out of the way. 'What are you up to?' Leo asks, when he has said his goodbyes to the driver and we are in the kitchen.

'I only just got out of bed. I was just about to make a coffee; do you want one?'

'That sounds great.'

'I thought you were resting this morning too? Weren't we just doing dinner?'

'I missed you,' he says, and I glance at him. He's staring at me intently. 'I was trying to reminisce but I kept running into blank space, so I thought I'd come and see you.'

'What were you reminiscing about?'

'I *think* I remember a lot of the months when we were dating. I actually remember now when you started the Foundation, and how hard you worked in those first few months. I remember being worried about you.'

'*You* worried about *me* working too hard?' I laugh a little. 'Good thing you don't know my husband then.' He smiles at my silly joke. 'So what was it you were trying to figure out?' I prompt, while I prepare the coffee.

'I can't remember how we went from "dating" to "engaged". Did I propose to you? How?'

Marry me, he'd whispered. Rain had been pelting down around us, and the adoration in his gaze and the reverence with which he'd whispered those words would have convinced me even if I had been at all uncertain. I glance at the window; lines of water are running down the glass in rivulets towards the ground. Suddenly I realise why Leo is here unannounced, and why I went for the wedding album this morning... He proposed on a day just like this one.

'Go through to the dining room,' I suggest quietly. 'I'll show you a photo.'

I collect the coffees and follow Leo. He is staring up at the wall of images.

'Do you know which one it is?' I ask him as I slide the coffee in front of him.

'Thanks,' he murmurs, and he shakes his head, confusion distorting his features. I point to a photo on the bottom corner. We are both soaked to the bone, our hair plastered to our foreheads, my make-up has run all the way down to my chin. We are smiling so hard that it hurts my heart just to look at it.

'Why are we wet?'

'I *was* working very hard.' I sit down beside him. 'But you didn't tell me you were worried about me. The Foundation had just bought the land for the Centre, and I had just hired Tobias and we were trying to pull together the plans for the buildings so that we could start looking for corporate sponsorship. You rang me one Friday afternoon and told me I needed to leave work early, but you wouldn't tell me why.'

'How mysterious and romantic of me.'

'Indeed. Well, we went straight to the airport, and you had booked two economy class tickets to Yulara.' He raises an eyebrow at me, and I laugh. 'I'd never flown economy class before. I didn't say anything to you at the time, but I was mortified.'

'Poor me,' Leo protests. 'That sounds like such a sweet gesture. I was taking you to Uluru?'

'We'd had a few conversations about it. You told me it was the spiritual heart of Australia and that it was negligent of me to have never visited.'

'That does sound like something I'd say.'

'Yep… So we flew in those cramped seats all the way to Central Australia and we stayed in the hotel there, and the next morning you woke me up at four in the morning so we could go and watch the sunrise over the rock. Does any of this ring any bells?'

'Not yet. But keep talking.'

'And the sunrise… it was breathtaking,' I murmur. 'The way the colours of the rock changed as the light hit it   It was an amazing experience. Later in the day, clouds came over, but we'd booked to do a walking tour around the base and you were pretty insistent that a bit of rain wasn't going to stop us.'

'We walked off from the tour, didn't we?'

I glance at him and smile. 'Yeah, you convinced me to break off and try to get all the way around before the rain started.'

'Was I trying to get you alone to propose? I don't remember that.'

'I think you were just trying to get me far enough along the walking track that I couldn't insist we turn back if it started to rain,' I laugh.

'So…'

'We started walking, and it was *so* beautiful. I was so happy, and so – content.'

'That's right… It was peaceful, wasn't it?'

'It really was. Until…'

'There was a crack of thunder.' Leo says slowly. Our gazes lock, and the atmosphere between us is as electric as the earth's had been the day of that storm.

'The rain clouds were obvious,' I whisper. 'But we didn't realise it was going to storm. The thunder started, and then lightning, and it didn't just start to sprinkle rain – it *poured*.'

We'd been drenched in seconds – not just by the rain, but by the instant waterfall that the sides of Uluru had become. Water was coming at us from every direction and the wind picked up too. It was hard even to keep our eyes open. Leo took my hand and made me run. So there we were, running along the track – red mud splashing up my calves – and shivering from the cold but laughing hysterically because – well, what else was there to do?

'I was going to shelter you in a cave,' Leo says softly. 'I remembered it from the first time I visited.'

'But you didn't realise it was much further ahead, and after a few minutes running, I started to complain.' *Leo, this is ridiculous! Are you sure this cave even exists?*

I'd been out of breath from the sprint I had to maintain to keep up with Leo, but still somehow, laughing. The joy of the adventure with him was brighter than the cold discomfort of the rain; more invigorating even than the adrenaline that surged through my body with each clap of painfully loud thunder.

'I remember now,' Leo says suddenly. 'I stopped to scoop you up into my arms, and I looked down at you and you looked like a drenched cat. But – you were still beautiful.'

'Oh, *please*!' I roll my eyes at him. 'I was a mess. But you *did* pick me up, and you stopped running and then while you were standing right there while the rain poured down all over us and the thunder raged above us, you just said…'

'*Marry me*,' he whispers, just like he had the first time. My heart leaps, and I realise with some shock that even if he proposed again right now – even knowing all of the heartache that would follow – I would *still* say yes in an instant.

'I didn't hear you the first time you said it. The rain was too loud.'

'Which was actually great,' Leo says softly, and he laughs. 'Because I'd said it without thinking. So when you shouted "What!", I stopped, and asked myself if this was really what

I wanted – and every single thing within me shouted *yes*! So I asked you again…'

I stare at him. 'You never told me that. I kind of figured it was impulsive; I didn't realise just how impulsive it was!'

'That's a *really* shitty proposal story,' Leo grimaces, and I laugh.

'I thought you'd lost your mind,' I grin at him. 'And yes, I think it possibly was the worst proposal ever.'

'At least this explains why I can't remember thinking about asking you,' he says, and he smiles to himself, as if satisfied by this realisation. 'I *didn't* think about it. It was pure instinct – it just felt so right.'

'So then we found the cave and finally got out of the rain, and you took that photo on your phone.' I gestured towards the wall. 'I was amazed that the phone still worked because it was drenched. We thought it was a good omen.'

'And then I dropped it as we walked back to the bus and the screen shattered,' Leo says, and he groans. 'Oh, God! What a disaster.'

'When we were walking back after the storm passed, and I complained about my wet clothes and how tired I was, you kept trying to convince me it was romantic,' I tease him lightly.

'Did I do something more romantic at some point to make up for that?'

'Not then, but you did surprise me with your grandmother's ring a few days later; and if I wasn't already madly in love with you, *that* would have done it.'

I raise my hand, and stare down at the solitaire above my wedding band. He'd walked into my apartment one evening and dropped onto one knee, and then wordlessly slipped the ring onto my finger. Later, he admitted that he'd stolen one of my other rings to get the size right, and he'd had to bully the jeweller into replacing the cracked stone overnight because he felt so bad he hadn't been better prepared.

'And we lived happily ever after?' Leo says now. I look back to him and swallow.

'Not exactly "happily ever after". The hero isn't supposed to lose his memory halfway through the story.'

'What if the hero losing his memory is the *start* to our story?' Leo asks me very quietly.

'You don't remember anything that happened between us, Leo.'

'All that I know is that I love you. If our life together has been disappointing to you, then I'm going to find a way to make it right.'

'I love you too,' I say unevenly. 'But you can't make promises like that to me.'

'Yes, I can,' he says simply.

'There's so much water under the bridge,' I whisper, and I feel rising panic because I know that I have to tell him now and it's going to break my heart. I raise my eyes to him, and see the love for me, right there, where I could almost reach out and touch it. 'Things between us aren't like you remember now, Leo.'

'What *is* it like, love?'

All of a sudden the panic inside me recedes and I accept my fate. Calmness settles over me. It is time to end this trip down memory lane once and for all. I can't prolong this anymore, leaving it even another hour will hurt us both too much. Leo waits patiently while I collect my thoughts, and then I take a deep breath, and I whisper, 'Leo, I'm pregnant.'

PART TWO

CHAPTER 24
Leo – August 2015

As soon as Molly says those words, I know that something is wrong.

I feel it in my body – a shiver of annoyance that does not at all match the words she is saying. And she is clearly anxious too – I can see her shaking. At first, I am too distracted by the sensation of displeasure to really absorb the meaning of her words – all I know is that, for some reason I can't identify, I don't like this news.

'Is this a good thing?' I ask her eventually. A tear runs down Molly's cheek and I automatically shift myself around the table to give her an awkward hug. I reflect on the tear-drenched weeks we've shared since we came back to Sydney. This emotional Molly does not at all match up to the memories I have recovered, something I'd not really considered until now… or perhaps I'd just put it down to the stress she'd been under since my accident. Now though the hormonal cluster bomb of pregnancy makes perfect sense, and I lean a little so that I can survey the shape of her body beneath her pyjamas. Molly's whole shape has changed from the memories I have of her – she has gained a little weight, and she is much curvier.

'We only found out a few weeks before your accident,' she whispers. She seems incredibly tense and I can tell she is still reluctant to talk to me about it, although I can't understand why.

'I haven't had time to even think about it. And I didn't know when to tell you – I didn't want to put any pressure on you…'

A baby. I try to understand what this is going to mean for me: I am going to be a *father*. On some level, I've always wanted children – I just hadn't expected to settle down well enough to have them. And with Molly? God, how could I possibly be disappointed – she's remarkable. So why do I feel so uncomfortable?

'Are *you* not happy about this, Molly?'

'With everything else that's been going on, I've just had to shelve it all for a bit. But you're doing so well, and I think I have to have an ultrasound this week… I'm going to start showing soon and I just can't put off dealing with this anymore.'

The shiver of displeasure is growing, not abating. I consider it curiously, studying the feeling as if it's something detached from me; simply a puzzle I need to figure out.

'How did I feel about it?' I ask her gently. Molly shakes her head. I think for a minute that she's not going to answer the question, then she says, 'It took some getting used to.'

'Was it an…' I almost say the word 'accident' when I realise how negative it sounds and so I correct myself, 'a surprise? Is that what you mean?'

She nods, but she's turned away from me now and I can't see her face, and the confused disappointment in my gut isn't shifting or fading. I force myself to stop thinking about the pregnancy so that I can start thinking about what it will actually mean: a baby, a child.

And I hate it that one of my very first thoughts is about how much more difficult it's going to be to leave when I need to go back to work. I don't dare consider what Molly would say if she knew what I was thinking.

'How many kids do we want?'

'We hadn't decided,' she whispers back. 'You wanted lots, maybe a few of ours... maybe some foster children too. Are you upset that I didn't tell you until now?'

'Hell, if you'd told me on that first day, I think I might have gone right back into the coma.'

She doesn't laugh. Instead, she turns back towards me and stares right into my eyes. 'Are you *sure* you're okay?'

'Is this why you've been...' I struggle to put into words the concern that I've not been able to shake. I have memories of us now – all the way up to our engagement, and I now remember a tremendous closeness with Molly that I've not felt since my memory has started to return.

It is as if I've reminded her of that fact with my question. She is a little slumped, leaning over the table as if the admission has drained the strength from her. Now though, she straightens and she turns back to face me fully, and I see fight in her eyes.

'There's more, Leo,' she says. 'I just – I don't know how to tell you the rest. I should have told you already, but it was...'

'It's okay, love,' I say gently, because she's in pain and although I am a little nervous about what more there could be, my first instinct is to calm her. 'You can tell me now.'

'You have to promise me you will try to understand, Leo. I only hid this from you because I didn't know how to tell you. I *have* tried to tell you several times, but...'

'Molly,' I whisper very slowly as I brush her fringe out of her eyes. I'm trying very hard to ignore the rising sense of dread as I reassure her, 'Whatever it is, I can handle it, okay?'

'We separated, Leo... You filed for divorce,' she whispers.

'We couldn't have,' I say instantly, and I pull away from her to stare at her – a hard stare, a questioning stare, because she is speaking utter nonsense. 'Especially if there was a baby. We just couldn't have.' There are tears in Molly's eyes now, and I am bewildered. I have just recovered the magnificent memory of her accepting my proposal. The world was our oyster five minutes ago – now she's trying to tell me that we let that slip away? It is simply impossible.

'It's not like *this* anymore, Leo.'

'What does that even mean?' I'm growing impatient. I have been frustrated ever since I woke up, but this is a different kind of frustration. It's an immense and overwhelming sensation, like being completely lost all over again just as I was beginning to feel I could understand my life, because I knew with absolute certainty that the central point of it was *her*.

I cannot imagine any scenario where I would allow us to be pulled apart. And she has said that *I* filed for divorce? I can't accept that; I *won't* accept it.

'Molly,' I say, and I force myself to speak calmly and clearly, 'What are you talking about?'

'That last year… has been really tough,' she whispers unevenly. 'We fought so much. It just wasn't working, Leo.'

'I would never have stopped trying, I just wouldn't have,' I say, almost to myself. I draw in a deep breath and hold it, as if fortifying myself for battle. 'Well, if that's true, then I am glad I had this accident because clearly I had lost my mind.'

The gaps in my memory are still extensive but I am undeterred – I am still certain of the love I have for her. Whatever happened between us, I refuse to entertain the idea that I cannot trust that love.

Molly stares at me. 'Leo,' she says, frowning, 'What are you saying?'

'If this is true, we have to fix it.'

'You can't possibly know that you want that.'

'The only thing I know is that I love you, and I know that you love me too. Surely everything else is just noise?'

'I might have said that too – once,' Molly murmurs, 'Back when you proposed, I remember thinking that life might be hard for us sometimes, but we'd always have each other. It just isn't that simple.'

'I'm afraid you are going to have to convince me of that, Molly,' I say and I shake my head, but then a new thought strikes me – the one thing that *could* change everything. I lean away from her a little, and ask hesitantly, 'Do you still love me?'

'I told you I do five minutes ago. I will *always* love you, Leo.'

'Then has it really become so bad that you would give up on us?'

'Can you remember any of it?' she asks me, her voice a bare whisper. 'Is any of this ringing any bells?' With some difficulty I drag my gaze away from her to stare at the polished floorboards. I concentrate as hard as I can, but succeed only in giving myself a headache. My every heartbeat triggers pain in my skull, and but for the fact that this is such a huge mess, I might have tried to put a pause on the conversation. But this did not seem like the kind of thing I could just walk away from and resume later after some painkillers.

'I can't imagine a time when you weren't a revelation to me,' I say, when my memory remains stubbornly blank. I think that the most recent memory I now hold is the proposal. We'd had squabbles when we were dating – every couple does – but the good times by far outweighed the bad. 'I can't even conceptualise how bad things must have been for me to walk away from you.'

'But you *were* walking away from me even when we were dating,' she says, and there's a barely restrained anger to her words. 'Every time you left for the field, every juicy story that you flew out to write, *that* was the start of where we wound up.'

'Are you trying to tell me that this was entirely *my* fault?' And although I'm telling her the truth and I do not remember a single thing of this, I know this defensiveness. I might not remember the incidents, but the urge to come back at her is strong – I have clearly done this a million times.

Is that what this came down to – did she try to force me to leave a job that I loved, and did I choose it over her? I find it hard to believe she would ever make me choose – but I also cannot be sure of what choice I would have made if she had.

'Being married is a lot harder than we thought it was going to be,' Molly murmurs.

'You mean it's a lot harder to be married to *me* than you thought it would be?' I say. I truly want nothing more than to sort this out right now and earn back the sparkling affection in her eyes but I'm still defensive, and as she recognises that I see Molly's eyes cloud over.

'We both made mistakes.'

'Do you *want* to fix things?'

'I don't know,' she admits, and my heart sinks. 'Since you woke up, I have had glimpses of the way it used to be. If we could be like that... If that is still who we are, then of course I want that.'

'But...' I can hear the word, even though she hasn't said it.

'But, Leo,' she gives me a pleading and watery smile then shakes her head, '*you* don't want this. As soon as your memory comes back, as soon as your legs are working again, all you are going to want to do is go back to work. And as soon as you go back into the field, we will be right back where we started.'

'Love, I can see that at least part of the problem was how much I'd been working. Obviously I'm going to be here, in Sydney, not working... for a while anyway. Do you think we could really focus on *us* while I'm here recovering? I *want* us to work, Molly. Can we work at this together?'

'So what does that look like?' She raises her eyebrows at me in a gentle challenge. 'How do you propose we "work at this"?'

'We *talk*,' I say, and when she grimaces, I ask hesitantly, 'You don't think that would work?'

She smiles sadly at me. 'I have no idea – we've never really tried it. We seemed to skip straight to yelling.'

I draw in a deep breath. 'So from today, we do things differently – we don't yell, we talk instead.' I exhale, and I offer her what I hope is a reassuring smile. 'We can fix this; I *know* we can.'

'You are so innocent without your memories, Leo,' she whispers.

And *she* seems so jaded. I hate it, and I hate knowing that I probably caused it. 'Is that a bad thing?' I ask her. 'Do you think I'm being naive?'

'No,' she says. 'I just... I really don't know if I can go through all of this again, Leo, not if we're going to wind up right back here.'

'We won't, I *promise*.' I release her gently, then run my hands over the stubble on my head as I exhale. 'God, this is not what I was expecting when I came over here today.'

'I'm so sorry, Leo,' she sighs.

I take her hand and hold it tightly between mine. I consider the softness of her skin against my fingers, and the burning fire of the way that I love her. Perhaps there is hard work ahead of us, perhaps there is a mess behind us that I cannot see yet, but I am not afraid of a fight – and I'm certain that if there's one thing in my life worth fighting for, it's Molly.

CHAPTER 25
Molly – December 2011

On the morning of our wedding day, I woke up in Leo's terrace. It was my terrace too by then, at least in theory. We had moved the last of my clothing in the weekend before, and we were going to be leasing out my apartment as an executive holiday rental accommodation. The terrace did not yet feel like home to me but we were discussing renovations. It was the smallest home I'd ever lived in and it would cost a fortune to make it a comfortable space for me but I knew I would build a wonderful life there... as long as Leo was happy.

He was lying on his side beside me, wide awake; he had been watching me sleep. I turned towards him and stared back at him in the early morning light. He'd had a haircut the previous evening, and except for a shadow of dark growth over his cheeks and neck, he was almost clean-shaven. Leo tended to let his hair and beard grow wild between haircuts, but I loved the civility of his look when he was newly shaved.

'Hey,' he whispered.

'Watching me sleep, huh?' I whispered back.

'I didn't want to go back to sleep in case I woke up and re-alised this was all a dream.'

I smiled softly and touched his cheek with my hand.

'I know how you feel.'

'Are you nervous?' he asked.

I shook my head. I wasn't at all nervous about marrying Leo, or the ceremony, or even the reception we'd planned – but I was nervous about Dad. He hadn't even responded to the invitation. I'd called Mum, and she told me he didn't want to come, but she was working on it. I'd asked her if she'd come alone if he refused. She didn't answer me.

I could not believe I was about to marry the love of my life without my parents there to see it happen. . . without my father there to walk me down the aisle. This wasn't how it was supposed to be.

'I just wish Dad was coming,' I said.

'I kind of wish that too,' Leo whispered.

'You *do*?'

'For you I do.'

'They might surprise me. Mum said she was working on him.'

'Will she come without him if he refuses?'

I swallowed. 'I really don't know.' I tried to keep my voice steady but failed as I whispered, 'I don't want to walk down that aisle by myself. It's the only part of today that won't be just as I dreamt.'

'It makes me so angry that they can't just be happy for you, Molly.'

'Maybe if we hadn't embarrassed them at the awards dinner...' I said. Leo's jaw tightened, and I added hastily, 'I didn't mean that you did the wrong thing. I just meant maybe if I'd been honest and told them upfront earlier, maybe things would have been different.'

'Things *couldn't* have been different because the awards dinner wasn't the problem, love. *I'm* the problem, you know that.'

'You are *not* a problem.'

'To your dad, I am. I don't fit in his world – I'm a worker bee, not royalty. You're marrying beneath you.'

I regretted bringing the topic up. I pushed Leo onto his back and straddled him, and when he looked up at me with surprise, I said, 'Well if I *have* to marry "beneath" me, I may as well make the most of it!'

CHAPTER 26
Leo – August 2015

As I'm pushing myself into the obstetricians for Molly's appointment, I realise that I have recovered a memory from the first year of our marriage. It happens like that sometimes – there's a feeling or some vague familiarity and all of a sudden I know about a moment that had been completely lost to me just seconds before.

It was a sense of being out of place that triggered today's memory. I was looking around, marvelling at the immense windows and the photos of celebrities nursing newborns on the walls of the lobby. I wondered how much this medical care was costing her – costing *us*, I corrected myself – and then suddenly I remembered terse discussions we'd had in the early days of our marriage about combining our finances.

Molly had been determined from the outset that we should just roll everything together. It didn't seem a big deal to her, just the logical next step. I'd been carrying on as I always had – automatically paying the bills on the terrace on my own. For me the best-case scenario was for us both to live at my place and for me to manage the bills on the house, and then we could just separately manage our private expenses. I didn't even want to know how her money situation worked – the trust fund, her shares, her assets – I wanted to stay ignorant.

I had set my heart on an outcome where I could continue to pretend that the vast difference in our net worth wasn't actually real. I'd always felt rich before I met Molly. I had no debts and plenty of savings – more money than I could have dreamt of when I was a kid. But then I married the love of my life and I couldn't escape the reality that, comparatively, I was still a pauper after all. It bewildered me why Molly was so determined that I should have access to her money, but over time, it became harder and harder to avoid it.

'It's *stupid* for you to pay all of the bills here, and impractical for us to try to split them. Leo, my money is *your* money. It would be so much simpler just to roll it all together now so we don't need to worry about a budget for the renovations. My tastes are expensive…'

Eventually I did as she asked, but only because I could see she was getting upset about my refusal and I still felt a little guilty about insisting she move into my terrace in the first place. We rolled my savings account and salary over into the trust fund and Molly somehow set up for all of our bills to go to her personal business manager.

I would never have to pay a bill again. The idea was less comforting than I might have imagined it would be. Was I technically a 'kept man' now? I didn't like that idea one bit. I did not marry Molly for her money – in fact, I had married Molly *in spite of* her money. If I'd had the ability to take her but leave the trust fund with Laith, I'd have done it in a heartbeat.

It bothered me immensely that the source of our wealth was Laith Torrington. If I had despised the man following my encounters with him around Declan's death, I positively hated him after he refused to come to the wedding. I wished I could have convinced Molly to just cut ties with it all and start a *real* life with me.

I am not surprised by these memories as they rise, but now, as I see her in the waiting room, I wonder if I've made peace with it all. I really hope I have, and that our former tensions were not a foreboding hint of things to come. She had been looking at her phone, but now she sees me approaching and the relief on her face is undeniable.

'Didn't you think I was coming? I told you I'd be here,' I say. She leans forward and I kiss her cheek.

'I know.'

'How's your day been?'

'Busy. Yours?'

'The usual. Failed PT, frustrating OT, lunch and then I escaped to come here.' Her smile is a little too sympathetic and I realise my self-deprecating humour hasn't translated as I intended. The lack of progress with my mobility is really getting to me. I was so sure I'd be walking again by now. 'Just joking. It's been fine. What happens today?'

'I don't know. They gave me a referral for tests to have this week but I can't remember what they were for...'

'You're about twelve weeks so I think it was probably the nuchal translucency screening scan and blood test,' I murmur, and I point towards the corridor. 'There's a sonography unit here and I saw a pathology collection room, maybe we can still have them done today.'

'You've already been reading, haven't you?' she says, and she raises an eyebrow at me, then narrows her eyes.

I grin at her. 'Maybe.'

She's right – I was up researching until very late. I am still a little ambivalent about the pregnancy but there's one thing I feel one hundred per cent sure about, and that's how I feel about Molly. I will make myself an expert on all things baby-related if only to support her as we move forward.

❖ ❖ ❖

In the next few minutes I learn that Molly's blood pressure is perfect, that she's avoided morning sickness for the most part but she feels a little queasy if she gets hungry, and that she's feeling utterly exhausted all the time. When she says that last bit, I frown at her because although I've noticed her tiredness, I had no idea how bad it has been. She avoids my gaze. Later, we go through for the ultrasound. It takes some shuffling to fit the wheelchair in beside the bed, but soon I'm holding Molly's hand while the sonographer starts waving the wand on her belly to locate my child.

My child. I keep saying the words to myself, trying to get used to them and trying to drown out my odd uncertainty about the whole idea. It's a human-shaped blob, really – but there's a steady heartbeat, and as the wand moves, four limbs come into focus. The baby does a sudden somersault away from the wand and we all laugh quietly.

'Is it just me, or is that a particularly athletic baby?' I say. 'Definitely gets *that* from me.'

I see the shape of the baby on the screen again and I suddenly picture my parents' faces when we tell them. I smile at Molly and ask, 'Can we get prints?'

She gives a surprised laugh. 'Settle down, Leo,' she says, 'Let's get the important stuff out of the way first.'

'You can have images, Mr Stephens,' the sonographer confirms. 'But your wife is right, we do have some actual work to do here first.'

My wife. My child. 'Absolutely,' I say, and I squeeze Molly's hand and look back at the screen. We watch as the measurements are taken and we share grins when the sonographer confirms that everything looks good. I see tiny little fingers that will wrap around mine one day and a tiny heartbeat that I want mine to beat in rhythm with. I'm so terrified and in love with that baby by the time the sonographer leaves to print off some images for us that I'm almost overwhelmed by the storm of it all. Molly seems so much calmer than I do. She's been watching the screen just as I have, but she hasn't shown much in the way of a reaction. As soon as we're alone, I kiss the back of her hand.

'That's one awfully amazing kid you've got hidden in there.'

'Leo,' she sighs. 'It's the size of a plum! You *can't* know if it's amazing yet.'

'Oh yes I can,' I assure her. 'I've met its mother. It's doomed for greatness.'

'Stop it,' she sighs, but she's smiling a little bit now. I kiss her hand again.

'Blood tests now and then if you're up for it, do you think you could spare me a few more hours?'

'Oh?'

'I know it's a big ask, but I'd really like to go tell Mum and Dad in person.'

Molly nods. 'Of course, Leo.'

'And when are you going to tell Laith and Danielle?'

She shrugs and sits up, then starts to button her shirt. 'I'll figure that out. I guess I'll go see them and thank them for letting me use the jet when you were sick… I'll go soon, anyway.'

'Do I ever see them?'

'No,' she says flatly. There is nothing subtle about her body language now; she's even leaning at an angle away from me as she fixes her clothing. Can we not even discuss her parents?

'It's never gotten *any* better?'

'No.'

Molly slides off the bed. She pulls her skirt up to her waist and smooths a hand over her hair.

'Is that Laith's fault, or is it mine?'

'I've never even tried to get you in the same room. Neither one of you would want that anyway.'

'What about when the baby comes?'

She glances back at me and shakes her head. 'I still see them occasionally, especially Mum. We'll figure it out.'

'And at his first birthday party? Will we just not invite them? What about his graduation, or his eighteenth?'

'*His?*'

I raise my eyebrows. '*That's* all you took from that sentence?'

Molly sighs. 'These are all things we have to figure out. It's going to be okay, one way or another. Lots of families have to have two parties for a child's special events.'

'I really don't like the idea of that,' I frown.

'*Really*,' she scoffs, and now she's glaring at me and I have absolutely no idea why.

'What?'

'You really don't like the idea of two happy birthday parties for a kid instead of one tense birthday party? That's pretty rich coming from the man who asked me for a divorce not so long ago.'

'Do you really think it's fair for you to throw that in my face when I don't actually remember doing it?' I say, as gently as I can. Molly's face turns beetroot and I can't tell if she's angry or embarrassed, until her gaze narrows. Definitely angry, but I'm not going to apologise – surely she sees my point?

'You and Dad haven't spoken a word to each other since that god-awful awards dinner, and I think it's better that we leave it that way,' she says flatly. She bends to pull her shoes on, and while she's crouched, I suddenly know that she's wrong.

'I spoke to him on our wedding day,' I say. Molly stands and shakes her head.

'No, you didn't.'

'I did. Twice, I think.' I'm still startled by this memory, and the detail returns to me slowly. I remember taking her phone while she was in the bathroom and copying his mobile number into mine. I called Laith the first time from the car on the way to Dad's house and he hung up on me as soon as I identified myself.

I was going to leave it at that, but it didn't feel like I'd tried hard enough – so standing in the lobby of the church just before our guests arrived, I blocked my number and tried calling one last time. I started the conversation with a pleading apology and then all but begged him to come, grovelling in a way that made me feel sick.

I'm sorry, Laith. Please. This isn't about me, or even you – it's about the one thing we have in common – Molly. Please.

I was ready that day to put *all* my hatred for Laith behind us. She'd been so fragile and so wounded as she lay in bed that morning, talking about how much she wanted her father to walk her down the aisle. I didn't get her need for his approval and his blessing and I didn't want to be taking my vows with Laith's disapproving glares on my back. But bigger and bolder and more important than *any* of that, I wanted Molly to be happy. I knew I'd forever regret it if I didn't try to get him there. I didn't want to see disappointment on her face as she walked down the aisle towards me to start our life together.

'I think you're mistaken, Leo,' she says now. She's got her handbag on one arm and her other hand on the door. I unlock the brake on the wheelchair but remain still.

'No, I definitely did. I tried to convince him to come to the wedding. It didn't work, obviously – but I called him. Twice.'

If you think I'm coming to give my blessing to the biggest mistake of my little girl's life, you've got another thing coming, Stephens.

Please, Laith, it means the world to her. Don't do it because I'm asking you to – do it for Molly.

Don't worry, I'll be there for her when she divorces you. I'll be ready and waiting.

'You never told me that,' Molly says. 'You hate Dad, Leo. You even hate that I still see them. You throw *that* in my face all of the time.'

'I must still be missing something – there must be a reason I've never told you this,' I sigh. 'I'm not saying I'm your father's biggest fan all of a sudden – it wasn't *that* big of a knock to my skull. I guess I'm just saying if you wanted me to try to reach out to them before the baby comes, I could. Give it some thought.'

She stares at me from the doorway, and then she says very quietly, 'Thank you.'

'Don't thank me yet. It might be a disaster.'

'It means a lot to me that you'd offer that. It shows me that you really do want to work on this.'

'I told you that last night.'

'I know. But – thanks.'

CHAPTER 27
Molly – December 2011

Leo left after breakfast to dress with Andrew at his parents' home, and Anne and Teresa arrived in his place They were giggling like schoolgirls from the moment they walked through the front door and for a while I forgot about my jitters about my parents.

'We never thought we'd see this day,' Anne told me more than once that morning. 'He's so old to be getting married, don't you think? But he loves you so much, Molly. I never thought I'd see him this happy.'

Just the thought that I'd made Leo happy made me feel light inside – and I floated through the morning with his mother and sister. I felt more beautiful than I ever had in my life.

I'd had a dress made for the day – I'd had a picture in my mind and nothing I'd found on the rack had done it justice. For the most part, our wedding would be a modest affair and at Leo's stubborn insistence we'd agreed to split the expenses down the middle. But I'd insisted on handling the dress on my own, and it was a good thing too – it had been incredibly expensive. It was an ivory lace gown, with a trumpet skirt and capped sleeves, and a little belt of a slightly darker shade of lace that tied right at the point of a deep V-necked back. I wore a tiny pillbox hat, which held in place a netted veil that covered half of my face. Teresa and Anne waited in the living room downstairs while I dressed alone, and when I walked down the stairs to show them, Anne burst into noisy sobs.

We'd chosen a small sandstone church only a few blocks from Leo's house. There was no bridal party – we'd only invited thirty people anyway, and Anne and Teresa travelled in the car with me to help me manage the dress.

When the limo stopped at the front door, Leo's mother and sister helped me out, and I looked along the street. It was a densely populated area and the street was lined with cars on both sides. I scanned in each direction, searching for one of the black cars from the Torrington fleet.

Suddenly I felt completely sure that Dad would come. Even if he loathed Leo, he wouldn't miss this – he just wouldn't. I was his only living child. I was his only daughter. I was his baby girl. If Mum and Dad didn't come, I would have no family there at all; it just wouldn't be right.

'Teresa,' I said suddenly, 'Can you go in and see if my parents are in there?'

She smiled at me and disappeared into the church. I walked up into the lobby too, but as soon as I was inside, a burst of anxiety hit me and immediately I walked back down the stairs onto the footpath again.

'Molly,' Teresa said softly, from the top of the stairs. When I looked up at her, she shook her head.

'They're coming,' I said. 'I'll give them a few more minutes. What time is it?'

'It's five past four, Molly,' Anne said quietly.

I closed my eyes and pictured the aisle, and imagined Leo waiting at the end, and I wanted desperately to go to him and start our life together. But the thought of walking into that church alone and giving up on my parents was unbearable.

'My mum isn't even in there?' I whispered. I couldn't cry – I *wouldn't* cry.

'I'm so sorry, Molly.'

'I'll just give them five more minutes,' I said suddenly, and I stood there on the footpath clutching my bouquet as I imagined how relieved I'd feel when their car pulled into the street. I heard movement on the stairs behind me and when I turned around, Leo was there. He was wearing the dark charcoal suit we'd picked out together, with an ivory tie the same shade as my dress. Because he dressed so casually most of the time, I was always startled by how handsome he looked in a suit.

'You're not supposed to see me,' I said stiffly. He caught me in his arms, but I tried to hold my face away from him so I wouldn't smudge my make-up all over him.

'They aren't coming, Molly.'

'But... I don't have *any* family here,' I whispered, and I suddenly felt all panicky – how could this be my wedding day?

'You *do*,' Leo said firmly. 'You're *my* family. And my family is yours now. And...'

He released me and he pulled back his sleeve and showed me the tattoo he'd had made for Declan. 'And your brother is with us, love. Somehow, he's here today, watching you – cheering us on.'

'I know,' I said, and I clenched my jaw. *Think happy thoughts*, Mum used to say, *just hold the big feelings in until you're in private*. 'They should be here, Leo.'

'I'm sorry, honey.'

'Dad's supposed to walk me down the aisle.'

'Molly,' Leo said slowly, pleadingly. 'You don't need Laith to give you away, sweetheart. You were never *his* to give.'

Leo looked so worried, and I thought about how excited he'd been that morning and how this moment of tension did not belong in *our* special day. I knew, with one hundred per cent certainty, that I was making the right choice and marrying the right man. I drew in a slow breath to fortify myself and press away the last of the urge to cry.

'Are we still doing this, Molly?' Leo asked me gently.

'We are,' I said, and after a few more deep breaths, I flashed him my most brilliant smile. 'Of course we are.'

'Then let's go,' he said, and he extended his elbow towards me.

'*You're* going to walk me down the aisle?'

He smiled at me. 'This day is about us, so let's do it *our* way.'

CHAPTER 28
Leo – August 2015

I am adjusting gradually to the bombshells Molly has dropped on me in the last week – a second wave of shocks after the initial shock of her presence in my life. There are so many parallels between my present situation and those moments back in Rome – I was initially sceptical that we were together, but I quickly realised that on some level, I knew it to be true.

Already I feel the same way about the separation. Looking back, I can see that there were signs all along in this last month that something wasn't quite right between Molly and me. Now that I understand it better, I intend to do something about it. Failure is not an option here – the only thing I am still struggling to believe is how I could ever have considered giving up on us.

I text Molly and ask her to skip our usual afternoon together the day after her scan, and instead, I ask her to dress up and come out for dinner and to bring our wedding album. When the van arrives in the laneway behind our house, I watch her walk from the courtyard into the laneway. She is wearing a stunning purple dress and pearl jewellery, with just the right amount of make-up. Her hair is rolled up tightly and pinned at her neck. She looks classy and polished and she's *mine*.

I imagine myself running to Molly and wrapping my arms around her, and as I do so, I am achingly aware the skills involved in that movement are as much a mystery to me now as the ability to fly is.

I have *lost* that, I realise, and this revelation is like a punch to my gut.

There is a chance that I will never again be able to stand to kiss her, or *God* – even to lie on top of her in bed while we make love, or to help her reach the jam on the top shelf of the pantry That's all gone, for now at least, and it's my fault. I chose to go to Syria, and according to Brad, I designed that assignment and I even convinced Kisani to let me do it. And now I can't sweep my wife off her feet to ravish her in the way that she loves to be ravished – the way she *deserves* to be ravished.

'Hi,' she says. I try to pull my thoughts back down out of orbit and focus on the other vital part of my life that I'm at serious risk of losing: *Molly*.

'You look amazing,' I whisper. She gives me a surprised smile, and thanks me demurely. 'But where's the wedding album?'

Molly hesitates and looks back to the terrace behind her. 'I already locked up…'

'Could you go back?'

'Really, Leo – there are so many locks on the door…'

I had particularly wanted to look through the photos with her over dinner, but she obviously has no intention of going back inside and *I* have no intention of starting the night by making her cranky.

'Maybe we can come back here after dinner then and look through it together?'

'If you want to.'

Molly clips her seatbelt as the driver closes the door behind her and I lift the bouquet of flowers we picked up on the drive over.

'What's this?' she asks suspiciously, and I present them to her with as much of a flourish as I can manage given that I'm literally stuck on my arse in a chair that's strapped to the ground.

'Beautiful flowers, for my beautiful wife.'

'Right,' she says, but the suspicion lingers in her voice until she takes the flowers and lifts them to her face. She inhales the scent, and when she lowers them away again, there's just the faintest hint of a smile left behind.

'There she is,' I murmur.

'There *who* is?'

'There's the Molly I remember; the one who could light up the whole world with a smile.'

She rolls her eyes and sits the flowers down onto the seat beside her, and while she's distracted, I blow out the last of my breath and push all thoughts of my useless legs to the back of my mind. I *will not* let self-pity ruin this night. It is too important to me – and to us.

'So where are you taking me? And while I'm asking questions, I should quickly check – who are you and what you have you done with my husband?'

'Our destination tonight is…' I trail off dramatically and then I wink at her, 'a *surprise*.'

'Not fair, Leo,' she complains, but she's laughing.

'Also – it's a mystery.'

'Well, you *are* the writer and I hate to pick you up on this but mystery and surprise, don't they basically mean the same thing?'

'Not at all. It's a surprise because *you* don't know where we're going. And it's a mystery because *I* don't exactly know why.'

'Aren't you a bundle of confusing lines tonight? I can't wait to see what you've got in store.'

I watch her face as the van makes its way down into Sydney's city centre. She's looking out the window, and the warm afternoon sunlight flickers across her face at times when it manages to get past the increasingly tall buildings otherwise blocking it. I think I can pinpoint the exact minute she realises where we are going and I'm pleased with her reaction. Her eyebrows lift with the corners of her lips.

'Figured it out?' I prompt, and she glances back at me.

'Maybe.'

'What a coy response.'

'I'm pretty sure I know where and why.'

'I hope so,' I say wryly. I've picked a bar that I can remember visiting, but I don't know what we were doing there. I only know that while I was there, I felt a pull towards Molly that was deeper and more intense than anything else I've ever felt in my life. I assume it was some kind of milestone moment for us, and I can't wait to find out what it was.

'So, tell me again why you picked "wherever" it is we're going?' she prompts.

'I've been trying to think of somewhere romantic to take you and I just kept picturing this place. I *can't* remember why it's special, mind you, which is where *you* and your fully functional brain will hopefully fill in the blanks.'

The van stops and Molly leans forward to look out the window. She sits back and frowns.

'Leo, where the hell are we?'

'I thought you'd figured it out?'

'No, I *thought* you were taking us to the hotel on the next block, which is where we had our reception. And spent our wedding night, actually. So what's *this* place? It looks like a bar.'

'It *is* a bar.' And a *very* upmarket one at that, which is why I assumed she had introduced me to it. 'Haven't we been here before?'

Molly frowns, concentrating. 'I'm pretty sure I've never been here before. Are you sure we're at the right place?'

'We definitely are,' I frown too. 'I have this vivid sense that it's special to us.'

Molly laughs quietly. 'Well, this is really awkward, Leo but – you've never taken me here. I've never even been here by myself.' I hear her sharp intake of breath, and she whispers. 'God, Leo! I hope you're not thinking of someone else…?'

I almost panic at that thought, and I can see from the way Molly's face contorts that she's panicking about it too. I try to calm myself with two reassurances. This feeling is definitely related to Molly, I'm sure of it. And I wouldn't have cheated on her, I know that – I can't even stomach the idea of it. But it doesn't matter how confident I am about those feelings – I still have no idea what I was thinking the last time I was here.

'It's definitely something to do with you,' I say, and I'm so frustrated at my own inability to join the dots that I groan and rub my temples. 'I'm sure something important happened here. Can we go in?'

'I'm a little nervous, but sure,' Molly gives a weak laugh. Inside we take a seat at one of the low tables placed around the room. I look at the drinks menu and I *know* that I've read it before. Molly is looking around the room.

'Familiar now?' I prompt hopefully. She shakes her head and gives me a bewildered shrug.

'I can say with absolute certainty I have never been here before in my life.'

I realise in an instant that she's actually right; I wasn't here with her – I was here *without* her. I still can't remember why I was in this bar, but I understand now that the reason this place came to mind was because of how far away she felt while I was here. I was missing her so deeply on that last visit that I could almost taste it... but the missing was all messed up with an overwhelming sense of guilt.

This is the first time I've had the emotional part of a memory return so strongly without any of the context, and even *that* odd fact seems to suggest that I might not want to remember the details.

'Remembering anything?' Molly asks, and I shake my head stiffly and lie.

'Not yet.'

I see her hesitation and now we are both wondering if I was having an affair again. I don't know what to say to her. I still feel certain that I wouldn't have been unfaithful to her – it doesn't seem to make any sense. But I can't deny the rock-hard pit of guilt that still lingers in my stomach. Whatever happened in this bar, it wasn't something that I was sure about – or even something I was proud of.

I sigh and reach for her hand. 'Well, this is a really pathetic first date.'

'First date, huh?'

'Oh yes. The plan was to romance you.'

'Did you forget that we're married again?' she teases. I am still unsettled by the things that I don't know, but I love the glint in her eyes anyway. I bring her hand to my lips and kiss it gently.

'Not this time,' I tell her. 'But I'd really like to *stay* married, so I thought perhaps I should put some effort in.'

Molly's smile fades a little, but she doesn't withdraw her hand from mine.

✦ ✦ ✦

'Do you know what this reminds me of?' Molly asks me, as we're finishing our meal. I glance at her cautiously, and she surprises me with a contented smile. 'When we were first married, in that first year, you weren't travelling much. I'm such a shit cook that when it was my turn to "cook dinner" I usually convinced you to come out somewhere and we'd sit in all kinds of restaurants and chat about absolutely nothing. And it was magical.'

'And it was *easy*,' I say. I don't remember all of the nights she's talking about yet, but I know the simple contentment they brought us.

'It *was* easy,' she echoes. 'Just like this. So, thank you.'

'What are your favourite memories from our marriage, Molly? That first year was good, was it?'

'Oh yes,' she says, and she hangs onto the 's' in the word a little too long, as if she doesn't even want to let the thought go. 'That year was a dream, we were so happy.'

'What were the best moments?'

'The simple ones. Moments like those long, lazy dinners out – and when we sat up too late drinking wine on the balcony off the bedroom when the jacarandas were in bloom. And when you washed up by hand, before we got the dishwasher, and I'd come up to you…'

'And wrap your arms around my waist, and rest your cheek against my back,' I murmured, and she nods and reaches across the table to rest her hand over mine. We share a smile, and in one moment, I fall completely in love with her, all over again. She's perfection – and she's *my* perfection.

I can't imagine ever *wanting* someone else. It doesn't make any sense that I would bring another woman to this bar. I try to console myself with the intensity of the guilt. If I *had* for some unfathomable reason met up with another woman here, there's no way I would have gone anywhere with her afterwards.

'I loved it when we watched TV together,' Molly continues with a smile. 'I loved how you'd be so engrossed in your book that I'd assume that you were ignoring the show altogether – and then something really stupid would happen and you'd suddenly have this in-depth commentary on the entire show and I'd realise that you were *totally* paying attention to it.'

'I loved the way that you snore,' I said, and she protests loudly.

'Excuse me, Leo. I do *not* snore.'

'You *do*,' I assured her with a grin. 'You always have, it was adorable – this classy, beautiful woman in my bed, and she sounds like a buzz saw as soon as she's asleep. And I read last night in this baby book that pregnant women tend to snore more, too. You probably sound like a dragon with a sinus infection now.'

'You're going to pay for that,' she assures me.

'Am I now?'

'You are. Literally. You can pay for dinner.'

I chuckle, then nod and go to the bar. As I return to Molly, I have a sudden impulse to take a walk with her. I'd love to link my fingers through hers and stroll together, swinging our hands between us gently. I look at my thighs, flat and useless against the wheelchair. They are already losing muscle tone and starting to shrink.

'What's up, Leo?' she prompts gently. I'm surprised she even noticed my discomfort, but it reminds me again how well she knows me.

'The biggest downside to being stuck in a wheelchair is that I can't hold your hand while I am walking,' I say. She stands and slips her handbag over her shoulder.

'Is that really the *biggest* downside?'

I laugh reluctantly. 'You make an excellent point,' I say. 'The *biggest* downside to being stuck in a wheelchair is, of course, being stuck in a wheelchair.'

'Hopefully not too much longer,' Molly says, and I glance at her.

'Do you really believe that?'

'Of course I do.'

'Even though I've not made any progress at all?'

She shrugs. 'I'm still certain you will eventually.'

'And if I don't?'

'I told you the other night, I won't think about that, and you shouldn't either,' she says, and she smiles. Her quiet faith in me is a comfort and a reassurance. 'Let's go home and look at some photos, hey?'

I'm relieved to leave the bar. Whatever secret it contains, I'm not sure either of us is ready to expose it.

CHAPTER 29
Molly – December 2012

At first, married life seemed amazing – just as I knew it would be. When Leo was home, everything felt right in my world – and when Leo *did* leave, he did so with obvious reluctance. In those early months I felt more adult than I had ever felt in my life to that point. I was a wife, with an amazing husband, and a house to renovate and a charity to run and laundry to do – by myself. No more dumping dirty clothes on the floor, knowing the housekeeper would sort it for me while I was out. I was finally – belatedly – a 'grown-up'.

Some nights, Leo and I would sit up late and talk about the future. I'd known him to be ambitious but I watched his determination to build his career take a leap to new heights as soon as we were married. He was *constantly* talking about the next big story.

'This could really build my career, Molly,' he'd say.

'Your career seems to be going pretty well already,' I'd assure him, but quietly, I was confused. His career *was* built. He was already world-renowned in the industry since he won the Pulitzer – what greater heights did he think he could achieve after *that* accolade?

'It's about making a name for myself,' he'd tell me, as if that was the explanation I was missing. We had the conversation often enough that I came to wonder if Leo was just trying to justify the constant travel to me, or the dedication he displayed towards his work. We were newly-weds, and I knew I had a lot to learn before I'd really understand my husband – that was part of the beauty of standing hand in hand and facing a life together. We had endless years to sort these confusing little things out. I was still finding my way with the Foundation in those days too, and I'm sure he was just as bemused by some of my ideas for my own work.

Sometimes, particularly in the intimacy of our dark bedroom late at night, we'd talk in whispers about the family we'd raise one day. It said a lot about our courtship that we hadn't even discussed kids until the early months of our marriage. I just assumed we'd agree on the subject, and we almost did.

'We'd never fit a kid in here,' I warned Leo, the first time we talked about it.

'No,' he sighed. 'We probably wouldn't. Although I reckon you could fit one of those little baby beds next to the bathroom?'

'Leo!'

'Okay, okay! But we can figure that out later, can't we?'

'Would you ever move into my apartment?'

He sighed and shrugged, but I already knew he didn't feel comfortable with that idea. I wished I could understand better why he hated my place so much. The Bennelong Apartments was one of the most sought-after locations in the country.

'We could buy something new,' I suggested. 'Well, something *old*, I mean – like this – I know you prefer this style. But bigger. With another bedroom.'

'Just one kid, then?'

'How many were you thinking?'

'I don't know. I've never really thought about it before... I didn't expect to find myself in a position where it would be a possibility. Maybe a few? Maybe we could mix our family up? Some of our own kids, and maybe foster some others?'

'I think we could do that.' I smiled at the thought. Leo was going to make an amazing father.

'So maybe one day we find an old place with *loads* of bedrooms. That way we're covered no matter what happens.'

There were so many things to learn about each other and so many compromises to be made – but still, my world with Leo felt close to magical. In that first year, I woke up every morning feeling amazed, and every night – even if Leo was somewhere godforsaken dodging bullets – I'd get some kind of communication from him, even if it was just a text or a note left on the pillow before he flew out. He was always home for longer between trips than he was away, and he was rarely away for more than a week or two at a time.

If that first year had been a taste of what the rest of our lives looked like, I would have been the happiest woman on earth.

CHAPTER 30
Leo – August 2015

'Tea?' I offer Molly as we step inside the terrace after dinner.

'Oh yes,' she says, and she kicks off her shoes and sighs as she wriggles her toes. 'That would be lovely. Would it be terribly unromantic of me if I change while you make it, though? I can't tell if it's the baby or too many carbs back in Rome, but this dress is definitely tight around my middle.'

'Go for it,' I say, and she disappears up the stairs. I shift myself towards the counter – and I instantly feel like a complete idiot as it belatedly occurs to me that I can't actually reach the tea bags *or* the kettle. Even if I could, I couldn't carry the cups anywhere while I operated the wheels on my chair.

If there's ever been a time in my adult life when I want to throw a tantrum this is it. I groan, but I take a few deep breaths and get the mugs out of the cupboard and sit them up on the bench near the kettle. I stare at the mugs, and then I try to pull myself up on the counter with my hands. If there's water in the kettle, I might be able to knock the 'on' switch. I can kind of lift myself, but I need both arms to do so, and my balance is terrible – I can only do it for a few seconds at a time before the room tilts. On my third attempt, I almost fall out of the chair and I realise I need to stop because if I do wind up on the floor, Molly is going to have to help me back up.

That is not going to happen.

Molly quietly joins me in the kitchen a few minutes later. I straighten in my chair, and point to the kettle. 'I can't reach,' I say, unnecessarily, because I can see from her shocked expression that she's just realised this too.

'It's okay,' she says. 'I'll do it.'

'I just wanted to make you a cup of tea,' I say. My words are forced – tightly wrapped in frustration and anger.

'Leo,' Molly says calmly. 'It's fine, we'll adjust.'

But I do not feel fine. I feel a thunderous sense of outrage that tempts me to run and hide from her. God, if she was already about to divorce me, what chance do I have of holding onto her now? I take myself to the couch and leapfrog onto it, but I have to adjust my thighs with my hands and this is so maddening that I want to give up altogether and just fall into a puddle on the floor. I see my wife approaching and I shake myself mentally. *Get your shit together, Leo. Be better than this, at least for Molly's sake.*

'You're okay?' Molly prompts, as she rests the two cups on the table and sits beside me.

'I'm fine,' I say.

She reaches under the coffee table and withdraws the photo album, and she gently places it on my lap. There's no dust on the cover, only fingerprints around the edges – and I realise that she's looked at it recently. I stare down at the image on the front for a moment before I can speak.

'God, Molly,' I breathe, 'look at you! How the hell could I forget *that* moment?' I run my fingers over the page and let them come to rest near her face. Molly and I are embracing in the photo, standing in a park somewhere with the sun setting behind us. She's staring at the camera and beaming that mega-watt smile. Her eyes are alight with love and happiness.

'It was a good day,' she murmurs. She's not looking at the album.

'What was your favourite part?' I ask her.

She shrugs and very briefly glances at the cover – but I notice the way that her gaze does not linger on it for long. The crease is back between her eyes and when she speaks, she's a little short with me again. 'The ceremony was beautiful. The reception was a lot of fun.'

'Where did we go on our wedding night?' I ask her.

'We stayed at a suite in the city right near where we were tonight. It seemed a bit silly seeing as our house was only a ten-minute drive away, but it was nice.'

'Did we…?'

'Did we *what?*' she asks pointedly, and when I just grin at her she laughs. 'Go on, *say* it!'

'Did we…?' I waggle my eyebrows at her in response and then say as suggestively as I can, 'order room service?'

She laughs and her frown disappears. 'We *did* order room service. And then after we ate it, we immediately fell asleep.' She's smiling again now. These memories amuse her. 'We had such grandiose plans for that night. I spent a fortune on lingerie that didn't even come out of the suitcase until we went on the honeymoon. But by the time you unhooked all of the tiny buttons on that dress, the most energetic activity we could manage was to climb into bed to sleep. We *did* make up for it on the honeymoon, don't worry.'

'We went to the Maldives,' I realise this as I'm saying it, and she nods enthusiastically.

'You remember?'

'I think I'm starting to,' I murmur. 'I remember several days where we barely left the hotel room at the resort.'

She laughs again. 'That's right. We didn't leave the villa for the first four days. We barely sobered up in that time, either. I seem to recall that when all of the fun slowed down we were both hung-over for days, and I think our room service bill was more than the accommodation in the end.'

I look back at the album and open the first page, and then gradually begin to make my way through the other photos. The whole album looks like something from a glossy magazine, bright bursts of colour and flawless skin in every perfectly framed shot.

'I remember *that* look,' I say quietly, and she follows my gaze. It's a photo of us staring into each other's eyes. For a while, we gaze at the image together and I slip back into the memory as easily as if it was never lost. I remember the scent of cut grass and the eucalyptus in the park around us – the feel of her soft skin in my arms – even the taste of mint on her lips when I'd kissed her. She'd been too excited to eat lunch, she told me, but she was starving after the ceremony and so she'd been devouring the only thing in her purse that was edible – a little box of breath-freshening mints. I remember the overwhelming sense of love, pride and amazement and – moments of pure intimidation.

I wait, wondering where that last bewildering thought comes from, and gradually, that thought clarifies too. Molly looked perfect that day, like a living portrait: she would stare at me as if I was a hero, and I both loved and was terrified by the expectation and hope in her eyes. She was the best blessing I'd ever known, but her happiness was now in my hands and the task of being worthy of that responsibility had seemed dizzying.

We talk for quite a long time before I can bring myself to ask Molly the question that now sits impatiently at the tip of my tongue. As soon as the conversation hits a lull, I ask her very gently, 'So, when did it start to go wrong, Molly?'

She's gradually moved closer and closer over the course of the chat until she's stretched herself along the lounge and now lies flat, with her head resting on my thigh. This position is familiar; I can remember her lying like this with me even in our earliest days together.

She stares up at me when I prompt the shift in the conversation's tone and the smile fades from her face. Then she looks beyond me, to the ceiling, then tentatively back to my eyes.

'Promise you won't get defensive?' she whispers.

'I *can* promise I'll try,' I whisper back.

'I actually think it started when you missed that first anniversary. You had good reasons for staying, but it was the start of a shift between us.'

She's told me about the anniversary when she told me about the motorbike. I still don't remember it though, and I hesitate to ask her, but the time has come for these painful conversations. Just like some nasty wound sustained in the field, sometimes some painful cleansing has to be done before things can heal.

'Tell me what happened?'

She shifts, and I watch the way her hands rest over her belly, as if she's protecting our baby from overhearing this discussion. I like that a lot, and I am momentarily taken by thoughts of the fantastic mother my wife is going to make. The distraction does not last long, because when Molly starts to talk, the stiffness has returned to her voice. I can see she's fighting it – fighting to stay warm and open to *me*.

I reach down to stroke her hair gently back from her face and she looks into my eyes again.

'You were coming home. You were going to get back the day before. I'd booked us a retreat, up in the Blue Mountains, and I thought we could ride the new bike up there.'

'So did I at least call you to tell you I wouldn't be there?' I ask her.

'You did let me know, but it was very last minute. I mean – God – we were on the phone the night before you were due to fly back and you didn't say a word about staying longer.'

I don't connect with this at all – it feels like she's telling me about the actions of a deranged lunatic, which clearly a man would *have* to be to voluntarily miss such an occasion with this woman. My memories still refuse to come to the fore. I know I can't force them – I spent a lot of time doing that when I first woke up and all fierce concentration seemed to do was give me a headache. Molly is my gateway to these memories. I try to focus only on her.

'So I didn't tell you on the phone that I wasn't coming back?'

'No. Actually, it was very late here, and I was lying in bed talking to you. I accidentally told you about the retreat, and you were laughing at how I had chatter-boxed my way into ruining the surprise. You told me you couldn't wait to see me. I went to sleep and woke up and you'd emailed me to say you weren't going to make it back.'

But I *know* this story only enough to know that she is missing the point. I don't know it well enough to know what 'the point' actually is. I keep my hand in her hair, winding the silky locks around my fingers, watching the chestnut lengths against my hand. But then I remember the retreat and in an instant, the story stops being nonsense too and I understand it completely. My first reaction to the flood of memories that return is to lie and pretend that I am still clueless – I don't want to tell her the truth about why I did not come home. The truth would show an insecurity in me that I'm not sure I would ever have been able to admit aloud before – not *even* to Molly.

I am all but squirming at the memories that arise because it is mortifying to recognise that I have allowed a weakness within myself to hurt my wife in such a brutal fashion. I can picture her waking up the day before our anniversary and smiling, and maybe checking her email on her phone as she rested in bed and finding the pathetic one-liner that I had sent.

I remember that too, now. It said something like *sorry, Molly, something has come up. Can you reschedule the trip?* – as if we had been talking about going to the grocery store together but now I was stuck at the office.

I remember too the punch of guilt in my stomach when I did make it home and she showed me the motorbike, and the automatic but dastardly resentment I felt at the very sight of it. I had wanted that bike forever and it was such an exorbitant purchase, but Molly could make it with a single phone call and not much thought at all. Instead of feeling blessed, I felt angry – and powerless, because this was just the reality – she was wealthy, I was not, and there was nothing at all that I could do about it. I knew that when I married her. I didn't need it rubbed in my face every anniversary – and yet, to say anything at all would make me a bastard.

These things about me are ugly and I feel shame, and I also feel defensive. There were genuine reasons to stay in Iraq at that stage too; a ground swell of dissent against the Iraqi Prime Minister was beginning, and even now as I look down at my beautiful, hurting wife I want to focus on *that* because it makes me seem noble. But that is not why I stayed. And if I really want to fix things with Molly, I have to do what I have promised her and avoid the defensiveness that is my automatic reaction to these difficult conversations.

'Molly,' I say. 'I remember that day.'

The pain in her eyes is heartbreaking – a stark contrast to the easy laughter and joy that I'd shared with her just minutes earlier. I realise that I am entirely responsible for the change and I feel sick.

'It is a small thing, in the scheme of things,' she says, obviously trying to console me, which only makes it worse. 'I mean, I know you had genuine reasons to stay, and I felt bad… I actually felt really bad for resenting your decision. You wrote some great articles on that trip, but…'

But I can't stand to hear this for a moment longer. I shake my head, and the slight pain in my skull as I do so is perhaps a fitting punishment for what I'm about to say. 'I need to tell you something, and this is really hard for me to admit… but I hope that you will see how committed I am to us fixing this. Okay?'

I'm talking too much – prolonging the moment, putting off what I need to say because I'm so utterly mortified to have to say it. The patient acceptance I see in my wife's gaze does nothing to bolster my courage. I raise my chin and I look at the television on the wall above the fireplace. It is huge and it does not belong in my house; it belongs in *her* house. This is *our* house, and that makes it *my* house. Every aspect of this moment pulls at me and I am torn up in knots inside that seem to be getting tighter as I procrastinate with thoughts instead of telling Molly the truth.

'I had planned a trip for us too, Molly,' I admit eventually. 'I was going to surprise you too.'

'You *were?*' I glance at her only long enough to recognise the shock in her wide eyes.

'I had hired a little cabin on the south coast. I couldn't wait to see you,' I admit. 'I missed you so badly, even talking to you on the phone was painful for me. I had visions of this love-fest in a sleepy village I'd found online. I Googled something lame like "*most romantic getaways, driving distance of Sydney*". It was a simple little place, secluded – no bells or whistles, just a big bed and a balcony over the water on this little inlet. I'd even booked a car so we could take Lucien with us.'

'You should have told me, that's so sweet…' she says, but then she shakes her head against my thigh. 'In any case, the "sweet idea" is all very well and good, but it doesn't make any difference because you didn't come home anyway.'

'You told me the name of your resort when we were on the phone, and I Googled that too.'

I remember the sinking feeling in my gut as I read about it, and realised just what kind of place she'd planned for us. I'd been imagining our weekend away to be just like that amazing trip we took to Uluru – staying somewhere comfortable but modest – somewhere I could afford to pay for myself. I didn't think the setting mattered until I saw what *she* had planned. I thought our focus would be on time together more than anything else.

'So…?'

'You called it a "retreat",' I say gently. 'But it *wasn't* a "retreat", Molly – it was an exclusive resort – the price for even the most basic room was thousands of dollars per night, and I knew you *wouldn't* have booked the most basic room.'

'I didn't. I wanted to surprise you – I knew how tough things had been for you in Iraq,' she whispered, and she shook her head again. 'I don't understand, Leo. It's not like we couldn't afford it.'

'I'd planned a humble, simple weekend away. You would have been so disappointed if it had gone ahead as I planned. No gourmet food, no butler, no private balcony with sunken spa, not a masseuse in sight. And Molly, I knew *I* was going to feel *very* uncomfortable in that place you had booked – but that was your expectation of a casual weekend away. I didn't even *know* about such places, let alone think to book them for us.'

'Are you telling me that you didn't come home because you didn't want to go to my resort?'

She sounds angry, and so she should. I hesitate a little. 'No, it was much more complex than that. There were good reasons to stay. There was genuine unrest brewing; good stories to write...' I dare to glance at her again and find her eyes swimming in tears. The breath leaves my lungs in a rush. 'No. Yes, Okay, Molly, I will be brutally honest with you. I stayed in the field because I felt powerful and capable there. And when I looked at your plans for our first anniversary, I felt completely out of my depth with you.' I force myself to continue – tearing myself open – pressing through the pain because it might be a way forward and we *have* to find a way forward, but the words I say come from a place so deep inside me that I could have hidden them forever and no one would have known. 'I don't think I have *ever* felt as inadequate as I did that day.'

Molly draws in a shuddering breath and a single tear rolls down her face. I'm breathing heavily because that admission was hard work and now I'm feeling exposed and unsure if it's even going to be worth it. I touch a shaking fingertip to dry the line of moisture that has run from her eye down into her hair, and suddenly I need to hold her: I need to wrap my arms around her and promise her that I will do better.

I remain still, because I am not at all sure I deserve to have that need met.

'If you had just told me this...' she says unsteadily.

'Surely you understand that I couldn't.'

'Why are you telling me now?'

'I *told* you,' I whisper, 'I will do whatever it takes to fix this. Maybe these conversations, as painful as they are, are all that was missing in the first place. Do you think?'

Molly sits up and she throws her arms around my neck and she presses her face into it.

'I'm so sorry, Leo.'

'No,' I whisper weakly. '*I'm* sorry.'

'I can see that.' We sit in silence for a minute or two, and then Molly whispers urgently, 'Leo, did you remember what happened in that bar yet?'

I shake my head.

'I don't think you cheated on me,' she says. Her voice is very small. 'And I'm not trying to attack you, but you really *weren't* in the country very much over those last few years. If you *were* unfaithful, there were months at a time when you could have done it with complete privacy in some foreign hotel. I can't imagine you'd wait until you got back to Sydney to do it.'

'*I* can't imagine I would have ever have even looked at another woman,' I murmur. 'It must have been something else. It *must* have been.'

We sit in silence for a minute. Molly turns, but then relaxes against me, resting her head in the hollow of my shoulder. I wrap my arms around her and rest my chin on her head.

'I need to ask something of you,' she says quietly.

'*Anything*, honey.'

'It's a big ask.'

'Okay,' I say. 'Go on.'

'Can you discharge yourself from the rehab clinic and come home?'

This is the very last thing I am expecting from her. I pull her gently away from me and she meets my gaze. Her eyes are dry now, but she is wearing a mask of determination that I don't understand.

'Here?' I say. 'But how? I mean…'

'No, probably not here,' she says reluctantly. 'I mean, you were too pissed off about the tea to notice, but I did get those chairlifts put in…'

I look at the stairs. 'Oh,' I say. 'Well…'

'The thing is, there's no room for equipment,' Molly interrupts me. 'And once you use that thing to get up there, you'll realise how frustratingly slow it is – they *will* get you up and down the stairs, but not in a hurry.'

'So – what are you thinking?'

'I know you'll hate this idea, but my apartment at Bennelong seems to be the best option. There's a pool there you can use and endless room for equipment and there are no stairs, just the elevator. I can get railings installed in the bathrooms and whatever else you need – I'm sure there's a way to lower the counters in the kitchen, but even if there's not, you could just call downstairs and the concierge would bring your tea anyway.'

She's speaking fast; trying to get all the words out before I can cut her off, I suspect. I wait until she's finished, and then I tuck a lock of her hair behind her ear and rest my forehead against hers. It feels amazing to be this close to her. Even the vulnerability of this conversation at some point stopped being painful and became its own reward.

'You really want this?'

'I do. *So* much. I can see that *you* really mean it – you do really want to fix things. Well, I am starting to think that maybe I do too. And I don't think we can do this unless we work at it together.'

I do remember the first time we tried to figure out where to live. We went back and forth about it for weeks – she was adamant she wanted to be at Bennelong, I couldn't think of anything worse, and nothing has changed – I still hate that apartment. It's a sterile, artificial home in a sterile, artificial world full of wealthy people who look down on me and who wallow in their lazy privilege. There's no spirit and no sense of community – no cheerful Mrs Wilkins next door, no beautiful jacaranda trees to see at the window.

But *Molly* will be there. I could wake up next to Molly every morning again. And her eyes are pleading me. She really wants this – maybe she even needs it. And if I'm there, I could take care of her and our baby.

'Okay,' I say.

'Okay, you'll think about it?' she asks hesitantly.

'No,' I say, smiling at her. 'Okay, I'll do it. When do we start?'

CHAPTER 31
Molly – December 2012

I woke on the morning of my first wedding anniversary and rolled over to see Lucien asleep beside me. I rolled again, to the other direction, where my phone rested beside the bed. I picked it up to check for a text from Leo, and when I found his email, I let misery and disappointment rush in at me. I thought how much I missed his presence in our house, and how empty life felt when he was away – and then out of nowhere, an idea struck me. I picked the phone back up and called my mum.

I hadn't spoken to her in a year – not since just before the wedding.

'Molly?' she seemed uncertain as she answered, and the sound of her voice was almost enough to break me.

'Hi, Mum,' I said. I was aiming for nonchalance, but was upset enough that the words came out sounding high-pitched anyway.

'Sweetheart, are you okay?'

'I miss you. I miss Daddy,' I said, and it was true. I felt much more than lonely – I felt *alone*. Mum didn't respond at first. When she spoke again, she was whispering, 'Darling, Daddy is never going to accept that man. He's just not. There's too much history.'

'I know. But do you think he can accept *me*? Can you? Leo is away so much; maybe I could meet you two for lunch sometime.'

'We assumed you wouldn't *want* to see us under those circumstances, Molly,' Mum said, stiffly.

'You're my parents. I love you. I hate the distance, Mum. Don't you? Can I see you if we don't talk about Leo?'

I had coffee with Mum that afternoon. It was a very tense catch-up, but I felt it had been a good start. Two days later, on the day I *should* have been travelling back to Sydney on the back of Leo's new bike, I went for Sunday brunch at my parents' mansion on the water at Point Piper.

Dad hugged me, but he didn't mention me leaving TM, and he didn't mention Leo. Instead, over Eggs Benedict and coffees, I automatically filled the somewhat awkward silence by talking about my new career. They did not actually acknowledge that I'd named the Foundation after Declan, but we talked for hours about the work I was doing. They seemed so interested – and I found that to be remarkably energising.

By the time I left that day, I knew my parents were proud of me, and that went a long way towards consoling the wound on my soul that had been left by Leo's absence. I wanted to tell him, but I knew instinctively that he wouldn't like me spending time with them. Whenever the subject of my parents came up, he'd clam up and tense up and then change the subject, as if he couldn't even stand to hear about them. So I decided that I would continue to meet with them occasionally, but only when he was out of town, and mainly to keep them abreast of the work of the charity I'd named for their son.

I didn't realise at the time that I was actually adding more and more layers of complexity and distance to what was gradually becoming a complex and distant marriage.

CHAPTER 32
Leo – August 2015

I am encouraged by the change in tone between Molly and me after the conversation about our anniversary. I feel that night marks the point where those catch-ups we have each afternoon become less of an obligation on her part, and more about re-connecting with me. We go out less, and we touch one another more. She is affectionate with me again, just as she was when we first met, and I can't hold her hand while we walk, so I hold it all the time as we sit.

I suspect that she is working a miracle for me at Bennelong. She won't let me see because she wants to surprise me, but she promises me that once she's done with that place, I will feel at home there. Given all of the energy I once threw into resisting this very thing, I'm surprisingly calm about my home being one of Sydney's wealthiest addresses. I am actually starting to suspect 'home' will be whatever building I am in when I wake up next to Molly again.

But even if I am making progress with my life and my memories, there's no denying that I am getting nowhere with my disability. I still cannot even stand independently. Sometimes I can stand for a few seconds – if it's early in the day and I'm not tired, and if someone else holds me straight because I can't balance myself, and if I have something to hold myself up on. I spend hours every day working at this, and the progress I've made feels like nothing at all.

It's pitiful and frustrating, and I am sensing increasing pessimism from my therapists at the rehabilitation clinic. Their focus is gradually shifting away from getting me upright again to convincing me I need to get used to being permanently seated.

'You're getting around so well in the wheelchair, a lot of patients don't ever seem as comfortable as you do,' the therapist tells me, and when he says it several days in a row, I finally snap.

'Is that your way of telling me I need to get used to it?'

'Well, Leo... for the time being, anyway, it might be better to accept this situation and find ways to cope with it, rather than focusing on changing it.'

I insist on a new therapist, but the second one isn't much better proposing a regime which focuses less on the mechanics of getting me back on my feet, and more on mastering ways of living that don't require it at all. The mood at the rehabilitation clinic has shifted, and it's an immense relief when Molly tells me that the apartment at Bennelong is ready for me to move in.

I visit at her office one afternoon, and we interview for a physiotherapist to work with me full-time at our new home. Out of the half-dozen that Molly and Tobias have selected for the interview, there's a clear stand-out.

'Tracy seems the best,' I tell Molly, and she raises an eyebrow at me.

'There were four men, one dowdy middle-aged woman and a stunning blonde. You *had* to pick the blonde?'

'She was definitely the most positive,' I protest, and Molly sighs.

'She *was* the most positive.'

'The others were all blabbing on about "coping strategies" just like those idiots at the rehabilitation centre. *She* was talking about aggressive therapy to get me back on my feet.'

'That's true. I just...' She glances at me and shrugs.

'Plus, this Tracy seems like a real professional. It's not *her* fault she looks like that.'

'Also true.'

'I mean, you're drop-dead gorgeous too, and you'd never blur the lines between your work and your personal life.'

'You're saying all the right things.'

'I'll pick one of the guys if that makes you more comfortable.'

'No, take the hot blonde. She did seem to be the only one who thought she'd get you back on your feet,' Molly sighs, then she mutters, 'But you should know, if we need to hire a nanny once the baby comes, I'm going to pick some gorgeous young guy with a six-pack as revenge.'

'I'm sure he'll have more going for him than a six-pack – a degree in child development, at least.'

'Let's see who applies for the position. I can be flexible about qualifications where there's a six-pack involved.'

'What was that I was saying about you being a professional who'd never blur lines?'

She grins at me, and kisses me. 'I'll call Tracy and offer her the job,' she tells me.

My whirlwind wife has organised everything for me. She had all of the kitchen counters and bathroom spaces lowered so I can access them, and the space I remember as one of her sitting areas has miraculously been transformed into a rehabilitation gym. I'll work out with the physiotherapist with a 180-degree view of Sydney Harbour to enjoy. Molly has even organised for a permanent dog walker, who will bring Lucien into the city to visit us a few times a week. She's thought of everything. The day the tradesmen move out, I pack my bag and have the van take me to my new home. She's waiting at the door when the elevator opens and we stare at each other.

'Welcome home,' Molly says. I move myself forward to her, push my bag off my lap onto the floor and take both of her hands in mine.

'It's *great* to be home,' I say, and I mean it. She shows me around and I survey the changes she's made with a sense of almost overwhelming awe.

'What do you think?' Molly asks me nervously when we return to the entrance.

'What do I think?' I repeat, and I grab her hand and pull her onto my lap. 'Kiss me. I love you. *That's* what I think!'

She giggles and gives me a very gentle, teasing kiss, then disentangles herself and walks back into the kitchen.

'You promised me a soufflé when you came home, Stephens,' she calls.

'This is a *lot* of effort to go to just to get a soufflé,' I say as I follow her.

'Pregnant women sometimes do some crazy things in order to fulfil their cravings. I would have thought you'd have learned that with all of your research.'

Later that night, after takeout and soufflés, we make love in Molly's bed – that same bed where we made love for the very first time. There are echoes of that night all around us, but it is inevitably a very different expression of our love.

I am, by necessity, a much more passive participant now. We find creative ways to work around my disability and Molly is very good at distracting me at moments when I might have fixated on what I *can't* do rather than the miracle of what *we* still can. We make it work – and somehow, the determined teamwork and communication required add a layer of intimacy that I hadn't expected.

Afterwards, she lies against my chest and I hold her so tightly that my arms tremble around her. Humbled by her, and humbled by the experience of being *with* her again, I kiss her hair and I whisper to her, 'I love you so much.' I squeeze my arms around her again. 'These have always been my favourite moments with you.'

'Really?' she sounds sceptical, and I laugh softly and kiss her again.

'Yeah, really. For me, these are the moments that make what we just did "making love" rather than "having sex".'

When we fall asleep that night, we lie on our sides and I tuck my whole body up close against her back. I rest my hands on her belly, over the place where our baby is nestled, and I feel completely at peace and completely content with my situation – thoughts of work and my legs and even my memory are far, far away.

❖ ❖ ❖

Living in Molly's apartment feels a little bit like a honeymoon, except of course for the hours of physical therapy I'm doing every day. I get up early and swim, then join her for breakfast. We read the newspapers together over toast and fresh coffee from the café, and then we each get to work – but now my work is my physical therapy with Tracy, and Molly's awaits her at the Foundation building in Redfern.

By mid-afternoon, I'm finished and rested, and Molly returns to the apartment. We have promised each other that we will spend the afternoons together – even if we do nothing more than lie side by side on the couch to read. Some days, we meet up with Brad and Penny or my family, or we go out for coffee or dinner. Most days we go for a stroll through the Botanic Gardens near her house and we talk.

'Can you tell me about a time when I was in the field and it was okay?' I ask her one afternoon. She looks at me blankly.

'*Okay?*' she repeats, and I shrug.

'Well, presumably you did get at least a little used to it. I mean, I was travelling to war zones from the first few months we were together and you were fine with it then.'

'No, I really wasn't. And I never got used to it.'

I just need a *hint* of positivity and her refusal to give it to me is frustrating. 'That's a bit overdramatic, don't you think?'

'I think *that* attitude is a big part of the reason I gave up on our marriage, actually.'

'That attitude?' I'm shocked, because I didn't even realise I'd shown her attitude. I repeat my own words back in my mind, but the mystery is solved when she stops walking and says flatly, 'That dismissive, arrogant streak that you have, which only creeps out when we talk about your work.'

I sigh and offer her an apologetic grimace. 'I'm just trying to keep this conversation balanced.'

'No, you're trying to *win*. For you the best-case scenario in these chats is that I have a revelation that it was okay after all and you sort your mobility out and things go back to normal. You can't talk me into that outcome. I didn't lose *my* memory; I know what it was like. I worried about you constantly. The more I showed you that, the less you updated me. The less you kept in contact, the more I worried and the more isolated I felt. There was no point when you were away in a war zone and I woke up alone and thought to myself, *well, this is nice.*'

'Okay, fine – but weren't there times when you were more proud of my work than you were frustrated by it?'

'I am absolutely proud of your work and now that I have a career I have a passion for, I even understand why you need to do it.'

'So, there were assignments that you *were* supportive of me going on?'

'I always *tried* to be supportive,' she sighed. 'But I love you, Leo. I wanted you *with* me. I married you to share a life with you, not to catch up every few months for a few days then feel you tear away again. Especially... especially *now*.' She touches a hand to the gentle curve of her belly, and I nod, but I don't say anything. The discussion remains unresolved, but I keep telling myself that we *will* figure out a middle ground, and a compromise too, and there will be a way that I can get back to my work and keep Molly in my life.

Because the more 'at home' I start to feel at Bennelong, the more desperate I am to get back into the field. It's not that I want to run away from Molly, it's just that I do love my job, and my days feel aimless without it.

I'm gradually reading back through the articles I wrote over the years I have lost. They are all familiar to me, but as I read them, I often remember the moments I spent in the field researching. This is bittersweet – because it makes me desperately want to return and that life feels so far away from me still. But it's an exercise that I undertake almost as a form of study, because even reliving those days gives me a hint of the *meaning* that's missing from my life.

One day, I read an article I wrote early in the Syrian conflict and I see an image Brad took of an old couple sitting among the rubble of their house. I remember a fleeting sense of frustration towards Molly as I see that photo and I show it to her when she comes home.

'Oh yes, *that*,' she sighs, and she offers me a sad smile. 'We fought about that photo.'

I sigh too. 'God, it just goes on and on. How did we fight about a *photo*?'

'You showed it to me when you came home from your trip, and I told you that I thought they looked similar – I thought they were brother and sister.'

'They do, I guess.'

'Your theory was that they'd lived a shared life – that because they farmed the land together they've had the same environmental exposure: they've eaten the same food, they've laughed and cried at the same time and life has weathered each of them in much the same way. So at eighty, or whatever age they were, they wound up looking kind of similar. And I think I said something like it wouldn't apply in *our* case, because the way you were going, with all the stupid risks you were taking, you'd probably be dead by then, anyway.' Her voice is flat, almost emotionless. 'And then you probably said something about my being so unsupportive of your career and that it wasn't forever... blah, blah, blah. Cue yelling and Lucien hiding with Mrs Wilkins until the noise quietens down.'

I focus not on the argument, but on a single aspect of it. 'You felt I was taking too many risks in the field?'

'I did. So did *everyone*, except maybe Kisani, who seemed to rather enjoy the bump in the magazine's popularity every time you got yourself injured and made the news.' I frown, and Molly sighs. 'I didn't mean that. She was devastated after your accident and she apologised to me for letting you go ahead with the assignment. Even she knew it was a mistake by then.'

'But *was* it a mistake?' I ask carefully. 'I mean, sometimes you do have to take risks in the field to get the important stories. And I was hurt in a car accident; that could have happened here in Sydney on the way to a Sunday brunch.'

Molly raises an eyebrow at me. 'But it didn't. It happened in Syria, while you and the militia you were embedded with were outrunning a squad of government soldiers who were trying to blow you up. Are you seriously going to sit in that wheelchair and try to tell me that pursuing the story that got you this brain injury wasn't a mistake?'

'Battlefields are dangerous places. And the important stories are never in the safe zones.'

Molly stands up abruptly.

'*Don't*, Molly,' I say, and I catch her hand. 'Stay, talk to me about it.'

'Don't you understand how hard it is for me to hear you say that? I thought you were going to *die*, Leo! I had to think through whether I could stand to fly back on the jet with your *body*,' she hisses, and she shakes my hand off hers. 'You're not even walking again yet and already you're justifying the next dangerous assignment you take. I just don't understand why you have to keep pushing the boundaries all of the time.'

'I *am* going to go back to work one day. You *know* this is my calling,' I say, and she groans and throws her head back in frustration.

'Well, Leo, I'll promise you one thing. The next time you're in a coma in a foreign country, it won't be *me* they call to deal with the aftermath. I'll be back at home here raising our baby and getting on with my life.'

She slams the door as she leaves the room and I sigh and look back to the article. I see my name on the byline, and I wait for the thrill I'd always felt at the sight of that, and the impatience that's hovering below the surface now that I'm grounded – the urge that is driving me to get well, and to get back to work.

Neither emotion surfaces this time. Instead, I can only think of Molly. I close the magazine and go after her. She's in the bathroom and the shower is on. I manoeuvre myself in through the doorway and watch as she tears her clothes off and throws them with force onto the floor.

'Is that what our fights are like?' I say, and she glares at me as she steps under the stream of water.

'That wasn't a fight,' she says, and she laughs bitterly. She lets the water run over her face and then turns to wet her hair. 'That was a friendly discussion by our standards but it gives you an idea, and as great as this has been between us the last few weeks, it shows that our problems are still there and that we haven't yet figured out a solution.'

'Yeah,' I murmur. 'We need to find a compromise.'

'There is no compromise.'

'What if I travel less?'

'You already promised me that once before. It didn't last long.'

'Do *you* have some ideas for a solution?'

'Yes.'

'Well?'

She pours shampoo into her palm and lathers up her hair before rinsing it off. The suds drain down over her glistening naked body and I follow their path, momentarily distracted from the very serious train of thought I'd been on.

'Leo,' she prompts, and I look back to her face. She raises an eyebrow at me.

'Sorry,' I mutter. 'Maybe you should just stay naked all the time. It would be really hard for us to quarrel if you did.'

'Even my naked body won't be enough to stop you getting on that plane the minute your legs are back in action.'

'So that's your solution? I don't work anymore?' I feel a tic start up in my jaw, and I reach to rub it. Molly is applying conditioner now and she doesn't answer me. 'Would you really have me stuck here and miserable about it?'

'I don't think you can regulate yourself, Leo. I think you get so caught up in that world that you disconnect from this one.

So yes, I think the solution is you not working in the field any-more. You can still write, you can still be a journalist, you could even be in a foreign posting if that was what you wanted – the baby and I would move with you. But you couldn't cover con-flict anymore – not in person – because your addiction to that adrenaline rush is our kryptonite.'

She flicks the shower off and steps out, and I pass her the towel. She wraps it around her body to dry herself, and I catch the edge of it again and very gently pull it back away from her. I run my eye back down over her body. Her belly is slowly but surely expanding, and she's glowing with a ripe fertility that is immensely attractive to me. I raise my eyes slowly up to her face and see her fighting against an answering response.

'We have to have this conversation eventually, Leo,' she whis-pers. Fleeting sadness crosses her face. 'Everything hinges on this for us.'

'I know,' I say, and I swallow. 'But we have *time* to figure this out. We don't have to come up with a solution right at this minute – or—' I drop my eyes again, and then I dare to offer her a grin as I glance back to her face, 'even in the next half hour?'

Molly sighs and walks away from me.

'Where are you going?' I call, and she throws a glance over her shoulder.

'To the bedroom, obviously. Try to keep up.'

CHAPTER 33
Molly – December 2013

Leo *promised* me that he'd be home for Christmas. It had been such a difficult year – we'd spent most of it apart, and I couldn't wait to reconnect with him. He had been gone for so long by that stage that I kept forgetting what his scent was like, and I'd taken to brushing my face along his clothes in the wardrobe every now and again, trying to catch a hint of it.

'Christmas,' he kept saying, whenever I told him I missed him or complained when he told me about yet another delay to his return home. 'I'll make it up to you at Christmas, I promise.'

With a few days to go, Leo emailed to say he'd be arriving in Sydney at six in the morning on Christmas Day – and although I never met him at the airport, this time could I make an exception? Everything was falling into place. We were going to have Christmas Day together, our first focused entirely on *us*.

I envisioned a sleepy day, cuddled up together in bed – and so it didn't worry me at all that I was so excited on Christmas Eve that I couldn't sleep. I considered staying up all night, but eventually drifted into a light doze. And then the phone rang at four o'clock on Christmas morning.

The shrill burst of the mobile on the pillow beside me sent me into an adrenaline rush and I was trembling by the time I pulled the handset to my ear. I tried to guess what the news was before I answered – plane crash? Car accident on the way to the airport? Stray bullet? Was he dead, or just injured?

'Leo?'

'Molly, honey – I'm so sorry. Everything is okay. I'm sorry to call so early but I had to ring while I had the chance. What time is it there?'

'*There*? Here? What do you mean? Why aren't you on a plane?'

His silence was all the answer I needed. Now I wasn't sure which was the nightmare – was it the dream I'd just been having, or this?

'I couldn't leave, Molly. Have you seen the news? There've been protests – thousands of people marching—'

'You mean, you *won't* leave.'

'I *can't*.'

Leo's frustration was palpable, and I was awake at last enough to hear how bad the phone line was, and I knew we weren't going to be able to speak for long. I wanted to rant at him, or at least to tell him how much he was hurting me and how miserable I was about it. Instead, I sat up in bed and pushed the hair out of my eyes. Lucien lifted his head sleepily to glare at me and then suddenly stood and walked until he was able to drop himself over my lap. I sank my spare hand into the softness of his fur and let the warmth of his body be a comfort.

I hated every single thing about that moment – even our dog was now so accustomed to me being upset and alone that he knew exactly what the signs were and how to help. Alone was bad, but alone for Christmas was a new low. I could have gone to his family but everyone knew how excited I had been to spend the day with Leo. I was embarrassed even at the thought of turning up and telling them all that he hadn't come home.

'So when *will* you be home?'

'I don't know.'

I did not respond. There was nothing I could say. I thought about the Christmas-tree shaped vegemite sandwich I'd made. It was a silly gesture – an innocent gesture – and I'd felt light as air as I cut the shape out clumsily with a knife. It was waiting for Leo in the fridge. Instead of being safely home to eat it, I thought a little hysterically, maybe I could serve it at his wake. There was absolutely no point in me trying to ask him not to stay; he had already made the decision. This was a courtesy call so I wasn't standing at the airport when his flight landed without him on it.

'I love you, Molly,' Leo said – at least, I thought maybe he'd said it, given the line was badly crackled by that point. I wanted to be silent and to make him see how livid I was and how hurt I was, but I was too scared that he would never come home and his last words from me would be an accusation – *why can't you leave?* That was always the thing. If I tried to make Leo come home, I was stopping him from doing his work. And his work was important – too important for me to stand in the way of. Even, apparently at Christmas.

'I love you too,' I whispered. I was crying, and Lucien stood again and tried to lick my face. Our damned pet was moved by my pain, yet Leo was never even there to see it. He was busy tending to *other* people's pain – other people's problems that were so much worse than mine and so much more worthy of his attention.

'I'll be home in a week or two, I promise. We'll have Christmas then, okay?'

But I knew that he would not be home in a week or two – not when the timeline was so vague. I knew that his vagueness meant that New Year's Eve and my birthday would also be casualties to his work this year. I murmured something as if I believed him and then I hung up the phone. I had stopped crying by then; instead, I lay on my back and let Lucien cuddle up on Leo's pillow. When I finally fell asleep again, I slept until eleven, and then I was awoken by a text from Mum.

Molly, Merry Christmas! I'm sure you are busy today, but if you do get time to get away on your own, please call past. We have a gift for you and we'd love to see you.

I didn't even bother to wake up properly before I called her.

'Molly! Darling!'

'Mum,' I said. 'Can I come for lunch?'

'Lunch? You want to come for lunch? *Today?*'

'Yes, Mum.'

'With… I mean, but – with—'

'No, Mum – Leo is overseas. It's just me.'

'Oh, yes, darling – *please* – come! Dad will be so delighted; this is going to be a wonderful Christmas!'

I popped next door to give Mrs Wilkins the audio books I'd ordered for her, and she smothered me in hugs and gratitude and then sympathy when I told her Leo wasn't going to make it home. Mrs Wilkins had bought each of us a gift but hadn't had time to wrap them – there was a hand-knitted brown jumper for Leo, a lovely purple throw rug for me and a horrifying pink collar with diamantes on it for poor, emasculated Lucien. I left Mrs Wilkins when her son arrived to take her for lunch.

I hadn't bought a gift for Mum and Dad – there was no point, really – they had enough money to buy any item in the world they might desire. Instead, as I walked into their dining room and saw the sheer joy break on their faces, I realised that my unexpected visit was the best gift they could have imagined. They lavished warmth on me that day – fussing over me at lunch as if I were a toddler. I felt a little guilty the whole time I was there, because I was only half in the moment and missing Leo's presence so dreadfully that I could barely stand it. Once or twice

I mentioned him because he was right *there* at the forefront of my mind – something I'd never done in all of the time since I reconciled with them. I learned that day that Leo's name had the same effect on my parents that Declan's once had; Dad would turn red and get snappy, Mum would freeze up and get teary. If I pushed it, the fragile bridge we'd built between us would disintegrate, and so as the hours stretched on, I tried harder to avoid his name – as if I were ashamed of him.

As we sat out on the deck afterwards and sipped champagne, Mum passed me an envelope. She and Dad were beaming, and I nearly dropped it when I realised what it was.

'Happy Christmas, Darling,' Mum whispered. She and Dad suddenly linked hands and I looked down at the cheque again and then back at them.

It was an obscene amount of money – more than my trust fund. I knew it was nothing to Mum and Dad in terms of their net wealth, but it would mean that I could expand the work of the Foundation immeasurably.

'This is…' I whispered, and I could barely breathe. When I looked up, Mum was still beaming at me but Dad was staring at the floor, his jaw stiff.

'We figured you didn't need anything for yourself,' Dad said tersely. 'And it's a tax deduction.'

'Dad, Mum – this means the world to me.'

'We know, darling,' Mum smiled at me, calmly and proudly, but without warning she burst into tears and threw her arms around my neck. Just softly enough that Dad wouldn't have heard, she whispered into my ear, 'You have done something for Declan's memory that I could never have even dreamed of. *Thank you.*'

It was the first time I had heard my mother say my brother's name in over ten years and although she was crying, I knew they were happy tears. Somehow, the work I was doing had given her some peace too. I wondered if this miraculous generosity would have eventuated had the Foundation been doing work with drug addicts or researching addiction, which was something I'd vaguely thought we might try to fund in the future. Still – it was a gesture that I could never refuse, and one that I hoped showed an acceptance of the person I now was.

I was still so angry with Leo, but as soon as I got home, I took a photo of the cheque and emailed it to him. *Leo, I hope you're still alive to read this. See the image? From Mum and Dad for Christmas. Isn't it wonderful? This is going to generate so much publicity – I'm sure more money will follow from their 'end of town'.* I almost hit the send button, and then I re-read my flippant intro to the email and softened. Once again I rested my hands on the keyboard and added a farewell. *Please be safe, love. I couldn't live without you. Come home soon.*

CHAPTER 34
Leo – September 2015

I wake up in the middle of the night thinking about our argument – *'friendly discussion'* according to Molly – and after a while, I realise I'm not going back to sleep.

I go to the kitchen for tea, fix the cup into the holder that's been attached to my wheelchair and take myself out onto the balcony. The sliding doors are in tracks that would have prevented me from getting out there, but Molly had ramps added. There's not a place in this apartment that I can't go, and not a thing I can't do for myself: she has thought of everything. It matters to her that I'm happy here.

I face the sparkling arch of the bridge and let the breeze fan the last vestiges of sleep from my mind. It's dark, and I feel alone with my thoughts. I haven't even thought about failure in this quest to rebuild a life with Molly so far; I do not actually consider it an option. I also haven't considered what my life would look like if I wasn't able to return to work at all. Sitting on the balcony nursing my tea, I let myself think about both possibilities for just a moment. Molly has not issued me an ultimatum – although I know she hates my job, I also know that she understands how important it is to me.

All the same, the conversation in the shower left no doubt in my mind that a serious change in my role is the direction her thoughts have taken. Was that what caused the break between us? I know I need to ask her about the moments that led to us separating, but that question is one that I have quite deliberately postponed. I know that it is going to be an intensely painful conversation and we need a level of intimacy and trust between us before we go there.

It is coming, and I will ask soon – but I still do not know what I will say if she tries to make me choose. For just a moment I imagine getting back to work. The vision that arises is one of the places where I have always felt most alive – I can smell gunpowder and dust and blood in the air. I can hear the explosions in the distance, and machine gun fire nearby, and Brad in my ear inevitably trying to convince me to pull back.

I can feel the adrenaline pumping through my veins and that strange sense of triumph when I finally understand the situation in a way that no one has understood it before. I picture myself at the computer later in the dingy hotel room, the words flowing out of me. I feel the satisfaction of that moment when the magazine is in my hands and it is *me* who has interpreted the conflict and brought it to light. It is me who has determined how history will remember that moment in time.

Those are the moments when I feel I am the most powerful man in the world. I have overcome the fear – but not just that, I am the *only one* who has overcome the fear. I have given a voice to the voiceless.

I love those moments – I love them with passion and strength and fire.

I look down at my legs, their form illuminated only by the light I left on in the kitchen. They are already wasting – the muscles fading away from disuse despite the hours of therapy I've been doing. I think about the headaches I get almost daily – throbbing pain that starts at the site of the fracture and that radiates all through my skull sometimes. I think about the mental tiredness and the fogginess that still creeps up on me unexpectedly.

I resist all of these things as if I can will them away just by refusing to acknowledge them, but they are very real, and some days they limit my ability to go about even this life here in Sydney with Molly. Usually I try to spin it so that she joins me and we can make it a peaceful, relaxing time of togetherness, but some days I have to nap just to get through the afternoon. On those days, I wouldn't make it through a working day even if my job had me sitting at a desk crunching numbers.

The neurologist has told me that all of these things are normal for someone with a brain injury – and even once I'm walking, and even once my memory returns some of these symptoms may persist for the rest of my life. This reality would be difficult enough to accept had the accident been some freak occurrence, but that isn't the case here.

I stop and I stare out at the water and for just a moment, I swallow hard. It is difficult to acknowledge, even just quietly within myself, but Molly is right: this accident happened because I was in a dangerous place doing a dangerous job. It could have been avoided. There is a chance that I will spend the rest of my life suffering the after-effects of an injury that I brought upon myself.

Even as I acknowledge this, the drive to return to the field resurges and I tell myself again and again that *it is worth it*. My job is amazing – it defines me – it is who I am. I sit in my wheelchair and nurse my headache and know that I brought all of that on myself and yet I *still* can't wait to get back to work.

I force myself to imagine what my home life would look like if Molly did issue me an ultimatum and I did choose the job I love. I picture myself returning to the terrace alone, but however hard I try, I can't even imagine it. I try to tell myself that life would simply go back to the way it was before her, but this lie is so unconvincing that I cannot even pretend to buy it.

I simply cannot imagine life after Molly. I do love my work, and it is fulfilling, but if it is all that I have, isn't my life actually empty?

And then, there is the baby… How would Molly raise a child on her own? She is more than capable of meeting the challenge, but I try to imagine what that would look like. I think about our childhoods and the different ways that we approach life. Ideally, our baby will have the benefits of both of our strengths, and the balance of both of our weaknesses. I suspect even Molly knows that she was spoilt by the excesses of her upbringing in the same way I know that I was damaged by the sheer *lack* in mine.

But would Molly even know to ensure that our child has a rounded education – not just the best schools, but a broad range of experiences? Would she push our baby too hard academically in the same way that her parents pushed Declan? Might she expose it to the things that she missed out on – would she ensure that it understands and appreciates its privilege, that it has an opportunity to be a person who understands the value of work, the value of saving, the value of possessions and achievements?

Would she even have a clue about the challenges faced by a black child, particularly if it went to a school full of wealthy white kids? There is no way around that: the baby needs *me* to navigate those aspects of its life.

Molly will love our child and she will nurture it and provide for it, but she is also soft, and she will want to spoil it – I know this with absolute certainty because she has even done so with me. She will throw birthday parties that are extravagant and give over-the-top gifts. We will argue about those things, I realise, and I feel the slow sinking of my gut. Even if we do restore our marriage, we will have to find ways – *healthy* ways – of finding the balance in all of these vast and countless differences. We have to get past the automatic reflex to speak louder and with more force, and find ways to connect, even when it hurts. That is not something that comes easily to either of us. For the very first time, it occurs to me that if the worst-case scenario does eventuate and if Molly and I cannot make our marriage work, we will have to talk about custody.

As I realise this, I am gripped by a fear that is every bit as real as an adrenaline moment on the battlefield. If we separate, if we cannot find a solution to the problem of my work, then there is a good chance that I would find myself in a custody battle with a woman of unlimited wealth.

I know that she would never keep me from seeing the baby altogether. But equally, I know that she is going to love that baby and it is going to be immensely difficult for her to part with it. Would I be forced into a situation where I only saw the baby when it suited Molly? What would that look like? A few hours on a Saturday afternoon? Every second weekend? A day here and there between my assignments?

Would I have any say at all in its upbringing if that happened? I am suddenly furious even at the thought of an outcome in this situation where I might completely lose control over my family life. I am going to be a good father and I won't let Molly take that away from me. One way or another I will be present in my child's life. As it occurs to me how utterly powerless I would be in that situation, I feel such anger towards her that I want to pack my things and go back to the terrace. The sheer loudness of this emotion is like a slap to my face, and I realise how far ahead of myself I'm getting. Molly is still trying to work all of this out, just as I am. Neither of us even wants to be apart from the other. I feel my pulse begin to settle and I have almost regained my equilibrium when the door behind me opens.

'Leo?' she calls softly.

I turn my chair back towards her and see the concern in her beautiful blue eyes. The last of my rage evaporates. She loves our baby – but she loved me first. For all of the pain that I have put her through, she is still trying. I reach for her hand and she steps out to join me on the balcony. The breeze whips her hair around her face.

'We need to make this work,' I whisper.

'I know,' she whispers back, and she gives me a smile. 'Please come back to bed, I'm lonely without you.'

I follow her back inside and we climb back into bed and I take her in my arms. She falls back to sleep, snoring softly against my ear, but I lie awake for a long time considering the sheer weight of the possibilities that lie ahead of us.

Molly warns me that she will be late home from work the next day. She's going to meet her parents for coffee to tell them about the baby.

'Have you thought any more about me trying to reconcile with them, Molly?' I ask.

'I have,' she says lightly. 'I'll try to run the idea by Dad this afternoon.'

When she comes home several hours later, Molly is upset, but she shrugs off my attempts to comfort her. She takes a bath, and when she emerges, she tells me quietly, 'I'm not going to see my parents any more, Leo.'

'But – why?'

She puts her hand on my thigh and she squeezes gently. 'I re-alised today how unfair it was for me to reconnect with them the way that I did. I did it because I missed them and I was lonely.'

'It's natural for you to want your parents in your life, espe-cially *now*.'

She shakes her head. 'I've made up my mind. If they can't accept you, they can't accept me. I should have said that to them two years ago, because I think by dropping back into their lives like that, I kind of condoned the way they treat you. It was a betrayal, in a sense, because I didn't insist that they respect you. And it's not okay, Leo. You did nothing wrong.'

'We've talked about this. About Dec. I get why they blame me.'

'*No*,' Molly says. Given how fragile she seemed when she walked through the door from visiting them, I'm amazed at the determination in her voice. 'I won't be a part of it. You have my loyalty, Leo – all of it this time. I mean it. You can trust me, I promise you.'

'What happened, love?'

'I asked Dad if he'd consider having coffee with us – both of us. I thought it would be better now, you know, because of the baby. But Dad can be such a hateful man. I think it's easier for him to blame you for what happened than to accept that it was actually Declan's problem. In any case, I told them that you and I are a package deal and that they don't get to treat you badly and have me or our baby in their lives.'

By the time she's finished talking, her voice is little more than a whisper and she's almost in tears. Then she sits up suddenly and groans in frustration. She wipes her eyes on her sleeves and growls, 'I hate being a weepy pregnant woman!'

'You know what will help with that,' I say, and she raises an eyebrow at me. 'Ice cream. With or without pickles, your choice.'

'Without.'

'I'll go out and pick some up, and then we can watch *The Bachelor* together.' She brightens considerably at this offer, so I caution, 'This is a one-time-only offer, by the way.'

'Thanks, Leo.'

'I love you.'

'I love you too.'

CHAPTER 35
Molly – January 2014

I woke up alone on the morning of my thirtieth birthday. Even Lucien had abandoned me that morning, having already taken himself outside, or to Mrs Wilkins's for breakfast. For a long time, I didn't bother to do much more than to open my eyes and stare at the ornate ceiling.

I felt as if there was a heavy weight on my chest that morning, even as I dragged myself out of bed and into the bathroom. I leant on the counter and stared into the mirror, surveying my bleary eyes and increasingly lined face. Maybe I needed a day at a spa. I glanced at my hair, and decided at the very least I needed a visit to the hairdresser – my colour was only a few shades lighter than my natural shade by then, but the roots were starting to grow through.

And then I saw it – a tiny patch of silver, right above my right temple – just a centimetre or two wide, so narrow that no one else would ever have noticed it. I lifted my hair and stared at it, tilting my head this way and that, trying to see if it disappeared. No, I was definitely going grey. I was thirty, and my hair was turning silver. Was it worry? Was it going grey prematurely like Mum's? Or maybe it was a perfectly appropriate thing for my hair to do, given I was now in my thirties?

There were balloons at work and flowers from colleagues and Mum took me out for lunch, but the whole time, I felt *forgotten*.

This was not how it was supposed to be. Leo should be home by now to make a fuss over me – instead, I got an email from him that was nothing more than a promise to call me later that night.

I went to Penny's house for dinner and we lamented our absent husbands while the kids bounded around and distracted us with hilariously poor tricks they'd been trying to perfect since receiving a magic kit at Christmas. But eventually Penny grew tired of dropping pointed yawns in my direction and told me that she had to go to bed. Shortly after I got home, Leo called and I listened wearily while he talked about the amazing interviews he'd been conducting and unconvincingly attempted to downplay the danger he'd been in outrunning a rebel squad earlier in the day. He did not seem to notice my depressed mood, or at least, if he did, he didn't bother to acknowledge it.

Later, I climbed the stairs to our bed and stared at the ceiling again. The house felt endlessly empty and I thought about the life and colour and sound of Penny's house, and the inevitability of my greying hair. I was aging, faster and faster by the day it seemed.

That's when I decided that if Leo was going to leave me for eight months out of the year, I would have to build my life without him until he was ready to settle down. So my thirtieth birthday drew to a close; I had a tiny patch of grey hair at my temple, but I also had the seed of a new dream in my heart.

I wanted to have a baby.

CHAPTER 36
Leo – September 2015

'Okay, we're going to get you up on your feet again now, are you ready?'

I'm concentrating so hard that sweat has soaked through my clothes and I feel it pooling in the curve of my lower back. I nod towards Tracy and grunt as I pull myself up to a standing position against a frame.

'One… two… three… four…'

My legs give way, and I collapse again. Tracy is operating a pulley system which easily catches me as I flop, and she is triumphant.

'*Yes!* That was almost five seconds before I had to assist you, Leo – that's brilliant progress!'

I am out of breath, and as she lowers me into the chair, I focus on regulating my breathing again. Tracy the physiotherapist might be an attractive young woman, but she's also a brutal taskmaster and I am finally making some progress. Rationally, four and a half seconds in a standing position does not seem like a victory, but it is *something* – and even though progress is still slow, at least I'm moving in the right direction.

'Again?' she says, as soon as I have recovered.

I grip the standing frame in my hands and take a moment to focus. Closing my eyes for a minute, I picture myself walk-ing – running – standing proudly on the karate mat – dodging a bullet on the battlefield – chasing a toddler down a hallway – standing to kiss Molly again. 'Again,' I say flatly.

Tracy adjusts the pulley in readiness and says, 'Go when you're ready.'

I haven't told Molly about the minor milestones I'm achieving while she's at the office. It's not that I'm deliberately keeping it a secret from her, rather I'm looking forward to surprising her one day. When I'm strong enough, I'm going to stand up to greet her when she returns from work one afternoon.

'You're the most motivated patient I've ever worked with,' Tracy tells me as she leaves that day, and I nod.

'I have a lot to lose and a lot to gain.'

'It *will* get easier the more we practise. Let's see if we can get past that five-second mark tomorrow. If you can stand for ten seconds, we'll start working towards a step, okay?'

Once the therapist has left, I shower and then go through to the office to do some reading. I've been working my way through my articles chronologically, and now I'm re-reading stuff that I wrote during our second year of marriage. It's been an interesting exercise and I'm gradually gaining an insight into my own state of mind during that year.

I hear Molly return to the apartment and I call out to her a greeting. She comes to the office and leans against the door. I see the shadow cross her face when she sees the pile of magazines on my desk.

'How was physio today?' she asks me quietly.

'Good,' I say simply, and she nods towards the desk.

'Any memories today?'

'I've only just started reading – Tracy stayed a little longer today.'

'Those editions are from 2014?'

'Yeah.'

'That was our second year married.'

I nod, and she enters the room and sits on the desk beside the magazines. She picks the top one up and surveys it.

'Do you remember much about us from that year yet?' she asks me.

'Kind of,' I murmur. 'What I remember most about you when I'm reading these is just a sense of missing you.'

'We were growing distant. I used to buy *News Monthly* so I could find out what you'd been doing while you were away. You never told me, not really.' She closes the magazine and rests it against her thighs. 'You know if you try to carry water in your hands, no matter how tightly you hold them, the water still runs through the cracks? That's what that year felt like to me. Our marriage was slipping away from me, more and more as the year went on.'

'I felt like that too,' I say, and she looks at me in surprise, then frowns at me.

'*You* pulled away. If you knew how much damage that was doing, why didn't you just stop?'

'I remember how I'd pause at the door as I left to go to the airport, and how hard it would be to force myself to walk through it, especially when things between us started to get rough.'

The magazine slides from her hands onto the floor. She slips off and bends to pick it up, and I see the awkward way she moves, avoiding a bend at her waist. Her pregnancy is still not showing yet – but the thickening at her stomach is obvious.

'Well, you never had a problem leaving anyway,' she mutters, as she drops the magazine back onto the desk. 'And you called me less and less as that year went on.'

'I remember times when I *could* have called you, but I didn't. It was too hard to hear your voice,' I admit, and because she's standing right beside me, I gently press my palm to her belly. 'I remember one time when I'd had a really rough few days, and I called you and as soon as you picked up, we had an argument because I *hadn't* called you for a week. Do you remember that?'

'That description covers quite a few of our phone calls, actually,' she whispers, and she sits her hands over mine on her tummy.

'Well, I can only remember one so far. I remember you were so angry with me, and I understood why, but Brad and I had seen this IED hit a troop carrier that afternoon and...'

I break off – startled as I remember exactly how brutal that scene had been. How many men died in front of me that day? Eight, I realise, as I remember the spider tattoo that I had added onto the back of my left shoulder.

'You never used to tell me about the things that went wrong, Leo. You never told me the specifics – this is the first time I've heard about an IED explosion right in front of you,' she frowns at me.

'It was ugly and frightening, and I thought you'd worry more if you knew how close I was to the danger.'

'I worried anyway,' she says. 'I never knew when you were safe, so I assumed you were at risk of death every second of every day.'

'I called you that day because I missed you and I wanted the comfort of a conversation with you. But then as soon as I called, we were fighting and I really didn't *want* to fight with you, plus you know, I'd crave the sound of your voice and then I'd hear it and I'd miss you more. So sometimes when I didn't call you, it was because *not* calling you was the only way I could bear to stay away so long.'

'That's completely bloody stupid, Leo.'

'Maybe.'

'Every time we talk now, I realise how easy it might have been. If you'd just opened up to me like this…'

'You know you're thinking about those phone calls and those arguments and you're thinking to yourself, *if only Leo had called me more and opened up to me more, we could have stopped things from getting ugly?*'

'Yeah?'

'Well, I was looking at those same arguments thinking, *if only Molly supported me more in my job, then maybe I'd call her more, and we wouldn't be drifting apart.*'

She stiffens, and pulls away from me. 'I *was* supportive,' she snaps, and when she continues speaking again, her voice is loud and her words are short, 'Do you know how many women would *tolerate*…'

'Molly,' I interrupt her very gently, trying to de-escalate. 'I *know* that was idiotic and close-minded of me. In hindsight, I can't believe how stupid I was, but from where I stood then, that was all I could see. I am simply telling you what I was thinking at the time. I had a blind spot. And maybe you did too.'

She stares at me, frowning, and then sighs and nods. 'I can see that.'

'We're talking now. We're opening up now. That's what's going to make the difference this time.'

She nods, and then she says, a little sheepishly, 'I'm starving, and it's making me cranky.'

Our gazes connect, and we both smile.

'Okay, let's get some lunch. Why don't you go get changed while I finish up here?'

She walks through to our bedroom and I pick up the magazine again. I open it up to the article I was reading and sink back into a memory of coming home. I was always thinking I'd take a few months off at some point to reconnect with her, but then there was always something more pressing to do – some bigger story to chase, some greater opportunity in the field that I just couldn't pass up. I hadn't realised it at the time, the faith I had in our love had actually left me blind to its fragility. I thought no matter the distance that grew between us, we'd always come back to one another when I *did* find my way home. That seems so selfish now that I want to go back in time and punch myself in the face. I sigh and put the magazine down.

Every time I went home and took her back into my arms, it felt like I'd never been away – but of course, I *had* been away, and she'd been carrying on with her life without me.

CHAPTER 37
Molly – February 2014

Leo came home on Valentine's Day after almost three months away – our longest separation ever. He was exhausted from the trip and had lost far too much weight during his travels, but the minute I saw him, I fell every bit back in love with him. The months of anxiety and fear and even anger disappeared. The second his arms were around me, I thought I had forgiven his every transgression.

I had taken the day off work and he was exhausted and jet-lagged, so we stayed in bed for a full day. I lay on Leo's chest while he slept and I listened to the sound of his heart beating against my ear, and I felt the hairs on his chest tickle my face when I moved. I stayed in that position until my neck had cramped and my joints were sore. I was afraid to take my arms away from around him, as if I was somehow anchoring him to me and that was all that was keeping him safe.

The love I had for Leo was still the most remarkable thing that I had ever experienced. I marvelled that it had somehow continued despite the separations and the fear. I hoped that our love might create a child that would manifest what was between us in a miraculously physical form. As I lay there that day, I could almost feel the movement of my imaginary baby beneath my heart. I could see it in my mind as if I already knew it. I could imagine Leo's joy at returning home to us and his pain at leaving us. I could see the ratio of *away* to *home* shifting and gradually reversing. Perhaps *I* wasn't enough to compete with his job, but surely our child would be?

A baby was the way forward for us, I was absolutely sure of it. I knew I had to pick my moment to raise the subject, but I also had a sneaking suspicion that Leo would be flying out quickly and I needed to talk to him about it in person. The other complicating factor was that I was more excited than I'd been about anything in quite a long time – apparently far too excited to plan my request. We made love on the morning of his second day in Sydney. My heart rate was only just returning to normal in the blissful moments of peace immediately after when I blurted it out.

'I want to have a baby.'

'What?' Leo jumped a little. 'What did you say?'

'I think I'm ready, Leo. I'm not getting any younger, and...'

'Molly...'

'Please, at least think about it.'

'Honey, this is really *not* the time,' he said gently. 'This year is going to be insane for me – you know that.'

'What about for *me*, Leo? What's this year going to look like for *me*?' If I'd planned it better, I would have figured out a way to keep the whiny, self-pitying tone out of my voice at least until we were further into the conversation. But I hadn't planned it better. I was not much more than a clucky, desperate, lonely mess.

Leo shuffled away from me in the bed and sat up, sliding his legs over the edge and turning his back towards me. 'I can't deal with this now.'

'When *will* we deal with it then? How long are you even going to be here for?'

'*Molly!*' he was immediately exasperated and I recoiled, confused by the sudden escalation of his impatience. 'I've only been home for twenty-four hours. I need to shave and shower and eat something and *then* you can start at me about how I've been working too hard and I'm not meeting your needs. Okay?'

He stood and walked into the en suite, slamming the door behind him.

❖ ❖ ❖

Later, Leo apologised. He came back to bed and he cuddled me, and he promised me he'd give it some thought. By the time he left again, we'd actually gone as far as to talk about seeing a GP together on his next visit so we could discuss any prenatal testing we might need.

'As soon as I'm back, okay?' Leo had promised me. And I smiled at him and I embraced him and in those moments, I felt more positive about our immediate future than I had in some months.

He was gone for five weeks on that next trip so I saw a doctor on my own. I started prenatal vitamins. I wondered if I was imagining a further drop-off in how often he called, and how long those calls lasted.

I didn't mention trying for a baby again while he was away, and when he came home, I did make a determined effort to hold back my enthusiasm until he'd had a chance to settle back in. In the end, I didn't need to raise the subject the second time. A few days later, we were in the bathroom dressing together when he saw the prenatal vitamins.

'What's this?' he asked, and he held the bottle towards me.

'We talked about it last time, remember? I saw the GP, she said to start them as early as possible.'

Leo put the bottle back in the medicine cabinet and closed the door. He didn't say anything else, but the furrow in his brow spoke volumes.

'Leo… don't you want a baby too?'

He sighed and rubbed his hair with a towel, looking at me from the mirror. 'I just don't think that this is the year.'

'We *can't* put this off forever. Do you really think next year is going to be any quieter for you?'

Leo hooked the towel onto the rail and turned to face me directly. 'Give me a year,' he said.

'A year?' I repeated. My heart sank. 'But…'

'Molly, I'm not ready. When we do this, I want to do it properly. I want to be here for you… with you. We'll talk about it this time next year, okay?'

He brushed a kiss on my cheek as he passed me, but he didn't wait for my reaction – he headed straight upstairs to his office.

'Leo,' I called, and ran up the stairs after him.

'On the phone,' he whispered, as soon as I entered the room, and then louder, 'Oh, hey, Brad! Yeah – how did that editing go?'

But I wasn't going to let him off that easily – I stood behind him for several minutes, and then when he continued to ignore my presence, I walked to his desk and pushed some paperwork aside to sit right in front of him. He frowned at me.

'Hang on, Brad.'

'You can't walk out on a conversation like that.'

'And *you* can't force me to be ready when I'm not,' Leo said pointedly. 'I'm on the phone, Molly. We will talk about this – and soon. But not right now.'

'*When?*'

He sighed impatiently, and turned his back on me to resume the phone call. 'Yeah, I'm back. No – nothing. Just Molly.'

❖ ❖ ❖

I convinced myself that the gradual fading off of Leo's communication with me was simply a consequence of our marriage now being a couple of years old, so over the next few months I decided I would make a determined effort to reach him more often.

When a day passed and he didn't call me, I'd send him an email, even if it was just a line or two asking how he was and telling him about my day. Sometimes he wrote back, sometimes he did not – but I felt better for having made the effort. When he called me one night, I asked him.

'Leo, can you call me more often?'

'Honey – it's so difficult, you know what it's like. I'm travelling all of the time and often not in the best circumstances...'

'Can I call *you*, then?' I had always been reluctant to call the satellite phone, knowing instinctively that I should save that intrusive method of contacting him for an emergency. His sigh stung and I was instantly defensive. 'Don't *sigh* at me! You were only ever going to travel for three weeks at a time, remember? Six trips a year, you said at one point? You're away *all of the time* now. I'm supportive – I'm patient – but you need to make some kind of effort.'

'I have a *job* to do, Molly, for Christ's sake!'

'Brad has the same job, Leo. And he calls Penny and the kids every single day.'

There was silence on the line and I thought it had dropped out altogether. I swore and moved to hang up.

'I'll try harder,' he said suddenly. 'I'm sorry, okay?'

'I don't mean to nag you, Leo. I just miss you so much.'

'I know, honey. I'll try. We can do better.'

For a week or so he did call more frequently, but the calls quickly dropped off again and so in June, I decided I'd mark his calls on a calendar so that I could track when I *did* hear from him. It seemed inconceivable that Leo might be distancing himself from me even more, but when I looked back at the end of the month and saw a clearly decreasing pattern of contact, I really started to worry. I emailed to ask him when he was coming home, and he replied quickly and told me it was still a while off. Upset, I called Penny.

'Sorry, Molly. I can't talk now. Brad and I are just taking Zane to the movies for a special—'

'Brad is *home?*' I shrieked the words, and then found myself breathless, as if she'd winded me.

'Didn't Leo tell you? He's been home for a few days – I thought Leo was coming soon too?'

'No,' I said. 'Sorry to interrupt you.'

When Leo called me two days later, I did not pick up the call. I hadn't emailed him since I'd learned that Brad was home, but that night I sat at the computer and I fired off a missive.

If Brad can manage to get himself home, then surely you can at least give me a date when I can expect you. I am sick to death of this. Do you not understand how difficult it is for me? You just have to find a way to bring some balance to our lives because I cannot go on this way.

And his response was waiting when I woke up the next day.

You knew what my job was when you married me, Molly. You know how important what I'm doing here is. This war is ugly and it's brutal. So I come home to you to make you feel better, who is going to be here? I'm doing this for us too. I need to build my career, you know that. I know you are feeling neglected and I will try harder but I am not coming home because you're having a hissy fit. I still have work to do here and my work takes priority over your tantrum.

When he called that night, I picked up the call, hung up on him, then turned my phone off. I didn't reply to his email and he didn't call again. Every other time we'd even squabbled while he was in the field, I'd hasten to apologise in case he was injured or killed before we could make up, but not this time. Days passed, and I felt cold inside, and desperate. Every midnight that rolled past saw me more hurt, and closer to resentment. I thought childish things – like *what if I just move out while he's overseas and see how long it takes him to notice?* And *maybe next time he comes home I'll get on a plane and go to the most violent war zone I can think of and hide out in a hotel for a week just so he can see what it feels like.*

All I wanted was Leo. I wanted the man he was, and I wanted the love we shared. I didn't want to change him; I just wanted to *access* him. A life with Leo was what I'd signed up for – not this endless series of pauses and delays.

✦ ✦ ✦

I got the 'flu that week. I think it was a combination of being stressed out of my mind over the situation with Leo, mixed in with a decent dose of bad timing – the staff at the Foundation had been passing the bug around since the cold weather began. I was on the couch under a throw rug watching soppy movies with Lucien cuddled up on my lap and tissues strewn all over the place.

I screamed when the door opened – which made Leo scream too, because he was no doubt assuming I was at work at 2 p.m. on a Thursday afternoon. After the initial shock, we both recovered and we spent the next hour falling over ourselves to apologise. By that stage, we'd been married long enough to have a few serious disagreements but we'd never let distance grow between us like that before and I thought the incident would be a wake-up call.

'You mean everything to me, Molly,' he said. 'I know this is hard, but I sometimes forget *how* hard it is for you. I just need to focus on my career for a little longer – after this Syrian stuff settles down, I can take a proper holiday and we can spend time reconnecting.'

That visit home was different for a lot of reasons. It was the first – and only – time he'd ever left the field because he was worried about me. I was so sure it was a turning point that I dared to bring up the subject of a baby again during that week. We were each making such an effort – being careful to nurture one another and to enjoy our time together. The timing felt right to me.

I raised the subject over breakfast one morning. Leo was reading on his Kindle while we ate and I'd made a point of clearing my throat a few times. Eventually he glanced at me. 'Are you still feeling sick?'

'I'm fine, I was trying to get your attention. Do you remember what we talked about last time you were here? I know you asked for a year but I just thought maybe we could think about it now.'

He sat the Kindle down and looked at me.

'I don't think it's the right time. I want to be *here* for you and the baby when the time comes.'

I took a deep breath, better prepared for this discussion than I had been the first time.

'It takes some couples years to fall pregnant and *we* are rarely in the same room, so I'm assuming it will take us a while. And even if I did, by some miracle, fall pregnant straight away, it takes months for a pregnancy to progress. You don't need to be *here* for the pregnancy.'

'Molly...' he pleaded with me.

My hand was on the table and I waited for him to reach for it, but he didn't, and for some reason that stung. I raised my chin. 'There are so many things that suck about being your wife,' I said flatly. 'I am here alone most of the year and I hate it. I am frightened for you all of the time. But you *can't* ask me to wait forever for this too. I can't miss my shot at motherhood because you love your job too much to let me have it.'

When we were talking face to face, there was never any doubt at all when I'd pushed Leo too far. His withdrawal was often a physical one – even when he didn't just get up and walk away from me, I could watch his expression close off.

'I'll think about it,' he said – but I knew that he was not going to think about it. I knew that he was simply paying lip service to my request. There was no doubt at all in my mind that if I did not ask again, he would never raise the subject.

'Do you not want children anymore?'

'You *know* I do.'

'I don't understand, Leo. I don't understand why we can't even talk about this now.'

'Because I'm not ready, Molly. It's not something you can nag me into, I'm either ready or I'm *not*.'

'You at least owe me the courtesy of an explanation.'

'You know how much my job means to me.'

'This has nothing to do with your *job*.'

'Are you seriously trying to convince me this *isn't* a way to guilt me out of travelling so much? Do you even want a kid?'

'You *know* I do!' I exclaimed, 'More than anything.'

'More than *us*?'

'What is *that* supposed to mean?'

'It means, if you keep pushing me like this, Molly – God – I don't know whether I can take much more of this. You *have* to respect my decision.'

I got up from the table and slammed my chair roughly back into place, then walked up the stairs, stomping my feet like a child. Leo didn't come after me – I didn't even expect him to.

✦ ✦ ✦

Even as the tension between us began to wind tighter over the months that followed, I still rejoiced whenever Leo came home. I'd be so excited when he walked in the door that I'd struggle to contain my enthusiasm, even if he was exhausted, even if he smelt like a man *smells* after weeks in a war zone. I'd force myself to wait up for him, or to wake up early so that I could greet him, but then when he walked in the door I'd have to give him space to make his damned vegemite on toast and take a few moments to decompress.

Inevitably, though, he'd join me on the couch and he'd pull me close against him and bury his face in my hair and tell me how much he'd missed me, and how wonderful I looked, and how difficult it had been to stay away so long. Those moments were the golden jewels that I lived for. The times in between were becoming more fraught by the day.

I told myself many lies in trying to deal with this reality. I could almost convince myself that he was just really caught up in his work. And he was busy – travelling regularly between Syria, Iraq and Turkey at that stage. He was excited that he'd been asked to consult on Middle Eastern affairs for *News Monthly*'s parent company. More frequently he started accepting invitations for television interviews, giving commentary and explaining the crises for an international audience.

So his career was soaring, but sometimes, when he rang, all *we* did was fight.

'You haven't called for six days, or emailed. The only time I've had any contact at all with you this week was when I saw you on television.'

'Molly, you know I'm busy—'

'I'm busy too!' I snapped. 'My work is important *too!* You don't ask about it, you don't even know about it anymore. My assistant knows more about my life than you do.'

'If you're wondering why I hardly call at the moment, it's because whenever I do, you're like this. I don't know what you think I can do about this. Do you want me to *resign*?'

And then we were talking over one another, and we were each rushing to speak fast so that we could fit more words in before we got cut off – and anything that even looked like communication between us stopped.

'I'm *going*! I'm standing in a war zone, for Christ's sake! Families are being torn apart by this war, get some perspective…'

'I want to *see* you, Leo. Can't you understand that? I want so much for us to be a family and…'

'I told you, I'm thinking about it.'

'Yeah, you told me. Plenty of times. Just how *long* does it take to make a decision? Do you even realise that time doesn't stop just because you're not here?'

'I'm going, Molly.'

'Fine. Fuck you!'

I knew that at least part of the reason he was pulling away was that I was pressuring him about starting a family. But in some ways my desire – and increasingly – my *desperation* for a child was not at all a rational thing. I thought about it constantly – every night I dreamt about what it would be like to be pregnant with Leo's child. It seemed as if every woman I knew was pregnant or thinking about becoming pregnant – Teresa had just given birth to River, there was a bunch of women at work who were pregnant too, but the most difficult pregnancy for me to deal with though was Penny's. She looked absolutely ripe with fortune and love – there wasn't any way I could have been more jealous of her. We'd become fairly close but I started visiting her more often, wanting to look once more at that lovely pregnant belly and to feel the movement of the baby beneath her skin.

Penny was always keen to catch up over dinner or coffee, even if we'd only seen each other a few days earlier. But the more I visited her, the more aware I was of how much better Brad was at staying in touch than Leo. He called at least once a day and he always stayed on the line or video chat long enough to talk to Penny and both kids. Somehow, she was *always* up-to-date with his travel plans and she seemed to know all of the details of whatever it was he was working on.

All I knew most of the time was that Leo was in danger. In fact, I only found out he was coming back because I was at Penny's house when Brad called, and Leo yelled from somewhere in the background, 'Tell Molly I'm coming too. Thursday night!'

I saw the look on Penny's face that night; she pitied me.

On Thursday night, I waited on the couch for Leo as I always did. The door opened and he stepped inside.

'Hi,' he said quietly.

'Hi,' I said. Leo dumped his bags on the floor and walked through to the kitchen. He made his vegemite toast and I waited there in the lounge. Every second I waited was torture, as it always was. I couldn't wait for him to come and sit beside me and to envelop me in those strong arms. That was the one moment in the awful cycle of leaving and returning when everything was okay.

Leo finished his snack and he started walking back towards the living area. I sat up – eagerly anticipating *my* moment. When he turned at the stairs and disappeared towards the bedroom, I finally realised that my marriage was in serious trouble. By that stage I was battling two furiously competing voices in my head whenever I considered our situation. There was the incessantly demanding voice that constantly suggested that only a baby would solve the difficulties we were facing. A baby would surely bring us closer together, return his focus to me, and to us, and that would mean a fresh start. Our love could be like it was – maybe even better.

The demanding voice also reminded me of all of Leo's flaws – of how much he'd hurt me over the years of our marriage by prioritising his work over me – of how guilty he made me feel when I complained, because how could my emotional needs possibly compare to the work he was doing?

Resentment had taken root in my heart, and it grew every time that demanding voice reminded me of the promises made on our wedding day, and how Leo seemed to have accepted without any fight at all that our emotional intimacy might disappear altogether. Resentment breeds disdain, and that's an ugly, toxic element in a relationship. It is the opposite of respect – the two things simply cannot exist in the same space.

Disdain meant that when I talked to Leo, I was bitchy and I was mean. Disdain meant that when he was dismissive of me, I felt I had the right to demonise him. I forgot the good in him and overlooked all of the fine qualities of the man that I had fallen in love with – when disdain took hold all I wanted to see was the *bad*.

Then there was the sensible voice – the voice of love. This voice was quieter and gentler. It worried for Leo. He had always loved his work but it had taken on a completely obsessive focus that I just couldn't understand. The sensible voice pointed out to me that Leo and I were barely communicating and that this lonely, tension-filled home was not a place to bring a child into. The sensible voice told me that the way forward was not a baby but the hard work of reconnecting with Leo and dealing with our issues.

The sensible voice had convinced me to enrol in a course of therapy. The demanding voice made me sit in those sessions with the very patient psychologist and play the victim, focusing on all Leo's faults, forgetting this was also the man that I loved with all my heart. Those sessions were not about me finding a way through the pain of our situation, they were about me convincing the psychologist that I deserved her pity because my situation was bad and entirely out of my control.

Every time Leo and I fought, the sensible voice grew weaker and the demanding voice grew in power. Yes, Leo was apparently fixated on his career but I was well on my way becoming irrationally baby-obsessed too. A long while after he went to bed that night, when I knew he'd be sound asleep and I wouldn't need to face him, I walked up the stairs to the bathroom and took the prenatal vitamins I'd been taking every day for over a year, and I stared at the foil contraceptive pill packet that rested behind it.

I hadn't actually stopped taking my pill. That seemed sinister – *evil* – unfair. Instead, I had become very forgetful about taking it and that month's packet represented a polka-dot pattern of inconsistency.

Leo was home for a week that time, and for all of our ups and downs, we'd never had a period like that before. Even when we were in the same room he felt distant, and when he looked at me his eyes were always cold, almost hostile. In the seven days he was home, he did not touch me once, not even an accidental brush of our hands. The one time I tried to get through to him we were walking from the car to Brad and Penny's house. I reached for his hand and he shifted away from me and stuffed it in his pocket.

'What was that about?' I demanded, stopping dead in my tracks.

'What?' he glanced back at me, but there was guilt in his gaze.

'You just *avoided* me when I tried to hold your hand.'

He frowned and shook his head dismissively, then knocked loudly on the door. Before I could push any harder, Brad and Penny's son Zane greeted us with wild excitement and it was time to go inside.

I couldn't miss the contrast between Leo and me and Brad and Penny at dinner that night. Penny was very heavily pregnant, and Brad apparently couldn't keep his hands off her. He kept making jokes layered with innuendo, which made her roll her eyes at him, and every now and again, I'd catch them just grinning at one another across the table.

Leo barely spoke to me. The one time I tried to make a joke to lighten the mood, it fell heavily flat.

'...So I said Brad could go back to Syria next week, Leo, but if he gets stuck there and he has to skype into the c-section next month, I'll castrate him the minute he gets back in the country,' Penny said wryly. 'That's a fair deal, isn't it?'

'That's so funny,' I said. 'Leo has decided the *only* way we'll have kids is if he can just skype into the birth. Right, honey?'

Leo stared at me expressionlessly, and then excused himself and went to the bathroom, leaving me to deal with the awkward aftermath with Brad and Penny. Brad made unconvincing noises about checking on their daughter Imogen, who had long since gone to sleep. Penny poured me a glass of wine and pushed it across the table.

'Drink this for both of us – I feel ill at having witnessed that moment between you,' she said.

I picked up the wine and drank it in one long motion.

'I don't know what I'm going to do,' I whispered when I'd finished the wine.

'Go home, put on some frilly knickers, and try to pretend that the last six months haven't happened,' Penny suggested quietly.

'He won't even hold my hand,' I told her.

She leant forward and whispered to me urgently, 'Then you *need* to talk to him, Molly, and figure this out. You two can't possibly go on like this.'

Leo returned then, but he didn't take his seat again.

'I've called the car,' he said. 'I need to do some work tonight, so we need to get going.'

We said our awkward goodbyes and travelled back to the terrace in silence. As soon we stepped inside, Leo made his way towards the stairs.

'*No*,' I said, with force. 'We need to talk.'

'I don't have the energy to fight with you tonight.'

'I don't want to fight either, I promise.'

We sat at the dining room table beneath the wall of photos from our life together. I was in the unfortunate position of facing the images, so every time I looked up, I saw a happy version of myself that felt like photographs from a past life or a parallel universe.

'What's going on, Leo?'

I listened to the clock on the kitchen wall tick as I waited for his answer. He stared at the table for a while, and then he raised his eyes to me. 'This isn't working anymore, Molly. We want different things out of life, don't we?'

'Don't say that. That's not true.'

'Isn't it? You want a baby, I want to focus on my career – I don't want to feel obligated to fly back to Sydney every five minutes.'

'*Obligated*?' I repeated, and I'd been so calm up until that moment, but the way that he said that made me feel like I was nothing more than a burden to him. My voice rose, and I knew that my promise of not arguing had been made in vain. 'I have been so patient with you, Leo.'

'But you *haven't*, Molly,' he said tightly. 'Not really.'

'Leo, I've put up with two and a half years of this part-time marriage. If that's not patient, I don't know what is.' I was so angry that the words shook in time with my hands.

Leo sighed heavily, as if I was being completely unreasonable, and then he spread his palms wide on the table. 'We are barely even friends anymore, Molly.'

'It doesn't *have* to be this way,' I snapped. 'If you don't like it, change it.'

'Well, how *do* we change it then?' he said, and he raised his eyebrows at me pointedly. 'Tell me, Molly – how do we find a way forward where I still travel as much as I need to, and you don't spend your whole life back here feeling hard done by?'

'You travel *less*!' I exclaimed. 'Surely it's not asking too much for you to prioritise your wife above your career for at least half of the year?'

Leo blew out a heavy breath, and then he said, 'Molly, that's not going to happen. Not any time soon.'

'Can't you see what this is doing to us? To *me*?' I gasped, and he tapped his fingers against the table impatiently and stared at me with visible frustration.

'*Obviously* I can. Do you think I like disappointing you?' he growled, then he sighed again and ran his hands through his hair. He looked so uncomfortable and frustrated in that moment that I barely recognised him. 'Look, I didn't know how to bring this up, but I think it's time that we ...' He tailed off and stared at me. He seemed to think that I could finish the sentence for myself, but I had no idea what he was trying to say.

'*What*?' I demanded furiously. 'Time we *what*?'

'Molly,' Leo said, pointedly calm again now. 'You need to think long and hard about whether you really want to stay in this marriage. I am not going to give up my career anytime soon.'

Once he said those words, it was like all of the fight and the air left my body at once and I deflated until I had slumped in my chair. Suddenly the loudest sound in the house was once again the ticking of the kitchen clock.

'You want a divorce?' I choked. I was beyond shocked – beyond stunned. Leo had completely blindsided me.

'I didn't say that. I don't know *what* I want – I don't know what the way forward is. I just know that neither one of us is happy, and we can't go on like this. I'm flying out tomorrow.'

At this I gaped at him. 'You're running away.'

'I'm not. We both need space. We need to figure out what it is we want and whether our goals for our lives even line up anymore… if they ever did. I'll be back with Brad when he comes home for the birth.'

He stood then, and as he turned to walk up the stairs, I finally lost the fragile hold I held on my temper. My hands were in fists and my voice was so loud that it echoed all through our apartment. I knew Mrs Wilkins and the students in the terraces next door would have heard me, but I didn't care one bit.

'How *dare* you drop that on me and then leave the country! You're a bigger coward than I ever realised, Leo Stephens.'

'Why don't you go talk to your parents about it, Molly?' Leo threw the words casually over his shoulder as he mounted the stairs, his tone mild again, as if we *weren't* having the most fraught conversation of our entire marriage. 'I'm sure you'd find a very sympathetic audience there if you want to discuss what a shitty husband I've been.'

'You're a *bastard*!' I hissed, standing so fast that the chair I was sitting on clattered down to hit the polished floorboards.

'And you are a spoilt brat,' Leo said flatly, and he glanced down at me from the stairwell. 'I'll pack now and sleep in the study. My flight is at six.'

I didn't want him to go. I wanted him to run down the stairs and sweep me up in his arms and kiss me until I couldn't breathe. I wanted to find a way to make everything okay between us again, because I knew that I wasn't going to feel okay until we did.

But I was left alone again – shaking with anger and frustration. I'd always assumed that we'd come through the rough patch eventually and life would be wonderful again. Until that night, it had never even occurred to me that I'd lose the battle if I ever tried to force him to choose between his career and our marriage.

Three weeks passed. He had asked me to think about what I wanted and I did – in fact, that was *all* I did. I watched the calendar tick down to the birth of Penny and Brad's child, knowing that Brad and Leo would be back in Sydney a few days before.

When Penny texted to let me know that Brad was back, I emailed Leo to ask him what time his flight was getting in. He called me a few hours later.

'I'm not coming home,' he said, without identifying himself. The hurt that rose within me was almost overwhelming. I wanted to lash out at him but I knew that I couldn't afford to do so. I still wanted to fix things with Leo – and if I was going to do that, I had to keep calm.

'Leo, please don't do this. Please come home.'

'Look, we agreed we needed some space anyway,' Leo said, and he seemed uncharacteristically awkward. 'I'm having trouble getting some resources for the next project, so I'm going to Istanbul instead to try to figure that out.'

'We've *had* some space,' I said. 'Now we need to talk.'

'Molly, I *need* to find a translator or the whole project stops, and we've put months of work into this. Brad is out for six weeks after his baby comes anyway. I'll try to get back during that time. That's the best that I can offer you.'

When I hung up that night, I felt a completely new emotion enter the equation of our marriage. All the lows and all the fear and all the longing had been bad enough but for the first time when I thought about Leo now, all I felt was panic.

That night on the phone, I realised that he was not just pulling away now – he was disentangling the last parts of himself that had been joined to me. I really was losing him.

Well, if he thought I was going to give up on our marriage without a fight, he was wrong. I walked to the computer and started looking for a flight.

CHAPTER 38
Leo – September 2015

Molly's belly becomes quite obvious over the weeks that follow. Soon it's a small but perfect curve that I can't seem to keep my eyes or my hands off, and I love even the idea that people can tell she's pregnant now just by looking at her.

I join her at the obstetricians one Friday morning for a check-up, and we get another brief glimpse of the baby on an ultrasound. This time, it waves its tiny hand towards us, and Molly's eyes get misty. 'You're not crying in public, are you?' I tease her, and she slaps my arm and tells me to shut up. The doctor and I laugh, and she rolls her eyes at us.

'You should be able to find out the gender at the next scan,' the doctor tells us, and Molly looks to me in surprise.

'We haven't talked about that. Do we want to know?' she asks.

'I kind of do,' I admit, and she grins.

'Okay, we'll find out.'

In the car on the way back to our apartment, I rest my hand on her bump and think about the movements of the baby beneath it. I can't wait for a few more weeks to pass so I can feel it kicking against me.

'Do you have a preference?' Molly asks me quietly.

'Nope.'

'What about names?'

'I like Henry for a boy,' I say, then suggest. 'Henry Andrew?'

'Oh yes,' she gives me a surprised smile. 'I really like that. And for a girl?'

'Maybe you should pick that name.'

'I've always liked the name Juliette – Juliette Stephens. It has such a nice ring to it, doesn't it?'

'I like that too.'

'Wow, that was easy!' she laughs.

'I have a feeling this kid was meant to be, don't you?'

Molly is clearly delighted to hear me say that. She gives this adorable shrug of her shoulders as she giggles, and says, 'I feel like that too.'

'I mean it's been such an easy pregnancy so far. You've hardly had any morning sickness and you *look* fantastic!' Her smile becomes a grin and I look down at my hand against her belly. 'And we just agreed on names like it was nothing. Plus of course... well, the fact that it was conceived at all is pretty much a miracle, right? Weren't you on the pill?'

There's a brief pause, but it's long enough that I look from her belly to her face. She nods quickly, but avoids my gaze. I frown. 'Molly?'

'I was,' she says, but she says it too quickly, and then she looks out the window.

'We haven't actually talked about that... About *how* the baby came to be,' I realise aloud, and I can't help but frown.

'I got lazy with my pill,' she admits. Her voice is very small.

'Like, you got busy and you got lazy?' I say, and then a memory rises – of Molly all but begging me for a baby, and then once the subject rose, it rose again and again and again.

Some of those arguments flood back at me now, and once I know it, I can't *un*know it.

I remember picking up the phone to call her more than once and putting it right back down again so we didn't have to discuss this very topic. And in the beginning, I'd actually been quite open to the idea – so open that I'd spent a lot of time wondering about it myself while I was in the field. But any enthusiasm I had for a baby quickly faded when Molly's calm request turned into an endless nagging that I just didn't know how to counter. She found a way to work the topic into any discussion and the more she pressured me, the less appealing the idea had seemed.

'It's okay,' I say now, carefully. 'You don't need to answer that. I remember.' She stares at her lap, and I exhale heavily and run a hand through my hair.

'I *had* been skipping my pill sometimes, for a long time,' she whispers. 'I went a little crazy, to be honest with you. River was a new baby, and then Penny fell pregnant, and it felt like everyone around us was having babies and it was all that I could think about. And at first you seemed keen on the idea, but then you weren't… and I just… It was selfish and stupid.'

'Yeah. It was,' I say quietly. I *am* angry, but not as angry as I might have been had I learned this information before I adjusted to the idea of the baby. I consider this and realise that the mitigating factor is that I do already *love* this child.

It was completely and utterly wrong of Molly to make the decision on my behalf, a betrayal of my trust, a manipulative and selfish move. It was the action of a spoilt child, far too used to getting her own way. But it doesn't matter how many phrases I apply to what she did, I can't make myself be as furious as I know I should be. Maybe it will come later, once this sinks in, or maybe I've just exhausted my reserves of energy for the day and I'll wake up furious tomorrow.

All I know is that I am not all that surprised by this realisation – maybe because as conscious as I am of Molly's strengths, I also understand her weaknesses. I wonder if on some level, I have known this all along.

'So I guess…' she murmurs. 'I guess that's done, then.'

'Done?' I repeat, and I glance at her sideways.

'This was the *thing*, Leo. This was what brought our issues to a head – what I did.'

'I think I can get past this,' I frown. 'This wasn't what caused us to separate.'

'Oh, it was definitely a factor.'

'So… you found out you were pregnant, and *then* we called it quits? That's crazy!'

She looks down at the bump of her belly and runs her palms up and down it a few times.

'You'd asked me to think about whether or not I still wanted to be with you and we'd barely spoken in the weeks since that conversation, but you were coming home with Brad when he returned for the birth. Then you called at the last minute and said you weren't coming home, so I got pretty upset. I went to Istanbul to spend a few days with you to try to reconnect.'

As she speaks, I remember a few things. I remember standing in my hotel room. I'd just put on my gym gear – I was in a foul mood, and hoping a vigorous workout would snap me out of it. I held a bottle of water in one hand, and I had the door key between my teeth. I swung the door open and Molly was standing there with a suitcase beside her. The sight of her was so unexpected that it startled me out of the trance-like processing I had been doing until I opened the door. *What the hell are you doing here?* I remember being as shocked by the rudeness of my own tone as I was by the sight of her, and I remember the way that her face fell. *I have been travelling for a full day to see you, and that's how you're going to greet me?*

'You weren't happy to see me,' she whispers, and then she clears her throat. 'I shouldn't have gone. It made things worse, not better.'

'God!' I say suddenly. I look at her in shock as I remember my next words to her. 'I told you to go home.'

'Yeah. We went into your room in that *shitty* hotel room you were staying in – it smelt like rotten socks and the bed had a popped spring in it and – it was just awful.'

'I just took the first room I found – I didn't want you to stay with me, not there.'

'I said I'd find something else so we could have a few days together. You told me not to bother,' she whispers.

Those memories are shocking, but jumbled pieces of the puzzle float around in my mind and I can't figure out how to make sense of it. I was furious with her for coming – I was miserable – I was stressed and panicked. Worst of all, I felt utter despair at the sight of her, which felt like an out-of-place emotion even then.

When I opened that door, I couldn't figure out what she was even doing there, standing in my hallway, looking at me with that desperate pleading in her eyes. I'd been ashamed to see her and to know that every new line on her face was *my* fault.

'You'd never come into the field before,' I say now, and she shakes her head.

'It's not like I walked through a firefight to meet up with you in Homs,' she sighs. 'You were in Istanbul, so it was safe enough. But I hadn't arrived unannounced before, no. We met up in Europe a few times during the first year, but you'd grown less keen on that as time went on.'

I'm frantically searching my memory, trying to figure out how that encounter ended. I can't think past sitting on the bed with her in the dodgy hotel room and being embarrassed at how bad the place was. She had looked so uncomfortable, and so utterly sad, and so out of place.

'I can't remember why you stayed,' I frown. 'Did you insist? Were you only there to…? I mean, did you know that if we…'

'*No,*' she says, and she gasps at me, as if I've insulted her.

I wince and point to her belly. 'Well… Molly, I mean… you did stop taking the pill. It's not such a stretch that you might have lined up a meeting for the right time to seal the deal.'

'It wasn't like that,' she says, frowning at me. 'I got *lazy* with it, I didn't *stop* taking it.'

'Is there any difference?'

She sighs and sinks back into her seat, then shakes her head. 'I know, it's still wrong. But I *promise* you, I didn't realise I'd missed enough for it to stop working.'

'So how did you end up staying with me, love?'

'You were angry, but then you realised what an arse you were being and you apologised, and we decided I'd stay,' she tells me. 'I found us a better hotel room and we moved across town, but you really only spent the evenings with me that week – you were busy all day.'

I have a vague idea that I might have made a point of staying out because I resented her decision to arrive unannounced and I hate the picture that paints of my mindset. I ponder this for a moment and another piece of the puzzle falls into place.

Trapped, I felt trapped. I felt exactly as though I was caught in a situation from which there was no safe exit – no way forward that didn't involve pain. I try to understand that, but I'm getting impatient and stressed now, and my mind refuses to offer more context. I sigh and glance back at Molly: she's the answer to the puzzle of my mind.

'So if you weren't there to get yourself a baby, what *did* you want out of that trip?'

She smiles at me sadly, and rests her hand over mine on her belly and squeezes my fingers.

'I just wanted to reconnect with you.'

'And we *obviously* did at least once,' I say, and I nod towards her belly.

'Not really,' she says sadly. 'I mean we were intimate again, yes obviously… but we didn't connect on the level we needed to. When we did talk, you only wanted to talk about the embed, and I *really* didn't want you to do it, so we kept arguing about it – which just proved the extent of the problem to us both, I think. I went there thinking that all we needed was time alone together, but by the end of that week…' she clears her throat. 'I couldn't wait to get home.'

'So did we decide to separate then?'

'Actually, no. You came home a few weeks later, and we had another big fight about the baby, and it just got so ugly… I think we both knew it was over then.'

'It *wasn't* over,' I frown at her. 'It will *never* be over.'

'I don't think we *know* that yet, Leo,' she whispers after a minute. Her eyes drop to my legs, and then return to my face. 'Unless you've suddenly realised you want to retrain as an accountant?'

We spend the rest of the car trip in silence. I can remember patches of that week in Istanbul now, and I can remember making love to her once or twice while we were there.

I remember missing her, even when she was with me – and I can completely understand what she meant when she said she couldn't wait to get home. I used to count down the days until I saw her, but that week, I counted down the days until she left.

I can hardly believe we let it get to that point – but I do remember the way that she had looked at me in Istanbul. There had been a confused blend of desperation and disdain in her eyes and every time I'd tried to share with her my enthusiasm for the assignment I was working on, I'd see even those emotions die altogether, until her beautiful blue eyes seemed dull.

I remember thinking that no one in the world had the power to hurt me like Molly did. She could cut me deeply with just a dismissive comment about not talking about my assignment, or a simple roll of her eyes when I tried to bring it up again. I knew that she didn't mean to, I knew that I'd hurt her too and she was acting from a place of pain, but that awful week was one long series of awkward conversations and each of us trying to reignite something that was too far gone to be reanimated. When she finally left, I was relieved.

That desperate, desolate relationship I am starting to remember is worlds away from the one I know now. These weeks with Molly have been alive with love and intimacy again – despite *all* the challenges we have faced in that time. How can things between us be so wonderful now, and yet in the ordinary comings and goings of our days the first time around, we let it fade away to nothing?

Even as I'm thinking about all of this, my mind drifts back to the moment earlier that morning when I stood on my own for exactly ten seconds, and I heard Tracy say those wonderful, magical words.

'Tomorrow, we take your first step.'

CHAPTER 39
Molly – May 2015

The emptiness of that awful week with Leo had been the wake-up call I'd needed. I was coming to terms with the reality that my marriage was dead.

The trip to see him had been a desperate act by a desperate woman, and when it turned out to be a bigger failure than I could ever have imagined, I realised that he was actually right. I still couldn't understand why, but there was no doubt that he was more committed to that job than he was to anything else – even a future with me, and even his physical safety.

When Leo did return from Istanbul, we shuffled around the house as if we were room-mates rather than spouses. We were each careful to stay out of the other's way, and we spoke to one another with an artificial level of politeness. But beyond the practicalities, we did not talk. I didn't want to be the one to bring up the subject of a separation – not *yet* anyway – but I had decided that when Leo did, I would calmly agree. I even called the management at my apartment building and had them cancel future holiday bookings and arranged for some things to be moved out of storage to prepare my apartment for my return, but beyond that, I made no plans.

For several weeks, we stayed in a polite but emotionless limbo. But then my period failed to show, and all hell broke loose.

CHAPTER 40

Leo – September 2015

I decide to surprise Molly a few days later, and I arrange for Tracy to come later in the day than she usually does. I skip my swim to rest all morning, and then just before Molly is due home, I greet Tracy.

'I hope she doesn't faint,' Tracy remarks, as she's setting me up in the supportive harness 'She is pregnant, after all. You should have warned her.'

'I wanted to surprise her.'

'Well, she'll certainty get that,' Tracy chuckles. A few minutes later, we hear the elevator doors, and Molly calls out, 'Hey, Leo! Are you here?'

'Yep,' I call back, and Molly follows the sound of my voice into the open living area where I have been training. Her eyes widen as she sees Tracy, and she gives us both a curious smile.

'What's this?'

'It's a surprise.'

'Oh,' she says, and I see confusion cross her face. I glance at Tracy.

'Ready?' I ask, and Tracy nods, so I put my hands on the standing frame and take a deep breath, and I rise. Once upon a time, I could run ten kilometres with less effort than it takes me to make two steps now – but I do it – I lift my left foot, and as I shuffle it forward, I whisper under my breath *heel*, and then I lower it slowly, and whisper again *toe*. My hands shake as I force the frame forward, and then I repeat the motion with the other foot.

After two steps, I am completely shattered and Tracy moves the chair behind me to catch me just as I collapse back into it. I am exhausted from this process in a way that still seems impossible – but I *did* it, and I raise my eyes to Molly, expecting to see excitement and joy and pride on her face.

Instead, I see a level of disappointment and fear that she cannot hide. This is not a micro-expression that I could have misread – this is a long, frozen moment that leaves me in no doubt at all what she thinks about my progress.

The wave of triumphant buzz I had been riding disappears in an instant as our eyes lock. I have felt like this before – disappointed by her, and disappointed in her – every time something wonderful happened with a story and she dismissed it or refused to even discuss it with me. My chest feels strangely tight.

'I… um… I should go, Leo,' Tracy says hesitantly. I nod, and she leans towards me and starts to unclip the harness.

'Leave it,' I say abruptly, and she scurries from the room as if the tension emanating from Molly and me might injure her somehow. I do not look away from my wife, not for a second. I am inexplicably furious with her, and I recognise that I am familiar with that emotion too.

This is the missing piece to the jigsaw puzzle of our life, that thing that I have not understood at all since I woke from the coma – it is the central piece upon which all of the other parts to *us* hang. She has said that our relationship broke down because I worked too much but I suddenly understand that for me the point of failure was actually Molly's stubborn, selfish refusal to *support* me. This brutally disappointing moment feels just like the dullness of her tone when I'd call her to tell her about some amazing development in a story, and the almost bored way she'd ask me every single fucking time I had to leave, *do you have to go?*

After everything we have been through, I cannot believe that today I have stood before her – against all odds, after so much excruciating work – and that she cannot even bring herself to be happy for me.

'Are you going to say something?' I prompt.

Her gaze drops to the floor momentarily, then she raises it stubbornly back to mine. 'I know I should be excited,' she says stiffly. 'And I know it makes me a terrible person that I am not. But *you* think you took two simple steps – *I* know that you just took your first two steps away from me again.'

'This is the problem. This was *always* the problem,' I snap at her. The hurt I feel is almost blinding – the sense of betrayal breathtaking. 'You have never supported me, Molly. You want me to be like some bloody pet that you keep at home to play with. Is the wheelchair a *bonus* to you because it anchors me here?' She raises her chin and stares at me, a fury rising that I know will soon answer mine, but when seconds pass and she does not speak, I try to hook a reaction out of her to hurry this argument to its inevitable conclusion. 'You never wanted me to walk again, you wanted me to be stuck here.'

'I *told* you,' she says, 'I knew you would walk again. I *knew* that you would never let this hold you back. And I also told you that we would end up right back here where we started – at the problem between us that has no solution. And if it makes me the worst fucking person on earth that I was hoping that your injury would mean you were stuck here safe with me so that we could be happy, then so be it.'

'How can you even say that to me?' I am all but snarling at her now, and I unclip the harness with furious, jerking movements, but I cannot get out of the portions that rest around my pelvis, so I leave them fixed as I wheel myself towards her. 'My job is everything to me and the fact that you could only give lip service to it shows me how little you understand me.'

I manoeuvre myself all the way over to where she stands near the kitchen and I stop a metre or so back from her. We stare at each other, and the silence and our breathing is ragged.

'Why are you so determined to kill yourself for that fucking job, Leo?'

She does not shout – the words are delivered with a deadly potency, she does not need to raise the volume of the sentence. I am incensed anyway by the selfishness of her anger, even as I feel my own frustration spiralling and building right along with it. My rage pulses red in my chest and my face feels hot. More than anything now I want to shout at her. I want to slam doors and storm out and go to the gym and punch a punching bag until my knuckles are bleeding.

But I can't. I can't do any of that, and even if I could, I wouldn't. Instead, I stare at her so hard that my vision goes blurry. I can't understand how she can miss such an obvious truth in all of these arguments about my work.

I have never understood her viewpoint on my job – but then again, I've never *really* understood why she wanted to be with me in the first place, or how she can fail to see what's so blindingly obvious about what drives me.

'I *have* to,' I say. My voice breaks and I don't know what that means – but I'm too angry to shut up long enough to figure it out. 'Don't you understand that?'

'But *why?*' she whispers, and at the desperation in her tone something inside me breaks free.

'It's for *you*! It's for you and your fucking father and all of the people in our lives who know that I'm not good enough for you! You know as well as I do that if I don't have this job, I am *nothing*.'

I seem to have stumbled upon a 'stop' button to our argument, because neither one of us knows what to say to all of that. I feel as though I have just accidentally left myself standing naked in front of an enemy at war.

'Leo,' Molly says. She's completely calm, and that should calm me – but it doesn't. My heart is racing faster and faster. I'm sweating – I *need* to get out of her apartment, away from this argument, before I lose whatever is left of my pride.

'Just leave it, Molly,' I groan, and I push the chair past her, into the hallway and towards the elevator.

'*No*,' I hear her say behind me, and then she takes the handles of my wheelchair and spins me round, and my anger resurges because I have *told* her not to do that and *fuck, I hate this powerlessness*. I might have shouted those things at her, but I can't speak – I can barely breathe. My chest feels ever-tighter and I am working so hard on keeping my face neutral that I can't really concentrate on much else. I certainly can't look at her. I won't see her pain in case it softens my anger, and I won't see her pity unless it pushes me over the edge.

Molly drops to her knees in front of me and she takes my hands in hers and presses the backs of my fingers against tears that have appeared out of nowhere to cover her cheeks. I lean back in my chair away from her and I still don't look at her – I *can't* look at her.

'I won't stop you going,' she says flatly. 'I won't *ever* stop you going. But before you do, you need to know something.'

She is waiting for me to make eye contact again, and I'm still not sure I can do it without showing her how deeply she has hurt me, and how furious I still am. But the seconds stretch and I realise that the only way I am getting out of there is to let her say her piece. I drag my gaze back to hers, and if I thought I was hurting before, I am in agony after I finally face the mirrored pain in her eyes.

'Leo Stephens,' she whispers, and then she gives me a teary, almost pleading smile as she chokes, 'You have never needed to be a hero to be *my* hero.'

I look away, and I feel the stupid tic at my jaw, and those words delivered with surprising softness land like daggers in me anyway. She's not done yet, either. I hear her draw another heavy breath and her voice is low as she adds, 'You promised me we wouldn't end up back here. You *promised* me there was a solution – a compromise. Well,' she stands suddenly, and she steps away from me. I look to her expectantly, and she raises her eyebrows as if issuing a challenge. 'Go *find* it so we can be a family.'

I ask the van driver to take me to the terrace. For a while I play with Lucien in what's left of my courtyard, and eventually Mrs Wilkins brings me a cup of tea and her legendary scones. We share them at the dining table. It's like an ordinary, pre-Molly afternoon in my old life, except that my apartment now looks like something out of a *Home Beautiful* magazine.

After Mrs Wilkins leaves, I stare at the chair-lifts on the stairs for a while before I lift myself onto the seat. It takes a while to figure it all out, but eventually I hook the wheelchair onto the side of the chair and turn the machine on.

Molly wasn't kidding when she said it was slow. It takes almost a minute to rise from the ground floor to the bedroom, and then another minute to get up the remaining stairs to my office – but the destination is worth the wait. I actually give an odd laugh of relief when I see my desk come into view.

I look at my books for a while, then take myself to my desk and I stare at the computer – the laptop is closed. I pull it towards me, intending to open it, but a letter was resting beneath it and that immediately captures my full attention. As I pick it up, I feel the definite shifting of something in my mind. All of the other memories have come back to me slowly – almost like an image loading on a poor internet connection, pixel by pixel swimming into focus. This time it's more like a bucket of ice water dumped unceremoniously over my head. As I stare at the piece of paper and I read the address, the last few pieces of the puzzle of my mind start to fall into place.

The letter is from Brokeshaw Solicitors and their office is right next door to the bar where I *thought* something special had happened with Molly. I don't read any further than the letterhead before it becomes completely overwhelming. I close my eyes – hoping I can slow down the barrage of memories by blocking out the visual trigger that's causing them: it doesn't work.

I'd arrived at the solicitor just in time for my appointment at 4 p.m. I had walked from the *News Monthly* office to give myself time to think. I thought I would be ready by the time I got there, but as I was about to walk up the stairs, my legs froze. I can stand in a battlefield and dodge bullets and feel only exhilarated, but *that* day, standing in an ordinary stairwell in a very safe city, for the first time in my life I felt a real sense of panic.

I couldn't do it; I just could not go in. So I slipped my phone from my pocket and I dialled, and I lied: I told the receptionist that I'd been caught up in a meeting and I would be at least half an hour late. Then I turned around and I walked into the bar next door. I sat at the bar and I ordered a Scotch and I stared into it as the ice-cubes floated around the top.

Molly. All I could think about that day was Molly. When I closed my eyes, I saw her in my mind – a montage of the extremes of the moments of our life together – screaming anger, hysterical sobbing, gentle smiles and radiant love.

She had betrayed my trust, and she had hurt me, and I was so burnt by the lack of support that she'd offered me. All I'd ever wanted was to be someone worthy of *her*. All I'd ever wanted was to deserve her love – but the harder I worked to be the kind of man to deserve a woman like Molly, the more I disappointed her It was a situation where I couldn't win because the very thing that I needed to feel worthy of my wife was the same thing that had destroyed my relationship with her.

In the bar that day I had wanted to fix things with Molly. In that moment, I wanted to be with her so much that it physically pained me to be apart from her. I had missed her – my *whole life* was missing her – but I felt crushed under the weight of failure and guilt, as if I had squandered a once-in-a-lifetime gift.

How had I let the best thing that had ever happened to me go to waste?

Eventually, I got up, and I walked next door and I went inside and talked to the solicitor. I gave him no details – he didn't need them. I just set the wheels in motion and told myself I was doing what needed to be done.

I open my eyes. My glasses have fallen onto the desk and there are drops of moisture beside them. I pick them up, and the text of the letter swims into focus.

Dear Mr Stephens

Further to your meeting with us, we have registered the date of your separation from Molly Torrington-Stephens as Thursday, 4 July 2015. As discussed, under Australian law you must be separated for a period of twelve months before you are able to file for divorce. To this end, we request that you contact us on or after Thursday, 4 July 2016 to continue with divorce proceedings.

We confirm your instruction that with regards to financial settlement you wish only to retain assets owned by yourself at the time of your marriage. We do suggest you consider this carefully over the coming twelve months as in the absence of a prenuptial agreement you would likely be entitled to a significant portion of Ms Torrington-Stephens' assets.

We also confirm your request that a formal custodial arrangement for a child will be required upon continuation of divorce proceedings and that you will give us further instructions with regards to this once the child has been born.

I put the letter down, and I think again about the man in that bar that day.

He was a man who truly knew what he wanted – he just didn't know how to get it. Or maybe he did, and maybe he just didn't have the courage to do what needed to be done.

I wipe my eyes with my sleeve and make my way back towards the stairs.

CHAPTER 41
Molly – June 2015

I had spent a lot of time that year thinking about what it would feel like to see a second line appear on a pregnancy test. I'd even stared at myself in the mirror and practised the joyous, maternal smile I'd wear when I told Leo our news. I had imagined his equally joyous reaction so many times that I felt like I'd seen it for real.

The reality of that moment in our lives was nothing at all like those fantasies. Leo was asleep in the recliner in the office when I went into the bathroom, and he was still asleep when I watched the second line appear.

I put the test in the bin and then I took Lucien for a walk into the city. He stayed close to me, which ordinarily would have suggested he was not in the mood for exercise, but that day I knew that he was picking up on the tightly-strung emotions that swirled around in my gut.

I couldn't think about the baby; I wouldn't let myself accept the reality of it. All that I could think about was the mess that I was in, and the added chaos that I had created.

I thought if I walked long enough, I'd figure out a way to make things right – but all that walk did was to convince me that there *was* no way to make things right. When Lucien started falling behind me, I called for my car and went home.

Leo was sitting at the dining room table, eating toast and reading the newspaper. He glanced at me when I stepped into the room, then looked back to the newspaper without a word. I stood opposite him and I did not take a seat.

'I'm pregnant,' I said. I didn't make excuses or deny that this was my own doing. I wouldn't insult his intelligence like that.

In the end, it wasn't anger I saw in his expression. It was a myriad of other painful emotions – hurt, confusion and realisation, and then right after that an icy and terrible hatred. Leo rose, picked up his wallet from the kitchen bench, and walked out the back door – slamming it behind him. The slam echoed in the empty house long after he was gone. I knew that it represented the death knell for my marriage.

He returned hours later, drenched in sweat and clearly exhausted. I knew he'd gone to the gym. I had a feeling there was a punching bag or a treadmill there that would probably need replacing.

I couldn't look at him. He came and sat at the other end of the couch.

'Are we going to get past this?' I asked him. My voice was hoarse.

'I don't know,' Leo admitted, and finally he looked at me.

'Is there anything I can do?'

'Just… give me space.'

'Okay,' I whispered, but it was frustrating beyond words. Leo *always* said that – *give me space* – and if I wasn't so broken, I might have asked him just how much bloody space a man could possibly need.

After a day a day or two, I actually started to wonder if we were somehow going to be okay. We had settled into a surprising kind of calm. The space between us felt fragile, but not as tense as it once had – not so taut it might shatter at any second – now it was a sensitive thing that we had to nurture carefully. We did not talk about the baby or what I'd done – although Leo returned to our bed, and I woke several times to find his hand resting on my belly.

And then, at dinner one night, Leo told me that he had booked his flights to return to Syria and that he and Brad had finalised the plans he'd been working on. He'd tried to tell me in Istanbul, but I'd been so resentful at that stage that I'd always cut him off or changed the subject before he could really explain the project.

My husband was planning to spend three weeks embedded in a group of jihadists.

He said it so calmly. If I'd listened to the tone and not the words, he might have been talking about something dull, and I might have missed the reality that he had signed himself up for a suicide mission. This was a whole new level of crazy and a whole new level of stupid. These were extremists who lived and breathed an irrational dogma that Leo despised as much as anyone.

'*No*,' I said. 'No, you can't. I won't let you.'

Leo looked up from his meal. 'You won't let me,' he repeated.

'That's not an assignment – it's a suicide mission. No one would have approved that.'

'Not that it's any of your business, but Kisani has worked through the plan as closely as Brad and I have. We're not even the first to do it, and I have a guarantee from…'

'*No*,' I said. I did not want to hear it – the false promises of his safety that he might give me, as if they would mean something. 'You can't do this. You're going to be a father, Leo – *Jesus*, Brad has *three* kids now! You just can't be so careless with your lives anymore. This wasn't Brad's idea, was it?'

'How does that matter?'

'Because you keep pressuring him into these things and one of you is going to get killed! I *won't* let you, I forbid you to do this.'

'You *forbid* me?' Leo scoffed. 'What are you going to do, Molly – go behind my back and stop me from going? Do my wishes count for nothing at all now, not even with my work?'

We both knew exactly what he was really referring to, but I couldn't believe how quickly the conversation had spun from me being terrified *for* him, to him attacking me over what I'd done. My face felt hot and my gaze drifted to the silk flowers on the table between us. '*Don't*, Leo!' I whispered.

'Well, what would you have me do? Do you want me to leave my job and do something that makes me miserable just because you've tricked me into fatherhood? I suppose a boring desk job is the last thing you've got left to manipulate me into.'

I gasped and stood so violently that my chair tipped over onto the floorboards behind me. 'You *bastard*!'

There was a minute flash of guilt over Leo's face, but almost instantly it was replaced by scorn.

'It is true, isn't it? This was what Istanbul was about, right?' That wasn't the case at all – but I couldn't deny the accusation of manipulation. I *had* tricked him into it – not as directly as he thought, but the little facts around our situation did not diminish my guilt one bit.

'If we're going to catalogue all of the things we've done to hurt each other, let's talk about *my* life the last year. Why don't we talk about what I have given up for you?' Pain twisted the words in my mouth until I was snarling at him. 'How about my family? How about my *home*? And for what, Leo? To live here, in this shitty shoebox alone for ten months of the year, with a husband who is so self-obsessed that he can't even be bothered to bloody call me every once in a while. I am so fucking sick of you treating me like this…'

'You "*gave up*" your family? *Please*, Molly, you didn't give up your *barely* functional family – your parents forced you out when you decided to rebel against your father by sleeping with me. And you still see them – do you think I don't *know* that?'

'I see them on special occasions, like Christmas. You might not be familiar with what that is – it's one of the many days each year when my husband doesn't bother to come home.'

When he didn't respond, I felt a completely fresh and unexpected burst of anger and I apparently decided to spiral the tone of the conversation down even further. When I spoke again, my words were a spiteful, awful hiss. 'You try to make it sound noble, Leo, and no one else can see through it – but *I* can. We both know that you only take the risky assignments because you *need* the adrenaline rush to make you feel like a *man*.'

I saw the pain in Leo's eyes at that last brutal insult and just for a second I felt triumph – I was glad to have hurt him. I wanted him to suffer like I was suffering.

'Maybe there's some truth in that. I certainly don't feel like a man when I talk to you these days. When was the last time you actually spoke to me as if I was someone you didn't loathe? *Why won't you come home more, Leo?* Because I *despise* being here with you, being reminded every fucking minute of the day how much you resent me. You should have listened to your father and stayed well away from someone of such poor breeding.'

'Fuck you, Leo! Fuck you and your false promises and your *goddamned* messiah complex! I *do* hate you, I can't do this anymore!'

'Then *go*, Molly! Go back to your ivory tower. Go and lament with your daddy what a scumbag I turned out to be and you can even have his approval back. Just fucking go!'

I burst into tears and then I ran up the stairs and lay on our bed and just sobbed. Lucien came and lay on the bed beside me and I knew Leo would be pissed off about it, but I let the dog comfort me and then when he fell asleep there, I childishly let him slobber all over Leo's pillows.

It was well after two in the morning when I heard Leo climb the stairs. I was still lying awake – although I'd long since stopped crying. He sat on my side of the bed right beside me and I thought he was going to apologise. Of all our fights, and there had been more arguments than I could count over that last year, we'd never been quite so cruel before – neither one of us, and I was as scared by it as I was shocked. It was a sign that all of those things that had been building – the disdain, the lack of respect, the contempt – even my betrayal of his trust – those aspects to our marriage had completely overtaken us.

'We can't do this anymore,' he whispered.

I sat up. Lucien sat up too, and then he saw Leo and leapt off the bed and disappeared down the stairs. Leo didn't move and he did not touch me. The room was semi-dark, illuminated only from the lights downstairs. I could see Leo's face, but I couldn't read it.

'I know,' I whispered.

'I know we always say this, but I promise you, Molly, I mean it. I don't want to fight again tonight.'

'I don't want to fight either,' I said, and I thought about how many times I'd said that to him over the years. There was a basic essential truth to the statement. I had *never* wanted to fight with him – it was the last resort when I grew desperate. I had only ever wanted to reach him, but it is so very difficult to catch up with someone who is always pulling away.

I waited, because this was the part where he was supposed to take me in his arms and we'd console each other. When Leo did not move to comfort me, I was actually confused.

'You know what my childhood was like,' he said, still very quietly. 'You know – that argument tonight? We could have had a five-year-old in the next room, lying in bed shaking with the fury of it, and we'd still have gone at it like that. We weren't in control of ourselves. We weren't respectful of each other and we haven't been for a long time. What we had, it's just gone, Molly… and what's left isn't worth repairing. I have seen what life looks like for a kid when a family revolves around anger. I want the defining moments of our baby's life to be filled with laughter and love, not fury and shouting. We *can* do that for our baby,' he stopped for a moment, and cleared his throat before he added, 'But we can't do it together.'

At this I lost my breath. I was forming a counter-argument even as I realised what he was saying was true. It was still habit to argue, but I had run out of energy for the fight.

'You told me you hated me tonight. You *can't* say you didn't mean it, can you? Face it, Molly, I've done a terrible job of being a husband – I'm a complete failure at this. All I have done is to hurt you and to disappoint you.'

'That's just not true, Leo,' I said, but I was surprised at the calm resignation in my voice. 'We did have good times – we had some *great* times.'

'We did. But we're a long way from those days now. I know I've already treated you badly, Molly – I know that as well as you do. But now there's this new thing between us that I just don't think I can forgive. If you think things have been ugly in the past… God, it can only get worse the way I feel now. The best way forward for us is a fresh start – *apart.*'

I knew I needed to apologise, but I also knew that the words would mean nothing at all to Leo now. I had taken something from him, and in so doing, I had damaged the trust between us in a way that could never be repaired. All that I could hope now was that if I could be mature about this, I might one day regain some of his respect.

Leo turned to face me, and I could just make out the shape of sadness in his eyes.

'This is who I am, you know. I can't change, I don't even want to – no more than *you* want to change. We've given it our best shot, and we could have kept trying for another year or two, even ten years, but the outcome would always have been this moment. Now that we are going to be parents, we can't afford to waste any more time trying and failing. I would rather see you happy and content and peacefully settled down with someone else...'

I couldn't imagine being with anyone else, but as he said those words, I suddenly realised that I couldn't imagine myself with Leo anymore either. He was right – the compulsion within him to do that damned job was always going to lead him back to a lifestyle that I could never accept. Our marriage had been doomed from the start.

'Okay,' I said, and while I was sure that we were in the right place and that this conversation needed to happen, that didn't lessen the pain of it one little bit, and I had to stiffen my whole body to try and force away the tears that loomed. We sat in a ragged silence for a moment or two, waiting calmly together among the ruins of our marriage and the life that we had built. I waited for Leo to leave, and eventually realised that he wasn't going to, so I sought for something more to say – a way to work the conversation around to an apology, in case that was what he was waiting for.

'We can rebuild a friendship before the baby comes. We can be civil.... friendly.'

'I really hope so,' Leo whispered, but then he surprised me as he added hesitantly, 'Do you remember when you said to me that you weren't looking for a happily-ever-after, and that whenever our relationship ended, you'd be glad for the time we shared?' I nodded, and a tear escaped my eye. 'I *am* glad for the time we shared, Molly. I *was* happy. It counts, even after it's over.'

I pulled him close, and though it felt like my heart was breaking right there in my chest, I wrapped my arms around him and then I kissed him carefully on the cheek. 'Stay safe, Leo,' I whispered, and a shuddering sob finally escaped my lips. I saw Leo clench his jaw and there was a raw pain in his eyes that even the darkness could not hide. And then he walked to the stairs, and disappeared into his study.

I moved back into Bennelong the next day. Maybe I hadn't meant what I said that night – maybe in that moment I didn't *really* hate him – but I certainly did in the days afterwards. I hated the mess of our life, but I hated Leo more for giving up on it. Things were apparently over and I still wasn't sure how I could have let the best thing that had ever happened to me go to ruin.

It was only a few days later that Leo emailed me to say that he'd seen a solicitor and to suggest that I see one too. I got the email when I was sitting at my desk with Leo's own father due for a meeting with me any minute. When Andrew came into the office, I could tell that Leo had not told his family what was going on between us, and I was so livid that I feigned illness and took myself home.

How could Leo be so unaffected by what was happening between us that he had calmly seen a solicitor before he had even told his parents? It was so typical of him to leave such a thing to me, but this time I was having none of it. I'd decided that under no circumstances would I be the one to break the news to his family. They were Leo's problem to solve – I had enough of my own.

So I ignored his email and I ignored his advice. I promised myself that I'd take as much time to grieve as I needed: I would start the steps to dissolve our marriage only when I felt ready to do so.

The next day I had my first obstetric appointment. I texted Leo to invite him and I was quite confident that he would come – after all, he had said he wanted to rebuild a friendship, and he'd said that he wanted to parent our baby together. When the receptionist tried to send me in and Leo was still not there, I asked her if one of the other waiting patients could go before me.

'My husband is coming,' I said. 'I'm sure of it.' It was a lie – I wasn't sure at all by then, but I felt I could see judgement in the eyes of the receptionist. Even when I did go into the doctor's room, I kept my eyes on the door. Leo did not come. I drafted several texts to him – but they were mean, because I was so disappointed that he did not show up. Eventually I deleted them. I knew that I couldn't afford to inject more tension into our relationship – we needed to find a new kind of peace before the baby came.

Before he flew out to Syria, Leo texted me from the airport. *I'm flying out. If there's anything else you need from the terrace, please help yourself before I get back. I've organised a walker for Lucien so you won't need to go to my house otherwise.*

✦ ✦ ✦

A week later my phone rang in the middle of the night. I heard sobbing as soon as I answered it. I did not know who the caller was, but I knew immediately that something had happened to Leo.

'He's dead, isn't he?' I said. I was calm. Pain and an endless grief would crash over me but the inevitability of the moment could not be escaped. I had *known* this was coming – I was prepared – I'd actually tried to imagine that moment already over the years. I had known that there would be a call or a knock at the door one day and he would be gone. Leo had seemed determined to martyr himself for his work.

'No,' the caller sobbed, and I realised it was Kisani. 'But he's injured.'

'Injured?' I repeated, and I sighed, imagining another bullet in his shoulder. 'What's happened, Kisani?'

'It was a car accident – Brad was sketchy on the details but it's bad…'

I heard the dread in her voice. This wasn't one of Leo's semi-regular 'flesh wounds'.

'How bad?' I whispered.

'I'm so sorry, Molly. They don't think he's going to make it. How quickly can you get to Rome?'

I was on Dad's jet by the time the sun rose and I didn't even think twice about whether I should go.

That's the thing about love. You can abuse it, you can dampen it, you can wrap it up in hate, or try with all your might to destroy it – but once it's been lit, an ember always remains.

CHAPTER 42
Leo – September 2015

It's late by the time I arrive back at Bennelong. The sun is setting over the city, and the living area is bathed in a warm orange light. The terrace has no western aspect and it's overshadowed on all sides, so it's much darker at any hour of the day. That warm light is the one thing I love about Molly's apartment – other than the fact that it's also *our* apartment, if she'll have me back.

The apartment is still and quiet, but I know she is home – the concierge told me as I came through the lobby. I wonder if she has cried since I left; I wonder if she will be able to see that *I* have. 'Molly!' I call, and I push myself towards our bedroom. I find her lying on the bed, staring away from me towards the window. She doesn't move when I enter the room, but I see the way that her hands are wrapped around her belly. I move towards the bed, and then I lift myself onto it and sit up beside her.

Molly moves slowly, reluctantly, until she's sitting up too. She flicks me only a glance before she looks away again.

'I wasn't having an affair, you know.'

'That's something, I suppose,' she whispers.

'The lawyer's office was next door to that bar. I had to go in for a stiff drink before I could bring myself to go see him. I *knew* I was making a mistake.'

'Was it a mistake, Leo? We're right back there again now. We've got exactly the same problem, only it's even worse now because we realise that we *love* each other again.'

'We don't have the exact same problem, Molly,' I say softly, and she looks at me properly now, but her gaze is openly sceptical. I reach into my pocket to withdraw a single page. I pass it to her and watch her face as she reads it. She gasps, and then looks back to me.

'Is this for real?' she whispers.

'It is.'

'You would do this for me?'

'No,' I say, and I shake my head firmly. 'I wouldn't do this *just* for you. I won't be any kind of husband if I'm miserable. I am doing this for our family – for you, for me, and for Henry-slash-Juliette.'

Molly passes the letter back to me and I skim it again myself. I remember now a time not so long ago when Brad accused me of having a magical ability to convince Kisani to approve any request I made at *News Monthly*, no matter how outlandish, but getting this one signed off in a single afternoon was a stretch even for me.

> *Updated position description, Leo Stephens.*
> *Role: Senior journalist and consultant on Middle Eastern affairs.*
> *Arrangement: part-time, three days per week, pending return to work clearance from medical team.*
> *Conditions of employment: no international travel will be required to fulfil the role – all assignments will be domestic in origin or will be researched by an assistant.*

'But I do want you to be happy,' Molly frowns. She looks at me. 'I want you to be happy more than I want you to be with me, Leo – even if it means you're constantly in danger. That's partly why I agreed to the separation the first time around – you'd made it so clear that you couldn't leave your job.'

'I know, love,' I say gently, and I rest my hand on her thigh because I just need to touch her again. 'But it's pretty bloody obvious that I can't work the way I have been *and* have you and the baby in my life.'

'Do you think you can be happy here with us?' she asks hesitantly.

'I know I can – I have been, haven't I? These last few months – even with all of the stress of the injury and my damned legs not working – I've been happy here with you. I love you more than anything, even my career. I feel like an idiot that it took me this long to figure out that just as I didn't marry you for your annoying wealth…' She rolls her eyes at my joke, but I press on, '*you* didn't marry me for my job.'

'God, Leo! *No one* would marry you for your job.'

'I think it just seemed too good to be true, you know? That someone like *you* would marry someone like *me*. And I wanted to – no, I *needed* to be someone for you.'

'You *are* someone, Leo,' she says, as she gazes at me.

I see both the pain in her eyes at the things I have just told her, and the sheer adoration that has always been there and that has always terrified me. Countless times I've accused Molly of failing to support me – but I realise now. She couldn't support my career, because it was killing me – but she always supported *me*. I am scared of this change that I need to make now; as scared as I ever was on the battlefield – but that isn't going to stop me this time. There is too much at stake, and I won't be adjusting to my new life alone.

'I loved that job, Molly. And I was damned good at it.'

'I know,' she whispers.

'But it's time for me to put *all* my energy into a new role, and I'm going to love this one even more.'

She glances at the page in my hand. 'Part-time domestic journalist and Middle Eastern correspondent?' she reads.

I shake my head. 'Husband and father,' I promise her. She breathes in slowly, and then the smile returns – the one that I have always felt could light up the whole world. 'We've never really had a life together, have we? But I want to grow old with you, Molly, until we have the same wrinkles and the same worn expression on our faces and people think we're siblings.'

'I don't think that's going to happen in our case, Leo!' She laughs at my stupid joke, and the freedom and joy she releases with that sound is the confirmation I've been looking for – it's not too late for us. I grin at her, and then finally take her in my arms.

'I want us to have one life, not two that meet up every now and again. And we could try this now and put every single thing we have within ourselves into it and we could still fail. But I promise you that this time around, I'm not going to give up on us unless we've given it everything we've got and there's nothing left to try. Will you promise me that too?'

'You know I will.'

We stare at each other. I watch a broad, teary smile transform her face and she is so beautiful in that moment that she steals my breath.

'So we're doing this?' I whisper.

'You bet your bloody life we are!'

EPILOGUE
Molly

'Say bye to Mummy, Henry.'

I am standing at the door, staring at Leo and our son. Henry is four months old and he's still the most adorable child I've ever seen. He has Leo's dark curls and brown eyes, and the months since his birth have been the best of my life. I love every delicious moment with him – sometimes, even when I am sat up feeding him in the small hours, I'm shocked by a fresh realisation that there is nowhere else in the world I would rather be and nothing I would rather be doing. Henry has given my life meaning in a way that I'd never imagined.

He is sitting on his father's lap now, waving with Leo's assistance, completely oblivious to the momentous first that we are experiencing. I have not spent more than an hour away from him in his entire life. Until today.

I am so close to tears. I knew this would be hard – but it is so much harder than I imagined. I shift my handbag on my shoulder and realise again that it's not the nappy bag I'm in the habit of carrying and I start to feel nauseous. It doesn't feel right – I'm never going to get used to this.

'Are you sure you're going to be okay with him?' I ask Leo, and he raises an eyebrow at me.

'You *know* I'm going to be fine,' he says. He is right, but still, I start to shake and I want to snatch the baby back up out of his arms and cancel the whole arrangement.

'I don't think I can do this,' I whisper thickly, and Leo shifts his wheelchair forward towards me. He can walk short distances now – usually with crutches or a frame – but it's still a slow and exhausting process for him even a full year after the accident. His one concession to his disability has been to accept a motorised wheelchair, but only since Henry was born, and only since he realised he would need one to get around while carrying his son.

There's still hope. His doctors say that it is still possible he will regain his mobility, but given how slow his progress has been, it may be years before his brain can rewire itself. Leo will never stop trying. He is undeterred by the thought of years of hard work to achieve a goal.

'It's completely up to you, Molly. If you're not ready, you're not ready. We can try again in another week, or another two – or however long it takes. I won't be upset, and I won't be offended.'

Leo cups Henry around his chubby belly with one arm, but takes my hand with his other. He squeezes firmly as the tears roll over onto my cheeks and down my chin. I have been staring at the baby, but now I glance at Leo and he offers me a gentle, reassuring smile.

'It's only half a day, love,' he whispers. I nod and go to turn away, but at the last second I lose my nerve again and I drop to my knees to bury my face in the baby's neck. Henry immediately turns his head to gum his wet mouth at my hair as if he might find milk there. After a minute or two, I rock back on my haunches and I look from my son to my husband.

'Maybe it's too soon for me to go back to work,' I say to Leo.

'That's fine if it is.'

'But we've arranged everything...'

'I don't care.'

'I'm being an idiot.'

'Not at all.'

Life is different now. We laugh at the same time and we cry at the same time. We stare down at our son in wonder together most nights. We live gently together – two lives entwined at last.

He is an amazing father, as I knew he would be – but more than that, these days Leo is the husband I knew he could be too. Somehow, after everything we've been through, we have finally settled into a life that suits us both.

Leo and Brad have been doing some incredible work highlighting Aboriginal people from around the country. They've been to remote communities and sat around campfires with elders who still live a traditional lifestyle. They've eaten burgers with kids on the streets of Redfern and they've interviewed executives at banks, and profiled brilliant indigenous artists and sportspeople. They've met families who are struggling but who have the courage to persist and hope for a better future. They have drawn public attention to so many strengths and challenges faced by the Aboriginal community, and this work is *good* for Leo. He approaches it with a kind of wondrous passion instead of the manic energy that drove his work overseas.

He has been working with his own community – but in doing so, he's been putting the pieces of himself back together too. Leo is starting to understand his own history in a way that I know he has always missed. And he will get back to that work again, some day, but *today* is supposed to mark a changing of the guard in our family.

I am returning to work part-time at the Foundation, and for the next twelve months at least, Leo will be focusing his energy on raising our son. So I *need* to leave them behind today – because the Foundation needs me, but also because it is Leo's turn to be the heart of our home.

I rise, brushing a kiss against Leo's cheek as I do. 'Actually, I need to do this. You two will be fine,' I say.

'We sure will. Won't we, buddy?'

'I love you, Leo.'

He takes his eyes from Henry and looks at me, and I see the softness there – the pride and respect and warmth and the openness that I was once sure I'd lost forever. These are rough and ragged parts of our history now. We are matured by them, and we are changed by them – but we have survived them. Just as Leo is ever so slowly trying to relearn how to walk, *we* are learning how to walk together too, and as a family unit now. We are better for having come through the tough times, as I am starting to suspect people usually are.

'I'm so proud of you, Molly,' Leo says, and I flash him a wobbly smile and finally call for the elevator.

'I'll see you at lunchtime?'

'We'll be waiting right here where you left us.'

I cry as the elevator doors close behind me, and then I cry all the way to the office and I'm still crying when I walk through the doors and Tobias is waiting in the lobby. He presses a coffee into my hands. 'Good to have you back, Molly,' he says, and I smile at him. I'm still crying, and he doesn't seem at all convinced as I say, 'It's good to *be* back.'

As I sit at my desk, I withdraw a photo frame from my handbag and I stand it near my monitor. It's a photo of my future and my hope – my beautiful son – and my hero, my wonderful, brave and complex husband. And with my boys watching over me, I reach for my keyboard and I get back to work.

LETTER FROM KELLY

Thank you so much for reading *When I Lost You*. I hope that you enjoyed reading Leo and Molly's story as much as I enjoyed writing it.

If you enjoyed this book, I'd be so grateful if you'd take the time to write a review. I really appreciate getting feedback and your review will help other readers find my books.

Finally, if you'd like to receive an email when my next book is released, you can sign up to my mailing list here. I'll only send emails when I have a new book to share and I won't share your email address with anyone else.

www.kellyrimmer.com/email

Kelly

P.S. You might also like my other novels, *The Secret Daughter* and *Me Without You*.

@KelRimmerWrites

Kellymrimmer

www.kellyrimmer.com

ACKNOWLEDGMENTS

I wouldn't have finished this story without the patient assistance of my genius editor, Emily Ruston. Emily, I can't thank you enough for your help in the development of this book. It has been a pleasure and an honour to work with you again.

To the team at Bookouture: to Oliver Rhodes, thank you so much for believing in my stories, being so generous with insight and advice into this industry, and for building a company that it's a privilege to partner with. To Lydia Vassar-Smith, thanks for keeping on my back with deadlines and getting things done. And to Kim Nash, publicity manager and all-round mother-hen-extraordinaire, thanks for *all* of the support.

A huge thanks also to my fellow authors with Bookouture, who have provided invaluable support on social media to get the word out about my books, as well as making me laugh constantly and helping keep me relatively sane (or possibly just making me *seem* relatively sane!). This story benefited greatly from the insight of friends and colleagues – to Helen, for giving me such a fabulous insight into the journalism world – so much of Leo's passion for his career was inspired by our chats. Thank you! Thanks also to my beautiful sister Mindy for the idea that lead to Leo's memorial tattoos, and to my dear friends Peter and Kisani for the late-night chat that inspired the story of the photo of the elderly couple.

On a practical note, thanks to Ryan and Rebecca for lending me their spare 'house' for my writing retreat when I had a looming deadline! And to Mum and Dad, thanks for always believing in me; also for lending me your dining room table and letting me eat most of the food in your house when I needed to knuckle down and focus.

Finally, to my husband Dan, thanks for believing in me, putting up with my crazy hours at the keyboard… and for taking up karate for my research purposes!